BURDEN OF VENGEANCE

A MAISIE LOCKHART INVESTIGATION

First published 2026

Copyright © Jack Hamilton, 2026

All rights reserved.

Hello, this is my husband's debut novel. Hope you enjoy reading it. If you do, please leave a review on Amazon. Thank you

Prologue

She came round suddenly, feeling confused and her heart pulsating with panic. Disorientated by the darkness, her limbs felt heavy and awkward, like they didn't truly belong to her. All she could hear was her own breathing and the occasional hiss and snap from the fire as the last of the heat escaped the dying embers. At first, she couldn't remember where she was, or how she'd got there. But as the stale, metallic stench of blood began to sting her nostrils, she was immediately transported back to the nightmare that was now her reality.

She heaved her contorted body up from the hard wooden floorboards. Aches and pains hammered through her body, an unpleasant reminder that the effects of the drugs were wearing off. Her left hand hurt worst of all. The sharp, agonising pain throbbed aggressively in unison with her heartbeat. As she held it up and inspected it against the remnants of the firelight, she was struck by a heart-jolting truth. Two of her fingers were missing. The third and fourth, cut cleanly from the knuckles. Like remembering the haunting fragments of a dream, she recalled the downward swing of the hatchet. The impact of the blade, and the blindingly sharp pain that followed, were the last things she recalled before she had been swallowed by the darkness.

As her eyes slowly became accustomed to the limited light, she searched the corners of the room. To her left, she could see the outline of his body, still leant against the wall. His head was slumped forwards and legs stretched out flat against the floorboards. She had to strain her eyes to see that his hands and feet were still bound in front of him. His bloodied hair was draped over his face, like tattered curtains, concealing all but the slightly pointed outline of his nose. He was unconscious, but still alive. She could just make out the sluggish oscillation of his chest, his lungs letting out the occasional wheezing sound as they scoured the stale air for oxygen. She wondered how much time he had before his body resigned to its inescapable fate.

Suddenly gripped by a flood of emotion, she fought back the tears as she felt a chasm of regret, deep inside of her. Thinking back to their first embrace, she wondered if, perhaps in another life, things could have been different. But this wasn't another life. Things were back to what she had always known. She was going to have to navigate her way through this. Alone.

1

Maisie Lockhart had an excellent memory for faces. Perhaps better than most. The sort of innate talent you don't recognise as remarkable until you realise that not everyone can see things the way you can. It wasn't something she paid much attention to. For her it was something that loomed in her subconscious. A game she played with herself from time-to-time, mostly identifying Z-list actors in films or instantly recalling where she had previously encountered a person in the street. But today was different. Today this wasn't a game. This time, this primeval intuition was screaming out to her, telling her something wasn't right.

As soon as she laid eyes on him, she knew instantly where she had seen him before. The first time had been three days earlier, only yards from her front door. He had been wearing a baseball cap and innocently walking a small terrier in the open parkland adjacent to her house. It was a yappy but rather cute little thing, and Maisie remembered thinking it looked distinctly out of place in his company. She had then seen him on each of the days that followed. Each time he had presented a different appearance, but she was certain it was the same man. And now here he was again, sat in the next bank of seating diagonally across from her.

The train pulled into its penultimate stop. Maisie had been standing in the central aisle since she boarded the busy commuter train. Half of the passengers pushed past her as they exited the carriage. One trod on her left foot – or, more precisely, the curved strip of titanium that had become as much a part of her as the limb it had replaced. The woman looked back apologetically without speaking the words and then carried on. But the act itself caused others in the carriage to stare, examining not just her foot but also the shiny, calf-shaped strip of metal beneath the line of her skirt. Maisie wasn't embarrassed. By now she was used to the attention it attracted. She knew they were not being deliberately rude. It was just a harmless curiosity. She imagined them wondering how she had come to wear it. Was she born with the disability or had it been the result of injury? Perhaps a car crash or some sort of road accident. That's what most people assumed. Some were even bold enough to ask. But Maisie didn't mind, not anymore. For her it had become a source of pride. She paraded it like a badge of honour. In many ways it had shaped her into the person she was today, and she had no desire to change that. Nor did she have any time for pity. By now almost everyone in her vicinity had taken at least a cursory glance, except for one person: the man whom she suspected of following her. She had been watching him the whole time and, although he must have felt her eyes on him, he hadn't looked back once. Just continued glaring impassively at his device.

He had a large, muscular build that bulged through his well-fitting suit. Whilst it looked expensive, Maisie guessed it wasn't bespoke on account of the slight rippling around the neck and shoulders. His slightly curved nose and sharply defined lower jaw gave him a slightly hawkish appearance. His eyes were dark, set close together and his ears were small and without lobes. From her estimation, he was in his late thirties, but this was based on their previous encounters. Today, the addition of a grey hairpiece – reasonably convincing to the casual eye – made him look a good ten years or so older.

The carriage lurched suddenly from side to side, triggering a burst of fear within her as the realisation of potential danger suddenly became more acute. If he was following her, maybe she should try to get away? At least walk through the carriages to create some distance between them. But realising this man knew where she lived, she reasoned it was pointless. Bigger than her fears was her desire to find out what he wanted. Even so, she felt afraid. Ever since a threat had been made on her life a month ago, fear had been her constant companion. And now she found herself constantly looking over her shoulder. Making mental notes of who was around and when. Some might have thought this to be paranoia, but she knew better. She had learned to identify true danger and to embrace that dull ache in the pit of the stomach. The chill that runs down the spine and tightens the skin.

The wheels screeched as the train manoeuvred round the buildings and onto the final straight over Cannon Street bridge where an uninterrupted view of the Thames broke through the train window. A thick veil of mist loomed over the city, concealing the tops of some of the taller skyscrapers, and beyond the imposing stature of Tower Bridge, ominous clouds gathered as a storm brewed from the east.

The train tripped clumsily over the last of the tracks, before gradually slowing to a standstill at Cannon Street station. Impatient commuters scrambled past one another. But Maisie waited and watched. The man seemed in no hurry to leave. Even when those sitting next to him got up and reached over him for their belongings in the overhead racks, he didn't flinch. But as the crowd began to thin, Maisie made her move. She slipped back into her overcoat and exchanged the comfort of the warm compartment for the sharp wintery air outside.

Leaving the station, Maisie glanced over her left shoulder as she turned the corner. She saw him behind her using the same exit she had. She looked at her watch. It was a quarter to nine. She decided to collect a coffee and some breakfast. This would be the first test.

She entered the busy coffee shop and stood in the queue, positioning herself with a good view of the street through the large windowpanes. There was no sign of him. She waited for her turn to order, all the time checking the entrance and the passing foot traffic.

After her name was eventually called, and she collected her black Americano from the counter. She checked her watch again. Seven minutes had passed since she had entered the coffee shop. The crowds were still flowing away from the station on both sides of the street. She scanned the line of shops opposite. There was still no sign of him, but that didn't mean he wasn't there.

She left the shop and continued on, following the most direct route towards her office. It wasn't far, but each step felt like a mile. She could sense he was near, that he was closing in on her. She just had to keep putting one foot in front of the other. She began to wonder: was she being paranoid? After everything that had happened maybe she was imagining threats that weren't real. But her gut was tight with caution, and she decided to listen to her instincts. After all, they had never let her down before.

As Maisie approached Lower Thames Street, the crowds had reduced to a scattering of individuals on either side of the road. Fewer people meant increased danger. She quickened her pace and checked over her shoulder. She crossed the street to continue left along the final straight, glancing at the reflections in the glass windows on the other side as she darted through the gaps in the traffic.

When she reached the pavement, she saw a flash in the glass in front of her. There he was. Thirty or so yards behind her, closing in. His expression was malicious and his movements purposeful like a predator stalking its prey. Her heart began beating harder and faster, feeding her senses with adrenaline. She took a deep breath and exhaled her anxiety. She had to get to the safety of her office before it was too late.

She resisted the urge to run. First, she needed a photograph. She retrieved her phone from her handbag and turned the camera on. Then she pointed it behind her and took a burst of images in rapid succession.

She felt vulnerable. The main road was uncommonly quiet for the time of day but there were still pedestrians travelling in both directions, and she remained in full view of the surrounding offices, with surveillance cameras monitoring the street. All things considered, this guy would be putting himself at considerable risk if he made his move now. And yet, Maisie knew it would only take a split second. Just the pull of a trigger or the thrust of a blade and it would all be over. Only for him to disappear into one of the many side streets, with no more than vague witness statements and obscure surveillance footage to prove he was ever there. Even an abduction could be accomplished with the appropriate speed and planning. And if he was who she thought he was, he might not be acting alone.

This made Maisie think. If she was going to be abducted, she should at least try and make it more difficult for them. So, she activated the tracking feature on her phone which alerted her exact whereabouts to a central security monitoring station. At least the authorities could track her if something did happen, she thought with defiance. Then she placed her phone back in her handbag and removed a bunch of keys. She gripped them so the teeth poked out from the knuckles of her right hand. With her left she squeezed the handle of her briefcase tightly. They weren't much, but they might at least allow her to put up some sort of fight.

Maisie sensed he was gaining on her. Time to act, she decided. It was now or never. She darted down a deserted side street. It was dark enough to provide some cover and perhaps allow her to launch some sort of counterattack. She crouched down, ready to pounce as soon as he turned the corner. She placed her briefcase on the cobbled stones beside her; it was too cumbersome to be used as an effective weapon, she decided. Then she waited.

Her heart was pounding against her ribcage, harder and faster with every second that elapsed. Heavy footsteps approached. A large shoe or boot. Then a shadow appeared over her. Maisie immediately sprung from her coiled stance, grabbed the person by the neck with her left hand, her right cocked and ready to deliver a blow to the face, the keys still poking out from between her fingers like a makeshift knuckle-duster. She looked into the eyes of her assailant, but something was wrong. His eyes were blue and filled with fear, not dark, predatory eyes filled with intent. She pushed him back towards the light of the main street to get a better look at him and immediately realised her mistake.

'What the hell's wrong with you?' the man exclaimed, the pitch of his cries slightly elevated and his voice shaken.

Maisie looked back at him with a mixture of horror and confusion, but she was unable to find the words to apologise. Fury was now her companion and the hunt her purpose.

She returned to the main street and searched all directions, but there was no sign of her assailant. No one was rushing in the opposite direction and no disgruntled drivers nor pedestrians that might have got in the way of his escape. He had vanished, and with him any trace he had been there at all.

2

Counting down the distance in her mind, step by step, Maisie eventually reached the entrance to Spotlight News, where she pushed her way through the revolving doors into the lobby. Then she stopped and checked behind her. Still nothing.

'Morning, Lionel,' she said, waving her pass at the security guard, 'how's the family?'

'The usual,' he replied, 'Bleeding their old man dry. But that's kids for you, ain't it? I can only hope they'll look after their old dad on his way to the grave,' he added with cheerful resignation.

'Lionel, do me a favour, would you?' Maisie said, cutting short their usual exchange. She took out her phone and presented the images she'd taken. 'If you see this man coming in, would you give me a call?' Lionel scanned the phone and looked up with a furrowed brow.

'Of course,' Lionel replied, sensing the gravity of Maisie's unusual request. 'Everything alright, Maisie?'

'Everything's fine. Just be careful, okay? Don't take any unnecessary risks,' she said firmly.

Lionel's eyes hardened as he nodded.

Maisie smiled to ease the tension and walked past the bank of reception desks and towards the security gates. Her slightly scuffed heels created a loud tap on the white marble floor, which echoed through the large atrium. She hurried up the small bank of steps, turned round and paused momentarily to take advantage of the elevated vantage point. Satisfied her pursuer was nowhere in sight, she allowed herself to relax. The danger hadn't passed, but at least, for now, she was safe.

Maisie stepped out of the lift on the ninth floor and was intercepted by her colleague Holly, who was hovering nervously by the reception desk.

'Jesus Maisie, are you okay? Ivan's just asked me to reach you.'

'I'm fine, just my last story catching up with me,' she replied with a slightly forced smile. 'I wasn't meant to see Ivan until ten. What does he want?' she asked.

'He's had calls from security. Something about your personal alarm being activated. He seemed worried. Are you sure you're okay?' Holly searched Maisie's face for answers.

Maisie cursed herself inwardly. She should have realised her editor would be contacted the moment she activated the alarm. And until she knew exactly what was going on, she would have preferred to handle this without him poking his hooter into her business.

'Absolutely fine, Holly. Nothing to worry about. But I suppose I'd better go see the old man right away and put his fears to rest. Nice to know he still cares.' She said flippantly, as she began making her way along the corridor to the main office, dread still inwardly weighing on her.

Maisie walked through the familiar bustle of ringing phones and clicking keyboards, blended with elevated voices. The engine room of a news media outlet. Maisie placed her briefcase on a vacant desk and hung her coat over the chair, then marched directly towards Ivan Leegood's office.

From the corner of his eye, Leegood could see Maisie approaching, but he stopped himself from looking up and kept his eyes aimed at his computer screen. Maisie knocked twice on the glass office door and entered, without waiting for an invitation.

'What the hell have you been up to?' He said furiously, before looking up from his screen.

'Up to?' Maisie replied, looking back with a casual innocence.

'Cut the shit, Lockhart,' he retorted, blood rushing to the vessels in his face, 'I've just got off the phone to our security team who say your phone tracking app was activated ten minutes ago. What the hell's been going on?'

'Oh, I don't know, it was probably nothing,' Maisie said unconvincingly, wondering as she spoke the words whether she should blame the incident on malfunctioning technology instead.

Leegood leant forwards in his chair, his eyes bulging from their sockets as though they were somehow capable of seeing into Maisie's very soul. 'Who was it? One of Conway's people?'

Maisie shrugged but Leegood remained silent, waiting for an answer. She had found herself in similar situations before, and Leegood always seemed to have an uncanny ability for extracting the truth. Worse still, once he thought he was on to something, there was no escaping his ferocious barrage of questioning. Maisie often wondered why he hadn't pursued a career in the security services, where he would have been quite at home exercising his interrogation techniques.

'Maybe. I guess the timing makes sense. He followed me off the train and towards the office. I managed to capture some images of him on my phone, so we should be able to get an ID from one of our contacts at the Yard.'

Leegood removed his glasses and used a small cloth to tend to the lenses.

'You were told that your life might be in danger, but would you listen? Would you accept police protection?' A smile appeared on Leegood's face. He shook his head, as if he was reliving the moment Maisie first came to him with her findings. 'I should never have let you talk me into going after Conway. Deep down I think I knew it would never be enough for you to simply cover the story. You had to be the one to bring down that fucking low-life drug dealer. You just couldn't leave it to the police, could you? And now you are the only remaining key witness between him and his freedom.' Leegood paused and looked out of his window, out over the gloomy view of the Thames, as if it could somehow offer him inspiration. 'Well, until this whole thing is over, you're going to have to keep a low profile, before you put yourself or anyone else in any more danger.'

A surge of frustration boiled in Maisie's veins as she considered her reply. 'Look, helping bring that bastard to justice remains one of the most satisfying moments of my career.' Maisie slammed both her palms onto his desk, as she leaned forward and stooped over him, 'and unearthing the activities of people like him is exactly what I'm in this for. If helping to prevent him from destroying any more lives means looking over my shoulder a bit more, I'm good with that. I have no regrets. And neither should you!'

Leegood didn't flinch, just smiled as he casually placed his glasses back onto his nose. 'Not much either of us can do to change it now, anyhow. But at least one of us must learn from their mistakes. I, for one, am not prepared to take any more chances. So, consider yourself grounded.'

Maisie opened her mouth to interrupt, but Leegood continued before she could. 'You're to report this to the police so they can find out who this guy is and why he's following you. In the meantime, I will find you something low-key to keep you occupied until this whole thing blows over.'

'And if I decide to take my services elsewhere?' Maisie asked, hostility building like the stormy clouds outside the window.

Leegood smirked, 'Go ahead. Be my guest, you'd be doing me a favour. But take my word for it, no one else will work with you right now.'

And with that, Leegood pointed to the door and turned his eyes to his computer screen, signalling the end of the meeting. Maisie shook her head and turned to leave. 'Oh, and Lockhart!' he called out, as she reached the door, 'try not to let your temper get the better of you this time, there's a good girl.'

Maisie released an involuntary growl of frustration. The large pane of glass twanged like a tuning fork as she slammed it behind her. She was almost disappointed when it didn't break. Then she took a deep breath and calmly returned to her desk.

3

Sergeant Niko Tamura looked down at his watch with heavy eyes. It was seven thirty, later than he expected to see. But hopelessly, he was still no closer to a breakthrough than he had been at the very start of the day. Looking out through the police station's glass façade, Tamura could see the darkness closing in. Soon it would be completely pitch black – the kind of darkness that only exists in rural areas, where the night sky is free from light pollution. Out there, when darkness falls, there was little sign of civilization at all. Just a scattering of solitary lights glowing in the distance, representing what little remained of this remote outpost. Now the, mostly empty, houses that lined the main road, were little more than a forgotten memorial to a once vibrant local community. Even the main road, which snaked its way past the station's entrance, witnessed no more than a handful of vehicles the entire day.

Tamura's eyes returned to the map in front of him. Illuminated by a small desk lamp, a handful of strategically placed red pins represented a sub-group of the search party. Each party consisted of three or four local volunteers, led by one of his own team. The small row of blue dots that trailed each red pin denoted the progress that had been made, updated at hourly intervals throughout the day. Unfortunately, today even fewer blue pins had been added.

Tamura had taken personal responsibility for overseeing the operation, down to the planning of the routes and systematic search of the area. Three days ago, they had started from where Akina Oshiro's vehicle had been abandoned. But so far, they had found no trace of her. Not even a trail leading away from the damaged wreck, found only meters from the road. Just the insinuation of a potentially violent crime.

Tamura leant forward and rubbed his eyes with both fists. He enjoyed his job. It gave him purpose, and through it he experienced a profound sense of duty. Never more so than right now. But time was against them, and the thickly wooded and rocky terrain would be far too dangerous for his teams to navigate in the dark. One party would soon approach a steep escarpment, carved by a section of the river over many millennia. Expecting them to continue would be irresponsible. The risks were high, and the chances of success not sufficiently high enough.

With the decision made, Tamura picked up his radio and issued a blanket instruction to all the search teams.

'This is Tamura. Today's operation is terminated. Return to your homes and we will recommence at five o'clock tomorrow morning. Acknowledge please.'

Each group had been assigned a number, and Tamura received confirmation from all four in ascending order, a process that had been well rehearsed over the past few days. As a precaution, he decided to wait an hour in case anyone ran into difficulties.

Tamura sat back in his chair and roughly massaged his temples to relieve the throbbing ache that pulsed under his skull. He was no stranger to working long hours, but he was not used to the stresses associated with a high-profile case. As a local sub-branch of the central office in Tokushima, Tamura and his team of four officers would typically deal with much more menial policing activities. Whilst his jurisdiction covered over two hundred square miles, the declining population now totalled less than a thousand. Mostly, he and his team divided their time patrolling the district, enforcing vehicle speed limits, investigating minor thefts and resolving trivial disputes. Never had they experienced anything like this.

Tamura's role was typically held by an older officer, one looking to wind down their career before retirement. But, as a younger man, he saw it as an opportunity for progression. A stepping stone. A way to gain leadership experience early on in his career before moving back to one of the larger prefectures. The opportunity to lead a case of this scale was certainly not lost on him.

Throughout the day, the Tokushima Prefecture Police Headquarters had been in constant contact, requesting progress updates and seeking assurances that everything that could be done, was being done. But the reality of the situation was becoming ever more apparent to him. As the radius of the search increased, they simply didn't have the resources to carry out an effective operation across the mountainous and densely wooded wilderness.

As he cleared his desk for the evening, the phone rang. The loud clangour shattered the silence and pierced his headache like a tolling bell. He answered without allowing the ring to assault him a second time.

'This is Sergeant Niko Tamura, Takakumi police.'

'Tamura, this is Inspector Kishimoto,' announced the voice at the other end.

'Inspector, how can I be of service?' Tamura replied reverently.

'Update me on the search for Akina Oshiro and the Englishman.' The instruction was decisive and formal, deliberately dispensing with pleasantries.

'Yes Inspector, of course.' Tamura had already updated Kishimoto's taskforce earlier that day, but this was the first time Tamura had spoken with the man in charge. 'We have completed a thorough sweep of the immediate area, from where Akina's car was found abandoned four days ago, up to a radius of approximately five miles.'

'Only five miles? Why so little progress?' Kishimoto asked.

'The dangerous terrain means progress is slow. But it's important that we are thorough. Earlier today the Search and Rescue helicopter joined the effort. Separately they have been scanning a much larger area, using their thermal imaging equipment to identify potential locations that can be followed up by the ground teams. But so far, all the potential leads have turned out to be false.'

'What about the car? Has it produced any forensic evidence?'

'The car was found just outside the village, crashed into a tree approximately thirty meters from the road. The passenger window had been smashed from the outside. It's not clear whether this was a result of the accident or the work of an assailant, but there were no other obvious signs of a struggle. The car has been taken to the Tokushima Prefecture Police Headquarters for forensic testing,' Tamura didn't like to point out that this was in the same building Kishimoto was calling from.

'Good. And what about the Englishman?'

'Edward Walker? He was employed by the Oshiro family as a geologist. Mr Oshiro informed us that Walker had been working on a personal project looking into whether a hydro-electric generator could be installed to provide power for his estate in the hills. Walker went missing a little over three weeks ago and we've been trying to retrace his steps. So far, there has been little to go on. One day he turned up for work, the next he didn't. Mr Oshiro didn't report him missing. He assumed Walker had abandoned his contract. He told us he had been disappointed with Walker's performance and general lack of commitment to his work. He said he had become unreliable and so was relieved when Walker abandoned his contract earlier than expected. It was actually Walker's father that first reported Walker missing. He visited the area looking for his son. Perhaps not surprisingly, his perception of his son's work ethic differed from Mr Oshiro's account. When we checked his lodgings in the village, we found Walker's room empty, and his belongings gone. We haven't been able to find any trace of him.'

'What about the owner of the Minshuku? What was their impression of Walker?' asked Kishimoto.

'Apparently, he was a good tenant. Always paid his rent on time and in full. He was quiet, respectful towards the owner and the other guests. He tended to keep to himself. No visitors or socialising the owner was aware of. Initially he spent most of his spare time in his room, but as the weeks progressed, he was there less and less. The owner believed that he was travelling outside of the village in the evenings. She didn't know where he was going. We're still looking into that, but so far there have been no material leads.'

'What about transport? Did he have a rental car?'

'Yes. I contacted the car rental company and the car has been paid in advance until the end of February. From their point of view, it wasn't missing. It was fitted with a tracking device, but it must have been faulty. It hasn't transmitted a signal for several weeks. They have agreed to send us what data they have in the morning.'

'What about the plates?'

'I contacted the Traffic Bureau to see if there have been any hits on the number plate. But so far, this has come back negative as well. They will contact me if they find anything. But right now, it's as if Edward Walker and Akina Oshiro simply vanished a couple of weeks apart.'

Kishimoto let out a short, pensive rumble from the back of his throat. 'The lack of progress on the investigation is unfortunate. I'm aware that you are short-handed. So, the decision has been made for me to join you in Takakumi. I will be taking charge of the operation and bringing personnel to strengthen the investigation. We will be at your office first thing tomorrow. Please ensure you are ready for our arrival. I will need you to begin by briefing my team on all that you have straight away.'

'Yes, Inspector. Thank you—' Before Tamura could say any more the line was broken, leaving just the dull hum of the dialling tone.

Whilst a part of Tamura was disappointed that he would no longer be overseeing the search, another part of him was filled with relief. At least now they would receive the support and resources they so desperately needed.

As Niko Tamura returned the phone handset to its base, his mind wandered. He knew neither Akina nor Walker particularly well. He had seen Walker occasionally around the village. The two had exchanged pleasantries, but no more than that. It was no secret amongst the villagers that Walker was working for Yoshi Oshiro of Oshiro Enterprises, although the details of his work were less conspicuous. Oshiro himself held considerable influence, both locally with the governor of the prefecture and with senior members of the Japanese Parliament. Tamura suspected that he must have used his influence to ensure extra resources were made available for the search and investigation.

Akina Oshiro, his daughter and only child, was in her midtwenties and lived several hundred miles away, outside Nagano on the mainland island of Honshu. She worked for the real estate arm of her father's business. Occasionally she would visit her father's residence, but she rarely ventured into the village itself. Oshiro had been unable to shed light on his daughter's recent movements and whereabouts. According to him, in recent weeks she had been staying at his estate on and off whilst she concluded a series of property transactions on the island. From what Tamura had observed, during the few occasions he had seen her, Akina seemed demure, unassuming, and awkward. Tamura tried to imagine her leading a multi-million-dollar negotiation, but he could never make the leap. But he had been a police officer long enough to know that sometimes people can surprise you.

It was approaching nine o'clock when Tamura decided to lock the office and head for home. Tomorrow would be an even tougher day.

4

The clinking of glasses and cutlery merged with lively chatter from the other tables, creating the unmistakeable ambiance of a central London restaurant at lunchtime. Maisie had chosen the venue for its good food and unpretentious atmosphere. Located halfway along Old Jewry street, Harland's was midway between Maisie's office, and the office of her friend and former work colleague, Fran Bletchley. Still on edge after the events of the morning, Maisie was keeping one eye on the people walking by outside, and the other on the diners inside the restaurant.

Almost all of the tables were filled. Mostly with work professionals in formal dress, engaged in polite conversation over what were likely to business lunches of some description. One table hosted a large party of women who let out an occasional synchronised burst of laughter. The staff were busy circulating the room, only stopping to take or deliver orders on their cyclical path to and from the kitchen. But none of the faces matched Maisie's pursuer from earlier.

'Are you absolutely sure about this?' asked Fran Bletchley. She had arrived just a few minutes before Maisie but was already on her second glass of wine. This was fast, even by her standards. 'I mean, this could all just be a coincidence, right? Some guy who you've happened to run into a few times. It doesn't mean he's definitely following you, does it?'

Maisie took a sip from her glass of Sauvignon Blanc and shrugged her shoulders. She was still on her first. She had expected Fran to react this way. Fran, always spoke with a strong accent of scepticism, and today was no exception. Right now, it was neither what she wanted nor needed.

'Okay,' Fran said, sensing Maisie's frustration from the subtle line that had appeared on her forehead. 'So, what do you think he was planning?'

Maisie didn't know how to answer and shook her head.

'If he *was* after you, today was a failure. Which means what …? He's going to try again?'

Maisie paused for a moment and stroked her napkin as she considered the question. 'I really don't know. But maybe it wasn't a failure,' Maisie said. 'What if he wanted me to know he was there? Maybe the whole point was to send a message. Back away from the trial, or else. A warning shot of some kind to scare me off.' Maisie took another sip of her wine.

She presented her phone to show Fran the images she captured from earlier. Fran took a perfunctory glance, then used her chin to purse her lips into an irregular shape whilst raising her eyebrows with a quiet resignation. 'Maybe,' she said, 'but if you're right that he's connected to Conway, one thing's for bloody sure: you're going to need to be more careful going forward.'

There was a brief hiatus as the main courses and Fran's replenished wine glass arrived at the table. Fran had chosen the halibut steak, Maisie the grilled sole with a Choron sauce. Maisie watched as Fran wasted no time in taking another large gulp from this her third glass. Fran had always liked a drink, but lately it was noticeable that the quantities had escalated considerably, along with the speed it was consumed. Maisie guessed it was Fran's money troubles that was taking its toll on her drinking, although they never spoke about either.

'Anyway, enough of all that,' Fran said, changing the direction of the conversation, 'What are you going to do about Ivan and his decision to sideline you like that?' she asked.

'I would probably do the same, if the situation was reversed,' Maisie replied.

'Not what I asked,' Fran retorted with a fleeting scowl.

'Obviously it's frustrating.' Maisie said with a slight snap as she cut into her fish. She was starting to wonder whether Fran was intentionally trying to provoke her.

'I hate to say this, but maybe he's right. I mean, about you taking some time out. You've got ample security at home, right?'

Maisie nodded. 'Top of the line stuff, all installed recently. Leegood insisted. The house now has more security than a bank vault. All externally monitored. I'm also pretty sure the Yard have put the local police on alert. I've certainly noticed more patrols passing my door than I used to.'

'So maybe it would be best to keep your head down and stay where you know you'll be safe?' Fran said seriously, the wine beginning to slur her words. 'Have you considered stepping down as a witness?'

'Out of the question,' Maisie said sharply, 'and I won't spend the next six months or more cowering away at home either. If the prosecution had their way, I would be locked away, under constant guard until after the trial. And it could be months, or even years before it's all over.'

Fran skewered some halibut onto her fork and swept it across the sauce on her plate, 'I could always try having a word with the old man myself?' she suggested, with a wry smile.

'Leegood? Absolutely not.' Maisie replied, dismissing the suggestion without bothering to explain why.

'Okay, I understand you don't want me sticking my oar in, but I might just have what you're looking for.' Her tone of voice had changed. She leaned in as if she were holding a pair of aces and was getting ready to lay them on the table. 'I've got a promising lead for a story that will take you far away from this miserable place. It might be just what you need.'

Maisie bit into her grilled sole and washed it down with the mildly chilled Sauvignon Blanc, as she tried to imagine a situation where Fran did not try and stick her oar in. But she knew she meant well. 'Fran, I'm grateful you want to help, but I didn't ask you here to solve my problems. I just wanted some drinks and perhaps some help to take my mind off all this bloody nonsense.'

'Seriously. It could be just what you need. You can keep working and no one will know where to find you, including this man who has been following you. This could be the perfect opportunity to keep everyone happy. Besides, this investigation relates to a missing person's case. Not our sort of thing as you know, so in truth you'd be doing me a favour. The information came via an old friend, and the family have hit a complete brick wall with the local officials. They could really use the help. Plus, you've always wanted to go to Japan, right?' Fran paused and took another sip from her glass, as she observed Maisie's reaction. 'Come on, this is perfect for you. Unless of course you don't think you're up to it right now?' Fran added, matching the wry smile she had produced several times already.

<u>5</u>

The fire had reduced to barely more than embers, but it still gave out just enough light for her to enjoy the outline of the cherry blossom. She was bordering on delirium, entranced by the delicate petals. Bunched together in an unassuming glass vase, the weight of the flowers caused the branches to arch gently downwards. Their proximity to the fire cast a faint silhouette across one half of the room, creating the illusion that the surrounding forest had breached the very walls of the cabin.

The delicate petals reminded her of her mother, pale and fragile. She stared at them in the dark. They were a welcome contrast to the otherwise dungeon-like conditions, their fragile beauty reminding her of the fleeting nature of life. But they also offered a small glimmer of solace. They gave her strength. They reminded her that she needed to get through this if she was going to have her revenge. And she wanted that above all else. It was the desire that boiled furiously within her veins. Right now, it was all that was keeping her warm. All that was keeping her alive.

She began to think about how she would get out. Get out and get home. First, she would have to find the nearest settlement. But in her now weakened state, would she make it? And, if she did, would she find anyone that could help her? Though her body was weakened and her limbs heavy, her mind remained determined. She knew she needed to focus on staying alive, getting through what each stage had to throw at her. Step by step. It was important she did whatever it took to punish him.

As the cold air penetrated her skin, she began to shiver. She wrapped her arms around her knees and pulled them tightly against her chest. The pain from her hand was getting worse. She wondered how long she could stand it before she passed out again. She looked across to the corner of the room, there was no movement. No signs of life. A knot of anxiety gripped her stomach, followed immediately by a rush of endorphins. She rocked nervously back and forth as she calculated her options. She would need to make her move soon.

She shuffled across the room. He was still propped up against the wall, his upper body slumped forwards. He was unconscious.

Silent. No movement. She shook him firmly by the shoulder. He didn't respond. She pressed her fingers against his neck like she had seen in the films, held them there for several minutes. His body felt cold, like all the life had already drained away. He was gone, and now she would need to move quickly to avoid the same fate. Now he was gone, she was free to leave.

The fire had now been completely extinguished by the damp air. Darkness was now her enemy. The doorway was her only way out and it would need to be broken down. There was no shortage of tools. They were difficult to see in the darkness, but she knew they were still there, leant against the far side wall. On her hands and knees, she felt her way through the darkness, guided by her memory of where the larger tools were. She needed something heavy. Not too heavy that she would be unable to swing it effectively, but heavy enough that she could break through as quickly as possible. Reaching into the darkness with her right hand, her fingertips navigated their way along a variety of tools until she located the cold, blunt steel head of a sledgehammer. She climbed clumsily to her feet, using the handle to steady herself, and then lifted it off the ground to evaluate its weight. She decided it would do.

The heavy head juddered over the jagged, worn floorboards as she dragged it across the room. The doorway was only visible from the faint moonlight that breached the cracks between the frame. By the time she reached it, her limbs were weakened by the labour of her task. She felt powerless and without strength, as though her body had nothing left to give. Clutching the handle with both hands she kept a steady breath against the pain of her throbbing hand. It was excruciating, but she fought against the agony and arced the hammer feebly back over her shoulder. This was it – she had to give this all she had. Using its weight to build momentum, she swung the sledgehammer downwards hard against the approximate location of the locking mechanism. The sturdy door shrugged off the blow with a nonchalant rattle. The vibrations transferred through the handle, into her body. Her hand felt sticky and wet. Blood from her open wound. She forced herself to press on and delivered another blow. Then another. Her hand was on fire as she swung again, screaming through the pain. The fourth blow resulted in a satisfying, crunching sound. Wood splintering.

And with the fifth she broke through the locking mechanism and the door swung open, hitting the wall with a violent clank.

Relieved and elated by her achievement, she dropped the hammer and cautiously crossed the threshold. The moonlight illuminated the small clearing around the cabin, but was too weak to penetrate the dense woodland beyond it. Standing silent in the still night air, the trees concealed a seemly endless and impassable darkness. But, through a single, tunnel-like hollow, the straight track led away from the cabin and towards freedom.

To the side of the cabin were the charred remains of the car. As she passed it, she wished she could drive it out of here and wondered whether she had the strength to complete the journey on foot. But she had no choice. She had to get out of here. Motivated by the sense of freedom, after a few lumbering steps, she limped into a wounded canter, forcing her starved and battered body to fight against fatigue.

She continued along the track, but within several minutes, she succumbed to the sharp and debilitating pain at the base of her chest. She fell to her knees and begged the heavens for strength. Her prayers were cut short by an unwelcome interruption. Behind her, the empty silence of the forest was splintered by a clanking noise that echoed through the trees. It was coming from the cabin. It was the same dull noise as when she broke through the cabin door. The sound of wood slamming against wood. The air was still, no breeze at all. She moved to the edge of the track to see if she could get a better look. Darkness was all around, so she was careful where she trod. She strained her eyes in the direction of the cabin but could see no signs of movement. As she sidestepped further away from the track, she discovered a better view of the cabin's front door, through the trees. The ground felt cold and uneven as her toes sank into the sodden mud. Still, she could see nothing. She moved a little further to her right, further into the darkness. Suddenly the ground gave way beneath her feet. First, she slid on her back. Then she was thrown into the air. A temporary sensation of weightlessness was followed by a heavy jolt to her shoulder as her body slammed violently against the forest floor. Then she began tumbling uncontrollably down the steep slope. Her head collided with the ground several more times, narrowly avoiding trees along the way as she summersaulted like a rag doll towards the base of the chasm.

Water broke her fall. The impact slapped her hard in the face and forced the air from her lungs. She thrashed erratically as the chill of the deep, icy waters engulfed her. She gasped for air, gargling as her body was pulled beneath the waterline by the fast-flowing currents. But as she fought desperately to breach the surface, she recalled her childhood water survival training. She filled her lungs with as much air as she could, tilted her head back and spread her arms and legs. Straight away she began to float, but it was not enough to stop the currents from pulling her back under as the speeding waters dragged her down river. She looked to the riverbank but the blur of the trees passing added to the disorienting sense of motion.

The cold steadily gripped her body, numbing her limbs. She rolled over and tried to swim towards the far bank, but the force of the current was too strong. If she could get close enough, she might be able to grab onto one of the low-hanging branches draped over the water's edge. She used her arms as rudders and slowly manoeuvred to the edge of the channel. Then pushing downwards with her arms and legs, she generated enough thrust to lift herself partially out of the water. There were plenty of opportunities to catch one of the branches, but as soon as one came into view, she had only a split second to react before it passed.

Her first few attempts were tantalisingly close but unsuccessful. She tried again and again, until eventually her persistence was rewarded. The branch she found was pliant and sharp against her hands. But she clutched it tightly, knowing the stakes if she let go. Every shift of her hands delivered an excruciating reminder of her injuries, but gradually she inched closer to the bank until her feet found traction and the strength of the current faded in the shallows.

She forced herself through the deep, sodden mud, using her arms and legs to paddle forwards on her belly, and became smothered in a thick layer of silt. It covered her entire body, cold and heavy. By now she was barely recognisable as a human being, completely camouflaged under the night sky. The wounds in her hand were stinging from the exposure to the mineral rich silt. She took some time to wash as much of the mud away from her hands and face, as she could. Then she carried on.

She assessed her surroundings. She had no idea where she was, or how far the river had carried her. Beside the riverbank was a high cliff face, impossible to scale in the dark. She decided to follow the river downstream. Eventually it would lead somewhere, she was sure of it. It was definitely her best chance of finding civilisation.

She regained her composure and pulled herself up off the ground, limping defiantly into the darkness, using the meandering watercourse as her guide, as it shimmered in the soft moonlight.

6

Hours passed; each one seeming longer than the last. Each step more strained. The parts of her body that didn't ache felt numb, either from the cold or loss of blood – she wasn't sure which. All she knew was that she was starting to lose hope. Her body couldn't take much more. Maybe she should rest a while. Sleep was calling to her, but she felt certain that if she gave in, she might never get up again. No, she had to keep moving. She lumbered on, pushing forward. Just as her agony reached a new level, her spirits were suddenly lifted by the appearance of a small collection of lights in the distance. Some were brighter than others. They were few in number and set randomly into the hillside, absorbed by the night sky like a solitary constellation.

As she limped on, the terrain began to level out into a small plateau, where the trees gave way to open, overgrown fields. She began to recognise the faint silhouettes of small wooden structures, partially illuminated by the occasional streetlamp.

It was like she was uncovering a forgotten city as she navigated her way towards the village, using her arms to clear a pathway through the dense meadow. Not far to go now, she reminded herself. Soon this nightmare would all be over.

She reached a clearing behind the main high street. There was a welcome feeling of the tarmac beneath her bare, bloodied feet, which made progress easier as she stumbled on, towards the buildings. She noted the scarecrows scattered across the village. She had never seen them at night. Their crossed, timber frames created the haunting atmosphere of a burial site, under the now misty moonlit sky.

She continued along the abandoned high street, heading directly to the police station. The illuminated sign appeared blurred through her tearful eyes, and she was hypnotised by the bright green neon glow. Reaching it had become her singular objective.

When she arrived, she pressed her face against the large pane of the window. There was no one inside. She shook the locked doors angrily and let out a frustrated cry. Then she noticed a small intercom system to the right of the door. It had a single button next to a bell-shaped icon. She pressed it firmly and was instantly rewarded with a loud buzzing noise, followed by the sound of an outgoing call. One ring. Two rings. On the third a voice at the other end answered.

'This is Sergeant Tamura,' said the sluggish and slightly dazed voice.

She pressed her mouth up close against the intercom, but was only able to conjure a strained whisper, 'Please. Please help.' Her weak voice was desperate.

'Who is this?' The voice replied.

'Please. Come, quickly.' She said, expending the last of her strength.

'Wait there. I'm on my way!' Tamura replied, this time with a more alert urgency.

She turned her back to the door and used it to support her weight as she dropped to the floor. Tears streamed down her cheeks in an overdue discharge of relief.

Within a matter of minutes, she could see headlights approaching from the other end of the village in the distance. Her eyes were still wet from the tears, distorting her vision, like looking through broken glass. Help is here, she thought. She dragged herself to her feet and stumbled unsteadily into the road. The car was approaching at speed and she could hear the throttle still being applied. She waved both arms to get the driver's attention. Still no sign of slowing. Four hundred yards. Two hundred. One hundred. Her body froze, as fear of the inevitable swept over her. She wanted to move, but she couldn't.

Time seemed to slow, as the bonnet of the car collided with her legs, followed immediately by the impact of her head and left shoulder with the windscreen. She was thrown into the air and momentarily suspended as the car passed beneath her. Then gravity crashed her down on the firm tarmac in a tangled heap.

The car slammed on its brakes, forcing it to a screeching halt, fifty yards or more further along the road. At the same time Sergeant Tamura arrived on foot, from behind one of the buildings, just in time to witness the incident. He ran towards the victim and skidded to his knees beside her. Cradling her head in his arms he wiped away the muddied, blood-soaked hair and immediately recognised the wide-set eyes, the soft, high cheekbones and narrow pointed nose. It was the same face he had studied every day for the past two weeks on his desk. It was the face of Akina Oshiro, the missing young woman he and his team had been searching for.

7

After her lunch with Fran, Maisie returned to the office to find an email from Fran already waiting in her inbox. This was unusually efficient and detailed for her, Maisie thought. But whilst she would only admit to having been partially drawn in by Fran's sales pitch, she wasted no time in satisfying her curiosity.

Missing Person: Edward Walker

Age: 32   Height: 6'2

Experienced geologist/ independent consultant and son to Jonathan and Jane Walker. No dependents. Contracted for three months to work for a private firm – Oshiro Enterprises – undertaking geological surveys in the village of Takakumi in the southern islands of Japan.

Parents not aware of the specific details of the job he was employed for, but likely to be related to either mining or infrastructure (i.e. Edward Walker's primary area of expertise).

Edward was in regular contact with his family throughout the first five weeks (typically twice per week). No signs of depression or unusual behaviour prior to his disappearance.

Last known contact was at 11:21 on Thursday 28th January (GMT) – a phone call between Walker and his mother. Walker's parents reported his disappearance to the British Foreign Office a week later after failing to make contact.

Having made little progress through diplomatic channels, Walker's father, Jonathan travelled to the region and managed to track down Walker's employer – a wealthy industrialist named Yoshi Oshiro. Neither he nor the local police had made any appreciable progress in tracking down Walker's whereabouts, nor the circumstances surrounding his disappearance.

Walker's whereabouts remain unknown.

Maisie inspected the attachment to the email. It was a photograph of Walker, taken at the finish line of a sporting event, possibly a marathon. He was handsome. Clean-shaven, with medium-length dark brown hair elegantly parted to the side and swept back over his head. He had chiselled features and the lean, muscular build of a long-distance runner or cyclist. His face wore a modest, thin smile that concealed his teeth, and his pale blue eyes carried the weight of a man twenty years his senior.

It was a strange situation, and Maisie was intrigued enough to spend the following two hours undertaking her own preliminary research. The village of Takakumi was small and remote; surrounded by vast, empty forests and mountainous terrain. She found only a few articles about the village, all following a common theme. They described a community plagued by misfortune: failing crops, a dwindling population, and accounts of other unexplained disappearances sparking suggestion that supernatural forces might even be at play. One article, dated only three days earlier, referred to the suspected abduction of the daughter of an eminent Japanese businessman, triggering a massive police search and rescue operation.

Strangest of all were the scarecrows. Hundreds of them had started appearing all over the village and nobody knew who was responsible, nor why they were there. But curiously, their arrival coincided with the gradual departure of the village's inhabitants. Maisie shuddered as she inspected a photo of one of the scarecrows. It was eerily lifelike and yet remiss of any human warmth. A round, intricately detailed face, made from porcelain or a similar material, was propped up on top of a clothed wooded frame and covered with hair. The features of the face had been moulded, as if from a cast, and subsequently painted to give it a lifelike appearance, despite exposure to the elements weathering some of the details.

Maisie felt a sudden rush of excitement paired with a hint of unease: the promise of emerging pattens and the lure of a puzzle yet to be solved. It was the same feeling she always got when she knew she could be onto something. She set up a series of alerts so she could stay up to date on breaking news that might be relevant. Her choices were uncomplicated: 'Walker', 'Takakumi', 'missing', 'British geologist'. Each would trigger an email to her phone, leading her to the related news article. Then she strolled purposefully towards Leegood's office with her signature self-confidence.

'Twice in one day, Lockhart? Quite the privilege.' Leegood said as Maisie forced her way through the heavy glass door without knocking. 'If you're here to talk me out of my decision, think again. My mind is made up.'

'Hear me out first, that's all I'm asking.' Maisie said, as she placed Fran's notes under Leegood's oversized nose. His eyes fell on the paper in front of him. With pursed lips, he began to read. She watched the subtle flicker of his eyebrows as his eyes concentrated on the text. Maisie took this to be a good sign and imagined a series of rusty iron cogs beginning to turn.

Leegood pushed the piece of paper back across the desk and lifted his glasses up over his forehead, 'So, what's all this about?' Leegood asked, 'you want to go gallivanting off to Japan, is that it?'

'I do,' Maisie replied, counting on him being in a good mood, 'but with good reason.'

Leegood's yellowing teeth appeared from behind a wide grin, 'very well Lockhart, I'll bite. There are hundreds of missing persons cases reported every day. What makes this one so special?'

Maisie sat down and began to explain. 'There are around eighty thousand reported every year in Japan alone. Remarkable for a population of that size. And that's the point. This is a real problem in Japan. So bad, in fact, a whole industry has emerged around it. Those who go missing are commonly referred to as "johatsu", meaning "evaporated." People who vanish without leaving any trace. Some people even choose to disappear. Escaping domestic violence is one of the more common reasons. It's alleged that one in three married women suffer physical abuse at the hands of their husbands. Others choose to hide behind Japan's stringent privacy laws, which make it easy to evade debt and allows them to start a new life. A high proportion of disappearances are believed to be suicide, a problem which is growing amongst young men. But perhaps most concerning of all is many of these cases remain unsolved.'

'So, what do you think happened to this Walker character? You think he committed suicide?'

'Unlikely in my view,' Maisie replied. 'On the surface, at least, he had no reason to end his life. A young, successful professional with a seemingly tight relationship with his family and no history of mental illness.'

'What then, murder?'

'Perhaps. That's what we need to find out. I think there is a compelling case for our own investigation into what has happened here. A British national caught up in an increasing Japanese social issue. Local police haven't made much progress and the company he was employed by doesn't seem to be cooperating. It's not clear whether this is apathy, incompetence or something else. Whatever it is, it feels like something we should look into.'

'I see. The infamous Lockhart gut instinct,' Leegood mocked, without declaring his position.

As she had not been completely shut down, Maisie continued her pitch. 'I have also done some digging into the area where he was working. It's a place called Takakumi – very remote and seems to be a hotspot for disappearances. In the last eighteen months the population has dropped significantly, and only a handful of residents remain. Strangest of all, as the population of the village has been dropping, large numbers of scarecrows have been appearing all over the village. Local reports suggest there are now hundreds of them, all within this small village.'

Deep frown lines reappeared on Leegood's forehead. 'Scarecrows? This all sounds a bit weird, Lockhart!'

Maisie nodded in agreement. 'Tell me about it. They're everywhere. Bus stops, public areas, schools, even abandoned houses. And they're not your run of the mill scarecrow, made from straw and tatty dungarees. These have a closer resemblance to the sort of thing you would have seen on London Bridge several hundred years ago. You know, heads on spikes.' Maisie took out her phone and showed Leegood the photo she had found online. As Leegood studied the image, Maisie witnessed the slight change to his temperament. There was no sarcasm nor pithy remark, just a subtle flicker of discomfort in his eyes.

'So, who's behind all this?' he asked.

'No one seems to be taking credit. Each one is unique, so whomever is behind it has gone to considerable effort.' Maisie said.

'Maybe it's a publicity stunt. Something to bring in the tourists?'

'That would make sense if there was a local business nearby that was attempting to capitalise on it. But there isn't. Not from what I've found so far.'

Leegood's wide grin returned as he shrugged off the residual disquiet, 'so, let me get this straight: you're expecting me to agree to let you travel to Japan because you think a load of life-sized dolls are, in some way, connected to the disappearance of a British geologist? Where did you get this from anyway? No, let me guess. I bet it was that bloody lunatic Fran Bletchley that put you up to this. Am I right?' Leegood leaned forward in his chair as he passed the report back to Maisie, looking somewhat pleased with himself.

'What does it matter?' Maisie replied with a passive admission. 'You must admit, it's mysterious. Whether this is a harmless prank or something more serious, it doesn't change the fact that Walker's missing. It may be a coincidence this has happened there of all places. But since neither the local authorities nor the company that hired him have shed any light on what has happened, someone ought to step in. Why not us?'

'Okay I get it,' Leegood interrupted, resignation in his voice, 'but did you hear me earlier? There is a credible threat to your life. And let's not forget that you were followed to this very building, just this morning. So, do you really expect me to condone you travelling thousands of miles to Japan? Somewhere you will be even more isolated and where you'll receive even less police protection than you have here? You don't even speak the language, for Christ's sake. Put yourself in my shoes and then tell me why you think this is a good idea.' Leegood looked back at Maisie with fierce eyes and waited for his answer.

Maisie paused. 'I agree, probably the best thing for me, right now, would be to lay low. But you know full well that I've no intention of hiding away, waiting to see if something happens to me. And the man who followed me this morning knows where I live. Which means he could get to me here at any time. But, by going to Japan, I will almost certainly be beyond his and Conway's reach. And I'm being productive, investigating an intriguing situation with ties to a missing UK citizen. It's definitely a story worth exploring. Win-win for the both of us. Right?'

Leegood got to his feet and began pacing from one end of the office to the other, visibly conflicted. Maisie knew she still needed to do more to win his approval.

'There's something else.' She added. 'Less than a week ago the daughter of a prominent Japanese businessman also went missing. This time it looks like she was abducted.'

Leegood shrugged. 'Maybe they ran off together? Happens all the time.'

Maisie paused. 'Maybe. But why disappear? Why would Walker put his parents through all this?'

Leegood pursed his lips together and nodded cautiously, without agreeing.

'And have you tried contacting the local police to find out what's going on?'

Maisie nodded, 'Several times this afternoon, but there was no answer. I may need to call in some more favours if we're going to establish some cooperation from local police.'

Leegood remained quiet, as though he was weighing up all the pros and cons in his mind.

'No need to agree right now.' Maisie said, still looking to persuade Leegood. 'First things first, I will need to visit the parents to gather the facts and hear their account directly. Let me do that and, if it all checks out, you and I can have a chat about how we will make this work. If it turns out to be nothing, I will drop it, I promise. Sound reasonable?'

Leegood knew if he agreed to the principle of her going, there would be no stopping her later. He pinched the bridge of his nose as if it were a pressure release valve.

'Very well. But I want to hear how it goes with the parents before you start booking flights and accommodation. Understood?'

8

Maisie shifted into a lower gear and pushed firmly down on the accelerator pedal. The burst of speed allowed her to comfortably overtake an idling vehicle before the line of cars in her wing mirror caught up with her. She enjoyed the satisfying crackle from the exhaust and the rumble from the plucky four-cylinder engine as she darted into the overtaking lane and created an instant gulf between herself and the cars behind. This was her first proper outing in her new John Cooper Works Mini, and the relatively clear roads were helping her to get a sense of what it was capable of.

The tuned two-litre engine delivered brisk acceleration on cue, whilst the short wheelbase made the handling sharp and nimble. The black interior was pleasant and functional, exuding the strong, sweet smell of a car recently off the production line. On the exterior, the gleaming jet-black bodywork was complimented by a few subtle red stripes that ran along the bonnet and side panels. She had also opted for the rally spotlights on the front bumper that, along with the slightly bulkier body kit, made the car look more aggressive and sportier than the standard model.

She changed up a gear and felt the shudder from the transmission before easing back to 85mph, where she held it at a cruising speed.

The previous day's events meant she was still very much on a heightened alert. As she weaved in and out of the traffic, deliberately putting more distance between herself and the other cars, Maisie regularly checked her rearview mirror for signs of any vehicles trying to keep up. Perhaps not immediately behind, but lingering one or two cars behind. That's how *she* would do it. But there was nothing obvious. Maybe the threat was real. Maybe it wasn't. For now, until she knew more of the facts, it was safer to assume it was.

While the threat still loomed over her, the fresh impetus of a new assignment was filling her with an exhilaration that overpowered any residual feelings of dread. It was days like these when the thrill of the chase gave her purpose and clarity of thought. It was what she lived for, and she was damned if she was going to let anyone take it from her.

Maisie took a moment to check her progress on the satnav. The Walkers lived on the outskirts of Sudbury, a small market town about sixty miles north-east of London. She had been travelling for a little over an hour, but she was still on schedule to arrive by eleven o'clock. She knew she would need to complete her interview swiftly to allow sufficient time to catch her late afternoon flight to Japan, already booked in anticipation of receiving Leegood's consent.

Suddenly the car's speakers erupted with the sound of an incoming call. The caller ID flashed up on screen as Nathan Roberts.

'Hi Nathan,' Maisie answered, 'let me guess, you're ringing to tell me you already have him in custody and he's confessed to everything?' Maisie said playfully, dispensing with the customary pleasantries.

Detective Inspector Nathan Roberts was Maisie's primary contact at Scotland Yard. Their professional relationship had spanned many years, dating back to when Maisie had worked under Fran as a rookie journalist. Fran had always taught Maisie the importance of a strong network of contacts and the value of sharing information on a 'quid pro quo' basis. More recently though, Nathan had become Maisie's point of contact for the Conway case. And protecting the case's key witness had become Nathan's priority.

'This isn't the movies, Maisie. You can't hand over a blurry image from a smartphone and expect me to have a satellite fix within minutes.' Nathan retorted with the hint of a smile in his voice. 'It wasn't easy, but we have commandeered the footage around the time you were in the area, including some from local office buildings. The coverage is certainly sketchy in places, but we were able to follow your movements from the station to your office.'

'So, what do you think?' Maisie asked.

'You were right, he does appear to have been tailing you.' Maisie felt her heart jump slightly, as she processed the news. She had mixed emotions. On the one hand she was pleased that she hadn't imagined the threat, but the fact was that there was still a threat. 'When you entered the coffee shop, he loitered in the entrance of an adjacent building smoking a cigarette and checking his phone. Then, when you left, he continued to track your movements, almost parallel to your position, from across the street.'

'That probably explains why I lost him for a while.'

'It's a simple but effective technique. And it avoided a possible confrontation with you whilst there were lots of people around. By the time you reached Lower Thames Street he was gaining on you. I don't want to frighten you Maisie, but it looked as though he might have had something in his hand. He seemed to be cupping his fist, as if concealing some sort of weapon.'

Maisie paused for a moment. Strangely, she didn't feel frightened. Not even a little. 'But he never made an attempt, why not and where did he go?' Maisie asked.

'When you turned into the side street, he turned and entered an office building. A few minutes later he left by one of the fire exits to the rear. He continued to head towards your office building, but you arrived a few seconds before he did.'

'He didn't try and gain access to our offices?'

'No,' Nathan replied, 'he walked past the entrance and turned left down a small street before London Bridge. We picked him up entering Monument Station, where he joined a westbound train on the Central line. He changed at Oxford Street and got onto the Bakerloo line. That's where we lost him.'

'You lost him on the underground? How's that possible?' Maisie asked, 'I thought all trains had CCTV?'

'Most do, but some of the older ones don't. My guess is he knew that and used it to cover his tracks.'

Maisie paused, taking a moment to digest the information, 'So why do you think he broke off his attack?'

'I guess he realised you were onto him and decided to change his approach. Maybe he wanted to make sure he had the upper hand, once he lost the element of surprise.'

'He called off the attack so he could come back and finish the job another time, when I'm not expecting it.'

There was silence at the other end of the line.

'Do you know who he is yet?' Maisie asked.

'Not much to go on at this stage. We've checked his likeness against Conway's known associates, probably the most obvious place to start given the circumstances. That's an extensive list, as you know. He used cash to pay for his Underground ticket, so we can't trace the transaction to a bank account. We've put an e-fit on our website, but unless he surfaces again, there's not much more we can do.'

Maisie slowed the car down to match the speed of the lorry in front, resisting the urge to overtake. 'So, it's true. Conway does have a contract out on me.' Maisie said, the weight of the words evident from her deliberate pronunciation, as if each syllable was becoming heavier on her tongue.

'Whilst that may be possible, we should keep an open mind that he wasn't anything do with Conway. It's possible this could be completely unrelated. We will need to continue to gather more of the facts until be jump to any conclusions here. What's most important is that you remain vigilant. Avoid your usual routine, vary routes to work and report anything out of the ordinary, however mundane it may seem.'

'Okay, but you must have a working hypothesis. Do you think Conway is behind this or not?'

Nathan let out a sigh of reluctance, 'I can't argue with the timing. Could Conway be trying to intimidate you? Trying to put you off testifying? I would say we shouldn't rule that out either.'

'So, what happens next?'

'We both know he's a dangerous man,' Nathan replied, 'I appreciate you don't want this trial to interrupt your life. But, speaking as a friend, I strongly urge you to go to ground for a while. At least until we can get a better idea of who this guy is and what he's after. Maybe even consider getting away for a while?'

Maisie smiled. 'Funny you should say that. As it happens, if my meeting goes well this morning, in a few hours I'll be leaving for Japan.'

9

Sergeant Niko Tamura stood perfectly upright, his hands crossed behind his back, as he looked out across the scenic views over the surrounding hillside. It was a welcome reprieve from the plain, utilitarian hospital waiting area where he had spent most of the night. By now he had abandoned any notions of sleep. But the dull ache lingering within his skull, together with the firm thumps from his heart, acted as disagreeable reminders that his body was exhausted. The events of the previous evening played out in his mind, over and over.

The person who had run down Akina was a taxi driver at the end of his shift, and was visibly shaken and fully cooperative. Leaving explanations and questioning for later, Tamura immediately focused on the severity of Akina's injuries and noticed she was losing blood, fast. Without hesitating, he ordered the driver to take them to the hospital at Kochi.

All the way there, Tamura did everything he could to stabilise Akina's condition. First, he removed his sweatshirt, tearing off one of the arms and using it to apply pressure to an open wound on Akina's abdomen. Then, using the remnants from a partially filled water bottle, he wetted the rest of the material and wrapped it around the top of Akina's head, where there were signs of a severe trauma. This would help to reduce swelling on the brain, a technique he had learned during an advanced first aid training course some years before – not thinking he would ever need to use it.

To help raise her body temperature, he wrapped her in his jacket and huddled her close to his body. He held her tight to prevent further injury as they rounded bends in the road and were thrown from side to side. Throughout the journey, Akina had let out the occasional incoherent groan as she drifted in and out of consciousness. Otherwise, she had been unresponsive to Tamura's basic response tests.

Suddenly, Tamura's wanderings were interrupted by the arrival of a police convoy. Three unmarked, black Toyota Crown saloons approached at speed along the main straight towards the entrance of the hospital. From his elevated position on the top floor, he could just about make out Inspector Kishimoto and a band of seven officers – three dressed in suits, the rest in uniform – hastily exit the vehicles and make their way inside. In less than thirty seconds they reached the top of the staircase and were pushing their way through the double doors at the end of the corridor. The fierce demeanour of Kishimoto, accompanied by his entourage, was a formidable sight.

'You must be Tamura.' Kishimoto said.

'Inspector Kishimoto, it's a great honour,' replied Tamura, reverently. Tamura knew the two of them had met before, two years earlier when he first visited the Tokushima Prefecture Police Headquarters. But seeing as Kishimoto clearly had no recollection, Tamura chose not to mention it.

'So, where's the girl?' Kishimoto demanded, getting straight to business. Tamura had already brought Kishimoto up to speed during a phone call less than an hour ago: the call from Akina, the collision, everything.

'Follow me Inspector. Gentlemen.' Tamura led the officers into a private room at the end of the hall.

'No security detail?' Asked Kishimoto, accusingly.

'Presently just me, Inspector. But a member of my team will be here within the hour.' Tamura responded.

Kishimoto aimed his finger at one of his uniformed officers and pointed to the vacant space beside the door. 'One of my men will remain here and relieve you. You will need to be available to assist me with the investigation and manhunt.'

'Manhunt? You mean for Walker?' Tamura asked.

'We'll get to that in a minute. For now, ask the doctor to join us, please. I'd like a full briefing of Akina's injuries.'

'Of course, Inspector.' Tamura walked to the end of the hall and returned swiftly with the ward's doctor.

All the officers congregated around Akina Oshiro's unconscious body. Her arms rested by her sides above the neatly spread sheets. An endotracheal tube connected her mouth to a ventilator and hissed intermittently as it forced air into her lungs, keeping time with the steady bleep from the life support machine. Her head was bandaged, leaving only her bruised face visible.

The doctor joined them and stood at the foot of the bed. 'So, Doctor. Please provide details.' Kishimoto demanded.

The doctor retrieved the clipboard from the end of Akina's bed. 'Where should we begin?' He said, raising both eyebrows to emphasise the extensive nature of her injuries. 'The area of most concern is the significant trauma to the head. Oshiro-san's CT scan revealed a small linear fracture to the right side of her parietal bone, the large region running from the top of the skull all the way to the back. The fracture is relatively small and there are no signs of splintering, which is good news. But it is the level of brain swelling that is causing us concern right now. During the night we took the decision to induce a coma, to try and get the swelling under control. We are monitoring the situation closely but for now her condition is stable.' The doctor paused briefly to refer to the clipboard again, before continuing, 'Other than the head injuries, she has a fractured wrist and two broken ribs. Her spine and lower body have both avoided major damage or broken bones. These are the types of injuries you might expect when a pedestrian is struck by a car.' The doctor paused again, 'She does have numerous other injuries that are less consistent with a typical traffic collision.'

'Other injuries?' Kishimoto said.

'Yes.' the doctor bent forward slightly and used his pen to point to her hand, 'the patient's third and fourth fingers have been removed from below the knuckles on her left hand.'

'Removed?' he said, 'you mean deliberately?'

'Yes, quite deliberately,' replied the doctor, 'The cuts were clean and, judging from the angle, they were made simultaneously with a single thrust of a large blade. Perhaps a cleaver or hatchet. Evidence of scorched flesh shows that an attempt was made to cauterize the wounds.'

'Why would someone go to the trouble of cauterizing the wound?' asked Kishimoto, contorting his brow.

'The "who" and the "why" is something I leave to you, Inspector,' the doctor retorted with an air of disdain. 'But, from a medical perspective, cauterization would be an effective way of minimising blood loss and the risk of infection. The initial toxicology report has identified traces of an opioid in her blood. So, it's possible she may not have felt much.' he added.

'So, whoever did this was trying to keep the victim alive? But why drug her?'

'Maybe the drug was used to immobilise her in the first place? As I said, Inspector, I will leave you to determine why.'

'Are there any more of these deliberate injuries doctor?' Kishimoto asked.

'Apart from her hand, it's difficult to say. She has extensive bruising all over her body, some of which could have been caused by the collision. But the inconsistent spread of bruises across her body suggests they may have been inflicted by other means. You see usually, when someone suffers a collision, the bruising is focused around the areas of impact. In this case, mainly the head and right side of the upper body. But Oshiro-san has bruising to her back, abdomen as well as random patches on both her arms and legs. It's therefore likely that some of these injuries occurred prior to the collision, although it's hard to say for sure. Other than that, she's severely dehydrated. It's likely she hasn't eaten for days. Overall, I would say she's incredibly lucky to be alive. This young man deserves a great deal of credit,' the doctor tipped his head towards Tamura, 'If it hadn't been for his quick thinking and decisive action, it's highly likely you'd be having this conversation with the coroner, rather than with me.'

Kishimoto ignored the doctor's praise and continued with his questions. 'How would you rate her chances of recovery?' Kishimoto asked.

'Unfortunately, there's no easy answer to that. With head injuries, each case is different. She is in a stable condition, but the next few days will be crucial. We won't know any more until she regains consciousness.'

Tamura's heart sank and Kishimoto let out a long sigh, which sounded like a growl.

The doctor's eyebrows and shoulders raised in unison. 'She is receiving doses of Midazolam to induce the coma. Once we start to see evidence of reduced swelling, we will begin lowering the dosage gradually. At this stage I would say it will be at least a week before we begin taking her out of the coma. But, when it comes to brain injuries, there are no guarantees. She may not react to the reversal of the drugs and if she does, it may be several weeks until she's ready to talk. Whether or not she can recollect the events …' The doctor let the shrug of his shoulders finish the sentence.

'Thank you, Doctor. Please contact me directly if there are any changes to her condition.' Kishimoto offered a card with his contact details, which the doctor accepted.

'You will excuse me. I need to attend to some of my other patients,' said the doctor, bowing his head before promptly exiting the room and leaving the officers at Akina's bedside.

'You've done well, Tamura,' said Kishimoto, in a sincere but forceful tone.

'Thank you, Inspector.'

'Nevertheless, there is still the matter of finding the Englishman. The superintendent has ordered me to launch a full investigation into Akina Oshiro's disappearance. Given her present condition and our limited leads, we must begin with Walker. The timing of his disappearance and links to the family make him the only suspect in her abduction. We must find him and wrap this up quickly, you understand?' he said rhetorically. 'I require your assistance in continuing to trace his last known whereabouts. I also want you to expand your search. Akina Oshiro must have been held captive somewhere relatively nearby; we must find that location. More officers will be arriving later this morning to support the search effort. I would like you to brief them on the area your team have covered and use your local knowledge to lead this part of the investigation. Can I count on you?'

'Of course, Inspector Kishimoto, it would be my honour.' Tamura said appreciatively, unable to conceal his satisfaction, a subtle asymmetrical ripple appeared at the corner of his mouth. This was the opportunity he had been waiting for.

10

Maisie arrived at the Walkers' shortly before eleven o'clock. She stepped out of her Mini, stretched her legs and sampled the fresh country air. The large, immaculately presented cottage with its rustic garden spoke of a simple, unpretentious affluence. Maisie had never considered living anywhere other than the city. She much preferred the bustle that came with a more urban environment and the convenience of having everything right on your doorstep. The knowledge that you were never alone. But in this moment, surrounded by the humbling expanse of rolling countryside bathed in the soft winter sunlight, the cottage put forward a persuasive argument for rural living.

Her boots crunched over the gravel as she made her way towards the front door and rang the bell. A few moments later a man and a woman, emerged from the doorway to greet her.

'You must be Maisie,' the woman said with warmth, reaching out to shake Maisie's hand. Meanwhile, the man lingered quietly beyond the threshold, with a slightly stern expression. The man was tall and thin, the woman shorter and slightly plump. They both had short grey hair, and Maisie guessed they were in their sixties. Their skin had a healthy, weather-beaten appearance, as though the outdoor life agreed with them.

Maisie accepted the extended hand and reciprocated the smile. 'Very pleased to meet you, Mrs Walker.'

'Please, call me Jane. Thank you for coming,' she said, sincere appreciation emanating from every word.

Jane Walker turned towards the man who was still waiting casually in the doorway. 'This is my husband, Jonathan.' He nodded as his wife ushered Maisie inside. The hall was pristine and decorated to a high standard. Paintings and family portraits hung from both sets of walls lining the large hallway, offering a snapshot into the lives of a proud family and their interests. They were arranged almost in a timeline. Some were of a much younger couple with their infant son, dating back three decades or more. Others, further along, were more recent and focused more on father and son, celebrating their achievements together. A fishing expedition, a mountain summit, the finish line of a marathon.

'This is very impressive,' said Maisie focusing on one of the more recent images.

'That's Edward there with his father, after completing their climb of Scafell Pike, part of the Three Peaks Challenge. Not really my thing, but they raised over £11,000 for charity.' Suddenly Jane Walker's face began to quiver as she spoke about her son. 'Come on into the living room,' she insisted, as she led the way, 'it's much more comfortable in here.'

In the living room, the décor was a pleasant blend of contemporary and traditional design, with subtle pastel shades of green and grey, contrasted with light oak beams, cabinets and tables. Two large sofas were positioned opposite one another, with a large coffee table in between, laden with a generous selection of sandwiches, biscuits and cakes. It was clear to Maisie that the Walkers were practiced in entertaining guests.

'Please, make yourself at home,' she said pointing towards the seating, 'what can I offer you to drink?'

'Coffee please. Black, no sugar,' Maisie replied.

Maisie collected one of the ornate china plates and began filling it with a selection of the sandwiches, which had been neatly cut into fingers, with the crusts removed. She had missed breakfast and was glad of the opportunity to stop her stomach grumbling.

'So, where do we start?' Jane asked, as she filled her husband's cup with tea, and then her own. Despite the sadness in her voice, she seemed to be consciously injecting a buoyant energy into the conversation.

'It would be helpful to know more about Edward. Perhaps a bit of insight into the type of man he is: his experience, relationships and interests, as well as what he had been employed to do in Japan. Anything you feel might be relevant. Shall we start with his profession? I understand he's a geologist. What's his specific area of expertise?'

'At university he studied Earth and Marine Sciences,' Jane replied. 'After that he worked for numerous organisations as an engineering geologist. He started small in junior positions, but as his experience grew, he began to lead more ambitious projects.'

'What sort of projects has he been involved in?'

'All sorts, I suppose. Although in recent years he's generally gravitated towards large-scale mining and infrastructure projects. Africa, the Middle East, Asia, his work takes him all over the world. A couple of years ago he set up his own independent consultancy business. It's small, but he has a growing list of large and high-profile clients.' Maisie noticed that reciting her son's achievements had elevated Jane Walker's mood once again, whilst her husband quietly sipped his tea.

'Is he married? Any children?' Maisie asked.

'No,' Jane said with a weighty sigh, as though she was looking forward to the prospect of both, 'he did get quite close to marrying someone a couple of years ago, but unfortunately it didn't last. He hasn't been close to anyone since.'

Maisie nodded as she made some notes. 'And does he live in England when he's not working abroad?'

'Yes, a flat in Shoreditch, close to his office.'

'And is this the first time Edward has worked in Japan?'

'Yes. Actually, his first time in Japan, full stop.' Jane Walker answered. 'From what Edward told me, there's not usually much call for foreign contractors. The Japanese typically manage their own projects, since they have no shortage of home-grown expertise,' she explained, 'but the country has limited natural resources of its own and so relatively little mining takes place there. As I understand it, they import most of the minerals needed to support their motor and technology industries … so I've read, anyway.'

'And this job, was it related to mining in some way?'

Jane Walker glanced to her husband, who answered, 'we're not sure exactly,' he said vaguely, 'he never shares any details of what he is working on until after the job is finished. He often had to sign non-disclosure agreements, which he always took very seriously. His employer told me that he was working on surveys for a hydroelectric generator, something that could power the whole area. But we haven't been able to verify that.'

Maisie sensed the suspicion in his voice, 'Did he ever give you a feel for how it was going? Whether he had run into any difficulties? Any personality clashes? Anything like that?'

'No. But then he never does.' Jane said. 'Never complains, just gets on with it. We actually thought he was starting to enjoy Japan. During his downtime he had been exploring the local areas. He visited Osaka, Kyoto and Tokyo. Much more than he usually does when he's away on business. Normally he can't wait to get home and so he typically works very long hours to complete the job as quickly as possible.'

'And when did you begin suspecting that something might be wrong?' asked Maisie.

Jane Walker's gaze strayed towards the ceiling as she tried to recall the answer, 'about four weeks ago,' she replied, after a brief pause, 'When he is abroad, on his own for any period, he always rings me. About twice a week.'

'That's why we knew something was wrong straight away,' Jonathan Walker calmly interjected, 'it's not like him to go so long without calling. He never has before. We rang his phone and left messages for him, but it always went straight to voicemail.' In Dr Walker, Maisie observed a calm, almost lackadaisical, composure. He uttered concise sentences only when necessary. But his eyes were sharp and inquiring, as if they were constantly assessing their subjects. Maisie imagined he was well suited to his profession as a general practitioner.

Maisie paused, took a few quick sips of coffee, and then continued, 'I understand that you went out to Japan to search for Edward yourself?' she said looking to Jonathan Walker.

'I didn't have much success,' he replied, creasing his forehead and letting out a sigh as he reached for his tea. 'I spent a couple of weeks trying to retrace his last steps. I hired a translator, as not many of the locals spoke English. I started with his accommodation, in the village where he was staying. Quite an extraordinary place. Beautiful, but quite bizarre at the same time.'

'By bizarre, are you referring to these scarecrows?' Maisie asked.

'That's right,' he replied, 'they were everywhere. I didn't really know what to make of them. Anyway, the room where Ed had been staying was empty and the owner said he had left suddenly. Apparently, one day an envelope appeared containing the exact outstanding balance for the room, as well as a note saying he wouldn't be returning.'

'So, he paid up and left without speaking to anyone?' Maisie asked.

'It would seem so.'

'And did you see the note from your son?' Maisie asked.

'No. I asked the owner, but she had thrown it away.'

'She wasn't able to shed any light on his movements leading up to his disappearance?'

'No. The owner indicated he hadn't been spending much time in his room at all.'

'Did you speak with anyone else in the village?'

'There was a young police sergeant who was very patient and tried to help. Otherwise, there were just a small number of residents in the village, most of whom seemed very unwilling to talk and claimed they had never seen Ed. I still can't decide whether they were telling the truth, or if they simply didn't want to get involved.'

'What makes you say that?' Maisie asked.

'They seemed nervous, like there might be consequences if they spoke to me. Nothing concrete you understand, just an impression I got. Like they were speaking to an outsider who couldn't be trusted. Only in this village, I might add. Everywhere else the locals would go out of their way to help you. The Japanese are famous for it. But it made the uncommonly cold reception that I got in Takakumi seem even more strange.' he paused briefly, leant forward and filled his cup with more tea, before continuing, 'Eventually I decided to pay a visit to his employer, a man called Yoshi Oshiro. He lived nearby in a vast estate situated high above the village in the remote hills. But he wasn't much help. Quite the opposite, in fact. He gave the impression that there had been some tension between him and Ed, but he wouldn't go into specifics, no matter how hard I pushed him.'

'We found this most unusual. Edward is always so personable. He never has any issues with people, least of all his clients,' Jane Walker added in her son's defence.

'He wasn't a nice man,' Jonathan said, 'egocentric, cold, apathetic. Perhaps a sociopath. Not a pleasant character at all.'

Maisie listed some of the words used by Jonathan Walker and underlined a couple of them. Even though he had every reason to be emotional, his calm demeanour made his account of Oshiro seem more measured, like he was diagnosing a patient.

Maisie paused, choosing her words carefully, 'Is it possible that the challenges of working with this man could have weighed on Edward's mental health? Did he show any signs that the pressures might be becoming too much for him?'

Jonathan Walker shook his head. 'No,' he replied, unequivocally. 'He's used to dealing with difficult individuals. He has a very thick skin. Very laid-back. Nothing ever seems to faze him. And he has no history of mental health struggles.'

'Even if he did, he would know that he could come to us,' Jane Walker interjected, 'he certainly wouldn't choose to … go missing.'

'And what about Yoshi Oshiro's daughter … Akina?' Maisie asked referring to her notebook. 'Did Edward ever mention her?'

The couple paused and looked warily at each other. 'He never mentioned her, no.' Jane Walker eventually replied.

Maisie sensed there was more. She held her attention on Jane Walker and waited patiently for more to follow.

'We did get the impression he might be seeing someone, though.' she added.

'Did he say anything?' Maisie asked.

'Not exactly. Call it a mother's intuition,' Jane Walker replied with wide grin. 'In previous relationships, Edward has always been very private. He doesn't like us poking our noses in. Not until he's ready to introduce us, anyway. But normally he wouldn't visit tourist sites or travel to other cities whilst he was working. That sort of thing doesn't really interest him. He would usually only do it at the suggestion of someone else or if he was trying to impress someone. I asked him whether he had met someone, and he was evasive, without denying it. Typical Edward. And that confirmed it for me really. Whether it was this girl Akina or someone else, I really couldn't say.'

'But you're aware that Akina has also gone missing in the last week?' Maisie asked.

Jane Walker nodded, 'only from what we've read in the local news articles. We monitor them daily in case there is any news of Edward,' she added.

'And you don't think the two of them could have, in some way, decided to leave together?' Maisie asked, finding herself tripping over her words as she tried to tiptoe around the subject.

'We did consider it,' Jane Walker said candidly, 'but it seemed unlikely, as the girl has only recently gone missing. Ed has been missing for weeks. But it can't be a coincidence, and the one thing that links them is her father, Yoshi Oshiro.' For the first time since her arrival, she sensed anger in Jane Walker's voice.

Maisie nodded, 'And what about the local police, have they interviewed this Mr Oshiro?' Maisie asked.

'Yes,' Jonathan Walker replied, 'but they achieved little more than I did. I visited the area where Ed was supposed to have been surveying the potential for the hydro-electric dam with the local police, and we couldn't find any evidence that anyone had even been there, let alone undertaken surveys. No tyre tracks, no disturbed undergrowth, just a vast expanse of impenetrable woodland on a hillside that fell into a deep ravine. We undertook a thorough search of the area for more than a week. But we found nothing.'

'Can you share the location of this area with me?' Maisie asked.

'Absolutely,' he replied, 'but bear in mind I don't believe this was where Ed had been working.'

'You think Oshiro was lying?' Maisie asked.

'I just didn't trust the man. My instincts told me that he was up to something. I've no idea what. But the area, where he claimed he was going to site this project, was miles from the village and his estate. The closest village was practically abandoned. I confess that I'm no expert in this field, but it just didn't add up. The costs would have almost certainly outweighed the benefits.'

'That's why we think you're our best chance.' Jane said, candidly. 'But it seems there may be some local politics to navigate. And we feel, to make real progress, we need to raise the profile of Ed's disappearance, with the help of the media.'

Maisie paused as she felt the weight of Jane Walker's words and the enormity of the task ahead of her. She was no stranger to navigating bureaucracy nor tracking down individuals. That was normal. Part of her job. But the fact that the Walkers would be relying on her to find their only son, made this altogether more personal.

Maisie closed her notepad and placed it on the table beside her, 'I fully understand,' she said, 'but I feel I should be straight with you as well. I will make the case to my editor. And I will do everything I can to try and find out what has happened to your son; you have my word. But I want to make it clear exactly what my role will be. My job is to uncover the truth and report it to our readers. That may include this man Oshiro, but it may also include some difficult truths about your son. I always try to be sensitive to those involved, but I will not be censored, in any way. That's why you may still want to consider other channels, including a private detective or support from your local MP.'

The Walkers searched each other's eyes for an answer and, without speaking, confirmed their understanding by nodding again in unison. 'Thank you, Maisie, we appreciate your honesty. Is there anything else you need from us?' Jane Walker asked.

'Yes. I will need all the information you have; the place where he was staying; where he was working; the plot of land you believed was a false lead. And I'll need to know the names of the officials you've spoken to, both here and in Japan. You also mentioned Edward had spent time visiting the local attractions in his downtime. Any details you can share with regards to when and where may also help.'

Suddenly, Maisie's phone pinged. She glanced covertly at the screen, careful not to cause offence to her hosts. It was a breaking news story. The headline read: '*Daughter of tycoon found alive – police continue hunt for missing British suspect.*'

Maisie excused herself and left the room, taking the opportunity to read the story in full. As the lines of text unravelled into an alternative narrative. What was originally a straightforward missing persons case, was already evolving into something altogether more complex. But the tone of the story was unequivocal. Walker was now very firmly viewed as the suspect, not the victim.

11

Tick-tock, tick-tock, tick-tock.

Yoshi Oshiro had become mesmerised by the rhythm of the ornamental clock in his study. Without realising it, he had begun matching its rhythm with his knuckles against his mahogany desk. He hated waiting, much less being told what to do. For the second time in his life, he felt his hold over a situation slipping helplessly from his grasp.

A gentle tapping, of heels against the polished solid wood floorboards, grew gradually louder, distorting the clock's tempo. His maid appeared at the large, opened-arched entrance to his study. She bowed reverently.

'What do you want?' he said, with an aggressive bark.

'Would you like me to prepare your supper, Oshiro-sama?' she replied in a calm voice, not remotely deterred by his tone.

'Didn't I make myself clear that I was not to be disturbed!' Oshiro growled, shaking his head in flustered fury. He had more important things to worry about. At any rate, he wasn't hungry. Nerves had already taken hold. He hadn't felt this way in a long time. And after years at the top as a captain of industry, he had little reason to. 'I don't want any fucking dinner,' he said, dismissing her with a single flick of his hand.

The maid bowed silently again and softly disappeared out of sight.

Oshiro's focus returned to the clock – five minutes to seven – tantalisingly close to the time he had been told to expect the call. He got up from his chair and walked to the window to calm his nerves. He looked down across the rolling hills, covered by dense coniferous forest as far as the eye could see. The three-inch thick glass pane created a subtle distortion of the outside world, making everything appear smaller. Dusk was taking hold and a mist had begun to rise from the forest floor, as the cold evening air descended on the valley. The thick haze concealed some of the lower areas, creating the illusion of an archipelago with only the elevated ground sprouting through.

Although it might have seemed a haunting sight for some, Oshiro was filled with a warm, reassuring sense of power and safety. From behind the ballistic-resistant glass, capable of stopping several 7.62 calibre rounds, he was comforted by the strength of his dominion. High up in the hills, surrounded by his vast estate, he was protected within the belly of his formidable citadel. No one could get to him here.

The call arrived at exactly seven o'clock. The sharp ring from the telephone sliced through his recently found resolve, and he rushed to lift the receiver to his ear. He said nothing as he waited for the voice at the other end to speak.

'Identify,' the assertive female voice demanded.

'Byakko,' Oshiro responded.

There was a brief pause and a ruffling sound as the receiver changed hands. Then a different voice, this time male, began speaking.

'Byakko.' he repeated with a pensively monotonous voice, 'that's an interesting alias. The white tiger. The god of the West. If I remember my mythology correctly, the white tiger served as a protector. A symbol of righteousness and bravery. Is that how you see yourself?'

Oshiro thought carefully before answering, 'Surely we all aspire to be viewed in such a way?' Oshiro answered, pithily.

'Perhaps,' the man replied. 'I prefer to see people for what they are, rather than how they would like to appear. That way, I'm less likely to be surprised when they fail to deliver their promises. Take yourself, for instance. Had I believed you to be the figure you present to the world – tough, resourceful, reliable – perhaps I might have allowed you to be central to the ongoing success of our arrangement. As it happens, I don't make such mistakes.'

Oshiro decided these theatrics were little more than posturing, designed to instil fear and ensure obedience. He had often used similar methods to instil discipline within his own workforce or to defeat an adversary. Yet, though he intensely disliked being spoken to like a lackey, he also recognised that this was a dangerous man. A man who should be respected and not underestimated.

'And how have I failed to live up to our arrangement?' he asked, adopting an assertive but non-confrontational tone. 'As I see it, we continue to make positive progress with our opposition. We are close to achieving our shared objectives. Meanwhile, the authorities remain unaware of our activities. You're also forgetting I have helped you amass a considerable fortune over the years.'

A brief and unnerving period of silence ensued. Oshiro sensed the echo of his words being swallowed by the ether.

The silence eventually broke. 'So, Byakko,' the voice continued, 'perhaps I do owe you an apology for wasting your time? After all, as you say, everything seems to be perfectly under control. No cause for concern. And yet there *must* be cause for concern. Otherwise, we would not be having this conversation, would we?' The pitch of the voice continued to maintain an almost perfect equilibrium. Emotionless. Without realising it, Oshiro had become drawn into his trap, relegating his ego to that of a small boy waiting to be scolded for misbehaviour.

'I assume you are referring to the activity surrounding my daughter?' he asked.

'And why do you think that might represent cause for concern?'

'I don't. In my view, there's nothing to be concerned about. She is nothing to do with our arrangement and knows nothing of our activities.'

'That may be so, but you have been foolish with the Englishman. And careless with your daughter. You should have been more cooperative with the police investigation from the beginning. Their lack of progress has increased the level of focus from England. And now the situation surrounding your daughter has increased the level of police presence, inevitably leading them to scrutinize your activities. Need I remind you that the success of our operation relies on maintaining fear amongst the locals and nominal police interference?'

Oshiro was surprised at how well-informed his associate was. Clearly, he had underestimated the resources at his disposal, 'I'm taking care of the Englishman,' Oshiro responded defensively, 'And after they lay my daughter's disappearance on him, I will have justice, the authorities will move on, and we can resume our business together.'

Once again there was a measured pause, 'You have one week to get this under control,' the voice said, 'And, let me be quite clear, this is your last chance.'

Without forewarning, there was an abrupt clunk at the other end, robbing Oshiro of the last word.

12

There was a sudden jolt to the cabin, as the plane skipped over a stretch of turbulence, providing a short bout of weightlessness. A calm voice from the cockpit attempted to reassure the passengers, whilst urging them to return to their seats.

Maisie Lockhart reached across to steady her gin and tonic, balanced on the fold-out table. She looked out of the window and into the darkness beyond the blinking lights on the wing. Whilst it was hard to tell, there was little evidence of stormy weather, although the lack of visibility below suggested there might be some cloud cover beneath them. She sat back in her comfortable seat, took another large mouthful of her drink and allowed the bitterness of the juniper to assault her taste buds. Six hours into the eleven-and-a-half-hour flight to Osaka, she was glad she had decided to upgrade to business class. While the countless journeys across the globe had made her familiar with the process, they had done little to improve her relationship with flying. Usually, the best she could negotiate from her editor was an upgrade to premium economy. And this flight was no exception.

'This isn't a bloody holiday, Lockhart,' Leegood's words echoed through her mind after their telephone conversation, 'I'm letting you go on your little wild goose chase, but don't think you can go lording it up with costly flights and expensive hotels. I want daily updates on your progress and expenditure. And if this story turns out to be nothing, you're coming straight home. Got it?'

Gone was the concern for Maisie's welfare, from the previous day. The Leegood she knew, and frankly was more comfortable with, had returned. She must have caught him after a budget meeting. Usually, the only time Ivan was even remotely concerned about costs was after a grilling from the publishers. Nevertheless, when Maisie arrived at the airport, she found that she had accrued sufficient air miles to upgrade her seat, and she intended to make the most of the fully reclining seat and steady supply of alcohol.

Whilst it wasn't particularly late, most of the other passengers had already turned off their reading lights and reclined their chairs. Maisie always found it difficult to sleep on aeroplanes. It wasn't that she was a nervous passenger, she was mostly indifferent to the whole experience. But even after years of flying, she found she could not get used to the constant, high-pitched whistle from the engines and decreased air pressure caused by the altitude. Added to that, details of the story were whirling round in her mind like the winds of a raging storm.

The disappearance of Edward Walker, the abduction of Akina Oshiro, the countless other disappearances in the area and the village itself with all its peculiarities. The scarecrows. Were these all linked or merely the product of coincidence? There was an irrefutable link between both Edward and Akina, but Maisie was troubled by the current speculation that Edward was the culprit.

The article she had read hours earlier, named Edward Walker as the suspect in the abduction of Akina and described a ruthless and unscrupulous individual with an unhealthy infatuation. These allegations were at odds with what she had learned about Edward from his parents, although she knew from experience that many skilled sociopaths had learned to hide in plain sight. Even so, one unshakeable detail was the timings of the disappearances. Edward had been reported missing weeks before Akina. Whilst this certainly didn't mean he could be behind her abduction, it made it much less likely. And what about the pattern of other disappearances that remained unresolved?

As she was unable to subdue her thoughts with sleep, she removed her laptop from her briefcase and reviewed her notes on Mr Oshiro.

During their meeting, Jonathan Walker's judgement of Mr Oshiro's character had lingered in her mind. Of course, he was biased towards his son, and yet he did not strike her as someone who was prone to exaggeration. Quite the opposite, in fact. Maisie would have to make up her own mind, but listening to others was important. Simultaneously she suspected everyone and accused no one. Not until she had all the facts she needed. That was her process.

An online search of the name 'Yoshi Oshiro' instantly returned various articles depicting a man who was widely celebrated in the world of Japanese business. He was the embodiment of the archetypal 'rags to riches' tale. From humble beginnings as the son of a fisherman, to becoming one of Japan's most successful businessman, Oshiro seemed every bit the homegrown success story for others to aspire to. Born in Kyushu, the most southerly of the five main islands, he was the third son of four boys. In the interview for *The Japan Times*, Yoshi Oshiro reflected on his relationship with both his parents. Oshiro remembered his father fondly as a peaceful and passive man, who had raised his children to avoid unnecessary confrontation and condemned acts of violence. In contrast, his mother he described as a 'fearsome woman', who had dedicated her life to raising her four boys and driving them toward success.

After completing his master's in economics, he worked briefly in an internship programme in London's financial district, before returning home when his mother fell ill with cancer, two months into his first posting. The young Yoshi Oshiro returned to Japan and took on a managerial role in a small consumer electronics manufacturing company, based in Osaka, close enough to visit her at weekends. She died a year later, but Oshiro remained with the same business and rose through the ranks quickly.

In his eleventh year, he achieved his first executive position. Five years later, after the death of the then Chairman and CEO, Oshiro took a controlling interest in the company, which he quickly renamed Oshiro Industries. Oshiro spent the next twenty years growing the business through diversification and acquisitions, enabling him to control the full supply chain for his products, from mining raw materials through to retail distribution. Equally impressive was the portfolio of properties owned by the real estate arm of the group, which included corporate office space and private rental properties in Tokyo, Osaka and London as well as an extensive retail presence across Japan.

Now believed to have an estimated personal wealth somewhere in the region of one billion US dollars, Oshiro clearly enjoyed celebrating his wealth, but was also well known for his philanthropy. Over a decade ago he had started his own charitable foundation, named for his late wife Sakura, who had tragically committed suicide following an apparently longstanding battle with mental illness. Under his personal direction, the foundation had funded a variety of different projects over the last decade, including scholarship grants to underprivileged children, housing for the homeless and support for those suffering with mental illness.

Both his success in business and charitable work had culminated in Oshiro being awarded the Order of the Rising Sun, one of the highest honours that can be bestowed upon a civilian by the Emperor of Japan. Maisie had located a news article that had covered the ceremony, which included a picture of Oshiro receiving the award from the Emperor himself, at the Imperial Palace in Tokyo.

Oshiro had never remarried after his wife's death and had only one child; a daughter named Akina. Maisie noted that the article covered very little about his wife, or his daughter. The only mention of his wife was in a separate article which disclosed she had been found dead by her daughter – a teenager at the time. The article didn't provide any more details surrounding the circumstances; only that medics had declared her dead at the scene and the police had not treated her death as suspicious.

Similarly, there was very little information available about Oshiro's daughter, Akina. Maisie had only managed to find a single picture of her taken over ten years prior, showing a shy, adolescent girl seemingly overshadowed by her charismatic father, whilst attending a business awards event.

Maisie was able to find out that Akina held a directorship role in the property arm of the business at Oshiro Enterprises, but she was not named as a shareholder.

Maisie used the information she had gathered to create a short profile of Oshiro, and his immediate family members. But as she finished her notes, her eyes were beginning to blur, and she had to concentrate to focus. She closed her laptop, placed it carefully in her briefcase. Then she took the last sip of her drink and reclined her seat fully into the sleeping position.

13

It was getting late, and Yoshi Oshiro was still in his study, hunched over his desk. After his earlier phone call, he had made a sizeable dent in his only bottle of Yamazaki 50-Year-Old Single Malt. With each decadent gulp, he paused and savoured the moment. He was not enjoying the flavour so much as the knowledge that each measure cost more than many would earn in a year. So far, he had drained enough of the bottle to numb his senses, but not enough to entirely suppress his trepidation. He knew what lay in store for him if he didn't remedy the concerns of his business associate.

This was not the first time they had threatened him. He had witnessed their wrath before and he was in no doubt what would happen should he fail them. Perhaps they would kill him anyway, he mulled as he took another swig from his glass. For some time now, he had been slipping deeper and deeper into their world. What had started, all those years ago, as an informal exchange of services – a way of getting ahead of the competition – soon developed into a partnership of sorts. Now they had become an intrinsic part of his life, influencing many of the decisions he made and the actions he took.

But his exposure to this world had also had a lasting impact on his own character. It had made him stronger and taught him that he too could be ruthless when the situation demanded it. Through his illustrious career, he had amassed considerable wealth and influence of his own. Perhaps then, they should be fearful of me, he thought, as he liberated the last of the liquid courage from the bottle and into his glass. Clearly, he would need to clear up the loose ends to ensure he would be absolved of any wrongdoing. But he had grown tired of leading a double life. It sapped his strength like a parasite. Maybe now was the time to consider his exit strategy.

Oshiro's mind returned to the present, and specifically to his daughter. A few hours earlier he had received a phone call from the CEO of the hospital. The man had made contact the very moment Akina had been admitted.

'Mr Oshiro,' the man had said, 'I will make sure that your daughter receives the very best care. I will also make sure you are kept appraised of her recovery.'

Oshiro had insisted on two updates daily. Once in the morning and once in the evening. 'Perhaps we should move her to a private hospital. One that has more resources available and more qualified staff.' Oshiro had stated plainly to the CEO, without pretending to care how his comments might be received.

'That is of course your decision, Mr Oshiro. However, my team are highly experienced. Particularly when it comes to brain trauma and spinal injuries. They tell me it would be unwise to move her at this crucial stage of her recovery. But regular reviews of what would be best for Akina's rehabilitation would certainly be wise.'

Today's call from the same man, was merely to confirm that there had been no change to her condition. She remained stable, in an induced coma. She was still on the ventilator, but her other vitals were strong. She was scheduled for another MRI scan in the morning, at which point they would check for any changes to the swelling to her brain.

'You're welcome to come and visit any time after eleven o'clock, should you wish to.' the man suggested to Oshiro, 'I'm sure you'll be anxious to see her? All we'll need to do is make the police guard aware, in advance. Security remains a principal concern, given the circumstances.'

Oshiro growled inwardly as he wondered whether the man was intentionally questioning his concern for his daughter. But he quickly realised that the optics may not be favourable were he not to visit at the earliest opportunity.

'I will be there at eleven as you have suggested. You will be good enough to speak with the police to let them know I will be coming.' Oshiro said, stating his expectations.

Oshiro had ended the call without any further pleasantries, so that he could turn his focus back to the more pressing matter in hand – Walker.

After an interlude to consider his strategy, and now fuelled by some of Japan's finest liquid gold, he retrieved his address book and dialled the number for the prefecture governor.

'This is Governor Saito,' a partially muffled voice answered the governor's private line.

'Governor, it's Oshiro.' He said plainly, unapologetic for neither the interruption, nor the hour.

'Oshiro, do you have any idea what time it is?' the governor asked incredulously, already aware of the answer, 'couldn't this wait until the morning?'

'It is the morning,' Oshiro said abruptly, 'and sleep becomes somewhat less important when your daughter is fighting for her life in hospital.' There was a pause at the other end of the line, and the governor realised he had been put firmly in his place. 'I haven't received an update from you.' Oshiro added, with expectation.

'We talked about this, Oshiro. You're going to have to let us deal with this. The superintendent has made this his top priority and put his best team on the case, but you can't reasonably expect instant results. They have been continuing their search for Walker, who is still considered the only person of interest at this time, as we discussed. However, as of this evening, there have been no new developments.'

Oshiro was pleased the investigation was focusing on Walker, as he had intended. But he was less pleased by the lack of cooperation and respect for his position, even if he was considered a mere civilian.

'And yet I have been one of your greatest supporters, have I not?' Oshiro asked rhetorically. 'I believe I am still your largest donor, by some considerable margin.' Oshiro had neither the time nor the patience to debate why he should be involved in the inquiry, and instead made it clear that this was not a request.

'I see,' the governor responded, pensively, 'so what is it that you want from me?' the governor asked.

'I expect daily progress reports, on what has been covered by the investigation team. Specifically, where they are with regards to the search for Walker,' Oshiro said.

'Very well,' the governor said submissively.

'I also want my daughter fully protected. That includes blocking unnecessary attention from the media, which could be harmful to her recovery.'

'Oshiro,' the governor became exasperated, 'you know we're trying to build trust among the media community, so asking me to shut down their involvement is not an option.'

'There are to be no further media conferences or press releases of any kind, without clearing it with me personally. Understood?'

The governor paused, sighed and conceded, 'Understood,' he said, reluctantly.

'And then there's the matter of this foreign journalist from England.'

'You *are* well informed,' said the governor, a little surprised, 'Yes, we understand she is coming to Japan at the request of Walker's parents. She has good contacts within the British police and they have asked for our cooperation whilst she is here. Politically, it would be unwise not to support the request. I see no reason why this will create an issue. She will not be granted access to any information that is deemed critical to the ongoing investigation. I suspect she may well want to meet you though, as Walker's employer.'

'Absolutely not,' he said, 'I won't be talking to any press on the matter.'

'That's your decision Oshiro-san. However, in my experience, it's better not to give these journalists any excuse. Best that you show you have nothing to hide.'

14

A man at the front of the cabin was yelling loudly at the woman beside him. Maisie remembered seeing the two sat together in the departure lounge whilst waiting to board the plane. The woman had been wearing sunglasses, and she was still wearing them now at 30,000 feet with very little sunlight penetrating the cabin.

Maisie couldn't make out what was being said, but she watched the erratic movements of the man's head above the eyeline of the headrest, as he delivered another irate barrage. She could see the awkward looks of the cabin crew, and the other passengers surrounding them, nobody quite sure how to react.

'You stupid fucking bitch!'

This time Maisie heard it with unmistakeable clarity. The sudden escalation stirred the other passengers, but still nobody intervened.

Maisie felt herself squeeze the armrest of her seat, as her blood began to simmer in her veins. She hated bullies being allowed to act with impunity. It was the reason she did what she did.

'How can you be so fucking stupid?' the man continued.

Maisie felt herself automatically rising from her seat, to get a better look of what was going on. It looked as though the man was holding the woman roughly by her shirt. Maisie searched each end of the aisle to see where the flight attendants were. The ones to the rear of the plane were oblivious to what was going on. The ones to the front seemed too scared to do anything, and were pretending they hadn't noticed as they continued serving drinks from the trolley. Her heart already pumping harder, Maisie decided to act. She strolled down the aisle until she reached where the couple were seated.

'Everything alright?' she asked.

Straight away the man turned to face Maisie. He seemed shocked, like he was unused to being challenged. The couple wore matching gold wedding bands. He had short grey hair, gaunt and slightly weathered features and a wiry physique. She had short dark hair. Her large, bulbous sunglasses covered most of her features.

The interruption from Maisie had given her the opportunity to straighten out the imprint on her shirt, left by her husband's fists.

'What the fuck has it got to do with you?' he eventually replied, slightly stumbling over the words and with a hint of slurring.

Maisie looked to the scattering of empty beer cans on the fold-out table in front of him, and then back into his menacing glare. He was leant forwards; both his hands gripped the armrests of his seat as if he were getting ready to pounce at any moment.

Maisie said nothing. She leant forward slightly and matched his glare. Then she stood up straight and shrugged her shoulders. She turned towards the two flight attendants, still only a few meters away by the drinks trolley. Both seemed to pretend they hadn't seen or heard anything. Maisie walked towards them.

'That's right, fuck off and mind your own business!' the man said, sensing his victory.

Maisie approached the drinks trolley and asked for a can of drink.

'Anything that's fizzy.' She added.

The flight attendant retrieved a can of soda and handed to Maisie. Maisie tapped the can firmly against the side of the trolley and then shook it in her hand for good measure. The attendant looked puzzled.

Maisie then turned and began walking back to her seat.

As she approached the man, he looked as though he was preparing to launch a fresh barrage of insults as she passed. But before a word could leave his mouth, Maisie cracked the can ajar. She used her thumb to direct the violent spray of liquid and bubbles; first at his face, then at his lap.

'I'm so sorry,' she said, with an overemphasised theatricality, 'clumsy of me.' As she leant forward, Maisie emptied the remainder of the can's contents.

The cabin fell silent, everyone watching in disbelief.

The man furiously wiped the spray from his face and leapt to his feet, automatically raising his fist, ready to attack.

Maisie's heart raced, but she didn't flinch. She stood firm without so much as a blink, just a hint of satisfaction evident from the upward crease at the corner of her mouth.

Maisie shook her head and tutted twice.

'I wouldn't do that if I were you.' She said.

The man froze, still with his fist suspended in mid-air above his shoulder, fury bellowing from his eyes.

'The police in Japan have a particularly low tolerance for gobby pricks like you. They might hold you for days, even weeks without charge. Not the way you'll want to spend your holiday, I expect.'

The man remained frozen in his stance, but now he wore a puzzled demeanour, like he was reassessing his standing within the universe – or something as equally profound.

Maise moved closer to him, holding eye contact.

'I'd suggest you go and clean yourself up,' she said. 'Otherwise, people will think you've had an accident.' Maisie smiled, as she tipped her eyes in the direction of his groin.

The man looked downwards, and observed the large patch on his trousers, still dripping with the contents from the can.

Maisie leant closer to him. 'And if you lay one more finger on her, I'll make sure you regret it,' she added, *sotto voce*.

The man immediately lowered his fists. He growled slightly as he witnessed the muted tittering laughter from the surrounding passengers. Then he turned and hurried in the direction of the toilet.

After watching the retreat along the aisle, Maisie turned to the woman, as she searched her pockets for a business card. She always had at least one on her, at all times. Then she leaned over the now vacant seat.

'If you ever feel trapped or you need any help, you make sure to call this number.' She said, as she retrieved a slightly crumpled and dog-eared card and offered it to the woman. 'I know people who can help.'

The woman looked back at her. She seemed shocked, like she was still processing what had happened. Then she smiled and nodded slowly as she accepted the gesture.

Energised by her victory, Maisie returned to her seat, receiving numerous approving nods from her fellow passengers as she passed through the aisle.

When the man eventually returned from the toilet, he said nothing. Just sat with his arms folded staring at the headrest in front of him, as he adopted the persona of a scalded child.

15

Yoshi Oshiro's jet-black Rolls-Royce Phantom wafted towards the main entrance of the hospital with an unapologetic air of superiority. Outside, a welcoming committee, led by the CEO of the hospital and three other men dressed in white lab coats, had already formed, ready to greet him. Oshiro hissed his frustration through his teeth, loud enough that it prompted a curious glance from the driver in the rearview mirror. He wasn't in the mood for this, but as he hastily finished his tonic and placed the empty glass on the burl walnut table, he decided he must put on a good show.

The car gently slowed to a standstill. The driver cut the engine and energetically got out to open the door for Oshiro, who slid across the soft leather seats and grabbed the driver's headrest to help pull his large frame out of the cabin. Once he was clear, the driver closed the car door behind him and returned to his upright stance in front of the driver's door, like a soldier standing to attention. Oshiro moved towards the group of distinguished hospital personnel and produced the smile he usually reserved for press events and public appearances.

'It was not necessary for you to go to so much trouble,' he said with false modesty, 'I would happily have found my way to my daughter's ward.'

'Not at all, Mr Oshiro. It is an honour to receive you. I only wish it were under happier circumstances,' the CEO of the hospital said, before introducing his colleagues.

Oshiro shook each of their hands but paid no attention to their names. Instead, he was mulling over the CEO's motives for making such a fuss. Clearly, he must be after something. Perhaps a donation towards the hospital or access to one of his many contacts? Oshiro knew these sorts of displays usually came at a price. But for now, he made a conscious effort to appear patient and courteous, rather than risk being seen as intolerant or, worse still, unsavoury.

'Please follow us, Oshiro-san. We will take you straight to up to see your daughter.' the CEO said.

As they walked through the main entrance, past the busy reception desk, Oshiro noticed there were no restrictions preventing members of the public from entering. It would be very easy for someone to enter unchallenged, he thought, as they all piled into the lift and rose one floor. Whilst he had noticed some dome-shaped cameras in the ceiling on the ground floor, on this floor there were none. It was only as they walked along the corridor to his daughter's room that he first became aware of a police presence in the hospital. The young man dressed in formal police uniform was quick to stand aside when he saw the party of doctors approaching, and made no record of who was entering the room.

All five men filed inside and gathered around Akina's bed. The most senior doctor began providing Oshiro with an update on his daughter's condition. Her fragile frame lay motionless on the bed, aside from the mechanical movement of her chest, as the ventilator pushed air in and out of her lungs. Her head was extensively bandaged, covering her entire hairline like some sort of headdress, and the features on her face were difficult to make out, due to the heavy swelling around her eyes and cheeks. A line of horizontal stitches on the left side of her forehead gave the appearance of a third eyebrow.

Oshiro quietly located the hand with the two missing fingers and observed the thick bandages that covered them. The sight instantly transported his mind back in time. To a time, many years ago, when he had first been exposed to this method of punishment. The memory triggered an unpleasant sensation that pierced his chest as his heart palpitated.

'Are you alright, Oshiro-san?' the CEO asked, noticing the sudden unsteadiness of Oshiro's stance.

'I'm fine,' he replied, removing his handkerchief to wipe his brow and dab his eyes before waving it at the doctor. 'Please, tell me the latest on my daughter's condition.'

'She's making encouraging progress,' said one of the doctors as he glanced awkwardly at his colleagues. 'From her scan this morning, we can see that the swelling in the right side of her brain has reduced significantly.' The same doctor held up an image of the scan whilst using his pen to indicate the area he was referring to.

'So where does this put her in terms of the timeline of her recovery?' Oshiro enquired.

'Well, it's hard to say exactly, when it comes to head injuries this extensive. I would encourage you to take each day as it comes,' the doctor said. 'For now, we will continue to monitor her progress, but so far things are looking very encouraging, given the severe state of her injuries.'

'You should be very proud of your daughter Mr Oshiro,' said the CEO, 'she is clearly a fighter.'

Oshiro nodded sombrely, as he repeated the CEO's infuriating platitude in his mind. If she truly was such an accomplished fighter, she wouldn't have found herself in this situation in the first place, he thought.

'Perhaps we should give you some time alone with your daughter?' the CEO suggested, sensing Oshiro's desire to be left alone. 'We'll wait outside if you need anything.'

Oshiro pulled up a chair and watched the door close behind them as they left the room. As he sat and observed his daughter, he found himself reflecting on how things could have got this bad, and what he must do to rectify the situation. But before he could answer his own question, there was a firm knocking at the door.

'Enter,' responded Oshiro, as he wondered who would be bold enough to interrupt him within such a short space of time.

His answer came when a middle-aged man pushed open the door and stood respectfully at the threshold.

'Mr Oshiro. My name is Detective Kishimoto. I can see that this may not be the best time ... I wonder if I might have a moment?'

Oshiro let out a small sigh before nodding to confirm his consent, without bothering to turn his head. Detective Kishimoto approached from the opposite side of Akina's bed. Oshiro was respectful enough to pull himself to his feet, and the two men bowed to each other.

'So, what can I do for you, Detective?'

'I am leading the police investigation that is focusing on identifying those responsible for your daughter's abduction.'

'You mean Edward Walker.' Oshiro interjected.

'Walker is a key person of interest in this case, yes. And now that your daughter is safe, finding him is our top priority,' Kishimoto said without agreeing with Oshiro's assertion.

'And so, what is the latest update on his whereabouts?' Oshiro demanded.

'We believe he's still in the country. We've reviewed passenger manifests for all commercial flights to the UK over the past two weeks and his name has not appeared on any of them. This has been corroborated by our contacts in the United Kingdom. We have also passed his details, and a recent photograph, to police at all of our international airports.'

Oshiro nodded approvingly, pleased that his words with the prefecture governor had been successful in initiating a national manhunt.

'We are also trying to locate his hire car,' Kishimoto continued, 'but, so far, nothing has come back on the number plates. It's possible the plates could have been changed or the car abandoned, but we will continue to pursue both lines of inquiry. We obviously hope your daughter will be able to shed light on events when she gains consciousness. But, since she had been travelling on foot, we are focusing our search on the immediate area, in the hope that we will discover where she was being held. When your daughter was found, her clothes were soaked and heavily soiled by silt, so we are tracing the river upstream for clues on which route she may have taken. Actually, the area we are about to enter falls under your ownership, so I wanted to check if you knew of any vacant properties that could help us to narrow down our search?'

'I own thousands of acres in this area and across Japan,' Oshiro said, with a slight elevation of his brow, 'I couldn't tell you the details of what is located within each of my estates. But I will put you in contact with my estate manager. He may be able to help you.'

Kishimoto's expression exposed a subtle hint of displeasure at Oshiro's dismissiveness. 'That would be very helpful, Oshiro-san. Thank you,' he spoke with a forced show of appreciation that betrayed his thoughts.

'And what of the driver of the car that ran my daughter down? Is he being dealt with?'

'Dealt with?' Kishimoto replied.

'Yes, will he be punished for his crimes?'

'Not for me to say,' replied Kishimoto, 'we are holding him on a charge of dangerous driving. We are also questioning him in connection with your daughter's disappearance. So far, we have nothing to suggest he is connected to the case. He is a taxi driver and he was rushing home at the end of his shift, having just returned a customer to the neighbouring village. His story checks out. Before the incident with your daughter, he was completing a three-and-a-half-hour airport run. The collision with your daughter seems to have been a genuine accident. My sergeant arrived at the scene shortly after and the two acted quickly to deliver her here.'

Oshiro nodded sternly, to indicate his understanding, 'It is right that he will be punished, of course. I understand that the incident with the car was what caused her head injuries and the reason she is now in a coma,' he said, ignoring Kishimoto's apparent leniency.

'Your daughter's injuries will factor in the severity of the driver's charge,' Kishimoto said, the sharpness of his words becoming more evident.

'And now that she's likely to be here in the hospital for some time, can you reassure me about the security arrangements?' Oshiro said, changing the subject slightly, 'how long will there be a man guarding the door, for instance?'

'I have arranged for an officer to be stationed here around the clock for the immediate future.'

'Good. Is there anything else, Detective? I don't want to keep you from your duties,' Oshiro added, keen to draw their engagement to a conclusion.

'Just one more item of business,' Kishimoto, said unapologetically. 'We have received a request from our English colleagues to accommodate a journalist who is looking into the Englishman's disappearance. We have agreed to receive her. My sergeant will be looking after her, and I have given him strict instructions not to divulge information that is sensitive to the ongoing investigation. Nevertheless, I thought you should be aware.'

'Just make sure they don't interfere in things that do not concern them,' Oshiro said abruptly, 'I want this mess cleaned up quickly.'

16

Maisie was about half an hour away from the village. Thanks to the clear roads, she was on track to arrive early, but it had still been a tedious drive along the stretch of dual carriageway that connected Kobe with Tokushima. A call from Fran had been a welcome distraction and had helped to break up the journey, if only for a short while. Fran had been uncommonly concerned for her welfare: where she would be staying, whether she was taking enough security precautions? Usually she hated fuss, but today Maisie didn't mind admitting that she found having Fran to look out for her, hugely reassuring.

Her destination was located within the easternmost part of the Shikoku Island mountain range. Already the urban areas had begun to give way to a more rural setting, and after passing through Miyoshi, she began the steady climb into the secluded, hilly and heavily wooded terrain.

Were it not for the occasional traditional Japanese wooden homes and farm buildings, with their distinctively tall, thatched roofs, the picturesque woodland would have reminded Maisie more of a European forest. Tall conifers crowded the edge of the road on either side, pointing like arrows toward the sky, and clumped so closely together they prevented the sunlight from penetrating the canopy. In places, large, jagged rocks crowned the peaks of the mountains, like the ruins of an ancient fortress.

Climbing further into the hills, the road narrowed to little more than the width of a single car. On one side there was a perfectly vertical cliff face carved out of the hillside, whilst on the other, a line of guard rails was the only thing protecting her from a sheer drop, several hundred feet to the bottom. As she caught a glimpse of the valley floor, Maisie was instantly reminded of her experience in the Zoji La mountain pass, in India, considered by some to be one of the most dangerous roads in the world.

Earlier in her career, while working as travel correspondent, she had naively taken the advice of a car rental firm to use the road which connected Ladakh and Kashmir.

'It's an experience you'll never forget,' he had told her, chuckling to himself as he handed her the keys to a tired four-by-four, caked in mud so thick that it concealed the eroding body panels and bald tyres. During that journey, on a stretch of road no more than six miles in length, she had her first encounter with extreme, unadulterated terror, as she had driven along the narrow ledge. The wheels had struggled for traction on the loose, muddy surface, whilst sliding closer and closer towards the edge. And there had been no barriers to protect vehicles from the sheer drop, thousands of feet down to the base of the mountain. Maisie could still imagine the jagged rocks displaced by the wheels, tumbling down the mountainside. But she also remembered the buoyant sense of satisfaction when she handed the keys back to the owner of the car rental, after her return journey.

'You were quite right,' she had said to him with a wry smile, 'a truly unforgettable experience.'

After that, there was not much that fazed Maisie, in a car at least. And whilst she certainly didn't have a death wish, occasionally she found herself yearning for that same feeling. The thrill of adrenaline you can only experience when you're on the edge.

The meandering roads were quiet and followed a cyclical pattern of steady climbs and slow descents to the foot of the valley. Eventually the trees yielded, allowing panoramic views across an expanse of rolling grass lands, dropping to a moderately sized plateau. The empty basin sunk beneath the surrounding hills and mountains. And, at the far side, a V-shaped gap, carved by the river over many millennia, continued into the distance.

Maisie checked the time on the car's digital display. It was almost five o'clock. The sun was at its lowest bearing of the day and the westerly side of the gorge had become darkened by its own shadow. Meanwhile, the eastern side and most of the plateau floor remained illuminated.

As she approached the village, the road began to even out. Quaint houses and commercial properties lined both sides of the road. On the right, behind the buildings, there was a large open stretch of overgrown pasture, with the river acting as a dividing line to the wild forests and rising hills beyond. Then she saw them. For the first time, the lifeless figures she had read so much about, came into to view. They were dispersed around the village like an invading force. All of them fixed to the same, rudimentary wooden frame, and each one dressed in their own unique ensemble, ranging from workman's outfits to suits, T-shirts to kimonos. The clothing was draped loosely over the frames and tied off at the middle to give the appearance of a midriff. But with no legs, the sets of torsos and heads, each supported by a single pole added to their macabre and somewhat disturbing appearance.

The frames of the scarecrows looked as though they had been thrown together in a hurry, but considerably more time and effort had been spent on the head and facial features of each figure.

Maisie pulled into a vacant layby and killed the engine. She checked her watch. She still had a few minutes before her meeting and decided to walk the rest of the way to the police station, which was visible at the other end of the village. It would be a good opportunity to stretch her legs, she thought, but also a good opportunity to see the village in daylight.

She left the car parked by the roadside and began walking towards the line of buildings that made up the main street. As she paced along the main street, Maisie was reminded of the Sergio Leone Westerns that often opened on a barren and sparsely populated scene, in a remote town in America's Old West. The whistling of the wind through the buildings and high-pitched squeaks and bangs that echoed from the abandoned buildings, all building a palpable tension. As if something bad was about to happen.

There were very few cars parked by the houses and those that had been left behind had deflated tyres and a thick layer of dust covering the windows. Maisie guessed they had been there for several months, perhaps even years. And yet the houses seemed in good condition. Their thick thatched roofs showed no material signs of neglect nor disrepair. On the surface, there were no obvious reasons for them to have been abandoned.

There must have been close to a hundred scarecrows that Maisie could see. Some were by the roadside. Others stood in front of buildings, in the playgrounds and in the overgrown fields surrounding the village. Many had taken on the roles of the former villagers. Some were posing as shopkeepers or huddled together as families. But when she located an entire classroom of schoolchildren facing a teacher, a sharp, discomforting shiver ran through her spine. It was almost as if these spectral figures had displaced the residents to form their own inanimate community.

She continued on, her list of questions without answers growing with each step, until she arrived at the police station. Its obtrusive architectural style was modern and utilitarian looking. Above the façade was a collection of Japanese symbols and the word 'Kōban'. At the rear of the building there was a car park containing several police vehicles.

As Maisie pushed her way through the glass door, the eyes of the three officers looked up from their workstations and studied her carefully with inquiring eyes. Two of the three were on the phone, speaking in Japanese. The third was standing hunched over a table, both his arms propping up his body as he studied a large map. He was a young man, probably in his late twenties or early thirties, and at least twenty years the junior of the other two men. The embellished epaulettes he wore, weighed more heavily on his shoulders than they did for his colleagues, and he exuded a quiet gravitas that spoke of a man in charge.

Voices repeatedly echoed through the radio on his desk. Combined with the fast-talking voices of the other two men, there was a tangible sense of urgency in the small space masquerading as an incident room.

The young man looked up with an expectant look on his face, waiting for Maisie to speak.

'Konnichiwa,' she said bowing her head, 'my name is Maisie Lockhart. I have an appointment with Sergeant Tamura. My colleague in London told me you would be expecting me.'

The young-looking man paused momentarily as he searched his distracted thoughts, as if he had forgotten the appointment. Maisie saw the precise moment when he remembered.

'Yes, you are the journalist from England,' he said with impeccable English, as he bowed his head. 'I am Sergeant Niko Tamura. Welcome to Japan,' he replied.

17

Multiple sirens sounded simultaneously in the distance, fracturing the calm in the chilly night air. A man known as Hunter stood on the balcony of his ninth-floor London flat. He used this opportunity to hone his acoustic senses. There were multiple vehicles. He estimated three, all of them police. Over his many years of experience, he had learned to distinguish their more rapid rhythm and higher pitched frequency, compared with those of other emergency services. It was something he knew might one day prove to be the difference between freedom and capture. Life or death.

Whilst the surrounding high-rise buildings distorted the sound waves, he reckoned they were a mile away, south-east of his position. And, judging from the gradually increasing pitch and volume, they were getting closer.

He wasn't concerned. One of the key reasons he had chosen this flat was the numerous escape routes available to him, were the need to arise. To the rear of the building, through his bedroom window, there was a fire escape ladder that led both to ground level, and to the roof. It would take a considerable police presence – one much larger than this — to cover all the possible exit scenarios simultaneously. Even once he had reached street level, he would have the choice between three underground stations and four bus stops, all located within a proximity of half a mile. Were he able to reach the basement garage, his Range Rover would be an effective escape vehicle, with both the power and weight to force most other cars out of the way.

Deep down he knew it was unlikely they were coming for him. If they were, they would not give up the advantage of surprise and announce their arrival.

The noise of the sirens became louder still, until he could make out the flashing lights refracting through the surrounding glass office buildings, as the police cars travelled at speed through the parallel streets. Within seconds, the noise had faded to a faint wailing, and tranquillity returned.

He took another large gulp of his whiskey and looked at his wristwatch. It was 1:35 a.m. The only reason he was still awake was because he was expecting an important phone call and wanted to be alert when he received it. He went back inside the flat, closing the sliding door behind him, and made his way through the living room and hallway, into the bedroom. In anticipation of his assignment, he had begun to lay out some of his belongings on his bed, ready to be packed. He had already decided he would travel in a formal suit, helping him to blend in as just another businessman on his way to Japan. Certainly, a less conspicuous reason for a man to be making such a long journey alone. He would also need a casual change of clothes, so he could later adopt a more tourist-like appearance, as he navigated the more rural areas of Japan as a foreigner.

Most important of all was money. Earlier in the day he had collected seven hundred and fifty thousand yen – equal to around five and a half thousand pounds – and the same equivalent in dollars. He had placed the order under a false name and bank account, and had the money delivered to a Post Office box in central London. He never used any payments that would leave a paper trail when he was working.

He moved approximately half of the yen into his wallet and placed the rest, plus the dollars, into the lining of the suitcase, securing it with a concealed fastening that he had fashioned for just such a purpose.

Suddenly his phone rang. He accepted the call but waited for the person at the other end of the line to speak first.

'Your meeting has been arranged,' said the electronically disguised voice. 'You have a green light to proceed with the deal.'

He made no reply. Not even a gesture of acknowledgement.

'Your car will be ready when you arrive,' the distorted voice added. Then the line went dead.

Seconds later his phone omitted a short ping. The text message read:

Today 01:37
33.85591, 134.019827. KIXP1093. BB0529

Whilst the phone call and subsequent text message were deliberately cryptic, he knew exactly what they meant. He opened his laptop and typed in the two sets of numbers into the search engine. This gave him the location of the target. The next set of numbers would be the reference for an airport parking bay in Kansai, where he would find a vehicle equipped with a concealed weapon. And the final set of alphanumeric characters related to the next SIM card he should use to replace the current one. Standard procedure was to replace it each time he was contacted by the Mothership. That's what he called it. A private joke that he shared with no one. Although in reality, the organisation he worked for had no name. Nor did it exist on paper. It was more akin to an invisible force. You might occasionally see evidence of its effects, but nothing more. Even *he* wasn't sure how big it was, but he knew that there were many others like him operating across the globe. He recognised their handiwork. The telltale signs that a suicide was not really a suicide and an accident not an accident.

He ejected the incumbent SIM card from his phone and snapped it in half. Then he disposed of it by carefully wrapping the remains in tissue paper before dropping it into the toilet bowl and pulling the chain. He returned to the bedroom and retrieved the pre-assigned replacement from a collection he kept in his safe and inserted it into his device. Then he emptied the remainder of his whiskey glass into his mouth before continuing with his packing and travel arrangements.

18

Maisie pulled up at the minshuku, at around 17:30. It was the Japanese equivalent of a bed and breakfast. This one was situated on the outskirts of the village and only a three-minute drive from where she had previously parked her car. The house was a large wooden structure on two levels, set into the hillside and partially concealed by the abundant bamboo, evergreens, oaks, and maples that carpeted the undulating mountain range. The well-maintained, but unassuming building, which had large plain glass windows and a gently inclined tiled roof, was perhaps a more modern design than the thatched buildings in the village. Nevertheless, it remained in keeping with its rural, mountainous setting.

Reaching it required a short climb up a steep track, where there was room for her to park alongside two other cars. Maisie got out and retrieved her luggage, before navigating through a carefully manicured zen garden, which boasted spectacular views over the valley. She was mindful not to disturb the gravel that had been painstakingly raked into decorative spiral patterns and followed the large stepping-stones that arced round to the entrance of the house.

Already waiting for her on the veranda was an older lady of small stature, who patiently watched Maisie approach. Her dark hair was tied neatly into a bun, and she wore a traditional Japanese kimono, made from a lavish blue silk and decorated with an intricate pattern of butterflies and flowers, tied off at the waist with a band of golden silk. From the moment Maisie first noticed her, she maintained a very broad, welcoming smile, and as Maisie approached the steps leading to the veranda, she slowly, but gracefully bent forwards.

'Konnichiwa,' the owner said with a spritely tone of voice, 'Agatte kudasai,' she added, gesturing for Maisie to come inside.

'Konnichiwa,' Maisie replied. 'Watashi no namae wa Maisie Lockhart desu,' she said in an uninterrupted flow, having spent much of the journey from the airport practicing her introduction, along with several other phrases that she thought might come in handy.

The owner nodded approvingly and responded with, 'Miyu,' whilst tapping her nose, to signify she was referring to herself.

It was obvious the owner didn't know a word of English and so it was likely hand gestures would be their main method of communication. Maisie had hoped she would be able to ask the owner questions about Walker's comings and goings. How he spent his time there. Whether anyone came to the house to meet him. His behaviour in the run up to his disappearance. Clearly this would almost certainly require the skills of an interpreter.

They entered a large open space with polished wood flooring. In the centre of the room there was an open fireplace, surrounded by a circle of cushions. A large steel hood, for catching the smoke was suspended from the wooden rafters, and connected to a long flue that pierced the ceiling. There was a traditional Japanese dining table, in one corner of the room, and a small collection of ornaments and sculptures. But otherwise, the décor was minimalist and immaculate.

Maisie was given a pair of traditional slippers to wear, which she immediately put on, placing her shoes neatly on a wooden rack by the door, alongside half a dozen other pairs. She couldn't help but notice the brand names of some of the walking boots on the rack, indicating there may be other Westerners staying.

The owner gave Maisie a brief tour of the other rooms on the ground floor, including a kitchen and room with nothing in it except for a series of long mats, presumably for exercising, Maisie assumed. The owner then led Maisie upstairs and opened the door to her room. The bedroom was large and generously equipped with a king-sized bed, a large wardrobe and a chest of drawers, a reasonably sized television and small seating area. There was also a desk by the window that looked out onto an impressive view of the picturesque valley and rolling hills, visible through gaps in the trees that enclosed the property. The window was slightly ajar, and Maisie could just about make out the soothing sound of water rushing over rocks at the base of the valley below them.

Maisie retrieved a photograph and presented it to the owner.

'Edward Walker stayed here?' she asked pointing to the image, not really knowing what else she could say.

'Hai, Edward Walker,' Miyu replied whilst nodding and pointing to the ground. Maisie had made a point of requesting the same room as Walker.

The owner continued to show Maisie the rest of her quarters, which included a small bathroom, with a bath and shower, and separate kitchen area with a sink and some basic cooking facilities.

Maisie nodded her approval. The owner then presented her with a menu card, which she used to highlight the time for dinner. Maisie shook her head, an attempt to articulate that she would not be needing dinner this evening. She had accepted an invitation from Sergeant Tamura, in her view made to get rid of her, so he could continue with his work. Sensing the hectic atmosphere, Maisie had seen this as a preferable opportunity to break the ice in a more relaxed setting.

The owner nodded politely to confirm her understanding and bowed once more, before leaving the room, closing the door behind her.

Maisie checked her watch. She had about an hour and a half before she would be meeting with Sergeant Tamura. Before doing anything, she intended to undertake a thorough search of the room; just in case any potential clues had been left behind by Walker and perhaps missed by the authorities.

After an extensive and exhausting search behind all the items of furniture in the room – inside the cupboards and drawers, behind the sculptures and artwork on the walls –Maisie had just about given up. She didn't really know what she was looking for, and deep down she knew it was unlikely that anything had been overlooked, but even the smallest detail could sometimes prove to be significant. A discarded receipt, a telephone number written on a scrap of paper or maybe even signs of a struggle. Any detail could potentially lead to something significant. Equally, she knew from experience that people could sometimes prove very resourceful if the situation demanded it.

As she sat on the floor with her legs crossed, looking around the room for inspiration, she noticed two slight indentations above one of the desk drawers – about the same width apart as the edges of the drawer itself. As she ran her fingers across it, she realised that the subtle scratches against the façade of the desk had been caused by someone attempting to slot the drawer back into place. Naturally she had already thought to check the inside of the drawers, but she had not thought to check underneath or behind them.

She removed each drawer, one by one, and placed them upside down on the bed. Nothing. Then she reached inside and ran her fingers along the panels. Suddenly, her fingers grazed something small, protruding from one of the corner joints. It felt sticky and irregular and noticeably different from the otherwise precise angles of the desk. She began tugging downwards with both hands. Whatever it was, it began loosening with every pull until the item broke free. She smiled to herself, as she inspected the small USB flash drive clumsily wrapped in electrical tape. Etched into the plastic covering were the letters 'EW'.

19

Before they had entered the restaurant, Maisie had imagined she would be dining at a low-level table, thirty centimetres or so from the floor, with traditional zabuton cushions to sit on. Instead, they were seated on high stools, facing each other across a thick, rustic wooden table. Otherwise, the décor was traditionally Japanese with an abundance of wood covering the floors and ceiling. Translucent white sheets on lattice frames, some bearing the restaurants motif, covered most of the walls and windows. Candlelight gently lit the tables and, with only a few other guests spread evenly across the open space, there was a muted, almost intimate atmosphere.

Tamura's body language gave very little away. He came across as a serious man, perhaps even a little aloof. But he had been generous enough to give up his evening. He had an athletic build, and carried a confident posture matched by a well projected voice and unwavering eye contact, which made him appear decisive, without being overbearing. But Maisie also detected a hint of gentleness in his dark hazel eyes. Maisie deduced that his stern exterior may only be a defence mechanism that might diminish once he realised, she was not a threat.

The waiter promptly arrived with their drinks order. Two frosted glasses of Japanese lager. Tamura's glass already wore his fingerprints where the ice on the outside had partially thawed.

'I understand you are famous in your home country Ms Lockhart. How would you say … a celebrity?' Tamura's face gave little away, and Maisie was not sure if he was attempting levity or sarcasm.

'Perhaps more infamous than famous, but certainly not a celebrity.' Maisie replied.

'I looked up your profile on the Spotlight News website earlier. Maisie Lockhart …' he paused before he began to recite the words he could recall from the profile, '… during her fifteen years as a journalist has been abducted, arrested, detained and shot at … is that how it goes?' Tamura asked with a wry smile.

'Let's just say I bore easily,' she said, taking a satisfying long sip from the chilled glass. 'And what about you, Sergeant Tamura?' she asked, 'how long have you been a police officer?'

'Four years,' he said without any supplementary detail.

By now Maisie had begun to focus on the sergeant's accent, which from the pronunciation of his vowels, carried the subtle hint of a North American rhythm. Although, in contrast, his choice of words, seemed altogether more formal.

'And your mother was an English teacher. Your father worked on the American airbase at Yokota.' Maisie said.

Tamura looked up suddenly from his menu. His eyes widened.

'You're not the only one who does their research.' Maisie added with a smile.

The waitress returned to the table to take their order. She spoke only to Tamura in Japanese and then returned to the kitchen.

'I ordered a selection from each of the courses for us to sample. I hope you don't mind?'

'Not at all,' Maisie replied, the words denying her true feelings. 'So how did you become sergeant of the koban in Takakumi?' she asked.

'I started my career as a police officer in Tokushima city. After I completed my basic training, I was encouraged to take part in a rotation of the various departments – traffic, vice, homicide – I worked in all of them. But then I was required to take on a permanent role. There were no sergeant's positions in the city at the time, so I had the choice of remaining in Tokushima city as a senior police officer, or to take the sergeant post that was available here.'

'It must be very different working here compared to a large city?'

Tamura nodded sternly, 'I knew it would be a lot quieter when I took on the position. Most of the time very little happens here. But now we are in the middle of one of the most high-profile cases this area has ever seen.'

Maisie began to realise that Tamura saw this investigation as being key to his career progression. It was also clear that the weight of this pressure was beginning to take its toll on him. Subtle signs of darkness around his eyes and the occasional squeezing of his temples and forehead – an action that he had repeated regularly throughout their conversation – both indicated long hours and maybe even sleepless nights.

'Are you referring to the disappearance of Akina Oshiro or Edward Walker?' Maisie asked.

'Both. We take all disappearances very seriously, whether they relate to Japanese citizens or foreign nationals,' Tamura said as if he were reading from a script, 'but they are almost certainly linked.'

'You mean, you believe Walker is the one responsible?' she asked, the local news article that had been released only yesterday still firmly engrained in her mind.

'Perhaps. We are exploring all lines of enquiry,' Tamura said without elaborating.

'And how is Akina? Has she said anything yet?'

Tamura shook his head, as he sipped his glass of beer, 'She is still in a medically induced coma, recovering in hospital.'

'But you don't yet have anything concrete on Walker?'

Tamura said nothing, but Maisie deduced from his silence and evasive body language that he was not entirely convinced Walker was behind it all. Maybe it was an order from above, or Oshiro himself. Maisie decided not to push it any further for the time being.

The first courses arrived at their table. One large bowl contained a noodle soup accompanied by strips of beef, a soft-boiled egg and a selection of steamed vegetables, a second contained some sort of small root vegetable in a chicken stew. Tamura encouraged Maisie to sample each of them in the empty bowl that had been laid out in front of her.

'So, what are you hoping to achieve from your visit here, Lockhart-san?' Tamura asked, as he began filling his own bowl.

'Simple I suppose. Find out what happened to Walker.'

'And what do you think has happened?' asked Tamura.

'Too early to say at this stage. Maybe he's behind it all, maybe not. But from speaking with his parents, he doesn't fit the bill of a psychopath. He has no history of mental health issues. And there doesn't a appear to be a plausible motive.'

'And yet, people can sometimes surprise you. Killers lying dormant for years. Abusers hiding in plain sight. This is not uncommon.' Tamura said as a statement of fact rather than a question.

'Actually, his parents seemed more inclined to believe he had found himself at the centre of a conspiracy, perhaps linked to Akina's father, Yoshi Oshiro. The man Edward was working for. Do you know him?'

'Yes, I know him. He is an important man around here. It would be a very bold person who hurled accusations like that at Oshiro-san. Certainly not without evidence.'

'I wouldn't have an issue challenging him,' Maisie said, with a hint of playfulness. 'As far as I'm concerned, he's fair game. Just like any other person, important or otherwise.'

'I, on the other hand need, to consider the evidence. And that his daughter has been the subject of a violent attack.'

'So, what evidence do you have on Walker?' Maisie asked.

Tamura ignored the question and the two of them continued eating the remainder of the first course, an awkward silence hanging in the air.

'I met his father a few weeks ago,' Tamura announced suddenly, 'Jonathan Walker, that is. He was understandably upset and very concerned for his son. I did what I could to assist him, but it was as if Walker had disappeared without a trace. We continued the search for his son, long after he returned to England, but the dense forests mean covering ground is painstakingly difficult,' he said defensively.

'What do you think happened to him?'

Tamura shrugged. 'I don't know. But finding him is our top priority.' Tamura said.

Maisie used her spoon to stir her soup, which was still piping hot. 'Well, perhaps there could also be an opportunity for us to help each other?' Maisie said, sensing an opportune moment.

'Help each other?' Tamura repeated.

Masie nodded. 'You're aware of my experience. I know where to look and what questions to ask. And because I am not a police officer, I am not constrained by the politics that you and your colleagues might be. You said yourself that this is the biggest case you have been involved in. I believe I can help you. You can take full credit for any leads that I identify, or information that I come across.'

'And what would you expect from me in return?' Tamura asked, a little taken aback by Maisie's proposal.

Maisie's phone began to ring. It was DI Nathan Roberts. She wanted to answer and hear if there was any news on the man who had been following her, but he would have to wait. She rejected the call, apologised to Tamura for the interruption, and resumed the conversation.

'I want to find out what happened to Walker,' she said simply. 'To do that I will need your help accessing individuals within your community, including Yoshi Oshiro, so that I can interview them myself. I also need access to updates from your investigation. How the search is progressing, the lines of inquiry, who you have spoken with, that sort of thing.' she added.

Tamura chuckled. 'It sounds as though you have got quite a lot to gain from this arrangement, given your present position,' he said with amusement. 'I don't know how things work in England, but if Japanese police leak information to the press without sanction from a senior officer, it usually results in disciplinary action.' Tamura paused for a moment, a ripple of lines appearing on of his forehead, 'I was surprised when I received the call from our central office, saying that they had spoken to police in London. They had advised that you would be arriving and asked if we could provide a local contact. It made me curious to meet you, seeing as you are clearly very well connected with the police in your England.'

'They are also used to working with me,' she said interjecting, 'and they have found that cooperating can be mutually beneficial. You can ask them.'

'Perhaps so. But I would be taking a big risk involving you in the workings of an active investigation.'

'If you are concerned about me writing about you or your team, Sergeant, don't be. I protect my sources, and my readers have no interest in hearing about how a Japanese investigation is conducted, unless there is widespread corruption. I shouldn't think that you personally would have anything to worry about in that respect,' Maisie said, taking a gamble she was right about his character.

Tamura paused pensively and took another sip from his drink before answering, 'I am happy to answer your questions this evening, but I cannot give you access to details relating to an open investigation. And if you want to speak to Mr Oshiro, I'm afraid you will have to find a way to make contact yourself.'

Maisie said nothing in reply, as if she was accepting Tamura's decision. Then she reached into her handbag and recovered the flash drive. She dangled it momentarily in the tips of her fingers, before placing it delicately on the table between them.

'What's that?' Tamura asked, gesturing with a nod in the direction of the item.

'I found this concealed in Walker's room at the minshuku.' she responded frankly. 'I've checked it and it seems to be his, but the files are encrypted.' she added. 'Now, there's nothing particularly unusual about encrypting files – fairly common practice I would say – but why would he feel the need to hide it, by taping it to the inside of a desk?'

Tamura said nothing. He just looked at Maisie curiously, as if wondering whether or not he could trust what she was telling him.

'I could arrange for this to be returned to England and the files decrypted there, but it might take several days before it is even received by my colleagues, and perhaps even a week or two before I would get the results. On the other hand, I'm sure you have people here who could look at it, meaning that both of us would get to see the information a great deal quicker?'

Maisie seductively manoeuvred the memory stick around the cutlery and condiments with the tip of her finger, letting it come to rest on Tamura's side of the table. Tamura's eyes met with Maisie's as he pondered his response. She could see him weighing the pros and cons carefully in his mind. Then, after a brief pause, he nodded with a solemn sincerity, to acknowledge the significance of the offering, before placing the drive carefully into his pocket.

20

The rigid tension that had loitered in the undertones of their conversation was suddenly gone. It was as if it had never been there at all. Tamura ordered another round of drinks, like he was celebrating a breakthrough, and the dialogue shifted from business, to more affable and informal conversation.

A team of waiters arrived at the table to deliver the main course. The first to arrive assembled a fold-out table, which was immediately used by the others to place the variety of dishes. There was red snapper in a sweet sauce, seared sliced tuna with a rare reddish-brown colour at its centre, a selection of skewered meats, boiled vegetables and soba noodles, a local speciality.

A ceramic bottle arrived at the table with two cups, the size of shot glasses.

'I thought you might also like to try this,' Tamura said as he began pouring the clear liquid. 'It is customary in Japan to pour Nihonshu for each other.'

'Nihonshu?' Maisie echoed, curiously.

'You may know it better as sake,' explained Tamura, 'but in Japan you would ask for Nihonshu.'

Maisie picked up the ceramic bottle and began pouring, surprised that the drink was ice cold.

'Ah yes, sake. I've heard of it, but I don't think I've ever tried it before. Isn't it normally served hot?' she asked.

'It can be,' he replied, 'but it depends on the type of Nihonshu, time of year and the preference of the individual. It is better cold with fish and white meats. But during winter, I might choose to take it warm.'

Maisie took a sip from the cup and was immediately surprised by the smooth, well-balanced combination of astringent and savoury flavours that were gentle on the palate. Suddenly she became quite conscious of her alcohol consumption. It was still relatively early in the evening and already she was beginning to feel a mild light-headedness and a slight loosening of the tongue. But it was an ideal way to break the ice, and aided a free-flowing conversation, unencumbered by inhibition.

Tamura had begun to play, nervously with his cup, using the tips of his fingers to rotate it several turns in a counter-clockwise direction before repeating the process in reverse. Maisie sensed he was building up to a question he was in two minds about asking.

'There was something else I read about you,' Tamura finally said, both hands still fidgeting with the cup. 'Something that happened during the terror attacks in London.'

Tamura gave a cursory glance in the direction of her left trouser leg, knowingly. 'Perhaps you don't like to talk about it.'

Maisie smiled, to ease the tension. 'Actually, it doesn't bother me in the least,' she replied as she leant down and teased the loose-fitting beige cloth to reveal the shiny metal beneath, where her shin should have been.

'I understand you were on the train when it happened?'

Maisie nodded. 'It was in my first year at university. The day it happened I was on my way to classes. The same journey I always took. I never paid much attention to the other passengers. Like most commuters I usually had my head buried in a book, oblivious to what was going on around me. But something about him made me look up. I can remember seeing him just before he did it. He can't have been much older than me – still just a boy. He sat down opposite me. I can remember seeing the fear in his eyes and wondering what was wrong. He kept looking up and down the carriage and fidgeting with the rucksack between his legs. The next thing I can remember is regaining consciousness. The explosion had thrown me clear of the carriage. I was laying on my back, covered in shards of glass, watching people scrambling from the burning carriage and making their way along the tunnel. I had a loud ringing in my ears – ruptured eardrums – but I could still hear the screams. A woman next to me had been badly burned and was writhing in agony. I wanted to help her, but when I went to move, I realised I couldn't. At first there was no pain at all. A man came to help me. His name was Samir. He was a trainee doctor who had been in the carriage when it happened. I can remember him looking reassuringly into my eyes. He was speaking to me, but I couldn't make out what he was saying. I knew I was losing blood. Then he tied a piece of cloth around where the leg had been severed and squeezed it tightly. That's when the pain kicked in. It was so severe I lost consciousness. The next thing I knew I woke in a hospital bed.'

'What was it like … afterwards?' Tamura asked.

Maisie sighed and took a mouth full of sake to help wash down the memory. 'It was tough, particularly in the early stages. I can't lie, there were some dark days. But time can be a great healer. You learn to accept the new status quo and to move on. Eventually I realised that I was lucky.'

'Lucky?' Tamura raised an eyebrow.

'Yes, extremely lucky. Sure, I was badly injured, but I met many others with both severe physical and mental scars. Many did not survive at all. My experiences were terrible yes, but I was able to rebuild my life and I came out the other side stronger. Do I wish it hadn't happened? Of course I do. Are there days when I wish I could get my hands on the men who did it, abso-fucking-lutely. But I don't want anybody's pity, I just want to get on with things. Otherwise, the people that did would have won, and I fear the thought of that more than anything.'

Tamura nodded slowly. Both drew pensively from the cups, looking back at each other as if they were waiting for the other to break the silence.

'There is one thing I've been dying to ask,' Maisie announced from nowhere, partially aware that her use of idioms might be confusing, 'What's the story behind the scarecrows?'

'I wondered when you would ask about that.' Tamura replied with a deliberate smile. 'Usually, it's the first thing anyone asks when they visit this place. Had you heard about them before your arrival?'

'Not until very recently, when I began looking into Walker's disappearance.'

'They have become quite famous locally,' Tamura said, 'and amongst some Westerners visiting the island.'

'I suppose many Westerners might consider them to be a little eccentric. But a more cynical person might say they were there purely to kick-start tourism, in a struggling, rural village.'

Tamura burst into laughter, somewhat shocked by the bluntness of Maisie's observation, 'I would tend to agree with you,' he said, in amusement, 'although some of the local residents certainly would not.'

'So, who has put them here, and why?' asked Maisie impatiently.

'Would you like the official response, or the unofficial answer?' Tamura said cryptically. As he spoke, Maisie observed the subtle signs of fatigue mixed with alcohol beginning to weigh down his eyelids.

'Sounds intriguing already,' commented Maisie, 'Both, of course. But perhaps the unofficial version first. I suspect that the official version will be far less dramatic.' she added playfully.

'Perhaps some facts to begin with. You are, after all, a celebrated journalist,' Tamura said with a smile, as he attempted to heighten the drama. 'At the last count there were precisely eighty-seven scarecrows, situated both in and around the village. Initially there were only a handful of them. The first of them began appearing almost two years ago and, at the time, the population of this village was considerably larger. You certainly wouldn't have described it as a bustling village, but there were a collection of shops and local businesses. The main employment was farming buckwheat, which is the main ingredient of these noodles we're eating,' Tamura said, pausing to sip from his cup of sake.

'The first sighting of the scarecrows was reported on 9th April, almost two years ago. I remember it because this date holds significance in Japanese culture. Specifically, the meaning of the numbers that make up this date. Some Japanese believe these numbers mean something bad will happen. The number nine can be a warning for pain and suffering. The number four – for the fourth month – can be a warning of death. In Japan this can be taken quite literally.'

'Do you believe in these omens?' Maisie asked.

'No, I don't. It tends to be more the older generations that believe such things. But it is still a widely held belief. When you visit a tower block in a major city, these numbers will mostly be missing from the elevator control panel. When the first scarecrows arrived on this date, the villagers saw them as a threat. Many shared this view after the incident.'

'Incident?' Maisie asked, impressed with Tamura's storytelling skills which had drawn her in and left her impatient for more.

Tamura paused momentarily. His slightly glazed eyes broke contact with Maisie's and dropped to a point in the centre of the table. His mood seemed suddenly more solemn and regretful.

'About a week after the first scarecrows were discovered, there was a severe fire at the home of an elderly couple. Both were killed. The investigators concluded the fire was an accident started by the couple's wood-burning stove. But some of the locals were more suspicious. It wasn't long before rumours began circulating that their deaths had something to with the arrival of the scarecrows. Some feared there was a supernatural cause. Others believed there was some sort of government conspiracy. But all followed a consistent theme. The scarecrows were here to force local inhabitants to leave.'

'Why would they think that?' Maisie asked.

'Who knows?' Tamura replied, 'In my experience, people don't need evidence to believe in the ridiculous.'

'So, what happened next?' she asked.

Tamura shrugged his shoulders and finished the rest of his cup, 'Their numbers grew. More and more. Sometimes a few weeks would go by and then lots would appear all at once. Initially we took them down, but they would just be replaced with more. After a while, the villagers stopped complaining. Now the scarecrows are part of the village, the same as the buildings and remaining villagers.'

'Aren't you curious to find out who is responsible?'

'We have more important things to worry about. Like finding your Mr Walker.' Tamura said, sharply. 'There's an old lady that lives in the village. Some believe she is behind it.'

'Why do they think that?'

'There's nothing to suggest that it's her. But she's seen as a little … how would you say … unusual. Some have said she makes them to replace the villagers that have left. Like she's building a community of her own. We have asked her about it, but she says they are nothing to do with her. Even if it was her, she's not breaking any laws. We don't get complaints now. As you say, some benefit from the tourists. Like the guesthouse where you're staying and local tour guides.'

'And what about all the inhabitants of the village? Why have so many left the area?'

'Mostly to find work, I guess. It's the same with many other communities across Japan. Nowadays there's more work in the cities. In the last twenty years bigger farms have replaced smaller ones that can't compete. So, people have moved away to find work.'

'And what about the large number of disappearances that have been reported in the area?'

Tamura let out a small sigh.

'Each one was investigated thoroughly. Most turned out to be people who had relocated and decided not to tell the other inhabitants or, in some cases, even their families. There are some open cases which we are continuing to investigate, but we are limited. Here in Japan, privacy laws prevent the police from accessing personal information like telephone records or bank account information unless there is a criminal case. If a citizen does not register their address with their local prefecture, there is no way of knowing where they have moved to, in the entire country. This can make finding individuals very difficult.'

Maisie pondered for a moment as she tried to decide what sort of man Tamura was. There was no doubting he was very intelligent, with a level of maturity far beyond his years. And yet, there was a certain naivety about him. When it came to the disappearances, Maisie couldn't decide whether Tamura was truly speaking his own opinion, or whether he was merely articulating the position of his superiors. For the sake of their newfound relationship, she decided not to push any further. For now, at least.

'And what would have been the official response?' Maisie asked.

'No comment,' Tamura replied with a smile, before calling over the waitress for an order of more sake.

21

It was a pleasant morning at Heathrow Airport. As Hunter was carried up the steep escalators towards the terminal entrance, he observed the unblemished blue sky. Blindingly bright light from the low sun reflected off the glass canopy above, and a thunderous rumble from the planes echoed around the concrete buildings. All boded well for his flight to depart on schedule, he thought.

The hire car he used had been rented under a false name and left in the long stay car park. He smiled to himself with a perverse sense of satisfaction as he contemplated the number of weeks, perhaps even months, that would likely pass before the car was eventually discovered.

He remained mindful of his surroundings and was careful not to draw attention to himself. Too many trained eyes would be checking his every move; from the moment he entered the terminal building right through to boarding the aircraft. One false move could lead to him being noticed, or worse apprehended. He needed to blend in. Be invisible to the casual eye.

As he dragged his small suitcase off the escalators and wheeled it into the terminal building, he felt prepared for every eventuality. He had completed the online check-in in advance, and so was free to go straight through to the departures area. This was where he considered himself at greatest risk. An area with a high concentration of police and border control staff. Even after he had passed through to the departures lounge, he would be confined to an area with heavy security and extensive CCTV coverage until he boarded the plane. And so, his standard practice was to arrive at the airport no more than an hour before his flight departure time. That way he never spent more time confined and observed than was strictly necessary.

He presented his ticket at the self-service gates, which took his image before letting him through to the queue for the security checks. He smiled to himself as he observed the frantic energy of the passengers queuing in front of him across the many lanes of security check points. This was good news for him, as the security staff would be under pressure to keep the flow of passengers moving. The only thing he really needed to worry about was his cash, hidden in the concealed compartment inside the suitcase. But this homemade feature had never let him down before. Even if it was discovered, the amounts were small enough to be shrugged off by a seemingly affluent and security-conscious businessman.

Ensuring he held strong but non-threatening eye contact with the airport officials, he passed through the metal detector without issue. He retrieved his suitcase and began making his way towards the departure lounge, the hordes of other passengers still providing good cover. He stopped to check the departures board, which showed his flight was already boarding at Gate 38. He cursed inwardly as he recalled this was one of the farthest gates, requiring him to walk to the separate satellite terminal. Even so, there was still plenty of time.

He followed the steady stream of passengers, filing down the escalators to the lower levels. Standing to one side of the escalator allowing himself to be carried downwards, he assessed his surroundings. The airport was a hive of activity, with families, individuals and large parties all moving at different paces. Some clearly in a hurry to be the first to board their flight, others keen to make the most of the duty-free shopping. Lots more were waiting on the long lines of seating, their eyes fixed on the screens, visibly willing the status of their flights to change.

As he scanned both the lower level and upper level behind him, he noticed a slightly overweight middle-aged man hunched over the railings of the mezzanine. The ill-fitting suit and identification hanging from a band around his neck suggested airport security. But the sidearm holstered in his belt, only partially visible through the drooping gap in his jacket, rang the siren of a police officer. Possibly even Flying Squad.

The officer was staring straight at him, tracking his progress with uninterrupted fascination as he proceeded slowly down the escalator. As Hunter reached the lower level, he decided to ignore the sudden attention. The secondary terminal was accessed via a separate corridor at the far side of the building, only a hundred and fifty yards in front of him. If he could make it there without arousing suspicion, he would probably be okay. But, as he approached the corridor leading to the satellite terminal, he noted the 'time to gate' was advertised as fifteen minutes away, plenty of time for a pursuer to catch him before he reached the plane. And the long narrow corridors would limit his chances of escape.

Using the pretence of tying his shoelace to assess whether the man was still watching him, he saw the officer was now making his way down the escalators. The officer uttered something into his radio, but his eyes remained fixed on Hunter. There were no signs of other police and security personnel. Just him.

Hunter's gut told him it was time to act. There would be no avoiding some form of engagement, but he must deal with this officer before others became alerted to his presence. Using the approaching crowd as cover, Hunter got to his feet and continued along the walkway, past the corridor to the satellite terminal and towards the entrance to the men's toilets. It was his best chance. Fewer people and no surveillance cameras.

As he turned left through the door, he checked behind him. The officer was less than fifty yards away, heading straight for him with a cumbersome canter, the firearm still visible in his belt as his arms chopped through the air.

Before the officer could catch up, Hunter pushed his way inside the toilets and quickly scanned the area. No one was visible, but some of the cubicles might be in use. He would have to make do. He removed his belt and hastily wrapped it around his hand, leaving a short length and the buckle free. Then he moved himself behind the doorway with his right arm raised up above his head. Frozen in position, he waited.

Within seconds, the door burst open door. A gun barrel emerged cautiously, immediately followed by the officer's hands clutching the grip tightly with both hands. This was it. Clenching the belt with his right hand, Hunter whipped his arm downwards, catching the officer's hands with the buckle, causing him to release a yelp of agony as he dropped the weapon. Then he unleashed a firm, precise jab to the officer's throat.

The officer dropped to his knees, struggling for breath, helpless to retaliate. Straightaway, Hunter grabbed his shirt collar and swung his head into the underside of the closest porcelain basin. The officer's body toppled over, his head thudding loudly against the solid floor. Writhing on his arms and legs like a wounded insect, the officer clambered towards the door. But it was no good. Time to finish the job, Hunter thought. Using both hands to grip the back of the officer's suit jacket, he hoisted the semi-mobile body into the closest cubical and slammed him headfirst against the base of the toilet. Then he wrapped both arms tightly around the policeman's head, and yanked his neck firmly in a twisting motion, until he felt the decisive click. The body flopped to the floor in a distorted heap. Hunter liberated the officer's radio and pulled out his ID. The laminated card read *Detective Inspector Nathan Roberts*. It was always sensible to know the name of his victims.

He pushed the body of DI Roberts up onto the toilet, locked the cubicle door from within and climbed over the side. Then he calmly washed and dried his hands and took a moment to unruffle his suit jacket and straighten his tie, before collecting his suitcase. Cautiously exiting through the only door, there was no sign of any other police or security personnel within the immediate vicinity. Checking his watch, he headed in the direction of the gate. He still had time to catch his flight. No problem.

22

Tamura instructed the driver to drop them at the police station. He paid the fare, having also refused to take any money from Maisie for dinner, and went inside to collect a torch, whilst Maisie waited by the entrance.

By now darkness had completely consumed the village. The few solitary streetlamps emitted a pitiful glimmer, otherwise, there were no other lights to speak of from the vacant properties. Thick fog blanketed the entire area. What little light there was illuminated the water droplets in the air to create a muted green glow that lingered in the atmosphere. Maisie observed the outline of the cross-shaped figures that occupied the open areas of the village, whilst the shadows created by the encircling woodlands completed a seemingly impenetrable perimeter. The two of them had come up with the idea to explore the village whilst in the restaurant. An alcohol-fuelled idea that sounded like fun at the time. An opportunity to perhaps catch the culprits in the act. But right now, having partially recovered her senses with the help of the chill night air, she wondered if this really was such a good idea.

Moments later, Tamura reappeared carrying a torch in one hand and a baton in the other, 'You can't be too careful,' he said, holding it up to show Maisie.

Up to this point, Maisie had considered the presence of the scarecrows to be little more than a hoax. But Tamura's caution, coupled with the eerie setting, suddenly made her feel on edge. Tamura led them away from the buildings towards an open field that spanned two hundred or so metres, all the way to the river.

Aside from the faint rustling as they trampled through the long grass, the distant sound of running water was the only sound in the still night air.

'Where are we headed?' Maisie asked Tamura.

'I'm taking you to see the first of the scarecrows. I thought you'd want to see where it all began?'

'Absolutely, I would,' she said appreciatively as they continued onwards, passing more and more scarecrows. Some were clustered together as if there were interacting with one another. Others were randomly placed throughout the field.

It felt almost as though they were searching for a grave, as Tamura continued to shine the torch to check each figure they passed, until they reached a small shrine on a raised platform, not far from the river's edge. A set of steps led to the top, which was crowned by a modest wooden gazebo, no bigger than a garden shed. To one side at the base of the steps, two inanimate figures stood, both with their backs to the village, looking towards the shrine.

'And here they are,' Tamura announced, 'the first ones to be found in the village.' Tamura set the beam from his torch on the figures as they walked around them, to inspect them more closely. Whilst it was more difficult to make out their features by torch light, Maisie could immediately see that their porcelain faces were far more weathered than some of the ones she had seen earlier.

'Would you mind if I take the torch a moment?' she asked, hoping to use it to get a closer look at their details.

The paint, used to define the eyes and mouth, had begun to fade, and there were large, speckled patches where the surface of the porcelain had begun to erode. Probably caused by rain. Another key difference was grey straggly hair and fine lines that saddled their eyes. They had been deliberately made to look older.

Maisie inspected the frame, which held up the arms and head. It seemed well-made and was more solidly put together than she imagined. All the joins had been precisely glued together and any rough edges carefully sanded down. The body, which consisted of a single vertical pole, was connected to a cleverly constructed stand, made from two intersecting lengths of wood, which were themselves fixed to the ground with four rusty steel pegs. Someone had taken time to craft these strange sculptures.

'I take it these haven't moved since they were placed here?' Maisie asked.

Tamura nodded. 'As I said earlier, we initially removed all the scarecrows that were placed here, but they were subsequently replaced with ones that looked the same, in the same place. After the first two times, we decided to focus our efforts on more important matters.'

'And you say that these appeared shortly after the old couple were killed in the fire?'

'Correct.'

'It's little wonder the conspiracy theories began circulating. Particularly when two scarecrows, dressed as an elderly couple, appear shortly after an elderly couple lose their lives.' Maisie pointed out, without fear of causing offense.

'I agree. But, as I said before, there was no evidence of a crime and the coroner concluded the cause of the fire was unintentional,' said Tamura, slightly defensively.

Maisie's attention returned to the scarecrow and the clothes they were wearing. All had their own individual style, almost as if their creator wanted to give them their own unique personality. Rather than wearing threadbare rags, many of the items they wore were well-made, some expensive. The elderly couple were dressed in intricately decorated traditional Japanese apparel, made from finely woven silk. And, whilst it was difficult to tell under torchlight, there was very little sign of wear – despite having been there for almost two years. Not the sort of clothing you would expect to be discarded, let alone chosen for a scarecrow, Maisie thought.

Suddenly, there was loud rustling of grass, thirty or forty yards in front of them. Maisie shined the torch in the approximate direction of the noise, but this only served to illuminate the dense fog with the white beam. She turned back to Tamura, but he was gone.

'Sergeant Tamura?' she called out, into the darkness. There was no reply. She arced the torch slowly round, turning a full three hundred and sixty degrees whilst continuing to move in the direction where the noise had originated. What was he playing at? 'I'm not in the mood for pranks.' she called into the darkness.

As she reached the estimated position of the first noise, she heard another. This time it came from the opposite direction, behind her. She stopped and pivoted round in a small circle. Still, she could see nothing. The fog seemed to be thickening even more, reducing visibility to no more than five or six meters and, were it not for the noise from the river, she would have been completely disorientated. Her spine began to tingle as she started to sense that this might not be a joke.

'Niko, this isn't funny,' she shouted, frustration in her voice. She began walking in the direction of the second noise. What sort of wild animals were native to Japan? Were any of them dangerous? Admittedly, having spent most of her life in busy towns and cities, she couldn't pretend to be particularly knowledgeable – nor comfortable – in the countryside, least of all one so alien as this. As she approached a wall of darkness in front of her, her paces instinctively slowed and became more considered, concerned that she might be approaching the edge of the riverbank.

The hairs on the back of her neck stood on end and a cold sensation rushed through her body, as she suddenly felt a presence behind her. Forcing herself to turnaround she was instantly startled by a large figure a little taller than her. She let out a short shriek and instinctively raised the torch in her hand to use as a weapon.

A hand intercepted her wrist and gripped it tightly.

'Maisie, it's okay. It's me!'

'You bastard!' she yelled, punching him feebly in the arm, as he lowered the scarecrow and let it fall to the ground, before bursting into laughter.

'You could certainly do with sharpening some of your senses,' he laughed, 'you should come along to one of my martial arts classes.'

'If it gives me an opportunity to exact revenge on you, I'll be there in an instant,' she said, as she attempted to settle her heart rate with some long, deep breaths.

23

Maisie awoke to the sudden, electrifying ring from her mobile phone on the bedside table. It echoed through her eardrums like a set of cymbals crashing together. The darkness of her surroundings and the unfamiliar setting, triggered a temporary feeling of disorientation and confusion, quickly followed by the realisation she was in her room at the minshuku.

She fumbled for her phone and could see that it was her editor, Ivan Leegood. Swiping the screen to accept the call, she held the phone to her ear while allowing her head to sink back into the pillow.

'Ivan?' she said, with dazed surprise.

'Maisie, thank God I reached you,' Leegood said, 'I'm afraid I have some difficult news.' He sounded nervous. Rushing the words like he couldn't wait to get them out and be done with it. He never sounded nervous.

Maisie sat herself up in bed and switched on the bedside light, one hand still holding the phone to her ear, the other sweeping her hair back off her face. In all the years she had known Ivan, he had never once referred to her by her forename.

'You're scaring me, Ivan. What it is it?'

'It's Detective Roberts,' he responded, 'he was found dead earlier today at Heathrow airport.'

There was a temporary silence on the line as Maisie processed his words. The shock of the news caused her hands to tremble, 'Nathan?' she was in disbelief.

'I know the two of you knew each other well,' Leegood said with a gentle affirmation, 'I wanted you to hear it from me, before the news story breaks in a few hours' time.'

Maisie paused again, the information still sinking in, 'How … why … what was he doing at Heathrow?'

'According to our source at the Yard, he was following a lead on your man from the other morning. The one that was following you. Apparently, they had stumbled upon some insider intelligence that someone in the London area would be targeting a journalist in Japan. A British journalist. Nathan was setting up a network of additional surveillance at the transport hubs with the best connections to Japan. As Heathrow is the main airport for direct flights, that was the priority. I'm surprised Nathan hadn't tried to make contact given the possible threat to your safety?'

Maisie thought back to the call she ignored. 'He did,' she admitted, regretfully, 'but I hadn't got round to returning his call.'

'Well,' Leegood continued awkwardly, 'Nathan was in the process of initiating a manhunt, with an increased presence from his team stationed at the airport. Apparently, a few hours into the first day, Nathan happened to be in one of the border control offices when he thought he recognised your man on one of the CCTV monitors. He went out to get a closer look and was seen chasing the target into the gents' toilets. When he didn't respond to radio calls, his team went to investigate and found him dead. Cause of death has yet to be officially determined, but the attack was swift and brutal.'

'And what about the assailant? Where is he now?' Maisie asked.

'He got away,' Leegood said, regret weighing down his voice.

'Fucking hell!' Maisie exclaimed, 'how on earth did they let him get away? He was in an airport, for fuck's sake.'

'The assailant boarded a plane, which took off only minutes after the attack. By the time Nathan was found, he was already in the air. It was hours before the authorities managed to find which flight he had boarded and where he was headed. They've apparently contacted the Japanese police, to try and apprehend him when the plane lands in Tokyo. I'm expecting to have an update on that, sometime later today.'

'So, what are you telling me Ivan? He's on his way here to get me?'

'I'm telling you it's time to come home. You're not safe.'

'What on earth for?' Maisie retorted truculently, 'it's not as if I'm any safer in England.'

'I don't want to frighten you Lockhart, but this guy managed to disarm and kill a highly trained and experienced police officer. Probably with his bare hands. He's clearly a professional. The police here are insisting that you go into protective custody immediately. For your own safety!'

'If he can get to Nathan in the middle of a busy airport, what's stopping him from getting to me in protective custody? And how long are we talking? Months, years, the rest of my life? You know I'm not going into hiding. Besides, things are already beginning to bear fruit over here. And I'm surrounded by police.'

'This isn't a discussion Lockhart,' Leegood said, this time more forcefully, 'get yourself on the next flight back to England. Got it?'

Maisie let the words hang in the air, before abruptly ending the call. Then she collapsed back into the bed and thought of Nathan and his wife and young daughter. A mix of sorrow and anger welled up inside of her as she curled up into the foetal position and pushed back the tears, trying hard not to blame herself for his death.

Maisie made the short drive in her car, arriving at the station within a few minutes. It was early, and the sun had only recently risen enough to reveal the remanence of the morning mist. She had not eaten and had barely slept. Rage was her only fuel. All she could think about was vengeance. To capture Nathan's killer and bring him to justice. And yet, she felt more powerless than she had ever felt before. This time she was the hunted. And he was coming for her.

But she also had a job to do, despite what Leegood had said about dropping the investigation and returning home. She intended to finish what she'd started. She felt that she owed it to Walker's parents, and to herself. She had never walked away from anything before, and she was damned if she was going to now.

One thing was for sure. If she was the intended target of Nathan's killer, at least she wouldn't have to go looking for him. He would find her. She was the bait. But she needed to be smart, not reckless. She would need to take steps to protect herself and make herself a harder target. A professional would undertake reconnaissance of the area beforehand, perhaps even try to observe Maisie's comings and goings to establish vulnerabilities. To move about at random would be a powerful defensive strategy.

She would also look to surround herself with police where she could, although she had already decided that she would tell Tamura what had happened. He deserved to know the gravity of the situation, before putting himself at risk.

The place where she knew she would be most vulnerable would be at her lodgings, and so she would need to consider a way to protect herself and raise the alarm. She had already positioned certain heavy object within easy reach across the room that could be used as defensive weapons. She would also make sure that she called Tamura before leaving the building. That way someone would at least know that she had gone missing within a fairly short window, were she to fail to arrive somewhere. One thing was for sure, knowing that he was coming for her meant she could be better prepared for when he did eventually strike.

Were it not for the hive of activity surrounding the police station, the village remained largely deserted. Gathered outside in a large huddle was a group of twenty or so police officers, receiving instructions from Tamura. As she pulled up, Tamura was finishing his briefing and sending them on their way to continue their search for Walker. When Tamura spotted Maisie, he acknowledged her with a casual nod of his head, before inviting her in for a coffee.

Inside the small station were the same faces as the previous evening, only this time her presence was met with a mildly welcoming, but still very formal, acknowledgement.

'It looks like you've been up for hours,' she said, breaking the silence.

'We have,' Tamura admitted, 'that's the second party to leave this morning. They will be starting from opposite sides of the gorge. Then by mid-morning they should come together and begin covering this largely flat, but heavily wooded area here,' he pointed to a seemingly large area of the map that had yet to acquire any pins.

Maisie noticed Tamura didn't seem to be showing any ill effects from the previous evening's indulgence of sake.

'So how many make up the search party today?' she asked.

'Almost fifty; the most we have had so far. As you can see, considerable progress is being made,' he said, pointing to the map again, 'but the search area is vast and made up of difficult terrain.'

'Are there any inhabited areas or structures in this area?' she asked.

Tamura nodded, 'Without doubt there will be numerous hunting cabins, but none are known to be occupied. No one goes out there anymore. Besides it's private property, belonging to Oshiro-san. He would not be pleased if anyone was found on his property.'

'So how much land does Mr Oshiro own in the area?' Maisie said inquisitively.

'Most of the land in the immediate vicinity, aside from the village of course.'

Maisie made a mental note as she took a satisfying sip of her strong coffee. She felt her heart rate flutter slightly.

'I've also sent the flash drive you recovered to our office in Tokushima, where they should be able to decrypt the files. As a thank you, and as agreed, one of my team will call Mr Oshiro's secretary, to see if we can arrange an appointment for you later today.'

'That's fantastic news, Niko,' she said gratefully. Looking around the busy office, she hesitated for a moment. 'I know you have a lot on your plate right now, but could I speak to you in private? I've had some news from home.'

24

It was late. Through the porthole there was only a vast darkness. Inside the cabin the lights had been dimmed for some time. By now all the passengers within view had adopted their sleeping positions, with most opting for eye masks. Even better, Hunter thought.

He had been waiting for hours. Ever since he'd noticed the medication belonging to the elderly man in the seat beside him. The pills that rattled in those unsteady hands alerted him to a potential weakness. The writing on the bottle was in Japanese but having covertly used the translation app on his phone, he quickly established it was Acebutolol – a drug commonly used to treat high blood pressure and irregular heartbeats amongst sufferers of acute coronary disease. Hunter immediately knew this was his way out.

While the other passengers had been watching films, he had been tracking the plane's progress on the screen in the headrest in front of him. It showed the altitude and speed of the aircraft, but most importantly, it showed the aircraft approaching the eastern edge of the Black Sea, about level with the Georgia-Russia border. They were now firmly within Asia. From here he would have multiple options to complete his journey. But crucially, he had decided none of them would include arriving by plane.

He looked over at the old man. His seat was partially reclined and his head tipped back. He had been asleep for the last twenty-two minutes. A sleep deep enough for him to remain unstirred by his own wheezing breaths that strained torturously through his nostrils.

One last check of his surroundings, in front and behind. There was no movement in the aisles and the flight crew were on their break. This was it; he might not get another chance. There was no margin for error. Twisting his body awkwardly in his seat, he silently leaned over the old man's motionless body, then with a sharp and powerful blow, he thrust his elbow into the old man's chest. As soon as he made contact, he heard a slight pop. The sternum snapped like a feeble twig. The old man immediately woke and began gasping desperately, confused and in a panic.

Instantly, Hunter adapted his persona to that of a concerned passenger. He shouted for help and pushed the overhead button to call for a flight attendant.

'I think this man's having a heart attack!' he yelled.

His other hand continued to apply pressure to the old man's chest. Within seconds the fiery look of betrayal in the old man's eyes was doused by the lack of oxygen to his brain, and both his limbs and eyelids slowly surrendered.

The flight attendant arrived briskly, clutching a red box against her breast. She clambered over him, to get to the old man. She quickly charged the defibrillator, ripped open his shirt and applied the leads to his chest. She checked his breathing, then his pulse, and huffed with disappointment. With a firm jolt, she discharged the first pulse of electricity into the old man's chest. Nothing. Again. And then again. But her repeated attempts to resuscitate him failed. As the old man lay motionless, she called to her colleague to inform the cockpit.

'Tell the captain we're going to need to land at the nearest airport, this man needs urgent medical attention,' she said, knowing it might already be too late.

Hunter smiled to himself internally. Exactly the outcome he wanted.

***

Tamura's team was able to arrange an appointment for Maisie to meet with Mr Oshiro later that morning, at eleven o'clock. Maisie was surprised by the immediacy of the meeting, and even more so when Oshiro's secretary had phoned again to pass on a message from Oshiro himself, saying he would be honoured to receive Maisie at his nearby residence.

Having told Tamura about Detective Nathan Roberts' murder, and the presumption that his killer may be following her to Japan, Tamura had become very protective, insisting that Maisie be accompanied by either himself or a member of his team at all times.

Although she was both touched and pleasantly surprised by his sudden concern for her welfare, she firmly declined the offer. She did however agree to join one of his martial arts classes; firstly, to soften the blow of her rebuff, and secondly because such skills might well come in handy, given the impending threat.

She had spent much of the morning strolling around the village to avoid outstaying her welcome at the station. And also, to give herself some time alone to grieve for her friend.

She had suffered loss before, but never under circumstances such as these. She was still very much in a state of shock. Only forty-eight hours ago she had been boisterously pushing Nathan to find out more about the man from the train. And now he was gone, leaving her with an acute emptiness inside, a hollow that would never be refilled. They weren't best friends, but they had worked together for years and had become close. She owed him a lot and had never told him how grateful she was. And, as she circled repeatedly around the village, her feelings of guilt were compounded as she repeatedly ran through the recent events in her mind. Were it not for her, he might still be alive.

***

Maisie set off for her meeting with Yoshi Oshiro half an hour early, armed with a set of uncomplicated directions given by Tamura.

'Follow the road up to the restaurant and keep going for another three miles until you reach a large entrance and set of security gates on the right. You'll know it when you see it, there's nothing else around for miles.'

Having experienced the road as a passenger the previous evening, it did not take long to pass the restaurant, and she continued climbing as she followed the road round the mountainside. At the peak, the road levelled out onto a long, arrow-straight ridge that seemed to stretch for miles.

To the left, there was a vast ripple of mountain ranges all the way to the horizon, all densely covered by forest. To the right, the branches from the trees on the higher ground, reached out over the road creating a long canopy that blocked the view of the sky above. Through the occasional break in the trees, Maisie began catching tantalising glimpses of a tall white structure ahead. A solitary skyscraper.

Suddenly Maisie understood why Tamura had been so casual with his directions. This was undoubtedly the 'large residence' he referred to, albeit a wholly inadequate description. 'Fortress' would have been more apt.

As she drew nearer, the thick woodland began to diminish until the trees gave way to an expansive clearing. A twenty-foot high wall ran parallel with the road for at least half a mile. With a base made from large granite slabs, and the rest covered in a smooth mortar painted white, it seemed more like a wall that might have guarded a fortified ancient city, than a private residence. Its proximity to the road, combined with its height, meant it successfully concealed all but the very top of the castle, which appeared to pierce the unblemished sky with its arrow-shaped crown.

She pulled into a grand entrance protected by double steel gates, ornately decorated with red paint and golden orbs. Either side of it, two life-sized statues of tigers, carved from white marble, stood proudly on separate pillars. She leaned out of her window to press the intercom button, and as she looked around, she counted five CCTV cameras fixed on her position.

'Good morning,' a voice answered in perfect English.

'Maisie Lockhart to see Mr Oshiro,' Maisie replied, a little surprised she would have no need for the Japanese she had been practicing on the way.

'Identification?' the voice demanded sternly.

Maisie held her journalist's ID up to the small camera lens on the intercom. She had been asked to send a scanned copy in advance; a strict protocol Oshiro's security staff had insisted upon.

'You are expected,' the voice said after a short pause, 'please drive up to the main building.'

The gates inched their way open to reveal the marvel of vast and immaculately kept gardens, consisting of undulating lawns, manicured hedges and decorated with a collection of large modernist sculptures. She followed the driveway that snaked up the hill towards the main building. She noticed a distinct lack of trees or foliage, uncommon in a setting as affluent as this. Any bushes or plants were kept manicured and small. Maisie wondered if this might be for security reasons, to prevent intruders using them as cover from the CCTV cameras.

The building itself successfully imitated the traditional sixteenth-century Japanese castles of the Sengoku period, standing imperiously on a solid base of stone, fifteen feet high. Its outer walls were painted in white, and it had six levels, each one narrower than the last, and divided by the characteristically exaggerated tiled eaves with their upward curves.

Perhaps standing over a hundred feet tall, the main structure was accompanied by slightly smaller interconnected buildings to the side. Together they formed a towering citadel, unapologetically intended as a symbol of wealth and power, subjugating everything that fell within its shadow, just as the original castles had hundreds of years before it.

Maisie parked her car at the edge of a large, gravelled area in front of the building and made her way to the base of the steps leading up the side of the stone platform to the entrance. Already waiting at the top of the steps was a young woman dressed in a black suit with a white blouse.

'Good morning, Ms Lockhart, and welcome to Oshiro-jo,' the woman said congenially. 'My name is Kiko, Mr Oshiro's Private Secretary. Mr Oshiro is expecting you, please follow me.'

Kiko escorted her through the large, heavy wooden doors and into the prodigious entrance hall. Straightaway Maisie's senses were overcome with the sweet smell of polished wood, which covered the floors and the grand staircase that rose up from the centre of the room. The hall was elaborately decorated with samurai swords and full suits of armour. The walls were decorated with tapestries, painting and woodblock prints, many of them antiques, depicting battle scenes and violence. Maisie thought it looked more like a museum display than someone's home. It was immaculate and looked brand new and barely lived in.

On each side of the hall were long separate corridors, each leading to a network of different rooms, concealed by traditional latticed room dividers.

'This is quite a collection,' Maisie commented to Kiko.

'Yes, Mr Oshiro is a great lover of art. These are some of his Japanese antiquities, but he possesses quite an eclectic collection throughout the castle. He has also recovered many of Japan's national treasures from private collectors and donated them to

Japan's national museums, including a famous sculpture of Japan's first emperor, Emperor Jimmu,' said Kiko proudly, who seemed well versed in promoting her employer.

Kiko led Maisie up the main staircase, leading to the first floor. Maisie looked immediately upwards to observe the many staircases that criss-crossed their way up to the gold painted rafters. On the first floor, there were more examples of Japanese artworks, intermingled with European impressionist paintings, as they navigated round the staircase towards another corridor. Halfway along was Oshiro's study, a large room in keeping with the décor of the rest of the property, with the addition of a large wooden desk, leather chair, and well-endowed bookcases covering the length of the left-hand wall. To the right of the room were a series of large, plain glass windows which spanned the length of the exterior wall. Oshiro was standing in front of the window, looking out over the valley like an emperor surveying his kingdom from the ramparts. He seemed to be lost in a daydream, unaware of their presence.

'Mr Oshiro. May I present the British journalist from London, Maisie Lockhart,' Kiko said, as if she was introducing a statesman.

The interruption jolted Oshiro from his musings and he turned to face them.

'Please come in,' he said with an exaggerated smile, 'and you needn't explain who our guest is, Kiko, I have read much of her work. You are quite the celebrity, Ms Lockhart. I suspect that it is as much a curse, in your line of work, as it is a blessing?'

Oshiro instigated a shaking of hands and gestured to Maisie to take a seat in front of his desk. He spoke with the familiar ring of home, and a charisma that Maisie had not anticipated. This greeting certainly did not align with the picture painted by Jonathan Walker, nor with the perception lifted from the pages of the articles.

'You're very kind Mr Oshiro. But I am certainly no celebrity. I've just been fortunate enough to cover some high-profile stories,' Maisie said.

Oshiro smiled artfully. 'Modesty. A rare commodity in today's world. I hear that you have been responsible for uncovering numerous political and criminal conspiracies. Not least your most recent exploits, exposing that emerging crime figure in London. A Mr Conway, I believe?'

Maisie's eyes sharpened. 'You're remarkably well-informed, Mr Oshiro. Details on that case have yet to be released to the public.' she said.

'Yes, well I have my sources. I suspect you have also done your research on me.' he said with a strong hint of expectancy.

'I have, Mr Oshiro, and I must congratulate you on your considerable achievements. Quite the rags to riches story. Perhaps one day you might allow me to tell *your* story?' Maisie watched as Oshiro's chest inflated with self-importance.

'I too have been lucky. But I suspect that perhaps the story would not be exciting enough for your readers,' he said with false modesty, 'just a simple tale of hard work and dedication.'

Already the vanity was pushing its way to the forefront of the conversation. Maisie began to study Oshiro's idiosyncrasies. The unnaturally wide smile contradicted the fierce dark orbs that seemed to penetrate her soul, and the animated hand gestures were reminiscent of some of history's worst autocrats.

Oshiro's secretary was still waiting patiently at the doorway and used the gap in the conversation to ask if they would like any refreshments. Oshiro requested a pot of tea and cake, without offering Maisie a choice.

'This is a truly impressive property Mr Oshiro – or should I say fortress?' Maisie stated looking around the room, in attempt to resume the tempo of the prior conversation, 'how long have you lived here?'

'This is one of a number of properties I possess, but it is undoubtedly where I feel most at home. I commissioned the build of this particular property a little over a decade ago. It was only fully completed in the spring three years ago. Building it required the expert skills of so many carpenters, the refurbishments for Osaka Castle were delayed by several years,' he said proudly. 'I designed much of it myself, although it was be built using traditional Japanese techniques, which date back to the fifteenth century: the Sengoku period. I have of course made some enhancements that make it more comfortable and appropriate for modern living. Obviously, we have running water, electricity, and central heating throughout, and far superior insulation. But much of the architecture is a marriage of old and new. Much like this room,' he said pointing towards the modern window, which had a sliding door leading to a large balcony, complete with infinity pool. But you didn't come her purely to admire my home, did you, Ms Lockhart?' Oshiro said, abruptly drawing the pleasantries to a conclusion, 'so how can I assist you?

Maisie shuddered inwardly. She hated being referred to as a Ms, almost as much as she hated the serpentine hiss that accompanied it.

'As you know, the main reason for my visit is to understand more about the whereabouts of Edward Walker and what is being done to find him. But first I wanted to ask after your daughter. I understand she also recently went missing and is now in hospital recovering from some serious injuries. How is she?'

'She's lucky to be alive,' Oshiro responded gravely, as if he were suddenly taking on a new persona. 'She remains in a critical condition, in a coma with very severe injuries. The doctors are keeping a close eye on her, but for now we must be patient,' he added.

'I wish her a speedy recovery, of course,' Maisie said, 'and that when she wakes, she will be able to shed some light on what has happened to her.'

Oshiro recoiled suddenly as if Maisie's comments were in some way intended to be an accusation.

'I remain positive that she will make a full recovery and be able to remember exactly what happened.' he responded.

Maisie took a moment to observe Oshiro's body language. Usually, she had good instincts for identifying dishonesty. Evasive or inconsistent eye contact or tone of voice, fidgeting or long pauses. If he was trying to hide his true feelings, he was putting on a reasonably good show.

'Do you have any idea what might have happened?' she asked.

Oshiro paused, his eyes searched Maisie as if he were trying to decide whether he was being cross examined.

'It remains a mystery,' he said. 'At first, when her car was recovered, I assumed she had been in an accident. Maybe she had become disorientated and wandered into the forest. Or maybe she might have even been discovered by a passer-by and taken to hospital. But when she didn't turn up at any of the local hospitals and there were no clues from the scene, the police began to suspect that she had been abducted. But I'm sure I'm not telling you anything you don't already know.'

'And you didn't receive any demands from anyone?' Maisie monitored Oshiro's body language as she delivered the question.

'No,' he replied, calmly with a firm eye contact, 'no ransom demands of any kind. I assume that's what you're implying?'

'Well, you are a wealthy and powerful man, Mr Oshiro. It would seem an obvious place to start. Someone with a grudge against you or your daughter? Perhaps in relation to your business dealings?'

'I am a respected businessman, Ms Lockhart. Why would anyone have any reason to target me?' he said.

'What about Edward Walker? Did your daughter become acquainted with him?' she asked.

'They may have met. My daughter has been staying here in recent months. But I don't imagine they ever spoke with one another.'

'Why would you say that?'

'She tends to be a very shy person. And, while she speaks English well, she rarely has the confidence to use it.'

'And your daughter is an executive in your company?'

'Yes, she's responsible for managing my company's property portfolio. Mostly commercial space that is either utilised by one of the subsidiaries or leased to other businesses. This was nothing to do with Edward Walker's activities.'

'So, as far as you were concerned, the two of them were not having a romantic relationship?' Maisie asked, directly.

Oshiro writhed in his seat, clearly discomfited by the line of questioning.

'Edward and my daughter? Don't be ridiculous.' he replied with a dismissive smirk. 'What on earth would have given you that idea?' he added.

'Just something his parents inferred when I spoke with them,' Maisie replied. 'That they thought he might be having a relationship with someone, not specifically your daughter.'

Oshiro said nothing and responded by firing a menacing stare at Maisie.

'And what were Edward Walker's activities, may I ask?' Maisie asked.

'I had commissioned him to undertake a survey for a hydroelectric power plant in the area. Nothing big you understand. Simply large enough that it could provide clean energy to my residence and the surrounding community.'

'Sounds admirable,' Maisie commented, 'and why approach a British company to do this work? Why not use local expertise?'

'Because he came highly recommended. And because I wanted to limit the risk of the information leaking out. You see, I wanted to avoid protesters poking their noses into something that I hadn't even decided on yet. When I built this place, it was met with huge opposition from environmentalist do-gooders. They gathered in their hundreds at the main entrance to hurl abuse at me and did their best to hinder the building work.'

'I see,' said Maisie, 'and did Walker complete this survey before he went missing?'

'He kept me apprised of his progress verbally, but I never received his final written report. His initial findings indicated it wasn't financially viable. The optimal locations for the generator were far too remote, which would have made the project complex and expensive.'

Maisie nodded as she scribbled in her note pad.

'I'm trying to get a sense of what Edward Walker is like, and what frame of mind he was in before he disappeared. Did he seem preoccupied or behave unusually at all?' she asked.

'Not having known the man previously, I can't say that I would be qualified to comment,' Oshiro stated. 'He was a man of few words, but I never got the impression he was anxious.'

'And when he didn't turn up for work, why didn't you report his disappearance?'

'I'm a busy man. I do not have time to micro-manage individuals. I paid him to do a job and I expected him to complete it.'

'Even so, Mr Oshiro, one minute a man is working for you and providing progress updates, and then his visits suddenly stop. Weren't you curious?' she said.

'I was losing interest in the project.' he said. 'Something I discussed with young Mr Walker. I assumed he had completed his surveys and was working on writing his report. Once I knew that I wouldn't be progressing with the project, it really didn't matter anymore.'

'I would be grateful if your team could provide details of when he last visited your estate. And the locations that were being looked at for the new plant.'

Oshiro shrugged his shoulders.

'You are welcome to talk to my security team.' he replied.

Maisie could see from Oshiro's restless body language that he was getting tired of their conversation, perhaps bordering on agitated.

'Just one or two further questions, I know you're a busy man,' Maisie said. 'Do you hold Walker responsible in any way for your daughter's disappearance?'

'You will admit that the timing of their disappearances is suspicious and must be linked to one another in some way.'

'Yes, it does seem that way.' Maisie agreed. 'And how is your relationship with your daughter?'

Out of nowhere Oshiro slammed his first down on the desk in an uncontrolled visceral release of emotion. 'What is the meaning of such a question?' he yelled.

There it was, a flash of anger. Maisie didn't flinch, just held eye contact with Oshiro.

'I'm trying to understand whether she would have confided in you if she was worried about anything, or if something wasn't right?'

Oshiro looked down, as he tried to calm himself with a series of heavy breaths.

'I suppose. I mean, I'd like to think she would.' he said as the anger in his voice turned to regret. 'I have a lot on my mind, as I'm sure you will understand.'

Maisie looked back at Oshiro and met the glare from his eyes. Was this a stressed father concerned for his daughter, or someone implicit in her downfall, trying to cover his tracks? Then she smiled to ease the tension.

'I do fully understand.' Maisie eventually replied. 'Thank you very much for your time, Mr Oshiro,' she reached out to shake his hand.

Oshiro shifted out of his chair uncomfortably as their hands met. 'Kiko will see you out. You can speak with my security team on your way out.' Oshiro said pressing a buzzer on his desk to call for his assistant.

Kiko arrived at the doorway almost instantly, as if she had been waiting around the corner. Maisie began to walk towards her but paused as she passed a large photograph of Oshiro as a younger man, accompanied by a woman and young girl.

'This is a great photograph,' Maisie said, allowing her curiosity to guide her closer towards the large portrait hanging from the wall. 'This must be you with your wife and daughter?'

'Late wife,' Oshiro corrected. 'And that was many years ago.'

Maisie nodded, 'I expect the two of them must have been very close?'

'Yes, quite inseparable,' he said, in a matter-of-fact tone, 'her death hit the girl very hard, as you would expect it to.'

Maisie smiled again, to show there were no hard feelings between them. Then she bowed respectfully in Oshiro's direction one last time, before leaving the room with Kiko.

As the pair walked along the corridor towards the main staircase, Maisie's phone began to ring. It was Tamura. Knowing it must be important, she made her apologies to Kiko before accepting the call.

'Maisie, I've got news.' he said with an excited whisper. Maisie guessed he must be within earshot of his colleagues. 'It's Walker. We've found him!'

25

The car jolted violently from side to side, stretching the limits of the suspension, as it inched its way along the uneven track. The tyres struggled for traction in the muddy grooves carved by other vehicles. Maisie hesitated, as she wondered whether she was in the right place. She had followed the directions given to her by Tamura to the letter, but having driven deeper and deeper into this heavily wooded area in the middle of nowhere, she started to think she had lost her way.

Before long, her perseverance was rewarded with the faint flashing of blue lights through the trees. And eventually the meandering track straightened out to reveal a small clearing. At its centre was a small, dilapidated log cabin, surrounded by police vehicles and a multitude of police personnel, most of whom were dressed from head to toe in forensic overalls and face masks. The area had been cordoned off and, as she drew closer, she noticed armed guards controlling access to the area. Clearly Tamura and his inspector were taking all the necessary precautions.

As she edged nearer, a police officer signalled for her to stop. He tapped firmly with his knuckles against the driver's side window. Maisie wound down the window and immediately received a barrage of Japanese. The words sounded tangled and sharp. Whilst she didn't understand, she guessed he must be asking for her credentials. So, she removed her UK press card from her handbag and handed it over. As the officer inspected her ID, Tamura emerged from the cabin and immediately called out to the guard, whilst gesturing with his hand to let Maisie in. Maisie manoeuvred her car as instructed, got out and walked directly towards Tamura who was engaged in conversation with another colleague. Judging from Tamura's upright body language and reverent expression, the man he was speaking with seemed to be his superior. Both were wearing forensic suits, but had pulled back their hoods and removed their face masks. As she approached, Tamura nodded to acknowledge her presence, as the other man glared at her warily. The man spoke to Maisie in Japanese, with Tamura acting as translator.

'This is Inspector Toyo Kishimoto,' said Tamura, 'he welcomes you to Japan and hopes you are being well looked after.' Tamura said with a dutiful formality.

Maisie bowed to the inspector. 'Thank you, Inspector,' Maisie replied, 'Sergeant Tamura has been very welcoming.'

Inspector Kishimoto nodded his acknowledgement and then paused briefly, staring at her as if details about her character were printed on her face and clothing. Then he uttered more words in Japanese.

'Inspector Kishimoto wants to make it clear that not every reporter is afforded such access to his team as you have been. He hopes you will remember this level of transparency when you write your report.' Tamura said without a smile.

Maisie immediately recognised the type of man Kishimoto was. A seasoned police inspector, whose experience had made him wary of the press, but who also clearly understood the politics associated with a missing foreign national.

'I am grateful for your assistance,' responded Maisie, 'Please tell the Inspector that my primary objective is to help the investigation and get to the truth. And that I always give everyone an honest accounting in my reports.'

There was a subtle glint in Inspector Kishimoto's eyes as he nodded sharply at Maisie. The two men then exchanged a few brief words with one another, before Kishimoto bowed his head to each of them and walked to his car.

'Thank you for contacting me,' Maisie said to Tamura gratefully, after the Inspector was out of earshot, 'I take it this is where you found Walker?'

'That is correct,' replied Tamura. His expression and voice were solemn, completely devoid of celebration. Not what she was expecting considering this significant breakthrough.

'Is everything okay?' she asked. 'Is it Kishimoto?'

Tamura looked around to make sure no one could hear him.

'He's concerned you're getting too close to the case. He thinks I'm being too trusting.'

'What do you think?' Maisie asked.

'I asked you here, didn't I?' he replied in a frustrated whisper. 'Just don't make me regret it.'

They continued walking towards the cabin, their body language suggesting a friction between them like two lovers in a quarrel.

'So where is Walker now? Can I talk to him?' she asked.

'When we found him, he was very badly injured. Barely alive,' Tamura explained gravely, 'he has been taken to the local hospital to be treated. We won't know how he is until the doctors take a closer look at him.'

'I must say, you seem rather less enthusiastic than when we spoke on the phone.' Maisie said, unable to conceal her observations.

Tamura ignored the comment. 'Would you like to go inside?' he asked, gesturing in the direction of the doorway with his arm.

The exterior of the cabin was made almost entirely from wooden planks, including the gabled roof, with the stone chimney adding a sense of permanence. Clumsy, and perhaps recent, attempts had been made to cover gaps where the aging wood had begun to rot away. To one side of the entrance was a table with a heap of forensic overalls draped over it. Maisie was asked to put one on by the officer in charge of logging access to the cabin.

'So, what is this place?' Maisie asked as she climbed into the overalls, 'does anyone live here?'

'No. Or, at least, not officially,' Tamura replied. 'There are many of these cabins in the area, built by people who used to live off the land. But when Oshiro bought the estate, over a decade ago, I'm told he ordered all of them to be vacated. No one is known to have lived here since.' Maisie made no reply as she inwardly reviled Oshiro and made another mental note against his character.

After wrapping herself head to toe in the disposable body suit, Maisie was permitted entry to the cabin. She followed Tamura over the threshold and was immediately struck by a stench strong enough to penetrate her think surgical facemask. It was a smell she recognised from the numerous crime scenes she had visited before. Decaying matter and a strong metallic tang caused by large traces of stale blood.

As the windows were boarded shut, the front door provided the only natural light. Portable electric lamps had been erected on stands around the small room that was itself no bigger than a shipping container. There was one other room to the right of the fireplace, which seemed to be a small kitchen area. Perhaps once a simple dwelling supporting an uncomplicated existence, the cabin now bore the scars of pain and suffering.

Maisie took the opportunity to study every inch of the room. Every item, every mark left behind. At this stage it was important not to rule out any detail. Large patches of dried blood stained the heavily worn wooden floorboards. Within them, small flags, closely grouped together, marked where there were thin indentations in the wood. Maisie guessed these must have been caused by a blade from one of the many tools scattered around the room. 'Was he tortured?' Maisie asked.

Tamura nodded solemnly. 'This is where we found him.' Tamura said pointing to the base of the doorway. 'He was lying face down on the floor, as if he was trying to make his escape. Maybe he collapsed from exhaustion or from the pain. Assessing the trail of blood, he must have dragged himself from over there,' Tamura pointed to another patch of blood in the corner of the room. 'His hands and legs were bound, we found deep cuts all over his body and some of his fingers and toes had been removed.'

'Has he said anything yet?' Maisie asked.

'He was barely alive when we found him,' responded Tamura, 'The doctors are not certain he will make it.'

'How long do you think he had been here?'

Tamura shrugged his shoulders with a mild resignation in his voice, 'difficult to tell with any certainty. Perhaps weeks? Judging by his condition, I'd say he's been here since he went missing.'

Maisie scanned the rest of the room and focused on the legless Japanese chair in the centre of the room. 'And is this where Akina was held before she escaped?'

Tamura nodded. 'We'll know for certain when we test some of the blood stains and fingerprints, but we found two of her fingers.'

Maisie walked over to the fireplace and inspected some of the tools and cutting implements that were still poking out from the ashes. 'So, the attacker was heating the blades, before they used them on Walker and Akina. Why? To stop the bleeding?'

'Probably,' Tamura replied, 'maybe not so successfully. Walker had lost a lot of blood.'

'So, the perpetrator was trying to keep them alive?'

'That's what we understand,' said Tamura.

'So maybe this *was* some sort of ransom?'

Tamura lifted his shoulders and forced his chin forward, in an exaggerated display. 'It's possible. But no demands were made. That we are aware of, anyway. And if so, why target both of them? Akina is a valuable enough hostage. You wouldn't need Walker.'

'Maybe he got caught up in it somehow? Maybe he witnessed what happened. In the wrong place, at the wrong time?' Maisie said speculatively. 'But, if that's the case, why torture him as well?' she added.

Tamura shrugged his shoulders, 'a psychologist from the prefecture office is working on a criminal profile, but there isn't much to go on right now. Based on the level of violence that has been demonstrated here at the scene, we are dealing with a sadistic individual. Maybe they were looking to punish the victims in some way. Or they simply gained satisfaction from the act itself.'

'What about possible motives?' Maisie asked, 'who might have a reason to do this? Had the work they were doing made them targets in any way?'

Tamura sighed deeply through a look of severe uncertainty. 'We were hoping Walker would be in a position to provide the answers. Between him and Akina, unless the forensic team turn up something substantial, we are reliant on them to tell us what happened.'

Suddenly it dawned on Maisie why Tamura appeared to be so downhearted. He and his team had been counting on Walker being the perpetrator. But now, all they had was a long list of unanswered questions and no leads. Worse than that, they still had a dangerous psychopath on the loose, without any viable suspects or working hypothesis.

'Have the forensic team identified any fingerprints?' she asked.

'Only Walker's, and the two fingers belonging to Akina. All the implements that were used seem to have been carefully wiped down.'

'In my experience, no one is that good at covering their tracks. They always leave some sort of trace. However subtle it may be.' she said encouragingly, as she began circling the room.

'What would you suggest?' Tamura asked sceptically.

'It could be any detail. From a stray hair to an obsessive and idiosyncratic tidiness. Not that the latter would apply here,' she added with a slightly regretted snigger. 'Sometimes it may be something the perpetrator would think nothing of, but would be strange to another person.'

Maisie scanned the room for inspiration. Aside from the blood-stained floorboards, the room was a complete mess. It was as if the whole cabin had been lifted off the ground and shaken violently, with the contents left to lie where they had come to rest. And yet amid all the chaos, there was something that stood out to her. It was a simple wooden vase, out of which sprouted the ends of several mid-sized branches. Ceremoniously placed in front of the fireplace, the delicate flowers, once attached, now lay scattered over the floor.

'This is strange.' said Maisie. 'What do you make of this? Some sort of cherry blossom?'

'Taken from the branches off a tree from outside.' Tamura said, with a muted reaction.

'But why go to the trouble of arranging this?' she asked. She looked more closely. While the large branches had lost most of their flowers, it seemed evident that someone had gone to some lengths to create a meticulously symmetrical arrangement.

'Perhaps to mask the smell?' Tamura responded tentatively.

'Unlikely,' commented Maisie, 'these flowers don't tend to a have a particularly strong odour. Not enough to overpower the smell of burning flesh and …' Maisie did not finish the sentence. 'Maybe it holds some significance for the perpetrator? Or perhaps taunt the victim?'

'We'll take a look to see if anything like this has appeared in other crime scenes.' Tamura said, not holding out much hope.

There wasn't much else to see inside, but Maisie jotted some short notes in her pad and began walking towards the door to leave.

Tamura followed. Before reaching the door himself, he stopped dead in his tracks. 'What's that?' he asked, not really expecting an answer.

Maisie turned back to find him crouched down, focused on a point in the floor.

'There, between the floorboards,' he said, pointing to the gap in the floorboards.

Maisie crouched down next to him. She saw it too. A tiny glint as the light from the doorway reflected off a small point in the floor, only a little bigger than a pin head. She watched him, as he used his ballpoint pen to carefully dislodge the object. As the item began to move, it became clear that it was two or three centimetres long, covered in blood or dirt, making it almost invisible against the aged wood and abundance of dried blood. It had a twisted design that was difficult to make out in the low light.

Tamura called to one of his forensic colleagues who rushed in. First, he took a photograph of the item where it lay. Then he marked its position. Then, with a pair of tweezers, he carefully collected the item and placed it in an evidence bag, which he logged on his clipboard. Tamura and Maisie then followed the forensic officer outside. Tamura took the evidence bag off the officer and held it up to the light.

'What would you say that is?' he asked Maisie.

Maisie shrugged. 'Some sort of jewellery? A pin or brooch of sorts? Maybe it belonged to Akina or …'

'… or the perpetrator,' Tamura said, before she could finish. He passed the evidence bag back the forensic officer and said something in Japanese. 'We'll get it checked out.' he said, turning back to Maisie.

They continued talking as they struggled out of their forensic overalls. 'So, whose car is that?' Maisie asked nodding towards the charred skeleton of a mid-sized four by four that was being inspected by three other members of the forensic team.

'We think it's Walker's,' Tamura replied, 'completely burned out. So, if there was any DNA evidence, there probably isn't now.' Tamura said. 'We think the tracker was deactivated before either Walker or Akina went missing. But the team are looking into whether this was a technical fault or done deliberately.'

'So perhaps the perpetrator used the car initially to transport Walker here, maybe even Akina as well. But how did they leave? Have you found any evidence of other vehicles coming and going?'

'Actually yes, my team are taking a plaster cast of some tyre tracks found near the front door. They do not belong to Walker's vehicle, so this could be a lead for our inquiry.' Tamura said. 'We will look to see if we can get a match to a particular manufacturer or wheel size, and also take samples of the soil. I'm told its chemical composition can be as unique as a fingerprint, in some cases.'

'Sounds promising,' Maisie said. 'So, what about Oshiro?' she added, 'will you be checking his car?' Maisie asked with a devilish smile.

'We will wait until we hear back from the forensic team once they have completed their assessment of the tyre tracks. At present there is no good reason to suspect Mr Oshiro's involvement in the abductions, particularly as one of the victims was his daughter.' Tamura stated dismissively.

'Perhaps there is no evidence to suspect him,' Maisie retorted, 'but he is currently the only obvious link to both victims. I would have thought that would have been a natural line of inquiry?'

'We already interviewed Mr Oshiro when both Walker, and then his daughter, disappeared. We will continue our investigation based on the evidence we gather, but right now nothing has materially changed from before. Yesterday, Walker was missing. Today he has been found,' he said calmly. 'Whilst he is not currently conscious, he is not dead, and so hopefully, he will be able to tell us exactly what happened before long.'

Maisie immediately recognised a parallel in Tamura's words, with those of a junior politician following the party line. But whilst they were almost certainly not his own, she also recognised the need to tread carefully. Far better to build an effective case through the meticulous gathering of evidence, than to strong-arm potential suspects, only for the case to be thrown out of court. But she also remained concerned that treading too carefully – as Tamura and his colleagues seemed to be doing right now – could lead to missed opportunities. Having now met Oshiro first hand, her gut told her that he wasn't to be trusted.

'By the way, the man your police were looking for in connection to your friend's death …' Tamura said, changing the subject, '… he never arrived in Japan.'

Maisie's eyes widened. 'What have you managed to find out?'

'The plane was forced to make an unscheduled stop in southern Russia after one of the passengers was taken ill. The passengers were allowed into the terminal building, but when they came back, one of them was missing.'

'So, he wasn't the passenger who was taken ill then?'

'No. That was an elderly gentleman. Japanese. *He* is in hospital in a critical condition. The person missing from the manifest was the same suspect your people were trying to apprehend. It seems he used the confusion to escape from the airport. The local authorities were not looking for him at the time and now have no idea what happened to him. He was lucky, we had over ten armed officers waiting to arrest him at Tokyo International Airport. So, it seems you will be safe from him.'

'You're assuming he's given up?' she said.

'He's obviously sensible enough to know that he wouldn't have been able to enter Japan without being captured.' Tamura said, pride emanating from his tone of voice.

'Perhaps he will simply look for another way to enter.' Maisie stated sternly, as she attempted to disguise her uneasiness.

'Unlikely. He would be putting himself at too greater risk. In any event, we have his photograph posted at every major international hub. If he does attempt to enter the country, we will identify and arrest him.'

26

The wheels of the carriage screeched in protest. The train pulled away from one station and on towards the next. Weighed down by the reins of fatigue, and having travelled through countless, anonymous places, each as barren as the last, Hunter had lost track of exactly where he was. But the sun was setting behind him, which meant he was heading in the right direction.

The plane had landed at Krasnodar Airport, in the Caucasus region of southern Russia. Not exactly what he had planned, but a happy coincidence. Now he would be able to travel the breadth of Asia, all the way to the Sea of Japan, without needing to cross any borders. Whilst this afforded some level of relief, his chosen route along the Trans-Siberian Railway would be long and tedious. It would take many days, perhaps more than a week, before he would reach his target. But he had planned for such an eventuality, and with plenty of cash at his disposal, he had treated himself to a private cabin. It was small, and hardly what he would have considered luxurious, but it had a bed and most importantly, it afforded him privacy.

As a precaution, he planned to change trains along the way, to avoid becoming a familiar face amongst the staff and other passengers. There would be a strong possibility that British police had circulated his image to the local authorities. And whilst no images had publicly surfaced online, he guessed it would only be a matter of time. Killing a policeman was a crime that was not taken lightly in any country.

Before boarding the train at Kransnodar, he had changed into his casual clothes, and retrieved the blond hairpiece from his suitcase, to make himself less recognisable. He would repeat this again with another change of identity when he boarded the next train to sever any potential trail, should the authorities begin to close in.

As he inspected the straw-like strands of hair in the reflection of the cabin's window, he contemplated what had gone wrong. He couldn't have been recognised by the British police officer through chance alone. And he was confident that he had not been followed on his way to the airport. After all, he knew how to detect a tail and had gone to careful lengths to avoid it. So how did they know he was going to be there?

It could only have been one of two possibilities. There had been a leak from within the circles of his own organisation, a tip off to the police. Or the leak had come from the client themselves. That's why he always thought it was best not to involve them in the planning process. He shouldn't have allowed himself to be used to intimidate the target. That should have been done by someone else, not by the operative who would be pulling the trigger. He had become complacent, overly confident with his own abilities, and it had cost him. In this game, when you reach that stage, it's time to get out whilst you still can.

But it was no use dwelling on the past. The matter in hand was to complete his original objective. Right now, he needed to focus on completing the job. Only then could he search for the person who had betrayed him. It was also a matter of pride for him personally. He never left a job unfinished. There was just one problem he still needed to solve, he thought, as he gazed out over mile upon mile of bleak and featureless landscape. How would he get into Japan undetected?

***

The intermittent bleeping from the two heart rate monitors had harmonised with one another, chiming in stereo. The only other sound in the large, dimly lit hospital room was the loud hissing from the ventilators. An overpowering scent of disinfectant hung in the air like a strong deterrent to visitors, making sure they didn't stay too long. Maisie Lockhart stared at the two motionless bodies lying side by side. They reminded her of the fragility of the human condition. How we only have one chance, and how easily it can be taken away. Something that should be respected, but not squandered.

'So why the same room?' Maisie asked Tamura.

Tamura seemed to be deep in thought as they waited for the doctor's arrival. So deep that it took him a moment to answer.

'I suspect Yoshi Oshiro will not be too happy to learn his daughter is sharing a room with the man he believes was responsible for her disappearance.' she added with a slight smirk.

'We now know Walker is not the kidnapper,' Tamura replied, 'and they both require protection. It seemed more practical to put them in together. I still need every available officer working to find the person who is responsible. Have you spoken with his parents?'

'Yes, I called them yesterday. They were obviously relieved to learn he was still alive but concerned about his condition. They are making travel arrangements to join him.'

'And has there been any progress on decrypting Walker's flash drive?'

'Not so far. The technical team tell me it should be possible to recover the information from the drive. But it does have a sophisticated encryption that may take time to crack. With any luck, it may be that we won't need them soon and Walker will tell us himself.'

The doctor entered the room and bowed to both Tamura and Maisie, and then began conversing with Tamura in Japanese.

'This is Dr Watanabe. I've asked him to go through Walker's injuries and treatment. He doesn't speak English,' Tamura said.

Dr Watanabe began speaking. He spoke softly. Little more than a murmur. But too quickly for Maisie to be able to make out any words for herself.

'Dr Watanabe says that Walker remains in a critical condition. He has extensive but shallow scarring all over his torso, where he's been repeatedly cut with a blunt implement. A number of his fingers and toes have been removed. Some attempts have been made to stop the bleeding, as with some of Akina's injuries, but he has still lost a lot of blood.'

'Has he said anything so far?' Maisie asked. There was a delay in the response as she waited for Tamura to relay the messages.

'Walker has not gained consciousness since arriving. He has been subjected to an overdose of some opiate-based drug, which is causing respiratory depression.'

'Any ideas what drug?' Maisie asked the doctor.

'He believes it's the same drug that they found in Akina's blood, although they are continuing to run tests to make absolutely sure.' Tamura said continuing the doctor's translation. 'In Akina's blood they detected a rare combination of opioids that may have been administered with an ethanol-based tincture.'

'Something like laudanum?' Maisie asked.

The doctor shrugged his shoulders and nodded tentatively, as he continued to converse in Japanese.

'The levels they found in Akina's blood were quite low, whereas Walker seems to have been subjected to a much higher dose. He says, it is likely that he has been heavily sedated for days, maybe longer. It is also likely he would have felt little or no pain during his ordeal.'

'But why drug someone and then proceed to torture them? And why would Walker have been subjected to higher doses?' Maisie asked aloud, without expecting an answer.

Tamura relayed Maisie's questions and waited for a response.

'The doctor speculates that the drug may have been initially used to subdue the victims, it's likely that Walker was the first to be drugged. Perhaps the perpetrator made a mistake by giving him too much and then learned from their mistakes with Akina. For someone with a low tolerance to the drug, you would not need much to cause a potentially life-threatening overdose.'

'And what are his chances of survival?' Maisie asked, 'is he going to pull through?'

'He was brought here just in time. Had he been there much longer, it's likely he would have suffered a respiratory arrest. He was also severely dehydrated. He is in a coma and his breathing is controlled through a ventilator. But he is in the best place for his recovery. It will be a few days before the doctor can be more certain beyond that.' said Tamura.

Maisie moved closer to Walker's bedside to inspect his injuries. He looked in bad shape. His face and arms looked thin and emaciated, like the limbs of a terminally ill cancer patient. His skin was pasty and blotted with bruising. The sharp crew cut and clean-shaven features were replaced by a tangled mop and craggy beard. It was hard for Maisie to reconcile the man in front her with that of the photograph of the marathon running athlete. But this was him all right. Maisie's eyes followed his arms, which lay parallel to his body above the neatly tucked sheets, down to his hands. The right was bare and showed little signs of injury, whilst the left was heavily bound with white gauze. His thumb, forefinger and middle finger were all visible, but the last two fingers were missing from the knuckles down. She then looked across to inspect Akina Oshiro's injuries.

'What do you make of this?' Maisie asked, looking to both Tamura and the doctor, 'they both share the same injuries to the left hand.'

Tamura came forward. His facial expression suddenly switched to one of grave contemplation. Then he fired a barrage of Japanese at the doctor and evicted him from the room. It was the first time Maisie had seen him agitated. Tamura's hazel eyes seemed to turn black as his pupils dilated, and he began to pace around the room frantically.

'What is it?' Maisie asked.

'I know what that is,' he replied abruptly, 'it's the mark of revenge. A mark of punishment.' he added, still pacing the length of the room, back and forth.

'What do you mean? A punishment by whom?' Maisie asked.

'It's the mark of the Osore Shirazu. One of Japan's most dangerous organised crime syndicates.'

27

It was late by the time Maisie returned to her room at the minshuku. The day had been filled with breakthroughs and, whilst there was a temptation to push through their fatigue, after leaving the hospital she and Tamura had gone their separate ways with talk of warm baths and a good night's sleep.

The first thing she had done when she returned to her room was to check her emails and any news articles. Anything remotely related to the death of Detective Nathan Roberts, and his killer. But so far there had been very little of any substance. CCTV footage had been released, showing how the events at the airport unfolded and eyewitnesses had been encouraged to come forward. But the artist's impression bore little similarity to the image seared into Maisie's mind.

Frustrated by the lack of meaningful progress, she closed her laptop and decided to get ready for bed. She unbuttoned her blouse and unzipped her skirt, allowing them to drop into an untidy pile on the centre of the floor. Then she went into the bathroom and began to run the shower.

As she gazed into the mirror to inspect the bags forming beneath her eyes, she heard her phone ringing. She went back into the bedroom and frowned at the name on the screen as she considered whether or not to answer.

'Hi Ivan,' she said, with the most innocent sounding tone of voice she could muster.

'So, where the hell are you then?' Leegood asked. After years of working together, Maisie had grown accustomed to his brisk and uncomplicated directness.

'I told you. I'm not finished yet.' she replied.

'Christ, Lockhart! What did I say when we last spoke?' he said, at the top of his voice. 'I said I wanted you on the next plane home. So, what exactly did you hear? Clearly something else entirely, or there wouldn't be an eight-hour time difference between us right now!'

Maisie said nothing. She knew that Ivan would take the disobedience of his instructions as a challenge to his authority, and this was his way of re-establishing it. Far better to let him get it off his chest, than to risk antagonising him further and make the situation even worse. She walked over to the bathroom and turned off the shower, sensing this wouldn't be a quick discussion.

'Are you hearing me this time? Get back here right away, or this is the end of the road for you and I.' Leegood added.

Maisie found herself visualising his red face and large flaring nostrils as she listened to the heavy breaths captured by his phone's microphone.

'Something's definitely going on here Ivan, and I need to find out what it is.' Maisie responded defensively.

'Rubbish,' Leegood countered dismissively, 'you went there to locate Walker's whereabouts, and he's been found. Not by you, but the authorities. What possible need is there for you to stay?'

'I only have half the story. Without knowing who is behind this and why, it's useless to us.'

'What? And the Japanese police can't get to the bottom of this without you? Do me a favour.' he remarked sarcastically. 'Look, cards on the table now, Lockhart. I never really wanted you to go out there in the first place. I thought it could be useful to keep you out of trouble, but it hasn't worked.' Leegood was beginning to sound nervous. Like he had made a mistake that he was now genuinely regretting.

'I'm serious, Ivan, we've had a potentially huge breakthrough. There might be a link to organised crime. This man Yoshi Oshiro is clearly in the frame somehow. And the police remain unwilling to bring him in. Besides, Nathan's killer is no longer a threat.'

'You're blind, Lockhart. Either that or deluded.' Leegood said, hoping his blunt and brutal honesty would force her to see his way of thinking. 'You think that a man who manages to bring down an airliner mid-flight to avoid capture is somehow going to give up on you? Listen to me when I say this: he is still coming for you. Do you understand me?'

Momentary silence.

'You're right, he probably is,' Maisie retorted, 'and if he is capable of bringing down an airliner and killing an armed police officer in the middle of an airport, I really don't see what difference it makes. I stay here and the chances are, he will find me. I come home, and no level of witness protection is going to help me. Let's face it, I'm fucked either way!' she said, with a slight escalation of hostility. 'But he has one definite disadvantage if he chooses to attempt it whilst I'm here. I'm more likely to see him coming. Plus, I'm surrounded by police. Trust me, there's no better place for me to be right now.'

There was a pause at the other end of the phone, whilst Leegood evaluated her argument. Maisie knew that she hadn't won the debate, but at times like this, he would respect her more if she stood up for herself and spoke her mind. And as very few others were bold enough to speak to him so candidly, such an approach still occasionally managed to catch Leegood off guard.

'Very well, you want more time. Convince me why it would be in my interests?'

Now they were negotiating, she thought, pleased by her gamble of the firm stance.

'For the moment, let's just say that you trust my judgement. And if I haven't got the outlines of a headline grabbing story within the week, I promise you I will be on the next flight home. Either way, you win.'

Ivan Leegood released a short hum as he mulled Maisie's proposal, secretly admiring her mettle.

'Very well, you can have the week. But I expect a progress report in my inbox within the next two days. This isn't some holiday for you, you know.' He added, before hanging up the phone.

Maisie rubbed her eyes and moved over to the comfort of the bed, phone still in hand. She noticed there were two missed calls and messages from Fran Bletchley. And so, in need of a comforting voice, and perhaps some inspiration, she rested her head on the pillow and waited patiently for Fran to answer.

***

It was Sunday. Maisie woke with a renewed impetus. She had many questions, but few answers, and she wanted to get to the bottom of all of them.

After her hour-long call with Fran, she had fallen into a deep sleep, not stirring until her alarm had sounded some thirteen hours later. Having not eaten a single meal during the previous day, her appetite had also returned. She wasted little time in getting down to the dining area where the owner of the Minshuku had prepared an impressive spread of fish, rice, eggs and freshly chopped fruit. She was so hungry she even consumed a large bowl of chestnut porridge, which initially she struggled to identify but found delicious, nonetheless. Today she would need her strength, as she was joining her first martial arts class with Tamura. As with most things she tried, she was instinctively competitive, and wanted to ensure she was at her best, physically and mentally.

At just after eight thirty, Maisie was the first to arrive at Tamura's house. They had time for a brief catch-up, over a cup of coffee, before the other students began arriving. They spoke about the investigation, although she could tell Tamura would have preferred not to.

When the other members of the class arrived, Maisie was immediately put at ease by the mostly adult demographic. Watching them as they entered, she guessed most were in their forties and fifties, with a few men and women in their twenties and thirties. They totalled twelve in all, by the time they settled in Tamura's front room, which he had cleared of tables and chairs and unrolled a large rubber mat across the floor. When all were present and assembled, the group looked like a small platoon, standing at ease as they awaited orders from their commanding officer. Maisie was conscious that she had not attempted anything like this with her prosthetic leg, but she had seen others with similar prostheses perform martial arts.

Tamura announced something in Japanese, which roused a burst of cheerful laughter as the whole room turned to face Maisie, who had somehow found herself at the centre of the group.

'I told them you didn't get the memo about the dress code,' Tamura said, smiling at Maisie.

Maisie was wearing her gym kit, which consisted of navy-blue leggings, a fluorescent pink top and matching trainers. The rest of the class wore the traditional white cotton jacket and trousers with coloured belts, each different. Tamura then announced something else in Japanese to the room, which elicited a collective response of 'Konnichiwa, Maisie Lockhart,' recited with an energetic and welcoming harmony.

Tamura then proceeded to lead the class in a series of stretches and exercises, starting with squats, crunches, rotating hips and shoulders, and then progressing onto leg kicks, and balancing exercises. Despite being impatient to get started with learning actual martial art moves, Maisie found herself appreciating the serenity of the movements. It was almost as if she had mistakenly joined a shared meditation group, with each member focused on perfecting their form. The only sounds were of controlled breaths and the occasional instruction from Tamura.

Maisie let her mind drift, and she thought back to her discussion with Fran Bletchley the previous evening. As was quite often the case, a conversation with Fran had the power to elevate her mood, whilst simultaneously helping to replenish her sense of determination.

Unlike Ivan, Fran was supportive of Maisie's intention to stay in Japan. And had been her usual blunt self when it came to her cantankerous editor.

'Ignore that old fucking dinosaur!' she had said. 'He doesn't understand what you're going through. You need to push on with this investigation, and once you've got to the bottom of it, you can divert all your attention to Nathan. Grieve for him and then, let's face it, if the police aren't up to the job, find the bastards that killed him!'

Somehow Fran always knew exactly what to say to push her buttons, whilst being able to deliver a satisfying contempt for Ivan. But, if truth be told, Maisie was not sure how she was going to live up to her promise of a substantial article within the week. Both witnesses had now been found alive, but it might be days, if not weeks before they regained consciousness. And that was assuming they had any recollection of their abductions. In her own mind, she remained resolute that Yoshi Oshiro was somehow involved, but she also knew she would need to find more of a persuasive reason for Tamura and his team to bring him in for formal questioning.

That was where Fran's clarity of thinking proved useful beyond measure.

'What about the other disappearances in the area, you told me about?' she had asked, 'surely these can't be pure coincidence. There must be some sort of link between them all, including Walker's abduction. If you really want to get to the bottom of this, you're going to have to follow the trail. And if your man Oshiro is somehow involved, he'll have left something for you to find. They always do. Nobody's that good.'

Fran was absolutely right. If one line of enquiry led nowhere, she should keep going until she found another that did. Looking for the detail that others might have missed or discounted. Having the confidence to recreate her past successes and do what she did best. Unravelling the truth.

'Are you with us, Maisie?' Tamura asked sarcastically, snapping Maisie out of her daydream, 'or are you volunteering to help me demonstrate today's self-defence techniques?' he asked, as if he were a frustrated schoolmaster, exercising a rebuke.

Maisie looked up from her forward lunge and felt the blood rushing to her face as the entire class focused their collective attention on her.

'Sure. Why not?' she replied convincingly. Tamura gestured for those at the front to make way, and Maisie moved through the parting in the pack to join him.

Maisie stood directly opposite Tamura, who spoke to the room in Japanese. She didn't know what he was saying, but she admired how effectively Tamura managed to command the attention of his students, as they concentrated reverently on every syllable. More surprising was the excitement, even levity, that he injected into his class. Whilst it had not been entirely absent from her encounters with him, this was a new level. His eyes seemed sharper and filled with guile, his movements fast and precise. Maisie decided Tamura took more pleasure from this pastime than he did his day job as a police sergeant.

After Tamura had finished addressing the group, both he and Maisie lined up opposite each other. Tamura looked directly at Maisie and explained in English.

'Firstly, I'm going to show you a sequence of moves, step by step. And then we're going to join them together. We'll start with you attacking me. I want you to come at me with both arms and try and grab me by the throat,' he said decisively, as he stood bolt upright, hand straight by his sides.

Maisie suddenly felt self-conscious. 'You're not going to hurt me, are you?' she asked, half in jest, and half seeking reassurance.

'You have nothing to fear. No one has ever been injured in one of my classes,' he said calmly, 'well except for that one time! Just try not to break any of my bones with that leg of yours,' he added, with a well-timed grin and a cursory glance in the direction of her left foot. 'Now grab me by the throat! As hard as you can!' he repeated.

Maisie reached forward and grasped Tamura by the neck, with both arms. She had both a height and reach advantage over him and managed to gain a firm grip around both sides. She watched his eyes, hoping to gain insight of where his counter move would come from, but he gave nothing away.

Expecting him to use his hands to prise her arms apart by force, she braced her arms and moved her right leg forward to give herself a stronger, better-balanced stance. Tamura remained perfectly calm and even took the time to congratulate Maisie's composure, commenting that it would be difficult to get out of this situation by force. He then looked towards the group and spoke in Japanese.

Tamura then returned his attention to Maisie and fixed his gaze with hers. Then he made his move. Rotating his body one hundred and eighty degrees, so his shoulders were perpendicular to hers, he took a single side-step away from her. And, with bullet-fast reflexes, he simultaneously grabbed her left hand and twisted it firmly counter-clockwise. Maisie now found herself locked in an inescapable position. His grip was gentle enough not to cause any pain, but she knew that would change, were he to apply more pressure. Maisie was astonished at how easily he had released himself from her clutches. And now *he* had the upper hand.

'No matter how strong your opponent,' Tamura explained, still restraining Maisie by her arm, 'it is quite impossible for them to prevent you from stepping away. You should then act straight away to gain the advantage.' Still using Maisie as his subject, Tamura proceeded to enact, in slow motion, examples of secondary moves that could be used to further overcome the opponent, including jabs to the throat or face, and forcing the head back by the chin. But by far the most impressive was the kick to the back of the leg, which destabilised the opponent's balance, causing them to fall to the floor.

'Now you try on me,' he said to Maisie. Firstly, they acted out the moves in slow motion. This took a couple of attempts until Tamura was satisfied with Maisie's technique. Then, from nowhere, Tamura lunged forward, grabbing her by the neck. Maisie was able to replicate his defensive technique, rotating her body and stepping away, whist catching him by the hand and twisting his arm. And with one swift kick of her right leg, she swiped Tamura from his feet, causing him to fall backwards onto the floor. The impact of his landing created a loud, satisfying thud, and Maisie felt a stimulating sense of achievement as she stood over him, victorious.

Tamura looked up at her with a combination of surprise and admiration. The rest of the class released a short burst of enthusiastic applause.

'Perfectly executed,' Tamura said, with emphatic praise, 'you learn very quickly.'

'I could see myself starting to enjoy this,' Maisie said, offering him a hand up.

28

For the next hour, Tamura supervised the other students, breaking them up into groups of two, rehearsing the routine like a carefully choreographed dance. He added alternative scenarios, including blocking a fist to the face and overcoming a neck restraint from behind, but it always ended the same way: with the aggressor ending up in a tangled heap on the ground in a dazed bewilderment.

By the end of the session, Maisie was exhausted, although she did her best not to show it. Today she had managed to rediscover muscles in her body she hadn't used since she was an aspiring gymnast as a teenager. But as she rested, sipping a glass of water, the release of endorphins by her body resulted in a sensation somewhere between incapacitation and euphoria.

After the other students had left, Maisie stayed behind to help Tamura pack away the large mats and reconfigure his living area. Afterwards, Tamura proceeded to describe the other, more advanced, defensive techniques which he insisted on teaching her.

'I certainly can't recommend trying to take on a man with a weapon,' he said, 'but I can provide you with some skills that could help you defend yourself should the worst happen.'

As she exchanged blows with him, Maisie was transported in her mind back to their first meeting. At first, she hadn't been sure what to make of him. He had been stern and aloof. But it hadn't taken her long to see that this was merely a façade. Under the surface he was thoughtful, generous and had begun to show that he cared for her wellbeing. Right now, she felt entirely comfortable in his company. Tamura might just be someone she could trust.

'There's something else I'm going to need from you,' Maisie said. She watched as the enthusiasm drained from his expression, regressing back to his familiar guarded guise. 'I need to know more about the other people that have been reported missing in the area. Their names and whether you have found any leads.'

'And what has this got to do with the disappearance of Walker?' Tamura asked, a slight curtness in his voice.

'Perhaps nothing. But you have to admit, there's a pattern here. And if there is a connection between this investigation and the disappearances of the other inhabitants, it would be better it's found sooner rather than later.' Maisie said, hoping to persuade Tamura that this would be in both their interests.

Maisie continued to study Tamura's body language as he deliberated her request.

'Okay, you can have the names of those reported missing in the area. I will not be able to share details of the police files. I'm sure you wouldn't want me getting into trouble, for divulging sensitive information on an open investigation?' he said with a wry smile.

'Of course not,' Maisie said, matching his smile, 'it will probably turn out to be nothing, but best to know either way.'

***

Later that afternoon, Maisie met Tamura at the police station, where he provided her with the details of the missing persons. There were twenty-two official reports in total, although Tamura admitted this didn't reflect the number of people that had vacated the area in recent years. That would have been closer to fifty. Maybe even a hundred.

The "official" list only related to instances when a family member or acquaintance had filed a formal missing person's report. Tamura reminded Maisie that, due to strict privacy laws, the local police had very few powers that could be used to locate people's whereabouts. If an individual moved to a new area, it was not mandatory for them to enrol their details with the authorities. Similarly, access to bank account activity or the use of more sophisticated measures like mobile phone tracking or CCTV were only permissible where there was evidence of criminality.

Maisie recognised the moral quandary of balancing the needs for protecting an individual's freedoms, versus giving the police the tools needed to do their jobs. Indeed, she often thought some Western countries gave away their freedoms far too easily. Electronic payment and website tracking, surveillance cameras, access to personal data, all made it far too easy for governments to monitor the movement and behaviour of civilians. George Orwell's worst fears realised. Whereas she found that nations that had experienced tyranny in their recent past, were typically less willing to place their trust in governments or powerful organisations. Even so, it was troubling how so many civilians could go missing, and so little be done about it. She also sensed that this did not sit well with Tamura either. Although he had been clear, from the outset, that the decision to deprioritise these disappearances had come from above, perhaps even the very top.

Maisie now had the full list of names, dates of birth, dates reported missing and last known addresses for each of the twenty-two people recognised as 'missing' by the authorities. Having returned to her room at the minshuku, she had spent several hours working her way through the list, scrupulously assessing each name on the list one-by-one and documenting her findings.

The list included a wide mix of different age groups who, on the surface at least, had no obvious links to one another, except for where they lived and that they were all Japanese. Young and old, singles, couples and, most shocking of all, young families. Maisie began her search by reviewing social media activity for the missing individuals. This was easier for the younger members on the list, but for some of the older ones there was little or no online presence. She spent time trawling through posts that included places they had visited in their free time, items they had purchased, items they were looking to sell, conversations about films and TV, even politics. All the things you would expect to see, albeit nothing of particular significance. What had become apparent was a real sense of community within the village of Takakumi. Locals worked together on community projects, helping other residents and enjoying social events.

Nothing summed this up better than the project to refurbish the local infant school, several years earlier. Photographs taken at the time showed evidence of a large gathering, with an abundance of smiling faces as they worked together to build an extension to the existing structure. The photos also portrayed a vibrant and attractive village with neatly cut grass, and well-tended flower beds. This was a community that was investing in its future, not looking to abandon it. It was a far cry from its current overgrown and dilapidated condition. So, what changed? She copied some of the images, so that she would have pictures to match all the names on the list.

One thing that was noticeable by its absence was the lack of any mention of the sudden incursion of scarecrows within the village. Maisie thought something this remarkable and eccentric deserved some sort of post from one of the locals. But there was nothing. The only reference she could find to the scarecrows had been by foreign tourists who had stopped off on their way to other local attractions, including the many temples in the area. This had been the same source of information she had used to research the region originally, before leaving the UK. Maisie checked for articles on the websites of both the local and national news, but there was nothing. Perhaps this sort of thing simply wasn't that unusual for this part of the world? Maisie floated the question but wasn't able to convince herself.

A subject with no shortage of media coverage was the problem of missing persons in Japan. Specifically in relation to people known as johatsu or 'evaporated'.

As a nation, Japan possessed a strong culture of uniformity; where the needs of the many are greater than the individual, and an enormous pressure to succeed in life is measured by your family and peers. For some, the indignity of failure was a burden too great to bear. Failed relationships, falling into debt, losing their job, or even failed exams. Every year in Japan thousands of men and women, of all ages, apparently orchestrated their own disappearances.

With the centuries-old tradition of the samurai, who would commit the suicide ritual of seppuku after defeat in battle, there remained many that still choose a similar fate. Maisie read about the infamous 'Suicide Forest' beneath Mount Fuji where hundreds went to end their lives each year, quietly in solitude.

But there were also others that chose to start afresh; assume new identities and a new life, using Japan's strict privacy laws to their advantage. Others with the money to do so chose to move to a faraway city or town where they would not be recognised.

It seemed those without money were not so lucky, and the demand for a new life had given rise to a shadow economy, operated by the criminal gangs. Such gangs preyed on the vulnerable, promising employment and protection in some of Japan's larger cities, such as Tokyo and Osaka, but the dream of a new life often fell short of the reality. Pockets of deprivation had emerged where the inhabitants provided what amounted to little more than slave labour, in return for anonymity and poor living conditions. This society concealed beneath a society could not be located on any map, but existed in plain sight as an unpleasant and unopposed open secret.

Maisie read one article that recounted the story of a young man in his early thirties. Married with a wife and two young children, the pressures of matching the lifestyle of some of his more successful friends and family had left him deeply in debt. His troubles escalated further when his daughter was diagnosed with leukaemia, resulting in spiralling treatment costs. After his wife's parents were forced to intervene and repay the family's debts, the young man vanished, never to be seen again by his loved ones.

Years later, the journalist investigating the story, described meeting the young man in his living quarters on the outskirts of Tokyo:

'We sat in a dark room with no windows, no bigger than a small single car garage, functioning as a kitchen, bedroom, living area and bathroom. With a broken spirit, the young man, who chose to be referred to as "Sasuke" reticently recounted the shame he had brought upon himself and his family. He explained how he could no longer live with the indignity.

"Each day I awoke to the same look of disappointment from my wife, knowing that I would never regain her, or her family's, trust," Sasuke explained, "I didn't want to leave my children, but I felt so worthless, that I believed they would be better off without me. I contemplated ending my own life, but I did not have the courage to go through with it. I had no money or anything of value that could be used to start a new life."

Sasuke chose to seek out the forgotten suburb, infamously known to locals as the Garandō – or void – where he was able to secure shelter in return for work. Two years on, Sasuke described how he remained trapped in "a hell of his own making", working endless hours in underground factories, earning no money, and paid only with basic food rations that he relied on to survive.

When I asked, why he stayed there in the service in the gangs, he showed me scars on his legs and arms where he had been beaten by his captors, "I once witnessed one of the gang leaders beat a man to death just to demonstrate to the new residents what could happen to them if they disobeyed them. They also find out information about your family, if you have them, and use that to control you. The only way to leave will be when I die, and I pray it comes for me soon."

It was clear that Sasuke was taking a considerable risk by sharing his story, and that he saw no way out of his current predicament. By him sharing his experiences he hoped that more could be done to raise awareness and prevent others from making the same mistakes he had. And yet I couldn't help thinking that he might also be mindful that by disobeying his captor's strict policy of not talking to outsiders, his actions may also serve to shorten his contract.'

Maisie rested her head in her hands and looked out of her window, pondering these societal pressures and unsustainable standards. And, whilst these specific circumstances seemed extraordinary, the wider issue was by no means unique to Japan.

She looked at her watch and was surprised when she realised it was almost three o'clock, much later than she thought. She hadn't eaten since breakfast and suddenly became aware that she was hungry. She recalled at least one small shop, located at the other end of the village, which looked as though it might sell refreshments – among other things – to passing travellers. She closed her laptop and decided to walk into the village, not really knowing what she would find.

29

In contrast to the previous day, dark clouds had gathered in the skies above the village. A light mist drifted above the treetops and through the valley, helped by a gentle breeze. Maisie was glad she had worn an extra layer as she walked down the driveway and along the main road towards the village. The road was quiet and not a single car passed her on the way to the main street. As usual the village was deserted, but still the lights of the koban were on, albeit today a much smaller contingent of two officers occupied the desks, visible through the plane glass windows. Seeing them provided Maisie with some comfort she was not entirely alone. As she monitored her surroundings and observed the haunting, skeletal remains of the village, she found herself shrugging off feelings of vulnerability. Something was going on here, she saw it. And she was going to have to get to the bottom of it.

Reaching the end of the village, the shop was still open. Outside, logs were stacked against the wall to the left of the entrance and, on the pavement, were a number of stands containing an assortment of different items, ranging from tea towels to umbrellas.

Stepping through the doorway revealed a small open space. There was just enough room for two sets of shelving, with numerous levels from floor to ceiling, stretching along each wall towards the counter. On the left-hand wall, the shelves housed an array of folded kimonos, T-shirts, baseball caps and a collection of sculptures carefully carved from wood into a variety of forms, including tigers, dragons, samurai figurines and Shinto symbols. All were intricately painted to a very high standard. On the right-hand side was a vast selection of snacks and confectionaries as well as a large open refrigerator with hermetically sealed sandwiches and portions of sushi. As Maisie browsed the items in the shop, an elderly woman appeared from a room at the rear of the building. She hovered behind the counter, watching Maisie as she browsed the displays. Maisie couldn't stop herself from peeking through the doorway and into a small, darkly lit room with a small bureau illuminated by a desk lamp. On top of the bureau were small sculptures and a collection of brushes poking out of a glass jar. Maisie returned to one of the displays in the shop and picked up one of the finished Shinto figurines. They were intricately painted and must have taken several hours, if not the whole day, to complete.

Maisie could feel the eyes of the old lady following her every move. She exuded a gravitas that more than compensated for her modest stature. As she monitored Maisie's movements through the shop, she made no attempt to acknowledge or welcome her. Quite the opposite in fact. Maisie smiled at her, with a single nod of her head, but the old lady maintained her unbroken and rather hostile stare. Maisie chuckled inwardly as she wondered how successful this sales technique had proven with other patrons.

She continued her search for something that would satisfy her growing hunger. Since she was unable to understand the writing on the sandwich packaging, she inspected the fillings until she came across one which she decided must be chicken. Then she browsed the other shelves before selecting a bag of dried fish and another of dried seaweed, and made her way towards the counter.

Placing the items carefully on the counter, she smiled again at the shopkeeper, but received nothing back. The old lady typed some numbers into a calculator and showed the screen to Maisie. As Maisie reached into her handbag to retrieve her purse, she caught a glimpse of a photograph hanging on the wall. She completed the transaction with the shopkeeper, and then took a closer look at the photograph. The large print was of a group of the villagers, which seemed to have been taken the day the local community came together to renovate the school. The subjects in the photograph had formed several lines, one behind the other, as if they were a football squad posing for a team photo. Maisie recognised Tamura in the photograph and a number of others from the images of missing persons she had found online. One member of the group, wearing a distinctive and slightly worn vintage Levi's T-shirt, also seemed familiar, although Maisie couldn't immediately place him.

Realising the photograph had sparked Maisie's curiosity, the shopkeeper quickly became agitated, waving her arms to shoo Maisie away from the picture. It was an unnerving and rather shocking display. This sudden erratic behaviour, only served to fuel Maisie's fascination, as she realised the photograph must in some way hold some significance.

She stepped away from the photograph and bowed her head whilst smiling apologetically at the shopkeeper. Then she took out her smart phone and held it up, gesturing to the woman to take a 'selfie' with her, hoping the shopkeeper would see it as the harmless gesture of an eccentric foreign tourist. The shopkeeper understood, but initially resisted, waving her arms in protest. Maisie persisted, and eventually the old lady reluctantly submitted. And after joining Maisie at the other side of the counter, Maisie put her arm round her and quickly took several images of the two of them together.

Maisie expressed her approval with a 'thumbs up' and as the shopkeeper turned away with an irritated growl, she reversed her camera, quickly zoomed in on the wall behind the counter and took a shot of the photograph. She was able to capture several complete images of the original photograph, without the shopkeeper noticing, before thanking the old lady and placing her smartphone back in her handbag.

Feeling pleased with herself, Maisie left the shop and began wandering back to the Minshuku, inspecting her handiwork as she walked. It took a while to enlarge the photo big enough see the original image, and Maisie made it two hundred yards or so before it struck her.

As she looked up from her phone, in the centre of the overgrown pasture, there it was. The Levi's T-shirt, identical to the one in the photograph. It was faded and had a small but distinctive tear in the right shoulder. Undoubtedly the same one. This time though, it was hanging from the wooden frame of one of the scarecrows. A scarecrow with an uncanny likeness to the man wearing it in the photograph.

30

The atmosphere inside the police station seemed lacklustre, and its workforce unproductive. It was as though the case had got the better of the officers and they had already accepted defeat. This frustrated Maisie, who believed she had stumbled upon a potentially significant development. Sitting opposite Tamura at his desk, she was disappointed with the impact her account was having on him. He seemed unmoved as he chewed on the end of his disposable ballpoint. His eyes were staring at nothing and he seemed preoccupied, as if he could have been deciding what to eat for lunch – or something equally unimportant.

'The old lady in the shop knows something about the disappearances. I'm sure of it.' Maisie said emphatically, trying to inject some energy into their exchange and snap Tamura out of his daydream. 'Why else would she be so concerned about me looking at that photograph?'

'The old shopkeeper's crazy,' Tamura said, with unguarded honesty, 'everyone around here knows that. Many times we have been called to the shop because she has become agitated or aggressive. She's well-known for it. But she's just a harmless old lady.'

Maisie tried to conceal her irritation.

'It seems to me that there's more to it than that. Even if there isn't, what's there to lose by going to talk to her? She could be a potential source of information.'

Tamura shrugged.

'Trust me on this, Walker and Akina may be able to shed some light on what happened when they wake up, but it would be unwise to place all your hopes on that alone. It might be days, perhaps even weeks before they regain consciousness. And what if they don't remember anything? You'll have lost critical time.'

'You're reading too much into this. They're just scarecrows. Someone's idea of a practical joke. Nothing more. You've found a link between a missing person and a scarecrow who is now wearing his T-shirt. What does that prove?' Tamura said.

'On its own, it's tenuous, I agree. But it's also possible to match the likeness of each missing person on your list to one of those scarecrows. In some cases, they're even wearing their clothes. The elderly couple you told me about for instance, who were killed in the fire. I found their surname printed on the inside of the clothes worn by the very first two scarecrows. You know, the ones you showed me on the first evening we met. Also, three of your missing persons are a young family, and there's a collection of three scarecrows by the school that match their likeness. These scarecrows have quickly been dismissed as a hoax, but nobody has established who has put them here and for what purpose.' Maisie produced her phone and shared some images to support her theory.

Tamura took the time to inspect the photographs in more detail. As much as he didn't like to admit it, there was no doubting that some of the carefully painted faces bore a striking resemblance to the individuals on the missing persons list. Perhaps the most haunting of all were the three that represented the young family. This forced Tamura to at least contemplate, if Maisie was right, this family might need help.

'Clearly, this can't be a coincidence.' Maisie said, as she continued to swipe through the images on her phone. 'The questions we need to answer is who is behind this and why are they doing it? Is it just some eccentric old lady's way of treasuring the memory of the former residents? Or could it be more sinister than that?'

'Alright,' submitted Tamura. 'Just tell me one thing, why are you so certain this lady is responsible for the scarecrows?'

Maisie smiled. 'Just a hunch,' she said, 'but, aside from the unusual behaviour when I tried to look more closely at the photograph, she also sells her own hand-painted sculptures. She has a studio in the back of her store. My father used to paint lead soldiers and it takes extraordinary patience and skill. The faces of the scarecrows have been painted to a similar standard to achieve a good likeness of the former residents. The old lady has the skill and means to produce them.'

***

Tamura made some calls before he was ready to leave the station. Maisie filled the time by checking the latest news headlines, as she sampled a rather disappointing cup of coffee from the station's dispensing machine. The thick, tar-like substance had a frothy top, like the bubbles formed from washing up liquid, and it left an unpleasant, charcoal aftertaste on the tongue. But it provided her with a much-needed hit of caffeine.

By now the murder of a senior detective at Heathrow was dominating the headlines of all the major news outlets. The public mood was reportedly one of shock and fear. If something like this could happen at the UK's largest and arguably most secure airport, what other vulnerabilities could there be? The police had released more images of a man wanted in connection with their investigation, last seen in Krasnodar Airport. The unscheduled landing of the plane had been caused by another passenger falling ill, as Leegood had said. This same passenger had later died in hospital and the police were now treating the death as suspicious. The news story had stirred up a frenzy of interest across the world's media, and already there was widespread speculation. One article suggested that the fugitive might be a spy. Another said that terrorist activity had not been ruled out. But clearly, they did not have any real facts to support either theory. Maisie still found it difficult to think about Nathan. It was such a shock. He was a good man who worked hard and didn't deserve the ending he received. Never seeing his daughter grow up. As the thought rose in Maisie's mind, she pushed it back down, along with the tears that threatened to follow. This wasn't helpful. She needed to focus on the investigation in front of her.

Maisie took a moment to study the image of the police suspect. Taken from a still of the airport's CCTV footage, the image was slightly burred and undefined. And yet, the harsh features, together with distinctive build and posture, left Maisie in little doubt that this was the man that had followed her less than a week ago. Maisie quietly tore the image from the page and folded it, before placing it in her pocket.

'Shall we go?' Tamura asked.

Maisie quickly finished the dregs of her coffee – which she immediately regretted – and followed Tamura out the door. They walked together in silence. Maisie sensed reluctance in Tamura's body language, as if he was carrying out an unpleasant domestic chore. Maisie imagined that it would not take much for him to abandon the exercise altogether. Whilst she didn't expect the old lady to say much, she hoped they would see something to make Tamura take her theory more seriously.

They reached the other end of the village and arrived at the entrance to the store. The door was open but there was no sign of the old lady inside. Maisie immediately noticed the photograph had disappeared from the wall, leaving only the misshapen rusty nail, used to hold it, behind. Maisie nodded at it suggestively to Tamura, who shrugged unenthusiastically. She knew he still needed some convincing, but inside she felt a warmth of reassurance. A feeling that told her she was looking in the right place.

Tamura rang the bell by the till and waited patiently. The old lady eventually appeared.

Without encouragement Tamura initiated the conversation with the old lady.

'I have explained to her who you are and the reason for my visit is to assist you in asking some questions for a story you are writing about the village.' Tamura said.

Maisie was impressed by Tamura's disarming approach, instead of the lazy and heavy-handed attitude that she had sometimes witnessed from others in his profession.

'What would you like to ask her?' he said, looking at Maisie.

'Let's start with the scarecrows.' Maisie suggested. 'Does she know who put them there?'

The question was met with an immediate but short retort, along with a convincing display of umbrage.

'She said that she's no idea who's responsible or how they got there,' Tamura said, still without much investment in the subject.

'Does she know anything about them at all? For instance, has she heard any rumours about why they might have arrived here?' Maisie asked, knowing full well that it would be improbable for someone in her position to deny any knowledge of even harmless tittle-tattle.

The old lady concentrated intently on Tamura's mouth, as if she were having to lip-read his questions. After he finished speaking, she paused briefly to ponder her answer. Then she uttered something snappily in Japanese at Tamura, whilst continuing to ignore Maisie's presence.

'She says the scarecrows are a bad omen. There is a rumour they represent the villagers that have moved on. She says new scarecrows are added every so often. And, when they arrive, villagers disappear.'

Tamura remained unmoved as he recited the old lady's comments. Maisie, on the other hand, found them more promising. At least now she was talking.

'Does she know what happens to the villagers that disappear?' Maisie asked, as she scribbled in her notepad.

The lady shrugged casually as if she didn't care.

'She says she doesn't know; only that they are never seen in the village again.'

'Does she know why this might be happening, here of all places?'

The old lady provided a long response to Tamura.

'She says that villagers are being punished by the Kami, for abandoning "Shinbatsu" or "the ways of the gods".'

'What are Kami?' Maisie asked.

'They're Shinto deities that are believed to inhabit both the living and the dead,' he said, without needing to consult the old lady.

'But why should they be punished?' Maisie asked, ignoring her own scepticism of the spirit world.

'She says that the villagers failed to heed the warnings and continued their ways of selfishness and disrespect. First the spirits took away the fertility of the land. But, even after this, the villagers failed to amend their ways.'

'I thought you said that the small farms closed because they could no longer compete with the larger ones?'

'That's true. But before that, the farmers were finding it harder and harder to work the land. It's not clear why. Perhaps a combination of over-farming and poor soil maintenance. I don't know the facts. It was before my time here.'

'Why the scarecrows?' Maisie asked, 'what purpose are they supposed to serve?'

Tamura asked the old lady and listened to her response.

'She says they are here as a warning to the other villagers and to those thinking of settling here.'

'And what about the elderly couple, why were they targeted?' Maisie asked.

'The coroner determined that their deaths were accidental,' Tamura replied, without posing the question to the old lady.

'And yet, the first scarecrows to arrive were made to look like them, wearing their clothes.' Maisie stated. 'let's see if she knows anything about it?' she added, gesturing with her hands for him to relay the question.

Tamura turned and asked the question to the old lady, who looked back at him coldly, with dead eyes, and shrugged her shoulders.

'Just one final question then.' Maisie said sensing that the old lady was running out of patience, 'If you believe the scarecrows are to ward off residents and potential settlers, why is it that you have chosen to stay?'

After listening to Tamura repeat the question, the old lady seemed shocked by his directness.

'She says she was born here and lived in the village for a large part of her life and considers herself a part of the land. In the same way that the rocks and trees are. She will never leave.' Tamura said.

Maisie looked back at the old lady as she maintained her defiant demeanour. She then picked up one of the delicately painted samurai figurines and placed it on the counter.

'Can you ask her if she paints these herself?'

The old lady nodded nonchalantly.

Maisie passed the shopkeeper the money to pay for it.

'Tell her they are very good and thank her for giving up so much of her time.' Maisie instructed Tamura. They both bowed respectfully to the old lady and promptly left the shop.

'I told you Maisie, it's just superstitious nonsense.' Tamura said exasperatedly. 'All this talk of spirits punishing the locals. It was a complete waste of time.'

'It's not unusual for people to resort to the supernatural in order to explain things they fear or don't understand,' Maisie said plainly. 'It happens all the time. But I certainly wouldn't describe it as a waste of time.'

'And why not?' Tamura asked. 'You think she knows more than she's telling us?'

'Without a doubt she does.' Maisie said unequivocally. 'Whether the explanation of the disappearances she provided was something she had dreamed up, or something she heard, she clearly doesn't believe it, otherwise why would she remain here herself? She didn't seem at all concerned for her own safety. Whatever the reason for the villagers going missing, she doesn't believe she will be targeted. That means she is either in denial, or she's part of it. My money is on the latter. At the very least, she knows more than she is letting on.'

'Part of what exactly?' Tamura asked. 'Why are you so convinced that people are being targeted? I told you before that we have traced villagers that have gone missing. And they had simply decided to leave in search of better prospects. There's nothing supernatural about that.'

'Because of the scarecrows.' Maisie explained, answering Tamura's original question, whilst choosing to ignore his subsequent comments. 'Concealed within the old lady's nonsense story about "the wrath of the spirits", was the reason they have been appearing here.' Maisie referred to her notebook and began quoting from it, 'the old lady said, "they are here as a warning to the other villagers, and to those thinking about settling here." Whoever is putting them here, and whatever the reason, they have managed to clear the village of its inhabitants very effectively, wouldn't you say? What if someone is trying to do exactly that?' Maisie said hypothetically.

'But why?' Tamura challenged.

'That's what we need to find out. But we're unlikely to get any more from the old lady unless somehow, we catch her in the act. And in the meantime, we need to follow the trail of one of the missing persons and find out exactly what happened to them and where they are now.'

31

They decided to wait until the following morning to make the journey into Tokyo. It took some persuading, but Tamura eventually relented to Maisie's impulse to find and question Chisato Tanii.

Tanii had been one of the alleged missing persons from the original police investigation, but had subsequently been found, alive and well, living in a small but smart apartment in Azabu-Jūban, in downtown Tokyo. Shortly after interviewing the old shopkeeper, Maisie searched the village for a scarecrow that matched Tanii's likeness. The one she identified not only wore overalls like the ones Tanii wore for his job as a carpenter, but a large dark mark had been painted on the scarecrow's left cheek which was an exact match to his prominent birthmark.

Even though Tamura remained resolute that Tanii was, in point of fact, not missing, he had settled on being curious enough to spend his day off accompanying Maisie into the city.

'What have we got to lose, except perhaps a few hours of our time? If we find him, we might learn something, even if it is to discount the relevance of the scarecrows.' she said.

The way Tamura saw it, at the very least he would be proven right. But, in the unlikely event that she was onto something, he would be there to make sure that she didn't get into any more trouble.

Maisie had also given Tamura the idea of using trap cameras, to catch the culprits behind the scarecrows in the act. Tamura had set his team the challenge of procuring and installing the cameras whilst the two of them were in Tokyo. Given that it would be near to impossible to do this without someone noticing, Maisie had suggested that Tamura's team set up a small number of decoy cameras that could be easily located. That way if someone were to attempt to destroy or remove them, they might mistakenly overlook those that were more covertly positioned.

Being a weekday, Maisie and Tamura had decided to travel after the rush hour, leaving just after nine thirty in the morning. This had given them sufficient time for a leisurely breakfast, and afterwards, they set off in Maisie's rental car for the first leg of their journey across Awaji Island, the waypoint to the main island of Honshu.

Having driven this route from the airport, Maisie was familiar with the roads, and they made good time, arriving at Shin-Osaka just before midday. There they caught the bullet train, which took them on an indirect route, firstly, travelling north-east, through Kyoto. Then, past Lake Biwa and Mount Ibuki, the line curled in a south-easterly direction towards Hamamatsu, before finally bearing north-east again, tracking the coast all the way to Tokyo.

Several hours into their journey, having passed through Fuji National Park, they began entering the outskirts of Tokyo, still within view of the magnificent mountain that was partially concealed by thick mist and dark, turbulent looking clouds. Tamura sat pensively in the aisle seat beside Maisie.

Other than during the martial arts class, this was the first time Maisie had seen Tamura in civilian clothes. He had opted for black jeans, a T-shirt and a biker style leather jacket. Not only did the outfit do an effective job of disguising his profession, it also accentuated his build and made him appear more formidable. Maisie guessed that might be a deliberate ploy, knowing he had chosen not to carry his police credentials. Today he wasn't on official police business. He was merely a civilian, assisting a foreign journalist with her investigation. Should they get into trouble, he would not be able to bail them out quite so easily as in the Tokushima Prefecture.

They had both started the journey full of optimism and excitement, as though they were embarking on an excursion rather than an enquiry. Maisie for one was eager to see Tokyo for the first time. And yet, even though this was a straightforward fact-finding expedition – retracing the steps of an earlier police investigation – there seemed to be a growing tension in the air. They were heading into a city renowned for being one of the safest in the world, and yet it felt as if the two of them were somehow travelling closer and closer towards an impending danger. But this was nothing new for Maisie.

Maisie focused her attention on the view from her window and the outskirts of Tokyo. They were still travelling at high speed, which allowed for only a glimpse of the scenery, from the elevated viaduct, as the train dissected the seemingly endless sea of low-rise buildings.

'It's so vast, isn't it?' Maisie said, with traces of a childlike wonderment. 'I mean, I knew it was a big city, but you don't appreciate just how enormous it is until you actually see it.'

Tamura took Maisie's sudden interest as an invitation to share some knowledge of his capital city.

'It's the largest urban area in the world, stretching over three prefectures and home to over thirty-two million people,' he said with a sense of pride. 'It was originally a fishing village named Edo, but it has been Japan's most important city since Tokugawa Ieyasu's victory at the Battle of Sekigahara in 1600, a very famous battle in Japan. From here the Tokugawa clan governed Japan until the nineteenth century when the Shogunate ended and Imperial rule returned to Japan. It was then that the city became known as Tokyo, which means "eastern city". Like many great cities it has experienced a mixed history of triumphs and disasters. Fire, war, earthquakes … The city has been destroyed many times, but it has always recovered. And become stronger in the process. Today Tokyo is one of the key financial hubs for the global economy, like New York and your London. Only here we have the most Fortune 500 companies in the world.' Tamura said, as if he could be narrating a promotional video.

'Remarkable,' said Maisie, as torrents of rain began beating like pellets against the window. She was slightly disappointed that they would not get much opportunity to enjoy it. 'Will it be easy to find Tanii?'

'I wasn't there when the investigating officers located Tanii, but I have the address in Azabu-Jūban from the file we had on him.'

'Did you know him well when he lived in the village?' Maisie asked.

'Not really. He was always quite shy. But people liked him. There weren't many people in the village who hadn't used his services. He was a talented carpenter from what I gathered. Respected.'

Maisie noticed Tamura's use of the past tense and wondered whether it was significant or not.

167

'I realise you're doing me a big favour by helping track down this man. In fact, everything you've done for me since I've arrived has been incredible. I appreciate this could all turn out to be nothing, but sometimes you have to make some guesses, even if they turn out to be wrong, before you get to the right answer,' Maisie said reassuringly.

Tamura nodded, before checking his watch. 'We should arrive soon. About another five minutes.'

Almost on cue, Maisie felt the train begin to shudder as the brakes were applied. Out of the window, she observed the low-rise buildings being gradually supplanted by towering glass edifices, as they neared their destination in central Tokyo.

The train arrived at Shinagawa train station, on schedule at precisely 15:45. Expecting most office workers would still be at work, Maisie was surprised by the crowds passing through the station at that time. Despite the bustle, there was a discernible serenity that set the concourse at Shinagawa apart from other transport hubs. A sense of order and courteousness as the hordes glided harmoniously through the walkways to the exits, like a colony of ants swarming with a shared objective.

'It might be better for us to travel the rest of the way by taxi.' Tamura said. 'I doubt you'll enjoy the experience of the metro at this hour. I would hate for you to experience the Oshiya.'

'Oshiya?' Maisie asked, with a puzzled look on her face.

'Yes, you would say "pushers". During busy periods, staff on the platforms will quite literally push passengers into the carriages to make sure that no train leaves that isn't filled with as many as it can manage.'

Maisie was no stranger to rush hour on London's tube network, where many of the passengers were themselves self-appointed "pushers", but agreed that a taxi would be the preferable option.

As they walked towards the exit, the rain could be heard crashing against the metallic roof, prompting Maisie to stop and purchase an umbrella from one of the concession stands. Afterwards, as they reached the exit, they witnessed the torrential rain cascading down from the skies like a wall of water, turning the roads into shallow canals and limiting visibility to no more than a hundred yards. Thankfully there was a plethora of taxis and only a short queue. Huddled under Maisie's umbrella, they dashed the short distance across the pavement and dove into the first available cab. Tamura immediately removed his notepad from his jacket and gave a short set of instructions. The driver responded with a nod of his head, and they were promptly on their way.

With the wipers whining continuously as they fought against the deluge, the driver proceeded cautiously. But with reasonably light traffic, it was no more than fifteen minutes before they arrived at the address.

The smart residential building, was situated in a narrow, cobbled street, lined with similar domestic buildings, some with integrated boutique shops, restaurants and bars at ground level. The heavy rain had cleared the streets of pedestrians and only the occasional vehicle crept respectfully along at low speed.

Maisie paid the taxi driver and proceeded with Tamura to the entrance. The front door was locked and next to it the intercom system was labelled with numbers. Pressing the button for flat number eighteen, they waited patiently, for a few minutes and then repeated the process until, after the third attempt, there was finally an answer.

'Moshi moshi.' It was a female-sounding voice with an inpatient tone.

Tamura responded by yelling loudly into the microphone as the rain lashed noisily down on the umbrella, Maisie gripping it with both hands to keep it steady. A lot of words were exchanged between them, and from Tamura's frustrated expression she got the impression that the person at the other end was not being helpful. But Tamura persisted, and Maisie heard him use her name in the same sentence as 'Spotlight News'. Then after a brief pause, the buzzer sounded and the front door opened.

'Interesting,' he said, almost surprised by his own success, 'your name really does seem to open doors.' he said with a smile. They went through into the large open foyer. Maisie took a moment to shake the droplets from her umbrella and swept her partially damp hair back over her head, letting it fall slightly to one side.

The wide, minimalist interior had a pristine cream marble floor with a large golden spherical sculpture in its centre, positioned in front of a set of lift doors, polished to such a high standard they could have been mistaken for mirrors. It seemed a very affluent setting, not at all what Maisie had imagined.

'She said to go on up to the tenth floor.' Tamura said as he summoned the lift car.

When the doors opened, they revealed a mirrored interior with a red carpeted floor. 'This is certainly more lavish than I was expecting,' Maisie commented, as she walked inside, thinking that Tanii had managed to land comfortably on his feet. 'Who's the woman? A partner or relative?'

'I found it difficult to hear, but it sounded like she didn't know Tanii. Maybe he's moved on.' Tamura said, as he pressed the button for the tenth floor. Maisie instantly noticed there was no ninth floor. No risk of pain or suffering in this building then.

With a faint hum, the lift carried them up and within seconds the door opened. There were two flats on either side of the small corridor – flat number 18 was on the left-hand side, its door closed. Tamura pushed the doorbell and was immediately surprised by the loud ring it gave out, which bounced off the concrete walls and marble floor. Maisie then heard the rattling of the chain and the click of the lock. The door was pulled open as far as the chain allowed and the face of a young woman appeared through the gap. Her hair was tied back in an untidy bun. Maisie detected a layer of foundation, but there were no other signs of make-up. She gestured an impatient, 'what do you want?' with the tip of her head, without offering any words.

'Konnichiwa,' Tamura said respectfully to the young woman, with a tip of his head. The girl didn't reciprocate.

Maisie looked directly at the girl. 'My name is Maisie Lockhart. I am a journalist from England investigating some disappearances in the village of Takakumi, including the abduction of a British national,' she said. She paused momentarily to allow time for Tamura to translate. 'I'm looking for a man that I thought was living here. Do you know him?' Maisie offered a photograph to the young woman. 'His name is Chisato Tanii.'

The young woman reached through the opening in the door to receive the photograph and took a moment to inspect it as she listened to Tamura's translation.

'He's not in trouble in any way,' Maisie continued, 'I'm just hoping to talk to him about his experiences living in Takakumi and see if he can help shed some light on what's going on there.'

The young woman's brow was weighed down by her temper. She responded sharply to Tamura, dismissively passed the photograph back to Maisie.

'She says she doesn't know who this is.' Tamura said.

'Can you ask her if she lives here? And if so, how long for?'

Tamura received another barrage of Japanese.

'She says it's none of our business.'

Maisie could see that she might be down to her last question, if she was lucky.

'Ask her if she knows anything about people being abducted and enslaved by criminal gangs in the Void, here in Tokyo.'

Tamura looked back at Maisie with uncertainty. Maisie responded with an encouraging nod.

The young woman took a moment to process the question, and then responded with a definitive slamming of the door.

'That wasn't very friendly. I thought helpfulness was part of the Japanese culture in Tokyo?' Maisie uttered sarcastically, as the two of them looked at each other.

'So now what?' Tamura asked sceptically.

'Across the street was a coffee shop. Why don't we wait out the rain there, while we plan our next move?'

***

They chose a table by the window with an unencumbered view of the entrance to the apartments across the street. Maisie ordered a black coffee. Tamura asked for the same.

'Did you notice her make-up?' Maisie asked.

'What about it?'

'Hair tied back, a layer of foundation applied. We disturbed her in the process of getting ready. Either she is on her way out, or she is expecting company. Let's see which one it is.' Maisie then used her phone to order a taxi.

'How do you know she will be in a car?' Tamura asked.

'Just a guess. If she's going to all that trouble to make herself look nice, I suspect she won't want to get drenched by the rain. If not, we'll leave the cab and follow on foot.'

'Are you sure this is a good idea? Following her I mean. This could be seen as harassment.'

Maisie nodded, 'It could. But her reactions to our questions tells me that she knows something. Particularly her reaction when she looked at the photograph of Tanii. I think she recognised him. Plus, she slammed the door when we mentioned abductions and organised crime. An innocent person would at least have asked us what we were talking about.'

'I guess so.' Tamura said. He remained sceptical.

'Don't tell me you've never been on a stake-out,' Maisie said with surprise.

'Yes, but if she was involved, the people she's working with now know we're here looking for them.'

'True. But I find sometimes you need to stir things up a bit if you want quick results.'

Tamura sipped his coffee nervously. 'What makes you think she will lead us to Tanii? Maybe she's just going out to meet friends.'

'Maybe she is. But this is probably our best bet right now.'

The taxi arrived, and straightaway Maisie received a text message to say that it was outside the coffee shop. Maisie responded asking the driver to wait. The translation within the booking app seemed to work well and the driver of the taxi acknowledged her message and turned off the engine. Maisie watched her phone a moment longer, as the fare for the taxi increased incrementally.

'What now?'

'We wait.' Maisie replied.

***

Half an hour passed and already the fare for the taxi had exceeded 5,000 yen. Two chasers from the driver had been answered and still he remained outside. But eventually, a Mercedes pulled up on the opposite side of the road. It was black, with blacked-out windows. The driver got out and stood by the curb. He had short, dark hair and wore sunglasses, even though it was still raining. A dark-coloured vest allowed him to show off a muscly physique, heavily decorated with tattoos.

'This looks promising,' she said as she spied the large koi scaling his left shoulder, 'are those gang markings?'

Tamura said nothing but nodded solemnly, his eyes remaining fixed on the man's position. The man looked around in all directions as if he was searching for something, the rain didn't seem to bother him as it soaked his clothes.

Moments later the young woman from the flat emerged from the apartment building. She opened the car door without acknowledging the man and got into the back seat. Maisie and Tamura, both jumped out of their seats. They waited for the man to get back into the driver's seat, before leaving the building and getting into the taxi.

The unrelenting rain provided good cover for Tamura and Maisie as they tailed the black Mercedes in their taxi. Both were leaning sideways, towards the centre of the car, so they could track the progress of the car between the gap in the front seats.

Maisie remained silent, expecting Tamura to acknowledge she was right at any moment. Tamura remained silent, expecting an 'I told you so,' from Maisie. Eventually the taxi driver was the one to break the silence. Tamura responded.

'What did he say?' Maisie asked.

'He's suspicious. He's asking why we wanted to follow this car. I said they are our friends. Their car was full, and we agreed to follow them to a club. He's not convinced, but he'll do it.'

Maisie said nothing, just continued watching the car as it navigated through the small streets.

'So, what do you think happened to Tanii?' Tamura asked.

'My guess is, whoever abducted him wanted you to think he had landed on his feet, in a luxury flat in central Tokyo.'

'But why?'

'Presumably to keep them off the scent of what they were really up to.'

'Which is?'

'That's exactly what we need to find out.' Maisie replied.

32

Within the short taxi journey, twilight had descended into night. The torrents that had endured since the afternoon had succeeded in dowsing the city's nightlife. The streets were bare, except for a residual scattering of drenched commuters who trudged through the streets as they returned to their homes.

The Mercedes stopped at the entrance to a pedestrianised zone. It waited just long enough to allow the young woman from the apartment to get out before driving off. By the time Maisie and Tamura pulled over and paid the taxi driver, she was already out of sight.

Maisie stood at the threshold of the pedestrianised street and admired the patchwork of bright neon lights that covered the building's façades, illuminating the wet tarmac with an eery, sanguineous hue. The blur of light was vast and all consuming, and Maisie felt as though she could be peering into an uninviting portal to another dimension. It was no coincidence the girl had led them here. Now she was certain: this is where they would find the man they were looking for.

'Do you know what this is?' Tamura asked.

'The Void?' Maisie guessed.

Tamura nodded slowly. Maisie could tell he was uncomfortable from the way he was inspecting his surroundings with a greater care than usual – like he was waiting for something bad to happen. 'This is the stronghold of the Osore Shirazu crime syndicate.'

'I know, I read about both in an article covering the story of a man who ended up here.'

'Then you know it's the most dangerous part of the city. Most of the crime in the whole city originates from this one area. Police only patrol the area in full protective equipment.'

'Do you want to go back?' Maisie asked facetiously.

Tamura shrugged, 'I just want you to know what you are getting us into.' Maisie detected the slightly higher pitch of fear in his voice. Maisie was aware of the risks, but delving into societies issues and dirty secrets was her business. It frustrated her slightly when others, in particular the police, were unwilling to address them.

As the two of them breached the threshold into this alien environment, there were smells of street food cooking from small kiosks and stalls. Besides them were a multitude of restaurants, bars and nightclubs – only partially filled – stretching all the way along the street. Maisie was unable to translate most of the signs, however many were of a more illustrative nature that was hard to misinterpret. The girl was nowhere to be seen.

'So, what now? Do we look for the girl?' Tamura asked.

'Maybe,' Maisie replied. 'Or maybe we should search for Tanii.'

'Why would he be here?'

'This is where the man, from the article I read, was brought. And if my theory is correct, this is where people from the village are being brought too. The girl has given us a link between where Tanii was last seen by police and this place. We should at least check it out.'

***

The hours ticked slowly by as Maisie and Tamura systematically covered the establishments on both sides of the street, speaking with proprietors, staff and even customers, whilst presenting the pictures they had of Chisato Tanii and the promise of a reward for any for information that could help to locate him.

Soaked through, and having covered almost a third of the quarter-mile long street without success, they decided to take a short break under the shelter of one of the many food stalls. They each pulled up a stool at the counter, underneath a large awning, and asked the owner for a selection of the chicken skewers, grilled squid and wheat noodles on offer, which they washed down with a glass of the local lager.

'So, now that we've spent several hours asking whether anyone has seen Tanii, are you ready to concede that he's not here?' Tamura asked, in a self-satisfied tone.

Maisie shrugged, 'It's still relatively early. No need to give up just yet, is there?'

Tamura said nothing.

'I take it from your reaction earlier, that you know all about this place?' Maisie asked. 'How local gangs are free to abduct individuals and force them into effective slavery. An open secret, feared by local police and ignored by government officials.'

Tamura rocked his head sideways and took another large swig of the lager.

'Is anything really being done to tackle it?'

Tamura shrugged. 'I guess. It's not something I'm involved in. You must have similar places in England? Sometimes these types of problems are bigger and more complicated than they seem from the outside.'

Maisie nodded. 'We do have similar places. But if you don't do anything to stop something, you can end up being part of the problem.'

Tamura said nothing, didn't argue. Just stared across the bar, pensively.

'Anyway, I often find if you ask enough questions in places like these, word tends to travel quite quickly,' Maisie added, with a hint of playfulness, as if she was enjoying Tamura's unease.

'That's what concerns me,' Tamura remarked as he drew another large gulp from his glass.

They finished their meal and prepared to continue the search for Tanii. And even if they didn't find Tanii, Maisie thought it would be worth learning more about 'the Void' and what sort of activities were taking place here.

Just as they were getting ready to leave, a boy Maisie guessed to be in his early teens arrived at the bar and sat on the stool besides Tamura. He ordered a drink for himself and pulled back the hood of his drenched sweatshirt to reveal his youthful face, partially concealed by a dishevelled mop of dark hair. He immediately leant towards Tamura and uttered something into his ear. Tamura urgently turned to Maisie and relayed the message.

'This boy claims to know where to find the man we're looking for. He said he will take us to him for a small fee.'

Maisie was both suspicious and intrigued simultaneously. 'Does he know his name?' Maisie asked.

'Tanii.' the boy replied with an enthusiastic nod, without waiting for Tamura to translate.

'And how much do you want?'

'Fifty thousand yen,' the boy replied.

'And how do you know this man?' Maisie asked.

The boy looked at Tamura blankly, then conversed quietly with Tamura. Clearly, he knew some English, but not enough to converse fluently.

'He says everyone knows everyone around here.' Tamura replied.

'Okay. Tell him he'll get the money after he's taken us to him.'

Tamura relayed the message. The boy paused as he thought about it, then he nodded and slowly climbed down from the stool.

Maisie paid the tab with a wad of notes, then they both began following the boy along the street. Further into the Void.

As they walked, Tamura leaned closer to Maisie and whispered into her ear. 'Are you sure about this? We could be walking into a trap.'

Maisie smiled back at him reassuringly. 'Then we should spring the trap,' Maisie replied unperturbed, 'besides it's the best opportunity we've had so far. Perhaps share our location with your colleagues? At least then we'll have something to use as leverage should things turn bad. Or you can wait here, while I go?'

Tamura frowned, 'But then who would translate for you?'

Tamura did as Maisie suggested and called one of his officers in Takakumi. The boy led them a few hundred yards further along the street, before turning right down a small alleyway between two restaurants. No more than a meter wide, the alley was part of a much wider network of side-streets that connected blocks of dilapidated housing, concealed behind the facade of the neon lights on the main street. As they trampled over shattered glass and fallen tiles, through the poorly-lit maze of brick and concrete, Maisie began to feel partially disorientated. It was like being spun in circles, blindfolded. The rain was subsiding, and so she folded her umbrella away and used its pointed end to shift some of the debris out of her path.

Eventually they arrived at a set of steep steps. The boy pointed up to the plain wooden door at the summit whilst muttering something to Tamura.

'He says Tanii is up there. Through that door.' Tamura said.

'Well perhaps he would be good enough to stay for the introduction.' Maisie retorted like an unimpressed schoolteacher.

The boy shrugged before reluctantly climbing the steps and slamming his knuckles firmly against the thin planks of the door, which rattled loosely against the latch.

There was a slight stirring from inside, but no answer. The boy knocked again until eventually there was the sound of footsteps approaching the door from inside. The latch clicked and the door opened tentatively inwards until there was enough of a gap to make out a slight, dishevelled figure. The face of the middle-aged man was only partially illuminated by the dim flicker emitted by his television set. But under the long thin strands of grey hair and overgrown beard, Maisie could just about make out the distinctive birthmark on his left cheek that she had repeatedly studied these past few days.

Tamura immediately sparked up a conversation, with the man supplying only short, subdued responses.

'What's he saying?' Maisie asked impatiently, having observed several exchanges between the two men, without an update.

'He denies ever having heard the name Chisato Tanii,' Tamura said dubiously, 'I know that to be false. This is definitely him. I have asked him to show us proof of identification.' The man obediently retreated into his home, leaving the door ajar.

The boy then spoke to Tamura.

Tamura waved him away and turned to Maisie. 'He's demanding his payment for finding the man we're looking for.'

Maisie removed her purse from her back pocket and counted out the fifty thousand yen, before passing the wad of notes to the boy. As quickly as he had appeared, the boy vanished into the alley.

'You still think this is a good idea?' Tamura said, as he followed the boy's path out into the darkness.

Maisie didn't respond but took Tamura's point. If this was a trap, there was little chance of escape from the dead end they now found themselves in. As she assessed the surrounding area, the only alternative exit might be to climb the fire escape and onto the roof of one of the adjacent buildings. Although, given its rickety condition, this would need to be an absolute last resort, she thought.

Tanii returned to the doorway brandishing an identify card which he handed straight to Tamura.

'According to his driving licence, this man's name is Tarou Yamada. It seems genuine and is correctly registered to this address.' Tamura said, slightly puzzled.

'Tell him he has nothing to be afraid of. We want to help, by finding out who is behind the disappearances in Takakumi. And to stop more from happening.'

Tamura translated Maisie's plea to the man, who looked compassionately into Maisie's eyes. He reached forward and held her by the hand as he spoke gently back to her.

'He says he's sorry, but he cannot help us.' Tamura said.

Maisie felt a folded piece of paper being pressed against her palm, which she gripped as she pulled her hand away.

'I understand,' Maisie said, 'can you tell him, if he changes his mind, he can contact me on this number.' She presented Tanii with her business card. Maisie and Tamura both bid the man, who they still believed to be Tanii, 'Sayonara,' as they turned and made their way down the steps. Then, following their original path, they navigated the alleyway and returned to the main street, turning left, back towards the line of shops and restaurants.

'So, what exactly happened there?' Tamura asked Maisie.

'What do you mean?' Maisie replied. She was only half listening to Tamura, preoccupied with how completely deserted the streets had become since their brief absence. By now the rain had entirely stopped, and yet now there were even fewer people around than before. The shops and restaurants that had previously been open and serving customers now seemed closed and had their interior lights turned off.

'What time do places tend to close around here?' Maisie asked looking at her watch. It was only just after eight o'clock.

'Not for hours yet. I expect most places around here would normally be open all night.' Tamura responded, still preoccupied by the conversation with Tanii. 'I saw him place something in your hand. What was it?' he persisted.

Suddenly Maisie caught sight of two riders on the back of a bright red motorcycle. It slowly prowled the promenade like a feline predator searching for prey. It was heading in their approximate direction. She could see the visors of each of the riders independently scanning both sides of the street in a forty-degree arc. Searching for something – or someone.

'Something's not right,' Maisie said calmly, 'do you see that bike up ahead? About a hundred and fifty yards to my one o'clock?' Tamura looked up, but before he could answer, the visors of both riders had fixed on their position. They had been spotted. The driver revved the engine aggressively.

'Quickly, behind that car!' Maisie yelled. They both sprinted towards the stationary vehicle parked at the edge of the street, twenty yards away. Simultaneously, the bike accelerated, explosively along the street, towards them. The noise of the engine created a deafening echo off the buildings, which grew louder and louder. Maisie could see the hand of the bike's passenger reach for something before extending his arm. Tamura and Maisie dove behind the car, just as the bike reached their position. Maisie rolled along the floor and took cover behind the front wheels. A burst of loud cracks echoed around the streets. Glass shattered above her head, and she curled into a ball to avoid the hailstorm of shells that whizzed aggressively past her head, and skipped noisily off the brick, concrete and tarmac. The incursion of gunshots ceased and was replaced by the tortured sound of squealing rubber, as the driver wrestled the bike to regain control in the waterlogged streets, allowing it to run on past its target.

Maisie got to her feet and looked over at Tamura. He seemed unhurt but was yelling something at her. His first attempt was inaudible, the piercing ringing in her ears overpowering all other senses.

'We need to move!' he shouted for the second time.

Maisie inched her head above the line of the bonnet and saw the bike slowing and begin the turn for a second run.

Maisie looked along the street. There were no alleyways nearby where they might make their escape. And most of the bars and restaurants had closed their shutters. Those that hadn't, more than likely would have bolted their doors. The only remaining cover were a few abandoned stalls.

'We're going to have to make a run for it,' she yelled, 'get as far as you can and then take cover behind those stalls,' she said pointing ahead.

'You're crazy! They'll gun us down!'

'No time to argue. Quick! Go!' Maisie yelled, as she collected her umbrella.

Tamura obeyed and began to make his run, just as the bike was lining up. Maisie wasted no time in following. Her senses had fully returned, and she could hear the throttle of the bike revving once again, the tyres struggling for traction on the cobbles. She sprinted faster than she had ever done before, spurred on by the sound of the bike closing in on her, as adrenaline pumped through her veins. Another burst of gunfire prompted her to hunch forward, but still she ran. Tamura continued on, twenty yards in front of her, unharmed. The bike sounded as though it was picking up speed and closing the distance. In a matter of seconds, it would catch them, she thought. More gunfire accompanied the whizzing of bullets above her head.

'Take cover!' Maisie yelled, as she dove to her left behind a stall, still grasping her umbrella. She waited as long as she dared. The roar of the bike's engine got louder, reaching a crescendo as the bottom half of the bike came into view from her vantage point beneath the stall.

This was it, she thought. She thrust the end of the umbrella between the spokes of the front wheel as it rushed past. Immediately there was a loud twang, and the umbrella was ripped from her hand. The engine revved uncontrollably as the rear wheel jolted upwards, and the bike somersaulted, propelling both riders into the air like synchronised human cannonballs. The momentum of the bike carried it onwards, cartwheeling erratically, until it smashed into a nearby bar, demolishing the glass frontage and much of the wooden furniture inside.

Maisie got to her feet. Her heart was pounding in her chest and her mind was fully alert.

'Tamura!' she cried out, as she began her search for him. He was lying face-down on the ground ahead of her, motionless. 'Tamura! Are you okay?' she rushed over to him, bending down to check his pulse before shaking his body firmly.

He groaned and began to stir, gradually rolling onto his side, 'Let's not do that again.' he said with an exhausted growl. 'Where are the riders?'

Maisie pointed to the two bodies that lay contorted on the cobblestones, only a short distance away.

'We need to get out of here and call this in,' he said, as Maisie helped him to his feet. Battered and bruised, they limped away from the scene arm-in-arm towards the end of the street. Tamura reached for his phone and began to make the call, while the two of them remained fully vigilant, mindful they were not yet out of harm's way.

'What was it that Tanii handed to you?' Tamura asked as he waited to be put through to one of his colleagues.

Maisie retrieved the folded piece of paper from her pocket, opened it up and showed it to Tamura. Inscribed faintly in pencil were two Japanese symbols. One vaguely resembling a stickman, and the other more intricate.

'What does it say?' she asked.

Tamura let out a deep, exasperated sigh, 'Oshiro,' he said as he handed the note back to Maisie. 'It says "Oshiro".'

33

Akina Oshiro awoke with a sudden jolt, confused and disorientated. Within a few seconds, her eyes adjusted to the dim lighting, and her vision slowly came into focus. The first things she noticed were the speckled ceiling tiles and the loud beeping from the machines beside her. Combined with the overpowering smell of disinfectant, she instantly knew where she was.

She tried to remember how she got there, but her memories were muddled and fragmented. The last thing she recollected was an endless forest of sakura trees in full bloom. She had been desperately trying to defend the area from an army of lumbermen. For days she had repeatedly tried to fend off their military-like advances as they chopped, sawed and crushed their way through the perimeter, leaving nothing but a path of stumps in their wake. But it had been no good. After attempts to negotiate and reason with them had failed, she had resorted to sabotaging their machinery by removing small but essential components. But it was not enough to stop them.

Eventually, her failed attempts drove her to more radical and violent action. And one night, under cover of darkness, she had set fire to the fuel tanks of the vehicles and machinery. At first, she had rejoiced at her own success, as the diesel ignited in the tanks and great fireballs engulfed each of the machines one-by-one. But quickly the fire had begun to spread. Firstly, to the dry fallen trees and then onto the trees at the edge of the forest. She recalled desperately trying to stop it from spreading but quickly the blaze grew into a wall of flames, higher than the trees themselves, consuming everything in its path. The last thing she could remember was the heat on her face and the smell of diesel fumes that had soaked her clothes.

That must be the reason she had been brought here, she thought. She must have been consumed by the flames. The fire *she* started. Akina panicked as she wondered how bad her injuries might be. She reached with both hands to check for signs of burns, but her face felt normal and untouched. She carried on exploring and detected bandages wrapped around the side of her head. The area it was protecting, to the left side of her skull, was sensitive and, touching it triggered an excruciating pain that forced her jaws together and her teeth to grind involuntarily. Something else was strange too. Both hands felt perfectly normal, and yet she detected an imbalance as the tips of her fingers made contact with her cheeks. She spread out both hands and held them up in front of her eyes. Two missing fingers. Immediately the memories came flooding back.

Her memory of the lumbermen and the fire was all an elaborate fiction. She had been in a coma, and perhaps the drugs had triggered the vivid dreams. Dreams so graphic, she was struggling to distinguish nightmare from reality. The irony of course was that her reality was one big nightmare. But one that should soon be over.

Akina continued to check the rest of her body for other injuries. There were bandages covering her abdomen, as well as both arms and legs. Underneath the dressings she could feel the lacerations to her skin, and her limbs felt heavy from the extensive bruising. And yet she still could not quite recall everything that had happened. She remembered her escape from the cabin. Her fall down the riverbank and into the river. Clambering barefoot across the thick, overgrown fields to the village. But what had happened after that? She strained her thoughts, but it was no good. Just an impenetrable fog of nothingness.

She gave up trying to remember – far more important was the here and now. And, working her stomach muscles to their limit, she heaved her body upwards so she could get a better look at her surroundings, resting on her elbows. The room was large, with a window to her left and only one door directly in front of her. Both were covered by closed venetian blinds. From the doorway, she could hear a faint whistling and the slow plodding of footsteps, both of which seemed to be getting nearer. Before long, a shadow was cast over the thin crack of light at the base of the door, and then both sounds seemed to fade away. Security personnel patrolling the corridor, she suspected. Perhaps even police, given the circumstances.

Checking the side of her bed, she saw she was surrounded by equipment. A monitor showing her vital signs was the source of the beeping. Her heart rate at fifty-eight. She guessed this was being measured by the clip attached to two fingers on her right hand. This was not the only source of noise in the room. From behind a half-drawn curtain, beside her bed, she could hear another independent set of bleeps indicating the presence of another life. Clearly, she was not the only patient in the room.

'Konnichiwa,' she called out, sotto voce, in the direction of her companion. But there was no answer. Not even a stirring in the bed. Wondering why she would be sharing with another patient, Akina clambered over the bed guard and lent over towards the curtain.

The fingertips of her outstretched right arm tickled the curtain, but she was unable to get enough of a grip to move it.

She heard a set of footsteps steadily approaching the door from the corridor. Quickly she fell back into her bed and resumed her recumbent position. Eyes closed. She heard a slight yawn from the hinges as the door opened, and the footsteps entered the room, pacing slowly towards her bed. She could feel a presence leaning over her and she detected a subtle scent of floral perfume. But she resisted the urge to open her eyes. Not even a squint.

For a short while, she heard some rustling of paperwork at the end of her bed. Then the footsteps moved away from her, and on to the bed beside her where the same routine was repeated. Remaining lifelessly still, and careful not to move her head in any way, she opened her eyelids a fraction, barely enough to see more than a haze through her eyelashes. The nurse completed her checks and promptly left the room through the unlocked door. As the closing spring eased the door shut, Akina caught a glimpse of the police officer stationed outside.

Until she had a better grasp of what was happening, she decided it was better that nobody should know she was awake. At least for the time being. She would have to remain absolutely quiet and be careful not to activate any alarms on the equipment. She guessed they might if her vital signs changed dramatically or if the clip measuring them became detached from her fingers.

Once again, she heaved her upper body out of bed and removed the covers to reveal her bandaged legs. Initially they were unresponsive and had to be coaxed to the side of the bed with the use of her arms. Gradually dropping down to the floor, she continued to hold the bed for support and allowed her weight to fall onto her feet. At first it felt as though the floor was swaying like the deck of a ship, but after a few careful steps her muscle memory returned.

Still connected to the machines, she inched closer to the adjacent bed and drew back the partition curtain to reveal the occupant. An icy feeling of dread struck her in the chest as she immediately recognised the sorrowful remains of the man she once knew. Walker? How could it be possible? The strong, athletic physique now looked weak and emaciated. His previously rugged, tanned face and arms had faded to a hue of pale grey, as if the life had been sucked out of him.

Akina leant over his bed and listened to his gentle, unassisted breaths, as she ran her hand through the mop of dark hair, trapping it behind one ear. Then she held him by the hand. She remained deeply conflicted. He was unlike anybody she had ever met before. Exciting and fearless, and yet caring and gentle. There was so much that she wished she had told him. Perhaps if she had, things might have been different. But she hadn't. And they weren't.

She listened for the whereabouts of the police officer. No sound or sign of him. Then she looked back at her bed to assess the distance and movements she would have to make to cover her tracks. She figured she could be back in bed without being caught, within a matter of seconds. Leaning further over the bed, she retrieved the clip, which fed his vitals into the machines, and placed it on her own left hand, next to the one she already had. It seemed to work, only now both machines sounded in tandem as they synchronised to her heart rate. Then she shook his body to test his response. No reaction at all.

First, she tilted his head backwards onto his pillow. Then she covered his mouth and pinched his nose. She felt the short pushing and pulling against her hand as his body instinctively struggled for breath. She tightened her grip as she realised the finality of her actions. Was she really ready to take a life in cold blood? After this there would be no going back. But she knew she had no other choice.

Within a matter of seconds, Walker's body began convulsing violently, like a large fish caught out of water. Akina strengthened her grip and used her body weight to subdue his movements. The bleeping from the machines intensified as her heart rate soared. Gradually the thrashing began to weaken. Tears ran down her cheeks, draining the last of her soul from her body as the life waned from his. Then it was all over.

She stepped back from the bed and felt the deep pit of regret in her stomach as Walker lay there lifelessly. Taking a series of long, emotional breaths, her heart rate began to drop, and she forced herself to keep going. She wiped away her tears, and then carefully reattached the sensor clip to Walker's hand. Without hesitation she lunged back into her bed, replaced the covers exactly the way they had been, and closed her eyes. She had made it, just as the alarms from Walker's bedside began to sound.

34

'So exactly where did this take place?' The police officer asked with a heavy hum of scepticism.

He spoke excellent English whilst simultaneously making notes in Japanese. Dressed head to toe in riot gear, both he and his team had only been at the scene a short while and already seemed keen to leave.

Maisie and Tamura had left the Void for no more than seventeen minutes, whilst they waited for the police to arrive. Maisie had been eager to return but it was Tamura's calm pragmatism that persuaded her to remain by the relative safety of the main road where there was a steady stream of passing traffic. By the time they returned to the scene, with the police, there was almost no trace at all the attack had taken place.

'This was where it happened. Right fucking here!' Maisie said, unable to conceal her frustration, and still over stimulated by adrenaline. 'The two riders were thrown from the bike and landed over there,' she pointed to the ground a few yards from their feet, 'the bike crashed into the window of that restaurant over there.' All their eyes followed the aim of her finger, towards the restaurant window. The security shutters had been pulled down, concealing the damage to the façade.

'I understand, Lockhart-san, but the owner has not corroborated your story.'

'How exactly does he explain all the damage to the inside of his restaurant then?' Maisie retorted, angrily.

'We have checked inside. It's almost empty and there is no sign of a bike. The owner says he's in the process of having the place refurbished.'

'Refurbished?! No kidding!' Maisie exclaimed. 'Surely someone else saw what happened? And what about the two men riding the bike? It's not as if they just got up and wandered off. If they didn't die from their injuries, at best they would be in intensive care by now. Have you received any reports of two crash victims being taken to hospital?'

'No, but we will look into it. This is a big city so, we get lots of calls.' the officer said in a slightly patronising tone.

Maisie took another look around and assessed the situation for herself. The previously deserted street was now home to a whole host of visitors enjoying their evening out. Eating, drinking, laughing. No wonder the police officer was sceptical.

'And what about the car we took cover behind? That will have been filled with bullet holes.' Maisie led the police officer and Tamura along the street to where she thought the car had been parked, but it was gone. 'Surely there must be some residue of the gunfire?' Maisie added checking the cobbles for signs of spent cartridges and the walls of the buildings for lodged bullets, but she couldn't see anything.

'Tamura-san, you were witness to this as well, aren't you going to say anything?' Tamura had remained mostly silent as soon as it had become clear that the scene had been wiped clean of evidence. He made no reply.

'This is unbelievable, why aren't you taking this seriously? I work for a respected news agency, and he is a police officer. One of your own. We wouldn't make something like this up. The two of us were followed here and barely escaped with our lives.'

'And what exactly were the two of you doing here in the first place?'

Tamura intervened without answering the officer's questions, 'Sightseeing. I was showing her around the city. Lockhart-san had heard about this place and I agreed to escort her.'

'Unusual place to bring someone sightseeing,' the officer commented with a raised eyebrow. 'Look, it sounds as though you may have witnessed some sort of accident. And perhaps you may have had too much to drink?' He said, looking at Maisie.

Maisie was furious, but Tamura stepped in front of her and gestured to her that it was time to leave. 'Do you have everything you need, officer?' he asked respectfully. The officer nodded and allowed them to leave.

'What the fuck just happened?!' Maisie exclaimed.

'Keep walking, before you get us into the sort of trouble I may not be able to talk us out of.' Tamura demanded, grabbing her arm and leading her away. 'You're clearly in shock, or you'd realise what's going on here.'

'What is going on?'

'This is clearly the work of the Osore Shirazu, crime syndicate. Only they could clear this up so quickly and force the locals to keep quiet out of fear.' Tamura explained, surreptitiously muttering into Maisie's ear as they walked arm in arm, careful to avoid others hearing him.

'But what about our account of what happened? Does that count for nothing?'

'No, but they have followed up our complaint and no one has validated it.'

'But you're a police officer?' Maisie said with continued exasperation.

'Yes but no evidence, no witness, a foreigner and an off-duty cop with no ID. Both have been drinking. These guys don't want to hang around here longer than they have to. And, right now, neither do I.'

'Fair enough.' Maisie sighed as they continued to walk away from the scene, her mind in overdrive. 'But we have learned at least three valuable pieces of information from today. One: the villagers are not merely migrating away from the village; there is a good chance they are being abducted, maybe even killed if they don't comply. And two: Oshiro is in some way connected to all of it. The disappearances in the village, the Void and most likely Walker's abduction.'

'And what was the third?'

'Never leave home without your umbrella.' Maisie said with a wide grin.

The two of them smiled at each other, as the realisation set in that they had just narrowly escaped an attempt on their lives.

The humour faded from Tamura's face, and a troubled look replaced it.

'But why would a respected and wealthy businessman like Oshiro be involved in something like this? Why risk his status and freedom by associating with organised crime?'

'Who knows? Maybe he's always been involved. Maybe that's how he became so successful. But at the moment, this is merely conjecture. We need to gather some firm evidence if anyone is going to take us seriously.'

'We need to be careful who we share this with.' Tamura added. 'Oshiro has political connections and contacts within the police.'

'Yes, I suggest we keep this between us until we have something more substantial to show.' Maisie agreed.

'For now, let's get the hell out of this place.' Tamura said, relieved with the prospect of returning home.

At that very moment Tamura's phone rang. He answered and began a short conversation. The satisfaction quickly drained from his expression and was replaced by a silent look of severity. He hung up the phone and turned to Maisie.

'That was my officer at the hospital. It's Walker,' he said gravely, 'he hasn't made it.'

35

It was only a quarter to eight in the morning and already Maisie was on her third cup of coffee. The mix of caffeine and sleep deprivation was causing her forehead to ache and her temples to throb. She had barely had any sleep at all, aside from forty or so measly minutes she had endured on the worn, leather couch in the communal area of the police station.

When they returned from Tokyo in the early hours, Tamura had insisted it would be safer to secure themselves within the confines of the police station, rather than return to their accommodation. He had locked all the doors and set the perimeter alarms before asking the central monitoring station to keep an eye on them. Meanwhile, Tamura had spent the night in his office, with a loaded revolver on the desk in front of him.

The moment they got back, the first thing Maisie did was to call the Walkers to inform them of the tragic news. In her mind, it wouldn't have been right coming from anyone else.

Walker's father had been sober and restrained. Perhaps deep down he had feared the worst all along, knowing the extent of his son's injuries and the doctors' concerns for his condition. But now, even hours later, Maisie was still haunted by the devastating wail that had echoed down the line, as Mrs Walker interpreted her husband's reaction.

'I'm so very sorry for your loss,' Maisie had said, having only delivered the positive news that he had been found, a couple of days earlier.

'Do they know what happened?' his father had asked with a heavy heart.

'Right now, that's not clear. The doctors were optimistic that he would make a recovery. He had been taken off the ventilator and had been breathing unassisted. There had been no signs of his condition deteriorating. But earlier this evening, he was found to have suffered some sort of respiratory arrest. The doctors tried to resuscitate him, but it was too late. They think it might have been acute respiratory distress syndrome, possibly brought on by a build-up of fluid in the lungs. But it's too early to tell for sure. I understand the coroner will be undertaking their investigation over the coming days. Either way, it's likely the police will be treating his death as a murder inquiry, given the nature of his injuries and the circumstances under which he was found in the cabin.'

Mr Walker had taken a while before responding.

'His mother and I had already booked our tickets to come out and see him. Only now it will be to make the arrangements to bring him home. Thank you for letting us know, Maisie. It was good of you to be the one to call.'

There was a final pause and then the call was ended with a clunking sound, as the receiver was placed on the base.

Having reflected long and hard this morning, Maisie felt powerless and foolish as she began to draft the first of what was to be a series of reports, starting with 'Scarecrow Valley'. Powerless because Walker had been the reason she had come here in the first place, and yet she had, in fact, done very little to help him. And foolish because, what the hell was the point in writing about something unless it could help find who was responsible?

As far as she was concerned, there was a time for shining a light on corruption and injustice. But this was not it. Now was the time to delve deeper into the conspiracy. To follow the leads and, where necessary, provoke. Only then would they be able to find out who was behind Walker's death. While her instincts continued to point to Oshiro – now more than ever – practically, she knew they had nothing that couldn't be easily shrugged off by a decent lawyer. Nowhere near enough to bring him in. And so, she decided Leegood would have to wait a little longer for her first instalment.

The lock to the station door clicked abruptly and then inched open. Maisie jumped in her skin, her nerves still raw from the previous evening's encounter. The door swung open, causing the temperature in the room to drop sharply, as the chilly morning air breached the perimeter. Sitting at one of the desks she had commandeered for her own use, she looked up from her laptop and immediately recognised the officer's familiar face.

She settled back into her seat and took another sip of her coffee. The two acknowledged each other without words, as he passed her on his way to report to Tamura. Tamura was still in the midst of a long telephone call – one which had lasted twenty minutes or more. But the officer waited patiently at the threshold until he caught his attention. Then the officer fetched a cup of coffee from the kitchen, sat himself at a desk on the opposite side of the room, and began what appeared to be a practiced routine of reviewing checklists, followed by a series of phone calls. Presumably he was checking in with the Tokushima prefecture office, Maisie thought, judging from the short but congenial tone of the calls. But she found herself more suspicious than usual and couldn't stop herself from monitoring his activities. After all, who could really be trusted?

When Maisie saw that Tamura had got off the phone, she took the opportunity to enter his office, closing the door behind her so the other officer would not hear their conversation.

'Tamura, I've been thinking. We need to act quickly on this, otherwise there's a risk Oshiro and his friends are going to cover their tracks again. Just like they did last night.'

'I agree. We need something more concrete to go on.' He said with a knowing smile.

'What is it?'

'You recall our first meeting, when you offered me that flash drive? Our technical team has finally managed to access the files from it.'

'And?' Maisie asked eagerly.

'It seems you were right to think it was important. It might just turn out to be the breakthrough we needed.'

***

Hunter arrived at the yachting centre by taxi at twelve thirty in the afternoon, having come directly from the train station. Outside the entrance to the main building, a man was leant against a set of railings, waiting patiently. Most likely the owner of the boat he was here to look at, he thought to himself, before paying the driver and exiting the cab.

He took a moment to fill his lungs with the coarse sea air and bask in the gentle warmth of the sun, as he appreciated the perfectly clear blue skies above. Up to this point, it had been one hell of a journey. First the incident at the airport, then the plane.

From Krasnodar airport, the train journey had taken a gruelling seven days, as far as the line would go to Vladivostok city, at the far east of Russia. There he had taken the slow ferry across the Sea of Japan to Donghae, South Korea, where he had boarded yet another train that had brought him here, to the busy port of Busan on the south-easterly tip of the peninsular. He had found himself with plenty of time to research and plan whilst on the train, and he had decided that it would be here that he would make the crossing to Japan. But as he stood by the docks, pleased with the miles that were behind him, he knew that his journey was far from over. Only a relatively small two hundred and thirty mile stretch of water lay between him and his objective. And yet, this part of the journey was going to be the most challenging.

'You must be Mr Hunter?' the man said in very good English, 'my name is Cheon Seo-jun,' he added, as the two men reached out to shake each other's hands. 'I know you are keen to get started, so shall we go take a look at her straight away?'

Hunter said nothing, just nodded his head. He saw no reason to try and ingratiate himself with the man. In his experience, spinning an elaborate lie meant you risked being caught out and only served to make a person more memorable, when part of his objective was to achieve the exact opposite.

Seo-jun led them across the partially filled carpark towards the entrance to the marina, 'You are English. Yes?'

'Australian.' he replied.

Seo-jun smiled nervously as he became momentarily trapped in Hunter's fearsome gaze.

'And are you here for business or a vacation?' he asked, immediately regretting asking.

'A little of both, I hope.' Hunter replied, again without offering an explanation. The two continued walking in silence.

They reached the security gate to the marina where Seo-jun punched in a code to release the lock. They filed along the wharf by the water's edge. It was a reasonably large harbour, home to perhaps two hundred and fifty motorboats and sailing yachts of varying sizes, all connected to the land by a series of floating jetties. Most of the boats seemed well-maintained and, whilst the surrounding skyscrapers conveyed an air of affluence, few of the boats were larger than forty feet.

The surface of the water in the harbour was calm and iridescent in the early afternoon sunlight, and the boats swayed peacefully back and forth in unison, making the occasional creak and splash as they pulled on their moorings. Above them the sound of squawking gulls echoed across the sky. Outside the harbour, a faint intermittent fizzing could be heard as the waves broke against the concrete barriers.

They reached the final jetty and Seo-jun led them down the gangway and onto the pontoons. He made some seemingly friendly exchanges in Korean with a couple of the other owners already aboard their boats. He stopped about halfway along.

'This is her,' he said proudly, as he held his arm out in the direction of the boat they were there to inspect.

It was a Beneteau Antares Series 9, a thirty-foot motorboat, complete with a fully enclosed cabin and flying bridge. Either could be used to operate the boat. He had chosen it specifically because of the cabin, and because of the protection it would offer on the open sea; the crossing would likely take at least eleven hours. The boat had a navy blue hull with a sharp, but wide bow, with stainless steel railings that ran almost the full length to the stern. The deck and cabin were white, and the windows were fully transparent. Hunter knew more recent models had tinted glass. In its day it would have been a handsome craft, but now, more than twenty years old, it bore the scars of servitude, with evidence of deep scuffs and scrapes on the hull and the deck. More than likely it had served as a fishing boat for tourists, who perhaps had not treated it as well as a proud owner might have. He smiled to himself when he saw the name of the boat. 'Liberty.' Perhaps chosen for their American clientele, it was very apt for the job he needed it for.

'She's just recently had a refit,' Seo-jun said with a salesman's optimism, as he lifted his leg over the side of the boat and stepped onto the aft deck. Hunter did the same and wondered exactly how extensive and how recent the work had been. Seo-jun then struggled with the sliding door, which eventually opened with a firm tug.

'She's well equipped with everything you need, whether you are looking to spend a few days, or even live on it.' Seo-jun continued as he began his tour of the interior.

Inside, the décor of the cabin was dated: an abundance of varnished wood and worn, cobalt blue coloured cushions. But it seemed relatively clean and included a small kitchen area, fixed table and benches. Down some steps, below deck, there was one cabin and a separate toilet and shower.

'How fast can she go?'

'Cruising speed is about twenty-two knots. Flat out, you might get thirty-five.'

'And how much?' Hunter asked, knowing full well what it was advertised for.

'Fifty-nine million won,' Seo-jun replied. Hunter knew this was the equivalent of fifty thousand US Dollars.

Hunter paused for a moment before continuing with a list of his requirements.

'I will need a dinghy with an outboard motor. Something that can be easily tied to the back of the boat. And some jerry cans with spare fuel.'

'Sure, I can get you that.'

'And I will need you to provide me with all the documentation I need by tomorrow.'

'No problem. Have you ever piloted a boat like this before?'

Hunter initially ignored the question and shifted across to the cockpit, where he located the ignition key. There was a deep growl from the diesel engines as it started first time, before changing tone to a continuous murmur that vibrated through the deck.

'Remove the moorings and you'll find out.' he said.

36

Maisie and Tamura had been studying the files from Walker's flash drive for almost two hours. There was a substantial amount of material, all meticulously organised into folders and subfolders. So many that they had decided to divide them up so that they could make better time.

Maisie had returned to her desk and taken the documents filed under "scope of work" and "full report". Meanwhile, Tamura had focused on the files contained within "correspondence" and "site surveys". So far, Maisie had scanned through numerous legal documents, including a non-disclosure agreement and a statement of work, both drafted by Oshiro's lawyers. She had also skimmed through most of the draft thirty-page report Walker had been preparing, which outlined both a summary and supporting detail of Walker's findings and recommendations. Meanwhile, Tamura had been perusing what appeared to be a complete record of emails between Walker and Oshiro's company. These went as far back as the initial enquiries made by Oshiro's firm, right up to the point at which Walker went missing. All were in chronological order. Walker had also kept records of surveys undertaken in various places in the local area. It was a gold mine of information.

Maisie got up from her desk to stretch her legs and make coffee, then proceeded into Tamura's office to compare and discuss their progress so far. She walked over to his desk and placed one of the cups to the right of his laptop, without asking whether he wanted it or not, and kept the other for herself. Then she pulled up a chair opposite.

'Find anything interesting?' Tamura said, his eyes still fixed on the screen.

Maisie pondered on the question as she considered which bit of information to focus on first.

'All extremely interesting in my view,' she replied eventually, 'and the more I read, the more questions it raises for our friend Mr Oshiro.'

'In what way?' Tamura asked, looking up from his laptop and taking a cautionary sip from the hot cup.

'When I interviewed Oshiro in his home last week, he specifically said Walker had been employed to undertake a feasibility study for a hydroelectric power plant he was thinking of building in the area. Something that would provide both his residence and the villagers with clean energy. I checked it back in my notes.'

'And?'

'There is absolutely no mention of that in Walker's files. Not in the scope of work nor anywhere in Walker's report. Instead, Walker's work seems to have been entirely focused on assessing the presence of yttrium.'

'Yttrium?' Tamura asked, puzzled.

'Yes, yttrium. I had to look it up. It's a "rare earth metal" used in a variety of different applications and industries, including electronic components and batteries. Extremely valuable,' she said, with an exaggerated frown to emphasise just how valuable. 'Perhaps even more so to a company like Oshiro's that specialises in electrical components.'

'So, this proves Oshiro was lying about what Walker was up to.' Tamura said.

'Yes. He obviously didn't think this information could find its way into our hands. Or anyone else's, for that matter. Walker was constrained by so many legal knots, he couldn't have disclosed this information without facing financial ruination.'

'I found a few things as well,' Tamura said enthusiastically, 'Walker recorded each of the surveys in great detail. Soil samples, photographs of the area, even the specific grid references, which show exactly where the work was carried out. I have been checking some of the locations this morning and plotting them on this map.' Tamura swivelled his laptop ninety degrees to allow Maisie a view of it.

'These dots represent the surveys that were carried out by Walker; there are ten of them in total. Some of them appear in the valley at the edge of Oshiro's estate,' Tamura used his finger to indicate the area, 'but by far the vast majority appear within the area of the village itself. Most are no more than a hundred meters from where we are now.'

'And who owns the land in the village?' Maisie asked.

'No one individual, the villagers mostly own the properties they live in. Or at least they did.'

Maisie leant back in her chair with an air of relief, sporting a satisfied smile.

'So, a rare earth metal, potentially worth hundreds of millions of dollars, is discovered in the area. Oshiro needs a specialist to verify the find and map out where to dig. But he can't use anyone local, in case the information leaks. Enter Edward Walker. But there's a problem. Walker confirms that a lot of this Yttrium is in the land beneath the village itself. Land that Oshiro *doesn't* own. Now, Oshiro can't simply announce that he wants to buy all of it. That would raise all sorts of questions and mean that the price of the land increases significantly. So …'

Tamura nodded emphatically and continued where Maisie left off. '… so, with the help of his organised crime contacts, he creates a plan to forcibly remove the residents from the village. Once he acquires all the land, he can begin mining it. The authorities dismiss the migration as people moving into the cities to find work – not uncommon in rural areas. And the scarecrows are used as a threat to help spread the rumour. Leave or be taken.'

Maisie smiled. The two of them were now completely aligned in their thinking. 'And anyone looking from the outside just assumes it's a quirky attempt to encourage tourism in another dying village in rural Japan. Any local tales of superstition can easily be dismissed as nonsense.' Maisie added.

'But where do the abductions of Walker and Akina come into this?' Tamura asked.

'Maybe Walker realised what Oshiro was up to. Maybe he was asking too many questions. From some of the files on the flash drive, it looks as though Walker had been looking into the sale of property in the area. Hundreds of transactions, all in the last three years and all by companies. No private individuals. That alone is suspicious.'

'What companies?'

'By the look of them, they are shell companies. But we will need to follow the ownership trail. See if it links back to Oshiro.'

'I can look into that,' Tamura said pensively. 'But what about Akina? Why abduct his own daughter?'

Maisie shrugged, 'Maybe she was helping Walker. Maybe her father found out and decided to punish her. When I spoke with Walker's parents, they were convinced he was in a relationship. Maybe it was with Akina?'

'But why not simply kill them? Why torture them first? The gangsters involved had no problem with trying to kill us last night.'

'Maybe Oshiro wanted to know how much they knew and who they had told first? Perhaps he wanted to humiliate and punish them first? Who knows what drives a man like that.'

There was another brief silence as Tamura leant back in his chair and stared at the ceiling. 'I don't know. This is all circumstantial.'

'Not if we can follow the trail of property transactions. That would prove Oshiro was up to something. That gives us the motive. Better still we need a witness. Someone like Tanii who will be able to testify that they were abducted.'

'Do you think that is likely, given last night?' Tamura asked. 'If he hasn't already run, the gangs will have got to him by now.'

'Then we will need to find a way to protect him and give assurances.' Maisie replied, aware of the hypocrisy of suggesting witness protection.

Tamura nodded in agreement. 'It makes you wonder, if Oshiro is behind this, how would he ever think that he could get away with it?'

'You'd be surprised how audacious criminal enterprises can be. And this fits the bill of an arrogant egomaniac. If enough powerful people are kept scared or given a vested interest, things can often be conveniently overlooked. I would put money on there being involvement from officials. Police or even politicians that have either been paid or blackmailed into looking the other way. It certainly wouldn't be the first time. That's why we need to be careful with this.'

Tamura thought carefully on that point, knowing full well the potential ramifications if he misjudged who to trust with this. After all, if Maisie was right and this was a far-reaching criminal conspiracy, who else might be involved?

'We do need to be careful who we share this with, but we can't keep this to ourselves. Otherwise, there's a danger they will try to silence us again. And, if they succeed next time, they will get away with it.' He said.

'Who do you think you can trust?'

'I will speak with Inspector Kishimoto. He will know what to do. And now we have the evidence from Walker, we have genuine grounds to bring Oshiro in for questioning. Meanwhile we need to get to work on finding some proof to support your theory that he's behind the disappearances.'

Maisie paused a moment. She thought back to the cabin, when Kishimoto was looking to get Maisie removed from the case. She wondered whether Kishimoto could be trusted. Then she searched Tamura's eyes for a hint of doubt, a sign of indecision. But there was none.

'Makes sense.' she said. 'How about we look into the trail of property acquisitions and take another look at the shots of the crime scene to see if there is anything that can link Oshiro?'

***

The moon seemed more massive than usual. It shined brightly, illuminating the surface of the calm sea as the small motorboat gurgled its way along, carving a vast V-shaped wake.

Having been satisfied by the demonstration earlier that day, Hunter had purchased the boat at the agreed price. Motivated by the promise of a quick sale, Seo-jun provided all the add-ons, allowing Hunter to leave that same afternoon. As Hunter saw it, he had already wasted enough time with the considerable detour through Russia and South Korea. He didn't have a moment to lose if he was going to catch up with the target.

Hunter checked his progress on the satellite navigation. From the point of leaving the marina in Busan, he had held the engines at full throttle for just over three hours, taking full advantage of the millpond-like conditions. He had already completed more than three-quarters of the 150-mile crossing, towards the mainland of Japan. He was aiming for the Kanmon Straits, a small stretch of water separating the islands of Honshu and Kyushu, and a short-cut to the Inland Sea of Japan. He was currently running parallel with the busy shipping lane, both to avoid the swell caused by the large ships and any unwanted attention. But he would soon need to converge with the route of the other vessels as he entered the strait. He would then pass between the cities that guarded the Inland Sea. Shimonoseki, on the southernmost tip of Honshu, and Kitakyushu, on the northernmost tip of Kyushu.

Once through to the Inland Sea, he had a further eighty miles before reaching the westerly coast of Shikoku island. There he had identified a small uninhabited island where he could moor the boat, out of sight from prying eyes. More than likely, it would still be dark when he arrived. Using the on-board dinghy, with its small outboard, would mean a less conspicuous arrival into the nearby fishing village of Honaicho Kikitsu, under cover of darkness. There he had already arranged for a car to be waiting for him.

Holding the boat's engine at maximum revs was taking its toll on fuel consumption, but including the reserves on board, he estimated that he had enough to complete the return journey. And whilst paperwork provided by Seo-jun would allow him to stop at a marina in Japan for fuel, he planned to avoid this unless absolutely necessary. After all, the main point of taking this route was so that he could enter the country undetected and minimise the risk of being challenged by border officials. Much better to limit his contact with anyone and ensure that nobody knew more about his journey than they needed to.

***

They had been hard at it for hours. Everyone in the station had been given a role to play. Only Maisie and Tamura knew the full picture. Now it was getting late, the fatigue was beginning to show on both Tamura and Maisie, but they were driven on by their determination and a steady flow of caffeine. Strings had been pulled and many phone calls made. But now they had the evidence they needed. Evidence that proved land within the village had been bought up by Oshiro's company, through a complex web of holding companies. During the search Tamura's team also uncovered some irregularities with the paperwork at the land registry body, known as Toki, indicating that not all the land had been acquired with the vendors' consent.

Meanwhile, Maisie had spent the afternoon reviewing the findings at the crime scene, including photographs and forensic reports. She was looking for something. Something out of place.

A clue that might shed light on the identity of Akina and Walker's abductor.

There were hundreds of images, most of them a graphic reminder of the horrors that had taken place. But two images stood out from all the others. One was the vase filled with the remanence of cherry blossom. No matter how hard she tried, it made absolutely no sense to her. It must hold some significance to the culprit, unless of course it was already there when they had arrived – and that seemed unlikely.

The second image was altogether more conclusive. It showed the item Tamura had found on the floor of the cabin and passed to forensics. A small, bloodied pin with a decorative crouching tiger, made from white gold. The blood had been identified as Akina's. But the partial thumb imprinted in the dried blood, clearly visible at the edge of the tiger's head, did not belong to anyone in the police database.

'This might just be the breakthrough we've been waiting for.' Maisie threw down the photograph onto Tamura's desk, unable to conceal her excitement.

Tamura shrugged, as he inspected the photograph, 'The tiger pin? What about it?'

'It's the only evidence that proves there was another person at the scene of the crime. And who it belongs to has been right under our noses all along.'

Tamura remained blank.

Maisie handed him another image that she had copied and enlarged from a newspaper article. Tamura inspected the photograph. It showed Yoshi Oshiro holding the 'Order of the Rising Sun'. He looked almost regal as he balanced the medal in his right hand, sat proudly in a decorative, throne-like armchair. But as Tamura looked closer, he saw it too. It was catching the light, probably the flash from the camera. It gleamed ostentatiously from the centre of Oshiro's left lapel.

'Fuck!' Tamura exclaimed, in an uncharacteristic release.

'Exactly.' Maise said in agreement.

37

The car swerved violently into the hairpin bend as the driver attempted to maintain speed, without losing control. With a dab of the brakes, he turned the wheel hard, followed by a firm thrust to the accelerator. The rear tyres squealed in protest and the tail veered towards the edge of the road. Clawing against the tarmac, the tyres once again found traction, and the vehicle powered on towards the next bend. The two cars repeated the procedure several times as they ascended the snaking mountain road, both drivers pushing the vehicles as fast as they dared. When they reached the summit, they powered along the straight, running parallel with the backbone of the mountain.

'Faster!' Tamura demanded impatiently, willing the needle of the speedometer towards the top of the dial. He had only informed the inspector and three of his most trusted officers that Yoshi Oshiro was being brought in for questioning. But he feared there was still an outside chance word would reach Oshiro before he could.

Tamura was in the passenger seat of the lead car, sitting beside the best driver on his team. Behind them two other officers were attempting to keep pace.

'Just a short way to go now. Come on! Faster!' Tamura encouraged eagerly, as they came within a mile of Oshiro's residence.

Mercifully, the narrow roads remained clear, allowing the two cars to glide over the uneven surface at high speed. Normally, he would have encouraged caution along this notoriously dangerous section of road but, right now, adrenaline and the desire to capture his target had won out.

As he spotted the entrance 200 yards away, he tapped his driver on the shoulder with his knuckles, signalling they were nearly there. Simultaneously he delivered instructions via his radio to the trailing car.

'This is it. Get ready for the next turning on the right.'

The cars slowed and turned into the entrance to the compound, stopping in front of the huge, black steel gates, guarded by the two life-sized white tiger statues.

The driver of Tamura's car wound down the window and pushed the button on the intercom. It rang for several minutes. Stalling for time, Tamura thought. Or were they simply demonstrating they hurried for no one. Not even the police.

'Please provide your identities and the reason for your visit.' said the voice from the intercom, sounding official.

'This is Sergeant Tamura, Tokushima police. We are here to speak with Mr Oshiro. Open up please.' demanded the driver on Tamura's behalf.

'I'm afraid Mr Oshiro does not receive walk-in visitors. Not even the police. But if you'd like to contact his secretary, I'm sure they'll make you an appointment.'

Frustrated with the time that was being wasted, Tamura broke his silence and shouted across the driver at the intercom.

'We have a warrant for Mr Oshiro's arrest. If you fail to let us in, you will be arrested for obstructing us in our lawful duty. Now open the gates immediately!'

The intercom fell silent and, for what seemed like several minutes, there was nothing.

'Right, enough of this nonsense. Ram the gate!' Tamura instructed the driver, furiously.

The driver responded with a questioning look.

'You mean …?'

'I mean we can't be made to look ridiculous just waiting out here. We have given them the opportunity to do the right thing. They haven't, so ram it down!'

The driver was initially sceptical and slightly unnerved by Tamura's uncharacteristically enthusiastic behaviour. Would a saloon – modified though it was – be capable of even denting the thick steel gates? But he could see Tamura was in no mood for a debate and so he did as instructed.

First, he reversed the car back down the road, about a hundred meters. Then he stamped hard against the accelerator pedal. The engine and rear wheels screeched. They were both sucked back into their seats as the car lurched forwards. Tamura watched the speedometer climb sharply, then the driver turned the wheel sharply to the right, just in time to make the turning and align the bonnet with the gates.

Everything happened in slow motion. The bumper of the car collided with the gates, setting off both the driver and passenger airbags. The thump to their faces obstructed their vision and disorientated them both. They heard a violent clang as the gates burst open and smashed against the walls either side. The driver, still struggling for visibility, instinctively applied his foot hard on the brakes. The car grinded to an aggressive halt, whilst spraying fragments of gravel into the air as the rear end began to skid sideways.

Tamura immediately prised himself from his seat and stumbled out of the car. He removed the revolver from his holster and checked his surroundings. They were in the compound, but there was no one around. No cars. No sign of Oshiro. None of his staff.

'You okay?' Tamura called back to the car.

The driver nodded, still stunned by the noise and impact of the airbag. He broke free from his seat slower than Tamura had and the other two officers pulled up in their car beside them.

'You two wait here and guard the entrance. Make sure no one gets in or out.' Tamura ordered. 'See if you can locate the security guard. We'll go for Oshiro.' The two officers acknowledged the instruction. Then they reversed the car and parked lengthways in front of what was left of the main gate – contorted metal that looked as though it had been blown apart by explosives.

Tamura and the other officer ran up the grass bank towards the entrance to the main house. As they approached, a member of Oshiro's household opened the main door and stood calmly, as if she were welcoming a regular guest.

Tamura and the officer slowed to a walking pace as they got within earshot of the maid.

'We're here for Oshiro. Where is he?' Tamura insisted, stopping in front of her as they reached the doorway.

'Mr Oshiro has asked me to escort you to his study,' the woman said politely, unconcerned by Tamura's brusqueness or the revolver in his right hand. 'Would you like to follow me?'

The maid's convivial manner instantly disarmed Tamura. Suddenly he found himself questioning whether he had allowed the excitement of the situation to affect his judgement.

'Of course. Please lead on,' he replied, humbly. The maid turned and began leading them through the reception hall and then up the grand wooden staircase. 'Can I ask what changed Mr Oshiro's mind?' Tamura asked the maid.

'I'm not sure I understand?' she replied, her gaze still focused ahead of her as they climbed the staircase.

'Why he is happy to invite us to his office, when only a moment ago we were refused entry?'

'Oh, you mean the main gate? Yes, you made short work of that,' she chuckled. 'Mr Oshiro has a standing instruction not to admit anyone without an appointment. I believe the security guard was just seeking his permission when you burst through.'

Tamura felt a dull ache in the pit of his stomach. Inspector Kishimoto was already on his way and would not be pleased to find that he and his team had acted with unnecessary force. Particularly against a man as influential as Oshiro. Worse still, what if he and Maisie were wrong about him?

Tamura holstered his weapon. He pushed his doubts to the back of his mind and concentrated on what he would say to Oshiro.

They reached the top of the staircase on the first floor and followed the landing to a side corridor. The maid led them into Oshiro's office. It was empty.

'Please take a seat,' she said, using the palm of her hand to point to the two vacant chairs in front of the desk, 'Mr Oshiro will be with you shortly. Can I offer you anything to drink?'

'No thank you.' Tamura replied on behalf of them both. He traversed the length of the large windowpane, unable to be still.

'Very well,' she chirped. Then she turned and walked back along the corridor, leaving Tamura and the officer alone in Oshiro's study.

'Something's not right.' Tamura said, turning to his officer.

Before he had time to respond, there was a loud noise from outside. A deep animalistic roar from a powerful engine echoed around the compound, repeatedly reaching a crescendo before dropping back to a pulsating burble. It was coming from the front of the building, and Oshiro's study only afforded a view of the rear.

'Quickly, come with me!' Tamura yelled as he passed the officer on his way towards the doorway. Tamura rushed back to the staircase, the noise still vibrating through the bowels of the building like the inside of a giant double bass. He found a window looking out over the front lawn. He traced the source of the sound to the edge of the gravel car park. A rectangular platform, camouflaged by a layer of gravel, was rising up from the ground. Beneath it, between some steel pillars was a black Rolls Royce, rising up from an underground car park.

Tamura couldn't quite make out who was at the wheel. The car had almost reached ground level but would remain unable to move until it did. Tamura darted along the landing, down the stairs, and out of the front door. He stopped on the gravel outside and looked across to the right. The car had almost reached the top. Inside, Oshiro's large frame was in the driver's seat, pounding on the throttle as he rocked back and forth in his seat, willing the elevator to reach the top more quickly.

Within seconds, the car made it to ground level. Oshiro released the brakes. The rear wheels spun and the heavy car lurched forwards, across the remainder of the gravel and then across the lawn. The wheels struggled for traction on the grass and the car slalomed down the hill, crossing the gravel road twice on its way to the base of the slope and then back onto the gravel again. He was heading directly for the main gate where the other officers were still standing either side of their vehicle, blocking the only exit. But now Oshiro was picking up speed.

Tamura removed his revolver from its holster and released the safety catch.

'Aim for the tyres!' he yelled to his officers.

The car was midway between himself and the exit, about a hundred yards away. Still accelerating. It was a difficult shot, even for a more practiced eye. He raised his revolver, clutching the grip with his right hand whilst steadying it with his left, and let off two shots in short succession. Both hit low down on the passenger door. At the same time, the officers opened fire, also missing their intended targets.

Oshiro was closing the distance to the gate and picking up speed. Tamura took careful aim and fired again. Two shots. The first was too far in front, but the second bullet pierced the front passenger-side tyre, sending the car veering out of control to the left. Oshiro could be seen through the rear window, wrestling with the wheel, but it was no good. His attempts sent the vehicle hurtling wildly in the opposite direction, towards the wall of the compound, before smashing head-on into the solid stone base of the twenty-foot perimeter wall. Accompanying the loud clang was the sound of glass shattering as the vehicle came to an abrupt end.

The two officers guarding the entrance began to close in on Oshiro. They proceeded cautiously, keeping their firearms trained at the vehicle's cabin. Tamura and the third officer ran down the bank to assist, revolvers still raised, ready to adopt a firing stance if necessary.

'Good shooting, Sergeant.' one of the officers said with admiration.

'When we close this case, you two should definitely get some time in at the firing range!' he replied in a rare display of banter, prompting a snigger from the officer beside him.

Tamura then went around to the side of the vehicle and observed the damage. Although the car had driven squarely into the wall, the front of the car had maintained much of its original form. The spirit of ecstasy remained defiantly upright above the grill. The windscreen was cracked and evidence of stray bullets scattered the wheel arches and side panels. Inside the cabin, the driver's airbags had deployed and deflated, leaving a dazed Oshiro resting his head on the steering wheel, looking straight ahead. His arms hung loosely from his hunched shoulders like a rag doll.

Tamura opened the driver's door with his left hand, keeping his revolver pointed downwards with his right. Oshiro's body remained inanimate. Only his eyes moved to meet Tamura's.

'Going somewhere, Mr Oshiro?' Tamura asked.

Oshiro sat up in his seat and wiped his bloodied nose.

'I hope you have good reason for breaking into my home and causing me to fear for my life, Sergeant?'

'We were just hoping to have a word, Oshiro-san? Is now a bad time?'

'You might as well enjoy the moment whilst you can. Your career is finished,' Oshiro said with a vicious growl and a grimace tainted by blood.

38

The door creaked slowly shut for the eighteenth time in the last two days. It had become an excruciating sound, much like the scraping of fingernails down a blackboard or a knife against a ceramic plate. Each occurrence seemed to last longer than the last.

Akina had been keeping count from the moment she had first gained consciousness. Not for any particular purpose, just one of the many distractions to pass the time and remain focused, as she lay waiting for the opportune moment. As of yesterday morning, the count of the officer's footsteps, as he paced along the corridor, had reached 2,973, until he had been replaced by a colleague more inclined to stay seated. Since then, she had resorted to counting the number of bleeps given off by her heart rate monitor. And yet, whilst all these sounds had now become torturous noise, Akina experienced a brief moment of euphoria each time the closing mechanism caused the door to slam. A clear signal that she was free to open her eyes, until the next time she heard footsteps approaching.

Akina looked around the room for something to drink. The intravenous drip she was connected to had successfully kept her hunger at bay, but it had done little to satisfy her thirst. Clearly her body was getting the nutrients and hydration it needed, but her mouth was dryer than she had ever experienced before. It had become an all-consuming sensation, and how to quench it was her singular obsession. As she inspected the room, the only liquid that she had access to was the IV drip itself. She reached across to the tube and unscrewed it from the needle. Then she held it above her mouth and waited in anticipation for the first droplet to fall. It was like a single raindrop landing on a parched desert. She squeezed the tube enough to moisten her tongue and the wall of her mouth. Then she reconnected it to the needle in her right arm and lay back in bed.

Her eyelids felt heavy, as though lead weights were weighing them down. Since she had woken two days earlier, she had deliberately prevented herself from falling asleep. She considered this a considerable achievement, seeing as she had been almost permanently recumbent, with her eyes closed. But she could not risk inadvertently alerting the hospital staff that she was no longer in a coma. Maintaining her pretence was her only alibi.

She had placed a pencil beneath her back, lengthways across her spine. This caused enough discomfort to make it difficult to drift off into more than a very light sleep. The only question was how long she could keep it up for.

As she mulled over the options, tempted by the prospect of ending this purgatory, she decided she should persevere for just a little longer. Another twenty-four hours would add more credence to her alibi, she decided.

39

Yoshi Oshiro hunched over the aluminium table, his head resting in his stout hands, as his legal counsel whispered into his ear. His head was bandaged, having sustained minor cuts and bruises after the collision. His expensive pinstriped suit had been reduced to tatters after being forcibly removed from his vehicle when he refused to comply with Tamura's officers. And yet his scarlet necktie remained defiant in place, as if it were the last remaining residue of his respectability.

It was no accident they had brought him to the police headquarters in Tokushima to conduct the interview. Not only did it have many cells in which to hold suspects – unlike the informal setting of Takakumi, here the rooms were sparsely furnished and drab. The small, dimly lit rooms were designed to make suspects feel confined and ill at ease and offered an unpleasant insight of what might be to come.

Oshiro lifted his head long enough to confirm his agreement with a nod of his head and then let it fall back into his hands.

'My client has no comment on the matter.' Oshiro's lawyer said for the third time on his behalf.

'Is remaining silent really the best strategy here?' Inspector Kishimoto asked rhetorically. 'After all, there is mounting evidence against your client. Already sufficient for a jury to reach a decisive verdict, I would suggest.'

Kishimoto then turned his gaze towards Oshiro, himself. 'Oshiro-san, we know you were aware of the presence of a rare earth metal beneath the land of the village. You commissioned the survey yourself. We also know you've been acquiring the land in and around the village. And we have your fingerprints at the scene where Walker and your own daughter where being held and tortured.'

Oshiro slammed his hands down angrily on the table and delivered a menacing stare from his bulging eyes.

'That's impossible! I had nothing to do with that! My daughter will be able to confirm that when she wakes up. I have never done anything that would harm her. Nor have I ever been to this cabin.' Oshiro declared emphatically.

'How can you explain the presence of this pin, found at the scene? This *is* your pin, isn't it?' Tamura asked, as he slid an evidence bag across the table. Inside the crouching tiger motif was still stained by dirt and blood.

Oshiro glanced at the evidence bag. Then at his lawyer. He said nothing.

'This is not a unique item,' said the lawyer. 'This could belong to anyone.'

Kishimoto didn't honour the comment with a response. Instead, he removed another photograph from his file then placed it on the table.

Both Oshiro and the lawyer looked at the photograph. Squinted to see the detail. It was a slightly higher resolution version of the one found by Maisie of Oshiro after receiving his Order of the Rising Sun decoration. A crude circular pen mark had been drawn around Oshiro's left lapel.

'There could be many like this, what makes you so sure this is the same one?' the lawyer asked assertively.

Kishimoto produced another photograph. This time showing an enlarged image of the pin. A thumb print etched into dried blood.

'What do you make of that?' he asked.

They both looked at each other, shrugged their shoulders.

'That is a thumb print made in the blood. The blood belongs to your daughter, Akina. We didn't know who the print belonged to until we were able to take yours here today. Now perhaps you could explain how your fingerprint could end up on this pin, covered in your daughter's blood and be found at the scene of the crime?' Tamura observed subtle signs of satisfaction appearing at the corner of Kishimoto's mouth as he delivered the news.

Oshiro paused for a moment, as if he was searching his mind for a specific memory.

'I have no idea. Someone must be trying to frame me.' he looked again at his lawyer, who seemed unable to offer anything. 'Even if I were crazy enough to abduct a man and my own daughter, surely you don't think me stupid enough to do it in my own backyard. Let alone leave evidence of my prints at the scene?'

'You'd be surprised how common it is for a perpetrator to make critical mistakes, particularly when we're dealing with amateurs. This is the sort of item that could easily be misplaced. But I suspect you weren't finished. Maybe you were intending to return to the cabin later. Clean it up and remove the evidence. But before you could, your daughter managed to escape, meaning you couldn't risk returning to the scene. Who knows, perhaps you were going to burn the cabin down once you were finished. That's what I would have done. What about you, Tamura-san?' Kishimoto added, now conferring with his colleague in a casual attempt to frustrate Oshiro further, and perhaps draw him into volunteering more information.

'That would certainly make sense. Much cleaner that way. Destroy all the evidence.' Tamura concurred, continuing Kishimoto's pretence.

'This is nonsense. I have never even been to that cabin,' Oshiro said in protest.

'If not you, then who else would it be? And why frame you?' Kishimoto asked.

Oshiro remained silent, as he searched inwardly for answers.

'We also have the black four by four vehicle that we found in your underground garage.' Tamura said.

'What about it?' Oshiro said impatiently.

'It hadn't been washed. We found the exact same mud on it that is found in the area by the cabin.'

'You mean the same soil that runs throughout Oshiro-san's estate?' The lawyer countered.

Tamura nodded, as if conceding, before delivering the fatal blow. 'The tyres of the four by four found in your garage also match the tyre tracks we found outside the cabin. There is no question the vehicle had been there.'

'That vehicle is used by my estate manager; I've never used it before.'

'We'll soon find out. We found hair follicles on the car seat. No doubt we will be able to prove they belong to you,' Tamura said confidently.

Oshiro didn't bother answering and just shook his head in disgust.

'So, we have compelling evidence that places you at the scene. Let's move on to motive. You employed Edward Walker to validate the find of yttrium. Is this correct?' Kishimoto asked.

Oshiro looked at his lawyer before answering.

'He was employed as an independent contractor to conduct an assessment into the feasibility of building a hydroelectric generator to supply my residence and the surrounding village with power. This included undertaking surveys and soil samples in a range of locations.'

'And did he find anything?'

'I was still waiting on his final report when he went missing.'

'So, he didn't tell you that he had found a rare earth metal, potentially worth hundreds of millions, maybe even billions, to someone with the right resources?'

'My client declines to comment,' Oshiro's lawyer interjected, 'he has already stated that he was awaiting the final report from Mr Walker.'

'We have seen the report,' Kishimoto disclosed, placing a copy down on the desk. 'Within it there is no mention of a hydroelectric generator. Instead, all it refers to is the yttrium and where it's located across the village. There is also a contract written by your company, noting that this was the specific objective of his assessment.'

Oshiro said nothing. He just sat there, holding unwavering eye contact with Kishimoto.

'And then there's the evidence that your company have been buying up property within the area of interest.' Kishimoto said, as he made a point of piling the documents on top of one another. The untidy stack was now over an inch high.

'The real estate arm of my company purchases land all over Japan. I am not involved in every deal.'

'Many of the purchases amount to more than ten million yen. As CEO of the company, wouldn't you be required to sign off purchases of that magnitude?'

'My company buys and sells property all the time. I don't have time to get involved in every acquisition.' Oshiro said.

The lawyer whispered in Oshiro's ear. Oshiro nodded back.

'If you're asking my client to investigate the accounting practices of one of his many businesses, that's a civil matter. Something which my client would be happy to investigate. This subject is quite separate from these unfounded accusations of abduction.' the lawyer stated.

'Murder.' Kishimoto said firmly. 'We are investigating the abduction and *murder* of Edward Walker. And the abduction and attempted murder of Akina Oshiro. We have reason to suspect that the motive for their abduction is linked to the discovery of the rare earth metal and purchase of property in the area. Some of this property may have been acquired illegally. But we think this conspiracy may be altogether wider than just your client. Maybe he is the one behind all of it. But there are also signs of involvement from organised crime. Maybe the Osore Shirazu crime syndicate. But so far, all our evidence points towards one individual.' Kishimoto adjusted his gaze to focus solely on Oshiro. 'Perhaps now you can see the predicament you are in and how everything seems to lead back to you, Oshiro-san?'

Oshiro and his lawyer both looked at each other and made no reply.

40

Akina was awoken suddenly by the distant sound of a door slamming in the corridor and heavy footsteps approaching. She cursed inwardly for allowing herself to fall asleep, although deep down she knew that it was inevitable. She tilted her head slightly to the left, whilst keeping the rest of her body rigidly flat on the bed, just in case someone was about to enter the room. The blinds were open and the low sun was casting a long beam of light onto the ceiling, by the window. Late afternoon, she thought to herself, still unaware of the exact time. She must have been asleep for at least an hour. Maybe two. And yet, as she inspected the covers in her bed, they remained neatly in place, with little or no evidence of movement.

The clomping of heavy boots got louder, before abruptly halting outside the door to her room. Then she heard the murmur of two male voices engaged in conversation. Maybe a changing of the guard?

She tried to concentrate on their faint voices, whilst the noise from the machines continued around her.

'You guys really got a hammering from the Giants last night. Did you see the game?' one of them said to the other.

'Just the highlights. Turned it off after thirty minutes. Too depressing.' the other replied.

'How did you ever end up supporting the Dragons anyway?'

'My father grew up in Nagoya. First game he ever took me to see was a home game against the Tigers. Been hooked ever since.'

'Bet you didn't beat the Tigers though.' joked one of them.

The other didn't answer.

'Anyway, have you heard the news?'

'News?' the other replied with a question mark.

'Yoshi Oshiro has been arrested. Tamura took a few guys up to Oshiro's place this morning. Caught him completely off guard.'

'Why arrest Oshiro?'

'Apparently some evidence was found linking him to the kidnappings, possibly even the disappearances in the village.'

'Old man Oshiro? No way.'

'When they arrived at his house, he was getting ready to run!'

'Run! Chance would be a fine thing!'

Loud laughter sounded in stereo.

'Not literally. In his car. He ended up crashing his Rolls into a wall after the boss shot the tyres. Completely destroyed it! Rolled it and everything apparently. Anyway, he's been taken to Tokushima. He's being questioned now by the boss and Inspector Kishimoto.'

As Akina lay in her bed, listening to the conversation, she realised that now was the time. She heaved her rigid torso up from the mattress and used her arms to keep her upright. Then she began taking short, quick breaths to increase her heart rate and give the impression of being in distress. Then she took one deep breath, filling the base of her lungs with air, and let out a long, high-pitched shriek.

The guards hesitated momentarily and then burst through the door to find Akina sobbing into her knees with her arms wrapped around her legs. The guards looked at each other in astonishment.

'Go and get help!' One said to the other. Then he entered the room tentatively and spoke gently to Akina, holding out one arm in front of him as if he was trying to tame a wild animal. 'Are you okay, Oshiro-san?'

'Where am I? What's going on?' Akina asked, feigning distress.

'You've been involved in an incident.' The officer replied reassuringly. 'You're in hospital, but you're safe now.'

***

It was getting late and there was a celebratory mood in the station. Two of the younger officers, present during the arrest, had spent much of the afternoon regaling the events to their colleagues.

Whilst Maisie was unable to join in the conversation, nor understand what was being said, the animated arm gestures enabled a partial translation and told a narrative of high-speed driving and gun shots with an explosive finale. Maisie watched and wondered to herself how much of the story had already been embellished, as events like these often were.

Tamura had been good enough to keep her apprised of the developments at various stages of the day and was himself extremely pleased with the result. Oshiro was in custody and, whilst he had not yet confessed to his involvement, with Akina out of her coma, it was only a matter of time before her father's deception unravelled.

Maisie had thought about going to visit Akina, but Tamura advised against it. Akina was still in a state of shock and unable to recollect any of the events leading up to, or during, her capture. The doctors had said it was likely she was suffering from mental trauma, which was not surprising given what the poor girl had been through. And so, for the time being, they were discouraging contact with the patient, to spare her further distress.

It was approaching six o'clock and already getting dark outside. Soon the numbers in the station would begin to fall away. Maisie found herself filled with mixed emotions. On the one hand she was relieved Oshiro was now in custody. Before long the wider conspiracy would be out in the open and the co-conspirators would likely be identified and brought to justice. And yet, a sense of danger still loomed over her like a dark cloud. Perhaps she was still a little shaken from Tokyo. Maybe it was exhaustion. Maybe it was what she had been trying to forget about the most: Nathan's murderer on his way to find her.

She pushed the thought away. It was time to rest. She packed her things away into her briefcase and went to leave for the minshuku. There she could enjoy a hot bath, a meal and hopefully a good night's sleep.

As she bid the others 'Oyasuminasai,' on her way to the door, she was stopped by one of the officers. He looked gently into her eyes and then attempted a sentence in English.

'I … am … to drive you?' he said accompanying the stuttered words with matching gestures. Tamura must have left instructions for his team to keep an eye on her, Maisie thought appreciatively.

Her hire car was parked outside and normally she wouldn't have dreamt of accepting the offer. But tonight was different. She would feel safer being escorted. And so, with a wide smile and keen nod of her head, she gratefully accepted the offer and waved to the others as she left.

Outside the sharp chill of the evening air bit at her skin. The clear skies allowed for the almost full moon to illuminate their pathway to the side of the station, where the three marked police vehicles were parked, side-by-side facing the road. The officer pointed to the large four by four Suzuki with his key, unlocked it remotely and they both got in. Then the officer started the engine and gently eased the car out onto the main road, turning left towards the minshuku.

Maisie felt a sense of guilt as she realised she didn't even know the officer's name. And as they drove out of the village, she attempted to communicate her first name to him, hoping that by doing so she would discover his. But she didn't.

The car began to pick up speed and she suddenly wondered if the officer knew where he was taking them. Presumably Tamura would have explained. As the car picked up even more speed, Maisie felt an uneasiness, followed by a sudden jolt in her heart as they passed the entrance to the minshuku.

She spoke out to get his attention and pointed towards the house, but the officer was unresponsive and maintained his focus on the road.

Shit, what's going on? Maisie thought, with a sense of panic. She tapped him on the shoulder and pointed again. This time towards the rear window of the car. The officer immediately slammed on the brakes of the car, and they came to an abrupt and uncomfortable stop. Then he held up his arms and uttered something apologetically in Japanese. Within a few moments, he had turned the car around and was driving up the small entrance to the minshuku. Maisie searched her tired mind for the word for thanks in Japanese, before exiting the car and making her way towards the house. She smiled to herself as she thought about how foolishly paranoid the recent events had made her.

Standing waiting for her on the porch was the owner of the minshuku. She had obviously heard the car arrive, and so had come out to greet Maisie. Meanwhile the officer, waited for Maisie to reach the front door, before reversing back down the driveway and screeching off, back in the direction of the village.

'Konbanwa,' Miyu said with a gentle but welcoming smile, illuminated by the light under her porch. 'Yushoku?' she asked whilst cupping one hand at chest height and using the first two fingers of her other hand to simulate the action of eating from chopsticks.

Maisie nodded gratefully as she walked up onto the porch and removed her shoes.

Miyu then held up seven fingers to articulate the time she would be serving, whilst folding her brow as if to pose the question.

'Mondainai,' Maisie said proudly, to confirm. Followed by, 'Doumo arigatou,' and a polite nod of the head. She then proceeded upstairs to her room.

As she entered, she turned on the lights and used her back to close the door. She released a satisfied sigh as she saw the large, comfortable bed, neatly covered by the thick duvet and deep pillows. Then she removed her jacket and her trousers, allowing them to fall carelessly to the floor as she walked into the bathroom and began running a hot bath.

As the water level rose, her mind drifted and she found herself wondering whether she would need dinner. Then her phone range. Maisie walked into the bedroom to retrieve it. She looked at the screen and hesitated a moment before answering it.

'Holly, I didn't expect to hear from you.' Maisie said, a little surprised.

'Sorry to disturb,' Holly replied, 'it's just the boss wants to know where you are?'

Holly sounded nervous.

'Where I am? In my room where I'm staying, if he really needs to know. What is all this about Holly?' Maisie said, wondering why Leegood had not bothered to ring himself, as he would normally. She liked Holly, and usually would make more of an effort to be polite, but right now fatigue had begun to drain the last of her patience. Now all she yearned for was a peaceful bath and a good night's sleep. The thought of sinking into the warm water suddenly prompted her to rush back into the bathroom to check on its progress. It was still only half-full and she sat on the edge of the tub and leant in to test the temperature with her fingers, as she continued the conversation with Holly.

'It's just he says you're to wrap things up, now that this Oshiro has been apprehended it's time to come home. You've got the story you wanted.'

Maisie removed her hand from the tub and twisted the tap to release an even hotter flow. Then she used the same hand to rest her head on as she squeezed her throbbing temples.

'You're kidding Holly, I'm just getting started. I'm not done at all, not by a mile. This story is just about to break, and we still haven't got to the bottom of all of this.'

Holly paused before releasing an indecisive hum to fill the silence.

'I'm sorry Maisie, I'm just relaying what he asked me to relay.' Holly added.

Maisie released and audible sigh down the line.

'No, I know it's not your fault.' Maisie said, with a hint of regret.

'So, is that a bath I can hear?' Holly asked.

Suddenly, Maisie heard a subtle creaking of floorboards. It felt close, possibly close enough to be in the bedroom.

'I'm sorry Holly, just hang on a moment would you?' Maisie took the phone away from her ear as she went to investigate, her senses now on full alert. She could still hear the faint echo of Holly, calling out for her.

Cautiously she guided the door open with her hand, careful not to make a sound herself. The room was mostly dark, with only streaks of moonlight glowing on the carpet by the window. She felt her way tentatively into the darkness, aiming for the approximate position of the overhead light switch. She was certain she had left it on. Perhaps it had blown? Maisie tutted to herself in frustration, as she tried the switch repeatedly, in vain. She moved towards the lamp by her bed and turned it on.

Her body froze. Immediately she sensed she was not alone. From the corner of her eye, she glimpsed a large figure standing motionless behind her. Within a flicker of an eyelash, she felt a damp cloth cover her mouth and nostrils, clamped in place by a large fist. Simultaneously, a large, powerful arm reached across her chest, lifting her off her feet and forcing the air from her lungs.

She flung her arms violently against the body, as their arms constricted her like an oversized snake. But it was no good. With each desperate gasp for breath, through the sodden gauze, she found herself weakening. Quickly she fell deeper and deeper into a dark abyss, until her limbs drooped inanimately to her sides and her body surrendered the fight.

41

It was completely dark. So dark that when Maisie opened her eyes, there was no appreciable difference compared to when they were closed. Maisie knew immediately that she was in the boot of a car from the unmistakable sense of motion, vibrations and tyre noise from the rear wheels, only inches away from her head. She couldn't move. Her arms were tightly bound behind her back. Her feet were tied too. Both were connected by a length of rope, which, together with the confined space, forced her body into a contorted S-shape facing the front of the car.

Maisie felt an overpowering sense of terror rise through her body, forcing a stream of tears down her left cheek. This time she was trapped with little chance of escape.

She had no idea how long she had been unconscious, but she assumed hours rather than minutes. She thought back to the attack in her room and recollected the gauze, soaked with a strong-smelling liquid. Chloroform, or something similar, she guessed, although she had never directly encountered the substance before.

Then she recalled the brief glimpse of her attacker. The large, tall frame, familiar hawkish profile and unmistakable, piercing eyes. There was no doubt in her mind that it was him. The man who had followed her and killed Nathan at the airport. But how had he found her? And how had he managed to get her out of the room without being seen by anyone?

Maisie's heart filled with dread as she imagined the worst. Maybe this time he had left no witnesses. Maybe she was the only one to make it out alive. But, as she cursed herself for putting the others in harm's way, she also realised that there was nothing she could do about it now. The most important things she needed to focus on were where she was being taken and how to stay alive.

Inspector Kishimoto and Sergeant Tamura returned to the interview room, following a brief intermission intended to allow Oshiro time to dwell on the gravity of his situation. Perhaps if they were lucky, he would reach the inescapable conclusion that his interests would be best served by assisting them with their investigation, rather than remaining obstinately uncooperative.

By now, Oshiro's dishevelled appearance had spread to his hair. It had become ruffled and misshapen from repeatedly using his folded arms as a resting place for his head.

The two officers each pulled a chair out from under the table and sat down in unison. They said nothing until after Tamura pressed the red button on the audio recorder.

'Interview of Mr Yoshi Oshiro reconvened at 20:32,' Kishimoto announced. 'Present at the meeting is …' Kishimoto then allowed each individual to speak their name for the tape, finishing with the reluctant and exhausted-sounding Oshiro.

'Oshiro-san,' started Kishimoto, 'I feel I must begin by sharing some news relating to your daughter's condition.'

Oshiro's eyes opened more widely.

'It is good news. I'm told she has awoken from her coma.'

Oshiro remained silent.

'The doctors say they are encouraged by her progress. So far, no signs of any long-lasting neurological damage. And they expect she will make a full recovery.' Kishimoto continued. 'The problem is, she seems to have no recollection of the events, either leading up to, or during, her capture. The doctors have said that they can't be sure her memory will ever return.'

Oshiro frowned and let out a faint grunt of frustration. 'I am relieved she is going to be alright,' he said, the words contradicting his expression, 'thank you for informing me of the news.'

'Whilst this is encouraging news. Unfortunately, at this time, she has no idea who was behind her abduction.'

'When she does, she will absolve me!' Oshiro said snappily.

'So you keep saying,' replied Kishimoto, sceptically. 'Let us move on to another subject. Are you aware of the scarecrows situated throughout the village of Takakumi?'

Oshiro remained silent and impassive.

'What can you tell us about them?'

'My client has no comment on the matter.' the lawyer interjected.

'Very well,' responded Kishimoto, before removing some photographs from his folder and placing them on the desk for Oshiro and his lawyer to see. They showed a series of low-resolution images, taken of the old shopkeeper from the village, as she constructed a scarecrow on the open common behind the buildings on the main road. They had been taken from the motion detecting trail cameras that were installed in various locations around the village. 'Yesterday, my team arrested this lady,' he said pointing to an image that clearly showed the face of the old lady, 'do you know this person?'

Oshiro pursed his lips together and shook his head, whilst maintaining a heavily frowning countenance.

'She seems a harmless enough old lady. Lives and works in the village. The owner of a modest shop. The only shop that remains in the village. But these photos, taken yesterday, quite clearly show her erecting two more of these scarecrows. One seems to bear a remarkable likeness to my colleague here,' he said pointing to Tamura, 'and the other could even be a representation of a visitor to the area, from England. I believe you've already met Maisie Lockhart?' Kishimoto asked.

Oshiro nodded, whilst inspecting the photographs more closely.

'The old lady is talented. You can see she has captured the likeness of Tamura-san. From the shape of his eyebrows and mouth, to the colour of his eyes,' Kishimoto said as he revealed two more higher resolution images. 'Originally these figures were dismissed as a harmless and eccentric distraction for the villagers. Something that might help attract curious tourists, and perhaps generate some much-needed business. But more recently my men have discovered a darker purpose. Any ideas what that might be, Oshiro-san?'

Oshiro kept quiet.

'These particular examples of the old lady's work,' Kishimoto said pointing to the photographs, 'were constructed around about the time both Tamura-san and Lockhart-san were attacked by two men with machine guns, last night in Tokyo.'

'Inspector Kishimoto, my client is a revered business leader, recognised by the Japanese state,' the lawyer said, 'I fail to see what any of this has to do with him.'

'We carried out a raid on her shop and home yesterday morning. We found tools and materials and moulds consistent with those used to create the scarecrows, along with enlarged pictures of many of the villagers, many of whom are officially on a missing person's list. We even found some freshly made examples that were in the process of being painted, based on the likeness of two of the remaining residents in the village.'

Oshiro shrugged, to protest his innocence.

'She was very quiet at first. But as soon as she realised she was looking at a potential jail sentence, she decided she would be better off cooperating with our investigation. She's told us everything. How the two of you met, what you asked her to do and why she agreed to do it.'

'I've never even seen her before.' Oshiro said dismissively, breaking his temporary silence.

Kishimoto paused. He glanced at Tamura and then back at Oshiro.

'Allow me to refresh your memory. The old lady was a close friend of your mother when you were growing up in Ine. She moved out to Takakumi almost twenty years ago after her husband died and opened a small shop. But she wasn't welcomed by the locals and for many years she was ostracised for being an outsider. According to her statement, when you first arrived at the village, she told us you attended a meeting in the local school. There you reassured the villagers that building your new residence above the valley would not disrupt their daily lives. It was then the two of you became reacquainted. And it was then that she told you about her troubles with the other villagers. But it wasn't until three years ago that you made contact again and shared your plan to help her enact revenge. That you would use your so-called "associates" to frighten those that had wronged her and force them to relocate. And that, when they did, she should use her skills to create scarecrows that look like the residents, as a warning to others. She believed that you were helping her to restore a spiritual balance to the village by ridding it of its heretical inhabitants.'

Oshiro did not flinch. Not even to dispute the accusations.

'Incredibly, it seemed to work,' Kishimoto continued, 'and when the police began investigating reports of these disappearances, you and your so-called "associates" left a trail that allowed us to find some of these individuals. Making it seem as though they had merely relocated. But, in actual fact, they remained under the control of yourself and your friends in organised crime.'

'These are very damaging accusations, where is your evidence Inspector?' asked the lawyer.

Kishimoto smiled.

'I'm glad you asked. We found some of the old lady's diaries detailing the whereabout and activities of the villagers before and up to the point they went missing. It details when she made contact and met with you and your associates, including times and dates, and specifically for how long.' Kishimoto said, pausing for effect. 'We also found burner phones. Several of them. Instead of destroying them, she kept them in a drawer for safe keeping, thinking they may be of use later. How right she was. We are in the process of analysing the numbers and call activity. It won't be long before we match the times with numbers and locations of where the calls were made. I guess we may see if any of these locations match your residence.'

'This is all nonsense!' Oshiro said angrily, 'All you have are the ravings of a crazy, disgruntled old woman. A woman I have never met before.'

Kishimoto paused for a moment and searched Oshiro's bulging eyes. Then he calmly produced another photograph from his file. This time a black and white image taken of a family gathered around a dinner table – three young boys and four adults. He pushed the image carefully across the table, and underneath the nose of Oshiro.

'I understand this is you,' he said, pointing to one of the young boys, 'these are your parents. And this here is the lady from the village. So, from where I'm sitting, her story seems to check out. We will also be checking out the veracity of the calls and meetings she logged, to see if they link back to you. Sure, it will take time, but it won't be too difficult to link all the pieces together.'

42

The endless swerving and acceleration followed by sharp braking had driven Maisie close to sickness, as she lay helplessly in the confined darkness. Her neck ached from holding it suspended above the coarse carpet lining the floor. It had already caused painful abrasions to her left cheek, as gravity slid her entire body from side to side in the corners. Her futile attempts to free herself from her bindings had left her limbs feeling weakened and her morale almost entirely depleted.

Remembering that most modern cars have a safety mechanism to release the boot from the inside, she tried to find it with her fingertips. But, after repeated attempts in the approximate location failed, she concluded that either this particular model didn't have one, or it had been deliberately removed.

Resigned to being unable to change her current predicament, she focused her attention on external factors in the hope that she might learn something useful about where she was, or where she was being taken. Maybe, if she listened carefully, she might be able to identify distinctive sounds that would provide clues. The presence of other vehicles, voices or loud music, the bustle of heavily populated areas. But no matter how much she concentrated, she couldn't hear anything except the car; the continuous whirring from tyres, interrupted only by the occasional high-pitched screech from the brakes. She concluded they were travelling too fast to be in a town or city. And the only indication to their whereabouts was the constant snaking and occasional undulation of the road that was becoming more and more pronounced as the journey progressed. All the characteristics of an anonymous rural road, she thought. And whilst she had established that she was being taken somewhere remote, it didn't answer the question of why she had been kept alive.

The car slowed sharply and veered right, off the main road. The force of the manoeuvre pushed Maisie's head tightly against the backs of the seats. The smooth tarmac was exchanged for a rocky and uneven surface, causing the chassis to jerk violently as the car moved forwards at a fraction of the speed it had been.

They seemed to drive in an arc, before reversing back on themselves. Wherever they were, it was clear they had arrived, Maisie thought.

There was a slam from the door, which sent a shockwave of vibrations through the shell of the car, immediately followed by a series of unhurried footsteps circling round the rear. Then there was silence, as if the man was waiting for something. Perhaps he was listening for signs of movement?

A loud metallic click broke the silence. Maisie recognised the sound of a pistol slide being pulled back and released, as it filled the chamber with a round. A sound she had become familiar with during her time spent in the gun ranges on the west coast of America.

The boot lid release delivered a loud thud, and the inner lights lit up, momentarily blinding Maisie. She felt the nip of the cold night air as it came flooding into the compartment. Sensing the presence of a figure standing over her, she attempted to rotate her body, to get a look once her eyes adjusted, but she remained unable to move from her forward-facing position.

An arm reached in, wrapped around her waist and clumsily lugged her body out of the boot, before dumping her carelessly on the rough ground. The left side of her pelvis landed on a sharp stone, and she let out a muffled cry from underneath the gag around her mouth. She felt the bindings being cut from around her ankles and she was forced to sit up with her back against the rear wheel of the car, her arms still secured behind her back. Maisie scowled as she tried to relieve the excruciating cramp in her right calf, by gently bending and stretching her leg repeatedly. As the pain gradually dissipated, she looked down to her prosthetic leg and wondered why the man had not simply removed it. Meanwhile the man got to work wiping his prints from the inside of the car with a scrap of cloth. Clearly, he planned to leave the car behind.

The night sky was clear and free from light pollution, which provided an almost magnified view of the stars above. The moon was directly above, bathing the ground with a muted, white glow that was enough to provide a moderate visibility of the surrounding area. They were in some form of car park on the edge of a forest. Two other cars lay parked along an area that spanned fifty metres or more. Initially, Maisie was shocked at how brazen he was to leave her in full view of the other cars. But as she inspected them more closely, she saw both were covered in a thick layer of dust and the one closest to them had flat tyres on all of the three wheels that were visible to her. Clearly these vehicles had not been driven for some time, and, just like her rental, this is where their journey had ended.

He finished wiping down the car and locked the doors, before tossing the keys into the wooded area. Then he dragged Maisie up onto her feet, placed a noose around her neck and tightened the loop, keeping hold of the other end with his left hand. She shuddered and tried to steady her breathing through the gag. With his right hand, he removed the pistol from his belt and wiggled it in the direction of the woods. Maisie remained complicit, although the futility of allowing herself to be threatened with a gun, only to be led to her death, was not lost on her either. But, for now, at least it bought her some time.

Maisie stumbled over the uneven surface like a wounded animal. Her limbs felt numb and crooked, but she continued on towards an opening in the trees. There she found a small footpath that cut through the woodland like a long tunnel that disappeared into the darkness. Maisie glanced at a tourist information board, hoping that it would reveal details of where they were. She could just about make out the silhouette of a map, as she stumbled past it. But, in this light, the writing was too faint for her to even attempt deciphering.

'Keep moving!' he demanded, whilst tugging hard on the noose to deliver a reprimand.

Maisie realised that, despite their numerous encounters, this was the first time she had heard him speak. His monotonous voice strangely complemented his icy body language. His face carried the same consistently inscrutable expression, void of emotion. His movements were efficient and precise, and yet unhurried like an apex predator. Fearing nothing, threatened by nobody. It all contributed to the chilling aura that loomed over him like a demonic presence.

Maisie found herself wondering what drove a man to become like this. She recognised the unmistakeable gait and posture of a military man. Possibly even Special Forces on account of his precise, feline movements and seemingly unyielding self-assurance. And someone with his affinity for killing, was unlikely to have gone unnoticed in the military. The precise, and almost over-pronounced, two words he had spoken indicated a British accent, with undertones of a privileged upbringing. At least some possible avenues to explore, were she to get out of this alive.

Twenty or thirty yards further, they came across other notices. Some contained both Japanese text and a telephone number. Others contained icons with large diagonal crosses, with words in Japanese and English prohibiting entry. It suddenly dawned on Maisie where he had brought them. It was the infamous Aokigahara, or the colloquially named 'Suicide Forest'. The place she had read about during her flight to Japan. A place where so many went to end their lives.

A sharp chill ran down Maisie's spine. Suddenly it all made sense. The abandoned cars and the noose. The forest and the use of her own rental car, with the clear intention of leaving it to be found by the authorities. He hadn't just gone to the trouble of bringing her all the way out here to simply kill her and hide her body. He planned to stage her suicide.

As she lifted her leg over the hanging chain, intended to prevent vehicles from entering, it felt as though she was crossing over a forbidden threshold. Before them the metre wider path was partially lit by the bright moonlight, whilst the skeletal trees cast tangled shadows on the ground. Maisie began to speculate how far into the forest the man planned for them to go. More importantly, how much time did she have left? It seemed he had kept her alive for his own convenience, so she could walk herself, rather than him having to heft her dead weight.

To make the suicide look convincing, he would need to select an appropriate location. She guessed he must have a target in mind. Something evocative and perhaps symbolic. Maisie recalled the article had referred to such a place; a specific tree where countless others had chosen to meet their end. A location known locally as the 'tree of forgotten souls'. Her gut told her they would be heading somewhere like that, in the heart of the forest, to give credence to the narrative.

Maisie found herself strangely respecting the elaborate and reasonably well-thought-out scheme. If executed well, no one would be looking for her killer. And no one would be looking at

Conway, assuming that was indeed who had sent him. But the thought of either of them getting away with it triggered a surge of rage through her veins.

The ground underfoot was becoming increasingly uneven, making it difficult to navigate in the dark. Maisie began to drag her feet and, simultaneously, pulled forwards against the rope around her neck. The man callously pulled back on it as if he were controlling a dog on a leash. Then the tip of Maisie's toe caught a rock, sending her tumbling, head-first, towards the ground. With both arms still tied behind her back, she was unable to break her own fall. And her left cheek bone caught the full impact of the hard ground, sending a dull pain through her skull, and partially numbing her senses. She feigned unconsciousness.

'Get up!' he ordered, whilst tugging violently at the rope, causing Maisie's upper body to jerk up and down like a broken puppet.

Maisie remained motionless as she ran through the potential outcomes in her mind. He might kill her there and then. But he would need to be careful not to leave any marks. Otherwise, her death would not look like a suicide. She guessed that would not sit well with a man who had clearly planned this out to the last detail and travelled many thousands of miles to execute it.

Really the gun was a last resort in case things went wrong. Maisie thought it more likely that he would carry her the rest of the way. Either that, or he would try and wake her and get her to her feet so that she could walk herself.

Eventually he gave up trying to wake her. Maisie heard a metallic click from the pistol, as he put the safety on and placed the weapon between his belt, behind his back. Kneeling down, he rolled her onto her back and proceeded to heave her over his shoulders. Maisie took some discreet pleasure in this small victory, in the knowledge that the act of carrying her would likely go some way towards weakening him.

The minutes laboured on as they drew further and further into the forest. Draped over the man's shoulders like an item of clothing, blood had amassed in Maisie's head, making it feel as though it might burst at any moment. The constant bobbing against his shoulder blade, became more torturous with every step.

And, with her hands still tied behind her back, the pistol stuffed under his belt remained tantalisingly out of her reach. She had begun to detect a subtle change in his breathing; it was deeper and more arduous. No doubt brought on by the slight incline, which was also affecting his walking pace.

Maintaining the pretence of her unconscious state, meant that she could not turn her head to see where they were going. But she was able to observe where they had been. Some time ago they had veered off the main path and onto a smaller trail, less than two feet wide. Tall, matchstick-like trees covered either side of the rocky path, which dissected the increasingly disorderly and precipitous terrain. Maisie wondered how he knew where he was going. Was he improvising or had he already rehearsed this very journey in preparation? She decided it didn't matter. What did matter was what she would do when they arrived.

Suddenly he stopped in his tracks and immediately threw Maisie to the ground, as though he was dropping a sack of potatoes. Maisie felt a crunch in her ribs. But she clenched her teeth together to prevent herself yelping from the pain. She wanted to maintain her pretence and so remained deadly still.

He stood over her as he gathered his breath. She opened her eyes a fraction, just enough to see she had been dropped near the base of a large tree surrounded by its network of bare roots. Around it was a small clearing in an elevated position where the moonlight granted reasonable visibility of the forest floor. At its edge, there was an expanse of darkness and the faint trickle of running water. Maisie guessed they might be on the edge of a precipice, perhaps with a stream at the bottom.

She could also make out items of clothing that littered the ground. The odd shoe, several ragged garments and jackets were carelessly scattered. Another haunting reminder of those that had preceded her.

The man moved away from her and moments later, she could hear the swooshing and creaking of the branches above her head. Evidently, her theory for why she had been brought here was correct. Time was running out.

She heard the man return. He grabbed her by the scruff of the neck and dragged her closer to the tree. Then he stood over her as he coaxed her upper body against the trunk of the tree.

Maisie realised this was likely to be the last opportunity she would have. It was now or never. Impulsively, she thrust her right foot upwards, as hard as she could, into his groin. The strike caused him to bend forward and cup the area, instinctively. He let out a strained, muted groan. Without hesitating, Maisie followed up with a firm kick to the head, this time using the solid metal tip of her prosthetic foot to deliver the blow. Her foot caught him on the upper throat, below the jawline. The impact forced him off-balance and sent him plunging to the ground. Maisie also heard a separate thud as the gun slipped from his belt and fell to the ground, lost somewhere in the nearby darkness.

Maisie scrambled desperately to get to her feet, but without her hands to steady her, progress was slow and cumbersome. This gave him time to regain his composure. Maisie was still in the process of pulling herself up from the ground, but before she could reach her feet, he launched himself at her, tackling her by the shoulders. The attack lifted her off her feet and onto her back. The force of the landing crushed her wrists between her lower back and the ground. Straight away Maisie felt a twang. First, she thought one or both of her wrists might have been broken, but she quickly realised the plastic cable tie had snapped under the stress of the fall, releasing both hands in the process. Instantly she used them to push against him as he straddled her body whilst grabbing her with both arms by the neck. His weight pressed down on her diaphragm as he squeezed her throat, tighter and tighter. Maisie clawed and scratched at his face, but it did nothing to deter the enraged, piercing eyes from their target.

The breaths that she was able to steal were encumbered by the gag still around her mouth, and pressure began to build in her skull. Maisie frantically searched the ground with her right hand for something to use as a weapon, her left hand desperately pulling against his grip.

The tips of her fingers made contact with something substantial. Perhaps a rock or a fallen branch? She stretched her arm as far as it would reach and used her fingertips to draw the object closer. Every millimetre of progress felt like a victory, and hope fended off submission. She had it. The rough texture of a big stone. Gripping it tightly with the palm of her hand, she swung the rock with all her residual strength against his head. The vibration through her hand, was accompanied by a loud hollow knock as it made contact with the side of his skull. He immediately became limp and dropped to the ground beside her with a heavy thump.

For a moment, there was silence. Then he began to stir, wheezing as he dragged himself away from her, in an arduous retreat. Maisie leaped forward in pursuit, the rock still firmly in her grasp. But he was still dangerous, and with one swipe, his large, clenched fist connected with the right of Maisie's jaw, knocking her to the ground again, several feet away. Maisie became aware that she had landed only yards away from the ledge. As she looked into the darkness, she could just about make out the faint reflection of light from the stream, some twenty meters below her.

Quickly she rolled onto all fours and began to pull herself to her feet. But he was quicker. His left arm hooked around her neck, from behind, and pulled her tightly against his body. He let out an aggressive growl from the back of his throat, as he diverted his remaining reserves into his biceps. This was it, Maisie thought, as she felt the familiar grip tighten around her windpipe. This time he would finish the job.

Struggling for breath, she started to submit, but then she remembered something. She reached back over her head and grabbed the neck of his shirt with both hands. With one swift movement, she arced her upper body forwards and bent her knees, yanking on his shirt as hard as she could. Instinctively she rolled forward, carrying his momentum over her shoulders. His body somersaulted over hers, and she felt a lightness and relief as he fell over the ledge and disappeared into the darkness.

43

The deep breaths sounded strained and painful. The bruising and cuts to the face and arms, somehow seemed more prevalent than before. Both were a disturbing reminder of the horrors this frail and defenceless body had endured. Tamura sat at Akina's bedside, pitying the cruelty that humans were capable of, as she lay flat on the bed with her head tilted towards him on her pillow.

Tamura had arrived at the hospital shortly after 11:30 p.m., having driven directly from the head office in Tokushima. The journey had taken over two hours, prolonging an eventful and seemingly unending day. He certainly would have preferred to have gone straight home for some rest, but the officer guarding Akina had relayed her repeated plea for answers. And so, reluctantly, he brought forward his plans to visit her in the hospital.

'I need to know … what's going on?' Akina was unable to muster much more than a whisper, interrupted mid-sentence by a strained gasp for air. 'Where's my father?'

For the time being, Tamura ignored the question and asked one of his own.

'What do you remember about your abduction? Is there anything you can tell us?'

Akina looked vacantly as she rocked her head, very slightly, on the pillow.

'I only remember fragments … like a nightmare.' Akina paused for a moment and let out an audible gulp as she attempted to relieve the discomfort in her throat, 'I can remember driving to meet Edward Walker. He was working for my father. And my father asked me to meet him in the village and provide him with some permits for the survey he was undertaking, something to do with a hydroelectric generator near to the village. But there was a car following me as I went to meet him.'

'What sort of car?' Tamura interjected, as he made notes in his pocketbook.

'A black four by four? I can't remember exactly what type. But a few miles before I reached the village, the driver pulled up beside me and rammed my car off the road. I must have lost consciousness. I don't remember much after that. I can remember waking up in a small room. Edward Walker was there too. I tried to get him out, but he was too heavy for me to move on my own. I intended to go back for him once I found help. Have you located him?' Akina asked with traces of optimism in her strained voice.

'We did. But I'm sorry to say he didn't make it. He passed a few days ago in hospital. The doctors believe he succumbed to his injuries.'

Akina remained silent. She broke eye contact with Tamura and faced the ceiling.

'Were the two of you close?' Tamura asked.

Akina nodded sorrowfully.

'We had become quite close in the short time he was working for my father,' she replied, turning her head to face Tamura again, 'I don't think father knew about it though.' she added innocently.

'He wouldn't have approved?'

'Father can be very protective,' Akina replied defensively, 'he's been that way since Mother died. Where is he? I keep asking to see him, but nobody will tell me where he is.'

Tamura paused and contemplated how much he should divulge.

'Your father is being held under arrest in Tokushima.' Tamura said.

'Under arrest? For what?' Akina asked, undertones of alarm evident even beneath her wheezing voice.

'We located Walker's files that prove he was not employed to help your father with a hydroelectric dam project. Instead, we believe your father had instructed him to validate and consult on the presence of a rare-earth metal in the valley surrounding the village. Something that would be very valuable, if you were able to control the mining of it. We have also found evidence your father may have been involved in a wider conspiracy, possibly linked to organised crime. Is there anything you might know that can help us? Perhaps Walker may have mentioned something?'

Akina turned her head away again and said nothing. Tamura could make out a faint stream of tears running down her cheek.

'We believe your father may have had something to do with Walker's disappearance. That perhaps he may have been trying to silence him in some way to protect his business interests and keep his criminal ties hidden.'

'If you believe that, you must also think he was behind my own abduction?' Akina said with a slight sharpness to her voice.

Tamura searched her eyes before responding.

'That was something I was hoping *you* might be able to shed more light on?' he said.

***

Maisie peered over the ledge with a sense of disbelief at what she had accomplished. A rush of endorphins warmed her spirit to a level of ecstasy she had never before encountered. She couldn't see him. But he was there, somewhere in the darkness.

She tried estimating where he must have landed, but the combination of foliage and limited visibility was hard for her eyes to penetrate. Even as her eyes adjusted to the light, she could see nothing at the base of the gully. She held her breath and pointed one ear in the direction he had fallen. But all she could hear was the sound of trickling of water.

Maisie found herself hesitating. Surely the fall alone would have killed him. At least incapacitated him to the point that he would no longer pose a danger. But should she use the opportunity to escape now, whilst she still could? Or should she check to make sure that he wasn't coming after her? She didn't mind admitting to herself that she wasn't the least bit concerned for his welfare. Not after what he had done to her. And to Nathan. But she had watched enough films to know you never leave the scene without first being sure the killer won't be following you.

In the end, her curiosity won out. Her heart began thumping harder in her chest as she decided to confront her fears. She needed to know, one way or the other.

Directly below her was an almost vertical drop. But a few meters to her right, some exposed jagged rocks, fashioned over the centuries into an oversized staircase, provided a convenient path to the bottom.

First Maisie searched for the pistol. She knew roughly where it had fallen and quickly located the faint, dark silhouette against the partially illuminated forest floor. She picked it up and immediately recognised the short barrel and angular design. A SiG Sauer 9mm, a gun she had fired many times before. She pulled back the slider, to check there was still a round in the chamber, then pressed the decocking lever and stuffed it into the front of her trousers. She returned to the spot she had identified to make her descent and slowly shuffled down the stepped rocks on her posterior.

The final step required a short jump to reach the stony floor. The slow-moving stream trickled past, just a few feet away. More large boulders and small trees, of varying heights and girth, lined the bank on either side. But there were no obvious signs of her man.

Maisie removed the pistol from her trousers, pulled back the hammer and held it with both hands, at eye level. Three small phosphorescent dots, one on the front sight and two on the back sights, made it easy to line the weapon up with a potential target in the limited light. She pointed it in the direction where she expected him to have landed, both arms stretched out in front to form a triangle. Slowly she began to navigate the uneven ground, vigilantly scanning her surroundings with every step until she heard a subtle, short groan. She followed the noise. A few meters further on, behind a large rock, she found him lying on his back, arched over a fallen tree, writhing like an injured serpent.

Maisie trained the gun on him as she inspected his injuries from a distance. His head had narrowly avoided a large rock, just a couple of feet away. Judging from the unnatural angle of his right foot, his ankle was broken. But the worst of his injuries was to his abdomen. He was impaled on a branch from the fallen tree. The sharp shard jutted vertically out from his torso. It was low enough to have missed his vital organs but would undoubtedly have pierced his small intestine. Maisie guessed the impact of landing on the trunk may have damaged his spine. But seeing his body in this weakened and vulnerable state did little to inspire sympathy, nor dowse her fury.

Her heart was still racing. As she stood over him, the gun still pointed at his centre of mass, she found herself fighting against the impulse to pull the trigger.

'Do it!' he said daringly. There was an undertone of despair in his gravelly voice as he spat the blood from his mouth, 'Do it! You'd be doing me a favour!'

His strangled words immediately dispersed any residual fear Maisie felt for him. Before her was neither a superhuman, nor a monster. But a fallible man, capable of bleeding. A man capable of dying.

'And why should I grant you any favours?' she replied dispassionately, without intonation.

'Because I killed the policeman. Your friend, right?'

'How do you know we knew each other?' Maisie retorted.

He lightly shrugged his shoulders, and immediately winced from the pain it triggered.

Maisie adjusted her aim so the gun was pointed at his head.

'I want answers.' she stated coldly.

He looked back at her and smirked, as if he was enjoying a joke that only he could appreciate.

'You can't threaten me with a gun, not when I'm in this state. Death would be a welcome reprieve.' he added.

Maisie paused for a moment to consider her predicament, still conflicted. On the one hand, she wanted him to answer for his crimes. The right way. The way she had always fought to protect. And yet, this was a chance to end things here and now. Once he was dead, he couldn't do any more harm. And with a man like this, there was always a chance he would find a way to escape justice.

Maisie imagined the gratification that would be granted from pulling the trigger and exacting her revenge. The visceral release of rage.

'You know, perhaps you're right,' she finally responded, in agreement, 'it probably would be easier for you to die.'

Maisie took the gag that was still hanging around her neck and looped it over her head. She glanced at it a second time, realising it had been fashioned from one of her own scarfs. But it was perfect for what she needed. She rolled it into a loose rectangle, then she shuffled closer to him, within reach of his torso, and used the scarf to apply pressure to the wound, whilst keeping the gun trained on his heart with her right hand. He let out an animalistic roar that echoed through the forest. Maisie kept her hand in place, using the scarf as a substitute for gauze, wrapping it around the branch where it had breached his belly to slow the bleeding. The pitch and volume of the scream rose to a gargled crescendo, before abruptly coming to an end as he lost consciousness.

In the silence that followed, Maisie smirked to herself as she realised the absurdity of using this item of clothing to deliver first aid. The same item that he had used to restrain and inflict suffering on her.

Maisie replaced the gun in her trousers, to free her hands. Then she lifted his left arm and used the dead weight of his hand to replace her own, holding the scarf in place. With both hands now free, she used the opportunity to search his pockets.

First, she located his mobile phone. It had a near full battery life and a surprisingly decent signal. After several attempts, she successfully manoeuvred his right thumb to gain access via the fingerprint scanner. Then she changed the password to an eight-digit number she would remember. In his other pocket she found his wallet. Inside was a wad of notes, several credit cards and an Australian driving license. As she removed it, she felt him stirring as he regained consciousness.

'Ashton Hunter. Is that your real name?' she asked plainly, as she inspected the photo ID, using the light from the phone.

He ignored the question and lunged furiously at her. But the failed attempt only served as a demonstration of how restricted his movements were. Maisie had only to take a single step backwards to avoid the reach of his flailing arms, but she took out the pistol once again as an added precaution. She balanced the phone and wallet in her left hand.

'I'd keep the pressure on that wound if I were you,' she recommended, like a teacher trying to instil good behaviour, 'I've seen that type of injury before. Years back I was covering the war in Syria. We were regularly caught in missile attacks and airstrikes. On one such occasion, I saw a woman thrown by the shockwaves and impaled on a shard of steel, protruding from a crumbled heap of concrete. In a sense she was lucky. The metal passed through her body without damaging any major organs, or her spine. It took several hours but eventually the medics were able to free her. She was taken to the hospital with the metal still protruding from her body. Several days later, I paid her a visit and she was making a full recovery.' Maisie paused for a moment as she found a nearby rock to perch on and take the weight off her ankle, still raw from being tightly bound by the cable ties. 'What I'm saying, Hunter, is that if you stay still and apply pressure to the wound, you may well survive long enough to be rescued. Try to move or free yourself and you will almost certainly die. Especially with that broken ankle.'

Hunter looked back at her with bewilderment, unable to comprehend what was going on.

'Why would you try to help me?' he asked, 'after everything I've put you through? Why don't you just kill me?'

'Who knows, it may still come to that. First things first, I want to know who you're working for and how you found me?'

Hunter said nothing and just stared stubbornly back at her.

Maisie sighed inwardly but did her best to conceal her exasperation. Feeling Hunter's phone pressing against her thigh reminded her to remove it from her pocket. She typed in the revised password and commenced her search of the phone book. It was empty. Then she checked the internet search history, emails, text messages: all deleted. The only evidence that the phone had been used at all was the pedometer, which showed intermittent activity over the last week. Then she suddenly remembered a hack that a tech colleague had once shown her for recovering data. She spent a few minutes searching the web. Then, after she had located and downloaded the suitable software, she began using it to scan the device.

Several minutes passed, until eventually Maisie's heart jumped with excitement as the first files began appearing as a short list on screen. At the very top were a series of outgoing calls made to international numbers. Maisie did not recognise the region codes. Then a small number of other items began appearing. This time some notes Hunter had made to himself that Maisie was not able to immediately decipher. The final entry was labelled as an inbound text message. She pressed the button to recover the data, and within seconds the message appeared on screen. It was dated two days earlier:

Tuesday 20:32

Target remaining in current location for maximum of 4 more days – cannot confirm beyond this point.

Staying at address 113 Takakumi, Shikoku Island, Tokushima Prefecture.

Maisie felt the unnerving jolt of betrayal strike her in the chest as a blend of rage and disappointment began brewing up inside of her. Fuck! How could she have been so stupid? So desperately naïve. A multitude of questions bombarded her internal monologue, immediately followed by overwhelming self-doubt. How could she be sure this wasn't just another trick? A backup plan in case he felt the need to manipulate the situation. But it wasn't, it can't have been. She felt like screaming, but stopped short of the indignity. Then when she had recovered her composure, she looked back to Hunter.

'You know deleted phone details are pretty easy to recover nowadays. Even someone like me can do it, and I'm definitely not the best when it comes to technology. It's far better to dispose of the SIM card or even the phone itself. But you probably already knew that.'

'Sure,' he replied, 'as soon as this part of the job was completed,' he added, in a dubious attempt to defend his professionalism.

'That was your second mistake.'

'What was the first?' he asked.

'Your choice of informer.'

He looked back at her with confusion.

Maisie stared long and hard at him.

'Now I understand how you've been keeping tabs on me,' she said.

44

Yoshi Oshiro sat perched on the edge of his bunk, staring at the imperfections in the concrete floor. Scrapes and stains tainted the painted surface, like a chronicle of past incidents. An unannounced search by the guards. A fight. Oshiro could only imagine the horrors suffered by his predecessors. Etched into the centre of one of the dark, reddish-brown blotches was the name 'Akuma'. Perhaps it belonged to the victim; the only memorial to an otherwise forgotten inmate. Or perhaps it belonged to the man who claimed the kill.

Oshiro had often feared his fall from grace. He had witnessed it happen to others many times. Watched from afar as a politician or public figure fell from the very pinnacle of their success. But even though he had been aware of the risks he was taking, he had never truly believed it would happen to him. He always imagined his money and influence would ensure his protection. It had always given him a comforting sense of invulnerability. But right now, he had never felt more powerless, nor alone.

A loud metallic screech startled him as the hatch at the base of the cell door opened suddenly. His dinner had arrived. But with a thoroughly defeated morale, and a knot of anxiety in his stomach, he was in no mood for food. But, despite his diminished appetite, boredom and curiosity forced him to his feet to inspect what was filling the cell with an unpleasant odour. A strong earthy and metallic smell mixed with decay. He closed the hatch to reject the offering. Then he aimed his ear towards the door and listened to the noise outside the cell. Yells from the other inmates echoed through the belly of this concrete manifestation of purgatory. He couldn't make out words, just angry screams intended to relieve frustrated energy and intimidate others. Oshiro wondered if any of them knew he was here and how long he would have before they would come for him.

More than twenty minutes had passed, in relative silence. The only sound had been the increasing regularity of Hunter's groans, as the pain from his injuries intensified. Maisie noticed he had resorted to holding the scarf against his wound to stop the bleeding. Not the actions of a man that wanted to die, she thought to herself. Eventually she was the one to break the silence.

'So, how did you do it?' Maisie asked, 'how did you manage to bring down that plane and get away with it?'

Hunter looked back at her as he decided whether or not to answer.

'You might as well tell me. It's not going to make any difference now. There's CCTV linking you to the crime scene at Heathrow and your photograph has been posted on every media outlet in Europe. Not to mention you've already admitted to killing Nathan. So, telling me about the plane is hardly going to make a difference.'

Hunter pursed his bottom lip against the top and raised his eyebrows, in acceptance.

'It was luck really. There was an elderly passenger on the plane who suddenly fell ill. Chest pains, I believe.' Hunter's face showed a faint smile in the darkness as he relived the moment in his mind. 'The crew were forced to land at the nearest airport. We must have been on the ground inside twenty minutes.'

'And how did you get away after that? Surely, the authorities would have held everyone either on the plane or in the terminal?'

'These sorts of situations can create confusion. And a man being rushed to hospital leaves no time for security checks. Neither does his concerned colleague. Once we were outside, it was relatively easy to slip away.'

'Impressive.' Maisie said with unenthusiastic, false praise.

Masie could tell that Hunter was enjoying recounting his exploits. She supposed he rarely had the opportunity to share them with other people.

Their conversation was interrupted by a growl from Hunter as he struggled to deal with the pain. He looked down at his waist and applied more pressure to the wound with the scarf. Maisie grabbed the opportunity.

'Okay, it's clear to me you're not ready to die. Right now, you're clinging to the hope that, however slim the chance, you'll find a way to get out of this. It's probably all that's keeping you going right now. Your survival instincts. But by now you will have realised that you are not going anywhere and without medical attention you will certainly die. Not quickly, mind you. It will be slow and, no doubt, very painful. So, here's what I want from you. You're going to tell me exactly what protocols you have for staying in contact with your informer. If you do that, I will call for medical assistance. Within twenty minutes I can have a chopper here.'

'And if I don't?'

'Then I will wait here with you until you eventually bleed to death.' she said callously.

'You're bluffing,' he replied with a faint chuckle, 'you couldn't just watch someone die. You don't have the stomach for it. I know all about you. You have principles. Principles you simply won't break.'

'I suppose you're just going to have to find out if that's true.' she replied.

'How can you be sure I will tell you the truth?'

'You'll have to prove it. I'll require a demonstration.'

Hunter thought carefully to himself. She could just about see the flicker of his eyes as he calculated the possible outcomes.

'All right,' he eventually conceded, with reluctance in his voice.

'Good. Let's start with how long you have been in contact with her?'

'About three months, maybe more.' he said carelessly.

'Is the communication always via text, or do you call each other?' Maisie asked as she continued scrolling through the chain of communication between them, spanning several weeks. Most of the messages from Hunter's phone were simple questions. Where Maisie was staying. Who she was in contact with.

'Only ever by text messages. Safer that way,' he replied, 'So long as you can't link the phone to the individual, it's more difficult to prove who sent the message.'

'And who is "Cousin Harriet"?' Maisie asked, noticing the name referenced in several of the messages.

'That's your codename,' he confirmed, 'there can be nothing that links directly to you, in case certain key words are being monitored by the authorities.'

'I see. And you always use the same phone and SIM card?'

'For the purposes of our communications we do. Otherwise, it can become very complicated to stay in contact, and I needed up-to-date information on your whereabouts.'

'And what if they'd become compromised? You could have been sent into a trap.'

Hunter nodded, 'I only ever use this sort of information as a guide. And I always proceed with the necessary caution.' he said, almost defensively. 'Besides, my organisation would have seen to that.'

'Organisation?'

'That's right.' he confirmed, without elaborating.

'So, how did you do it? Was it the threat of death or something else?'

Hunter laughed, followed immediately by a wince of discomfort at the effect on his wounds, 'What makes you think I needed to do any of that? What makes you think anyone was acting against their will?' he replied.

Maisie felt a repeat of the jolt in her chest she experienced earlier. This time it echoed through her body, like she had just touched a live wire. She had not even contemplated that someone so close to her would be acting of their own free will or, worse still, that they had actively betrayed her. But she quickly reminded herself that she would need to gather the facts, rather than take everything Hunter said at face value.

'There's one thing in particular that has been troubling me,' Maisie said, curiously, 'why did you choose to come all this way to get me? I mean, I know it was you on the train and before that you were outside my house. What was stopping you from abducting me in London?'

Hunter gave a lazy shrug of his right shoulder, before answering.

'Really it came down to risk. I knew that, although you had rejected police protection, the police were still monitoring your daily activities. Your home was alarmed and regularly patrolled, and I know you were given a personal alarm, which gave the authorities your whereabouts, in real time, to within a few feet. And, when you did leave your house, your movements were generally random.'

The thought of Hunter watching her with impunity sent chills through her body. While she knew he had been watching her, clearly there was a lot that she hadn't been aware of. In that moment, she wondered if she would ever feel safe in her own home again.

'Getting you to travel here would get you away from all of that,' Hunter continued, apparently still enjoying the destructive impact of his revelations. 'Somewhere you didn't know. Out of your comfort zone. Somewhere you could be made to disappear without too many questions being asked. This place was perfect. Chosen by so many as a place to end their own lives. And if you were found, you would be just another victim of this forest. Everyone would have understood, of course. Particularly the pressures you have been going through with the Conway case. It's unlikely that anyone would have looked too closely.'

'So that day I saw you in London, what was that? Just for show?'

Hunter smirked, 'Something like that. We needed something to help you on your way. You had the story about Walker, which was the carrot. I was the stick.'

Maisie filled her lungs with the chilly night air and looked up at the stars above, attempting to cleanse her mind of all her fury. Then she checked the phone for the time. It was 1:23 a.m. It would be several hours before there would be any sign of daylight. But she guessed that, in all probability, Hunter would not last that long. She would need to contact the emergency services now if he was to survive and answer for his heinous crimes.

'That will be enough for now.' she said, closing down the conversation as she pulled herself to her feet. 'Time we contacted the emergency services.'

The minutes that followed the call passed slowly. The temperature had dropped to the low single figures, forcing Maisie to wrap her arms around her knees, which she pulled tightly against her chest for warmth. She fantasised about tracing her steps back to the refuge of her car. To simply drive away and leave this all behind her. And yet she remained stubbornly at her post, standing guard over Hunter. Even though he remained helplessly pinned to the trunk of the tree.

More than half an hour had passed, and Maisie had expected the emergency services to have arrived by now. She had given the coordinates to their exact location, using the phone. And now she listened for the unmistakeable sound of a helicopter. But so far there was nothing.

Hunter's condition was deteriorating. His entire body convulsed intermittently, and his increasingly laboured breaths were regularly interrupted by fits of coughing. The light wasn't good enough to see how much blood he had lost, but Maisie guessed it could well have been several pints. She remained conflicted about offering him her help. But she had chosen to break off some low-hanging branches from the surrounding conifers and used them to cover his body, in an attempt to stave off the cold and help to stabilise his condition.

'I underestimated you.' Hunter said from nowhere. His voice had become coarse, the volume barely louder than a whisper. 'That was my biggest mistake.'

'What?'

'You said earlier my biggest mistake was to have trusted my informer. That wasn't my biggest mistake. My biggest mistake was underestimating you.' Hunter continued. 'I mean, where did you learn to fight like that?'

'Actually, I learned that fairly recently.' Maisie replied nonchalantly, reluctant to engage in small talk with him.

'I know you probably think I'm a monster.'

'Yes.' Maisie answered instantly. 'You are a monster! Are you going to try and tell me none of this is your fault? That you were just following orders?'

'Of course not. But sometimes things are not always as simple as they seem.' Hunter said cryptically.

There was silence between them again for several minutes.

Hunter broke the hiatus again, but this time with a fit of coughing that didn't stop. Initially Maisie ignored him, but after a couple of minutes it was clear something was wrong. And it had become important to her that he stay alive.

'What is it?' she asked, jumping to her feet, 'what do you need?'

'Water!' Hunter was unable to formulate a sentence between the loud painful expulsions and desperate gasps, 'Water!' he pleaded again with a coarse whisper.

Maisie looked around. Clearly there was plenty of fresh water. But what to use as a vessel? Perhaps a large leaf like she had seen in the survival documentaries. No, there was no time. She hurried to the stream, cupped her hands together and collected some water, before returning to Hunter and kneeling beside him. He was continuing to cough involuntarily but attempted to position his head so that she could begin pouring. It was difficult to see Hunters lips in the limited light, but she made an approximation and tipped the contents of her leaking hands towards them. She heard Hunter take a gulp and then he turned away to expel some of the water that had gone into his lungs.

Then, from nowhere, Hunter grabbed the neck of Maisie's blouse and threw her backwards. Caught completely off guard, Maisie fell back in a heap, her head only narrowly avoiding a large rock. Hunter snapped the branch pinning him down and launched himself on top of her.

Maisie tried to struggle against him, but his weight was too much for her. And, once again, he had managed to get a firm grip around her neck. His thumbs pushed down hard, closing off her windpipe and preventing blood from circulating.

Maisie reached behind her back to where the gun should have been, but it was gone. It must have slipped out when she fell, she thought. Frantically she searched for it, flailing both arms against the ground with a familiar desperation.

Maisie's temples began to throb as blood became trapped in her skull. At that moment, she heard a faint, thunderous clapping noise. It was distant but drawing closer at speed. Within seconds, the noise of the rotator blades, chopping through the air, was right above them. The downdraft rustled the tops of the surrounding trees, roaring over their bodies and causing Maisie's hair to be swept over her face in a tangled mess. Like night switching to day, a blinding light from above instantly illuminated the forest floor to reveal the location of the gun, laying a couple of feet out of reach of her right arm. Hunter momentarily released Maisie from his gaze and looked up at the chopper. Maisie immediately acted on his lapse in focus. With her left hand she reached down to his waist and tugged on the piece of branch still attached to Hunter's body.

Hunter screamed to the skies at the top of his voice.

'Bitch!'

He struck her with all his weight, across her jaw. But Maisie had already used the opportunity to reach for the weapon. Hunter tried to grab her arm with both hands. But it was too late, the gun was already pointed at the centre of his chest.

Maisie felt an immediate jolt, accompanied by a deafening crack, as she pulled the trigger. The gun discharged a round from the barrel. Straight away, the full dead weight of Hunter's torso collapsed on top of her, smothering her face.

She rolled his body off to her side and discarded the pistol. Then she collapsed in a heap of exhaustion. A tight, uncomfortable sense of remorse gripped her chest and stomach, but were quickly purged by the overwhelming sense of relief as she gazed up at the welcome sight of the rescue helicopter. Finally, the nightmare was over.

45

Roars echoed outside with the ruthless anticipation of several hundred hungry men. Oshiro's eyelids prised themselves open reluctantly. He guessed he'd slept no more than an hour, maybe two. And yet, this morning his outlook had changed. In the night he had been touched by an epiphany that had purged his fear. He was a wealthy man, and a wealthy man in prison can afford protection, even certain luxuries. Most importantly, he hadn't talked, and his associates would know that by now. He knew he was still valuable to them and the wider operation, and it was important they remained aware of that fact.

The roars grew louder and more intense, and Oshiro sensed something was about to happen. Was a riot brewing? Or was this merely the dawn chorus of prison life? Something he might have to get used to, for the time being at least.

He heaved his torso up from its recumbent position and hung his legs over the side of the lower bunk. The frame creaked as he shifted his weight over it, as it had done all night long. The thin mattress, covered in a layer of worn plastic, offered little more comfort than sleeping on the floor. He was amazed he had managed to get any sleep at all. But when you are tired enough you can sleep on anything.

A buzzer sounded and the door emitted a heavy, metallic clunk. The sound of doors being flung open, echoed throughout the prison as they slammed against the adjoining wall. Within seconds, the roars grew louder as they approached his cell and then died away again – each voice with its own unique song.

Oshiro got to his feet and approached the door. Opening it cautiously he saw the passing chain of inmates. He expected more attention from them. Surely, they must know who he was and why he was there, he thought. News of his arrest must have made the newspapers, perhaps even been televised. But each individual passed without so much as a glance, like they knew he was there but were too afraid to make eye contact. Oshiro puffed out his chest and opened the door fully, before picking a gap and filing along the gangway and down the galvanised metal staircase to the open canteen and dining area. His appetite had returned and, as he approached the queue for the breakfast line, the smell of cooked rice and fish grew stronger and more alluring. He wasn't sure whether the smells were any better than the meal from the previous evening, or whether his intensifying hunger just meant he was prepared to eat anything.

Everyone in the queue took a single pace forward. Before Oshiro could do the same, another inmate stepped in front of him. His proportions were gigantic. He was almost a foot taller than Oshiro and perhaps twice as wide. A combination of muscle and enormous bulk, he waddled with the sort of nonchalant confidence that signified he was at the very top of the food chain. Oshiro noticed the scaley tail of a koi carp decorating his right forearm where his sleeves ended. No tattoos went above his neckline, but the back of his cleanly shaven head showed extensive signs of scarring from old wounds. Evidence that others had tried and failed.

Oshiro immediately recognised the challenge. One that might define his standing in the pecking order. Here things were simpler, yes, but it was no different to the outside where you had to prove your strength, to survive and thrive. Still no different after millions of years of evolution. No different to the animal kingdom where the rules were born. He knew, if he did nothing, it would be seen as weakness and would invite others to prey upon him. But get this wrong and he might not walk away from it.

He decided to act. He tapped the man firmly on the shoulder without being aggressive. The man slowly turned his head and looked sternly at Oshiro, as if touching him could have severe, perhaps even painful, consequences. Oshiro decided that words might dilute his message. Instead, he made a short jolt of his head to the left, to signal he wanted him out of his way. Initially the enormous man was shocked. Clearly this was a situation he rarely encountered and Oshiro could read the indecision in his eyes. But after a moment's thought, he stepped aside and allowed Oshiro to pass him, without an apology and maintaining the stern glare. Oshiro walked forward, concealing the thrill of his success with a matching glare, as he felt the entire room witness his victory.

Oshiro allowed the inmates serving to fill his tray which he then carried to the only vacant seat at an otherwise already filled table. His choice not to sit alone was deliberate. The others, already sat eating, watched him arrive and sit down. They said nothing and he said nothing in return. Inwardly he began to relax. He knew he was not clear from danger, but he hadn't faltered.

It started suddenly and from nowhere, all within a fraction of a heartbeat. One second, they were eating breakfast in relative calm; the next there was chaos. Oshiro watched it unfold in slow motion. Two men sat opposite one another, at the other end of the table, began squaring off. First, one stopped eating and stared at the other, then the other stopped eating and stared back. They exchanged the sort of looks that suggested they each wanted to hurt the other and were just waiting for an excuse to do it.

Then it happened. One of the men changed his grip on his fork and thrust it directly into the other's left eye. There was blood everywhere. It squirted violently out from the man's wound, covering the table and those closest to him in a thin veneer. Some droplets caught Oshiro in his eyes, partially impeding his vision. Then the guards descended on the perpetrator who continued to grip the fork and wave it around as a defensive weapon. The other inmates instantly scattered, like there was a practiced protocol. No one came to the aid of the victim, as he lay on the floor, cupping his eye and screaming in agony as a small pool of blood formed under his head.

A few of the other inmates joined in the fight, but most hurried to return to the safety of their cells. Oshiro did the same. The innate need to preserve his life kicked in and he hastened towards the stairs, as quickly as his bulky body could. As he reached the stairs, he tussled with the other inmates as the fleeing herd forced its way up the small stairway. Oshiro felt tugging on his shirt and received numerous stray knocks to the head as arms and elbows flailed in a frenzied display of fear.

Eventually, Oshiro made it to the top of the stairs, just as the loud siren began blasting from the tannoy system. He stopped and looked back down over the escalating riot in the open area below. The piercing pitch announced the arrival of more officers dressed in full riot equipment. They were released from behind a locked door and immediately employed their batons against the crowd still putting up a stand against their colleagues.

Oshiro pushed on to find his cell. He hesitated. He wasn't sure which one was his. This was not the time to get it wrong. He searched his mind and quickly recalled his was the fourth along from the stairs. He hurried towards it and pulled the door closed behind him. He held himself there clutching the dull metal ridge his fingertips had found as his forehead rested on the cold metal. Relief.

But, as he peeled himself away from the door and stepped backwards, he realised he wasn't alone. As he turned away from the doorway and towards the inside of his cell fear struck him again like a thunderbolt. There were four of them. Each of them huge, muscular specimens. One of them was fashioning a small rope from strands of material taken from his mattress, another was using parts from the partially disassembled bed frame to create some sort of hook. The other two immediately launched themselves at him, tackling him to the ground. Pinned against the floor Oshiro struggled against their enormous, combined weight, but it was hopeless. This was it. This was his reckoning.

46

Maisie Lockhart had pushed past the point of tiredness and was now being kept alert by a cocktail of adrenaline and caffeine. Each breath reminded her that two of her ribs were broken on her left side. All her limbs were sore. She had not looked in the mirror, but judging from Tamura's fleeting look of horror when he arrived, and the nagging ache in her jaw, she guessed her face must be badly bruised. She decided she'd rather not know just how badly, for now.

'Don't tell me. I might have to put my modelling career on hold for a few weeks?' she asked Tamura with a faint smile, as he sat down by her bedside. The young sunrise was beginning to direct its rays through the Venetian blinds that hung over the only window in the plain hospital room. Her tired eyes were sensitive to the light, which triggered a mild ache in her forehead.

'Don't expect a call any time soon.' Tamura replied with a wry smile.

Maisie smiled but stopped when she felt the pain.

'So, I leave you alone for one afternoon and this is what happens?' Tamura said. 'Seriously, are you okay?' he added sincerely.

'I've been worse,' she answered, without much thought as to whether her words were accurate. 'At least the list of people who want me dead is fewer by one!'

'My team told me this man was attacking you when the helicopter arrived?'

'They saw that?'

Tamura nodded, all traces of levity gone from his expression.

'They were using an on-board camera to scan the ground. They saw him beating you, and then with his arms around your neck, moments before you reached for the gun.'

A sudden, deep twang of guilt reverberated through the pit of her stomach like the strings of a guitar, as she relived the painful blows to the head and then the satisfying punch from the gun as it recoiled.

'You have nothing to worry about.' Tamura added reassuringly, as he read Maisie's body language. 'We will need to take a statement when you're ready, but it's the clearest example of self-defence I've ever come across. Inspector Kishimoto agrees, as does the Public Prosecutor's Office.'

Maisie nodded, grateful that Tamura was thoughtful enough to consider her feelings. She wriggled painfully to move her body further up the bed, so she could sit up. Without offering, Tamura rearranged the pillows behind her.

'So how have things being going with our friend Mr Oshiro?' she asked.

Tamura paused momentarily, the expression on his face primed to deliver bad news, 'He's … dead.'

Maisie frowned in disbelief.

'I received a call no more than half an hour ago. It happened sometime this morning, having been moved to the general population in Tokushima prison.'

'Dead?' Maisie asked, both struck by the shock of the news and also disappointed he might have gotten away lightly. 'How did that happen?'

'It's still under investigation. Suicide hasn't been ruled out.' Tamura replied guardedly.

'Suicide? What do you think would have been the motive? And what in God's name possessed you to transfer him to a prison? Why not keep him in the holding cells where he was being questioned?' Maisie asked.

Tamura looked towards the doorway, to check that no one was listening before answering.

'I don't know,' he replied candidly, 'he had admitted nothing during questioning, and, in my opinion, he didn't have the look of a man who was contemplating suicide. And you're right, he shouldn't have been transferred to the local prison. The shift supervisor is blaming an administrative error.'

'Administrative error? That's putting it mildly!' she said.

Tamura nodded in agreement. 'Inspector Kishimoto was furious. He's suspended the supervisor and his team.'

'So, he suspects foul play?'

'He hasn't said anything to me, but you can tell from his behaviour that he thinks something isn't right. He's more guarded than before, like he doesn't know who he can trust,' Tamura said, still with a furtive whisper.

Maisie took that as a good indication that Kishimoto was not in on it himself.

'What about the old lady from the village? Has she said anything?'

'She is cooperating. And she claims she will be able to identify the gang involved in the abductions. Although it's unlikely she has come into contact with any high-level members from organised crime. But right now, she's our only line of inquiry. Kishimoto is not going to make the same mistake with her as he did with Oshiro. She is being moved to an undisclosed location. One thing is for sure, suicide or not, Oshiro was the key to all of this, and his death certainly seems to have solved somebody's problems. He was vital to finding out just how far reaching this whole thing is. So, for now, the trail has gone cold.' Tamura said with fervent disappointment.

'Let's not forget what a big player Oshiro was in all of this.' Maisie said, in an attempt at optimism, although secretly disappointed herself. 'You have uncovered the central conspirator and dismantled his whole operation. You should be proud of what you have achieved.'

'But what about the others?' he asked, looking for reassurance with childlike eyes. 'What about the ones that were behind Oshiro, behind all of this?'

'You'll find them. As we discovered before, keep digging hard enough and eventually they'll find you.'

'That's what worries me.' Tamura added with a deflating sigh.

'One thing's for sure. They'll think twice before trying anything on *your* patch for a while,' Maisie said, a warmth in her eyes.

Tamura produced a half smile, as if he wasn't quite convinced but appreciated Maisie's attempt to improve his mood.

'So, what are you going to do now? Are you intending on staying a while longer?' Tamura asked, almost posed as a plea, rather than a question.

'My editor will almost certainly want me back; there's no doubting that. And there's the matter of Hunter's informer to deal with. Providing the doctors give me the green light to fly, I will have to return to the UK in the next couple of days.'

Tamura's eyes hardened as he concealed his disappointment.

'Perhaps before you go, you will allow me to escort you on a visit to Kyoto? It's currently Hanami, a Japanese celebration of the cherry blossom. I would say we have both earnt a break. Plus, the city of Kyoto itself is steeped with Japanese history. Can I tempt you to one last adventure?'

Maisie smiled to confirm her acceptance.

'Before we do that, I'd like to meet Akina – now she's awake, that is. She may be able to clear some things up, including her relationship with Walker. Is she still here in this hospital?'

'No. She was discharged yesterday at her own request. She's now in protective custody.'

'How soon can I speak with her?' Maisie asked.

47

They arrived at Akina's house at a little after two p.m. Tamura had managed to grab some much-needed rest in the comfort of his own bed, only to return and collect Maisie just a few hours later.

Maisie had wrongly assumed Akina would be at her father's enormous mansion – or rather *her* enormous mansion now – in the hills above Takakumi. But instead, she was surprised to learn that Akina had returned to her residence in Nagano, situated almost four hundred miles away.

First, they had driven to Tokushima, where Akina had arranged for a private helicopter. Maisie was no stranger to helicopter travel, but mostly in former military aircraft brought out of retirement to taxi reporters across war zones. Never had she travelled in a Sikorsky, which by stark contrast was modern and luxurious.

The two-hour journey took them over the cities of Osaka and Nagoya, across the vast mountain ranges of Central Honshu to Nagano airport. The scenery breezed past their windows whilst they sipped expensive champagne from the comfort of their sumptuously soft, white leather armchairs. After all that had happened, Maisie didn't mind admitting that she was enjoying herself, finally feeling able to relax, with the threat to her life now behind her.

As the wooden automatic gates to Akina's residence opened inwardly, they revealed a small, circular gravel driveway and, beyond it, a single storey oblong building. It was built in a minimalist style, with a mostly glass frontage and a flat rosewood roof which seemed to levitate above it. Only two sets of large structural supports, positioned at either side of the centre, interrupted the symphony of glass that allowed the construction to blend almost seamlessly into the rich vegetation of its surroundings. While unmistakably lavish, the architecture was clean and modern, with a hint of modesty and understatement that had been well and truly lacking from her father's fortress.

The chauffeur of the Mercedes S-Class, sent by Akina to collect them from the airport, pulled up beside the squad car, parked overtly at the front of the property, and killed the engine. A watchful officer in police uniform appeared at the entrance to the property.

'If there is a possible threat to Akina's life, why bring her here?' Maisie asked with chords of concern mixed with disbelief, 'surely you must have more secure locations than this? If someone was trying to get to her, this is the first place they'd look.'

'I agree,' Tamura replied, 'but Oshiro-san insisted. There is no need for concern, two officers are stationed here around the clock. And we have a car patrolling the area which is in contact with the officers inside. They have also been instructed to undertake hourly checks of the perimeter.'

Maisie was not convinced, but she nodded all the same.

As their feet crunched their way through the deep gravel, the officer called out something in Japanese, his gaze focused on Tamura. Tamura responded by removing his warrant card from his pocket. The officer maintained his stern expression as he examined it more closely, before delivering a sharp but accepting nod of his head. No pleasantries. Then he led the two of them inside the bungalow.

'He seems pleased to see us!' Maisie chuckled sarcastically.

'Kishimoto's instructions.' explained Tamura, 'they have been warned to expect attempts to breach the compound and not to break protocol. These men are specialists in witness protection.'

They were led into a reception room and left to wait for Akina. Maisie didn't feel like sitting and took the opportunity to inspect the room's contents. The medium-sized oblong room was in keeping with the design of the building itself, minimalist and devoid of clutter. What little furniture she had was contemporary in design. Two cream-coloured settees sat facing one another in the centre room, separated by a small coffee table where tea, coffee and a selection of sandwiches and sushi had been laid. Ordered in, Maisie guessed.

They each remained silent. Tamura gravitated towards the windows, casually making his own assessments of the security of the premises. Meanwhile, Maisie continued to inspect the room more closely, with her usual measure of curiosity. On one wall there was a traditional Japanese tapestry depicting colourful rural scenes of woodlands and streams. At the edges of the room, against each of the three glass walls, there were matching cabinets, each host to obscure sculptures of twisted wood or metal. Their distorted shapes were chaotic and painful, and strangely at odds with the straight lines that dominated the otherwise obsessive devotion to symmetry.

Throughout the room, picture frames of various sizes captured a snapshot of a young woman, and a child at various ages. The young Akina and her mother, Maisie deduced. The pictures captured snapshots of happiness. Childhood memories of playful experiences in picturesque surroundings. Against one of the glass walls was another cluster of photo frames, all carefully arranged in a symmetrical display on a cabinet. Above them, hanging from the wall was a much larger portrait of the same woman who had appeared in almost all the other photographs. At either side of the portrait, were matching vases, containing incense sticks recently burned. As Maisie's eyes scanned the various images, she noted that none of them included Akina's father. Perhaps he was taking the photograph, she wondered?

'That is a portrait of my mother.' said a timid voice from across the room. Maisie turned to find Akina stood at the doorway. Still carrying some of the scars of her ordeal, she looked pale and emaciated. Her dark, dishevelled locks mostly covered her face. But from what Maisie could see, her face was without make-up with heavy swelling beneath the eyes, as if she had been crying.

'She was a very beautiful woman.' Maisie said politely, just remembering to use the past tense as the word left her mouth. Maisie and Tamura both offered a bow that was quietly reciprocated by Akina. 'And from the photographs it looks as though she was joyful too.' Maisie added.

'We were always happy when we were together.' Akina replied awkwardly.

'And you both shared many different interests?'

Akina forced a smile and nodded. 'She was a very important part of my life. I still miss her.'

'And what does this writing mean?' Maisie asked inquisitively, pointing to the kanji symbols engraved on a wooden plaque beneath the portrait.

'It means: "Beautiful Sakura, never forgotten". That was her name.' Akina explained.

Maisie smiled and redirected the conversation. 'It's good to see you looking so well again.' Maisie said. 'It is truly phenomenal that you managed to escape your captor.'

'I was lucky to receive such good care. And that Sergeant Tamura found me when he did. I owe him a great debt.' Akina said, with a pursed smile as she looked fondly at Tamura.

Tamura shuffled uncomfortably as he tried to conceal his embarrassment.

'It was my honour to be of service, Oshiro-san.' he said formally.

'You seem to have experienced trouble of your own?' Akina said with a slight brazenness, as her eyes inspected the bruising on Maisie's cheek.

'Yes, I was also lucky. Thanks largely to some martial arts training and the swift response by the police.'

'Perhaps I will also look into that. The martial arts training, that is. Father always saw it as unladylike.' Akina said, her expression suggesting the words left a sour taste. 'Can I offer either of you anything?' Akina asked, gesturing half-heartedly in the direction of the coffee table.

They all sat down and Maisie proceeded to pour coffee for Akina, Tamura and then herself.

Tamura was first to break the awkward silence.

'I know this may be difficult for you, but I was hoping you would be ready to talk more about your father?'

Akina remained silent. Just gazed vacantly at the table.

'It's over now, Akina. He can't hurt you anymore.' Maisie said reassuringly. 'We think Edward Walker found out what your father was up to. But he must have had help. Someone with an intimate knowledge of your father's dealings.'

'I don't understand.' Akina said, confusion muddled within the words. 'What is it you think he did? Are you suggesting he had something to do with my abduction?'

Tamura and Maisie looked at each other, surprised and somewhat confused by her response.

'We have compelling evidence that places him at the scene in the cabin. Where you and Walker were being held.'

Akina's expression crumbled. 'I can't believe it. Why would my own father do that? And what was it that Edward found out?'

'We think your father was at the centre of a conspiracy,' Maisie interjected. 'A conspiracy to forcefully acquire land in and around the village of Takakumi. Possibly with the help of organised crime. Is none of this triggering any memories?'

Akina's hands began to shake uncontrollably as she burst into tears.

'I can't believe it! It can't be true!' she cried as her head fell into her hands.

Maisie removed a tissue from her handbag and held it out for Akina who grabbed it from her, turning away as she dried her eyes.

'I realise this must be a lot to take in right now.' Tamura said, apologetically. 'We can do this another time, if this is too soon for you?'

Akina shook her head.

'No. I need to hear this,' she said, 'please continue.'

'We think Walker found out what your father was up to. We assumed you had provided him with this information?'

'No. I wasn't aware of any of this.' Akina replied plainly.

'What about you and Walker?' Maisie asked cutting in again, 'were the two of you in a relationship?'

Akina nodded her confirmation.

'We had become very close. He was such a fantastic person. Poor Edward!' she said, as she broke into more tears.

'Did your father know about the two of you?' Tamura asked.

'No, I don't think so. We were keeping it a secret from him. He wouldn't have approved.' Akina replied, as she dried her eyes again.

'Why not?' Maisie asked.

'He was very protective of me. He wanted me to marry an influential Japanese man. A politician. He had been trying to arrange something for some time. Knowing that I had become close with Edward would not have pleased him.'

'Did your father ever mistreat you, Akina?' Maisie asked pointedly, attempting to unwrap her seemingly euphemistic language.

Akina's head dropped.

'What do you mean?' she responded evasively.

'Was he ever violent or controlling towards you in any way?'

Akina failed to answer.

'I can't believe he would have anything to do with this. Why would he abduct me?'

'Perhaps he found out about you and Walker?' Maisie speculated. 'Perhaps he thought the two of you were working against him? Maybe he wanted to find out how much you both knew and what you may have been planning?'

A look of terror descended upon Akina's countenance.

'You think it was my father who tortured us?' Akina asked as she looked inwardly in search of her memories.

'We found this at the scene with your father's fingerprint on it,' Tamura held up a picture of the blood-spattered tiger pin. 'Do you recognise it? The blood on it belongs to you,' he said gravely, 'the fingerprint in the blood belongs to your father.'

Akina looked anxiously back at them.

'I want to help. But I just can't remember!' she said, expressing her frustration with a frenzied shaking of her head. She took a sip from her tea and seemed to calm down.

'I understand the last thing you do remember was being rammed off the road. Is there anything more that you remember about the car or who was driving?' Maisie asked.

Akina's head fell into her hands.

'Still only fragments. It was a dark coloured four by four, I think.'

'Do you remember if the driver stopped?'

Akina looked blankly back at her.

'What about the collision?' Maisie said.

'What about it?' Akina replied, confused.

'How did it happen? Were you hit from behind? Did the driver pull up beside you, and hit you from the side?'

Akina shook her head, vaguely.

'From the side, I guess. It's so hard to remember.' Akina looked to Tamura to rescue her from the overwhelming bombardment of questions.

Maisie read her body language and eased herself back.

'I'm sure it will come back, in good time.'

'Maisie's right, don't feel pressured. You've done amazingly well to show this much strength. Take your time. Besides we have a witness who is cooperating with our investigation.' Tamura said with reassurance. 'It seems she had some involvement with your father. She claims to have known your grandmother, all the way back to when your father was living in Ine, as a child. She claims the two of them had been working together and she has confirmed your father played a role in the abductions that took place in the village. Possibly with the help of contacts within the criminal underworld.'

'Where is she now?' Akina asked, 'Would I be able to speak with her? If she knew my family, maybe it would help if I spoke with her?'

'Not at this moment,' Tamura answered, 'she is being held in protective custody for her own safety, in case there are others involved in this that might still be out there.'

A deep dread shrieked from Akina's eyes. 'That's why I'm in protective custody, isn't it? You think my father was murdered. You think they will come for me as well, don't you?'

'No.' Tamura said definitively. 'But until we have concluded our investigation it would be safer to accept the additional security.'

Akina nodded vaguely as she stared at the bare floorboards. She looked weary and let out an audible yawn.

'Pardon my rudeness.' she said.

'It is us that should be apologising, Oshiro-san,' Tamura said, 'we should allow you to get some rest. You have my number if you need to contact me, or if you think of anything else that could assist our investigation.'

All three of them rose from their seats in unison.

'One other thing I was going to mention ... It is a little delicate,' Maisie said, with a hint of reservation in her voice. 'I have been informed that Walker's parents will be coming out to Japan to accompany him to the UK.' she said.

Akina looked back at her blankly, unsure what Maisie was expecting from her, nor what her reply should be.

'I was wondering whether you wanted me to pass on your contact details? I imagine you will want to attend the funeral. Perhaps even be involved with his funeral arrangements? I'm sure his parents would be keen to meet you, seeing as you had become so close to their son?'

Akina maintained a perplexed expression, as if she were being asked a trick question. Eventually she blurted out a clumsy response.

'Would that be wise?' she asked Tamura.

Tamura shrugged. 'I can't see why not. Although I would suggest you speak with the officers assigned to you. They may want to go with you,' he said.

Akina turned back to Maisie, to answer the original question.

'In that case, yes please do pass on my details.' she replied, in a matter-of-fact tone.

Maisie and Tamura then offered a bow to Akina and began making their way to the front door, to leave. On their way, Maisie made a conscious effort to observe the other photographs hanging on the wall of the hallway, looking for at least one image of Akina's father. But, whilst there were many others that contained a combination of Akina, her mother or both, none of them contained Yoshi Oshiro.

Perhaps it wasn't so unusual for someone to hold such fond memories of a loved one who had passed, particularly when it had been at such a young age. But the absence of Akina's father faintly troubled Maisie's subconscious.

Tamura was first to reach the doorway where he and Maisie filed outside onto the elevated porch. Maisie turned one last time to Akina.

'I just wanted to offer my sincere condolences for your father,' she said as she held Akina by the hand, maintaining eye contact, 'I'm sure this is extremely difficult for you, whatever he may be accused of.'

Akina stared back at her without offering any words, eventually settling for a gentle nod.

'Fair well,' Maisie said to Akina, 'I do hope our paths cross again in the future,' she added with a smile, before turning and joining Tamura by the car.

'So, Kyoto next?' Tamura asked, hurling his words over the roof of the car.

'Kyoto.' Maisie replied with a smile, as she entered through the passenger side rear door.

48

A sanguineous hue had emerged at the edge of the horizon, encroaching on the otherwise unblemished blue sky. Maruyama Park was a hive of activity. Maisie and Tamura had sought refuge from the busy crowds under the vast canopies of pink and white blossom in full bloom. Along the wide promenades that navigated the greenery, street vendors had constructed temporary stalls that offered a variety of food and drink. Everything from takeaway tapas to more formal meals with table service. Meanwhile, every inch of lawn was occupied by a patchwork quilt of picnic blankets. Visitors from across Japan, and some international tourists, sat and enjoyed the majestic setting alongside city workers, still dressed in their formal attire.

Sat at one of the many tables beneath the canopy, Maisie inhaled the fresh spring air, which carried the faint scent of vanilla, lilac and rose, laced with the tantalising smells from the kitchen.

'Welcome to Hanami.' said Tamura, raising his cup of sake in the hope that Maisie would do the same.

'Hanami?' Maisie asked, whilst tentatively raising her own cup.

'Yes. It is the festival for flower viewing. Specifically, the viewing of the cherry blossom.'

'It's very beautiful,' Maisie admitted, 'why cherry blossom in particular?' she asked.

'It is the delicate flowers themselves and their transient beauty, lasting for little more than two weeks. A metaphor for life itself. That it is to be cherished and appreciated. It helps regain perspective for what is truly important.'

'And what would you say is truly important?' Maisie asked.

'I suppose … family, friendship. Love.' Tamura replied, adding the last word with a hint of embarrassment.

Maisie wasn't sure what she should say in reply and so decided to change the subject.

'So, what did you think of the meeting with Akina?' Maisie asked. Now out of earshot of Akina's driver and the helicopter pilot, she was keen to get Tamura's thoughts on their meeting.

Tamura had come to recognise the tone of suggestion in Maisie's voice.

'Not a great deal. She was nervous and afraid. And she remains in denial about her father's involvement in either her abduction or his other criminal enterprises. I would say both are natural reactions, given the circumstances.' he replied.

'Don't you think it's strange she doesn't remember anything about her abduction? I mean, nothing at all.'

'The doctors don't seem to think so. She has suffered a serious physical and mental trauma. She had a head injury.'

'You're right, it's perfectly possible,' Maisie conceded, 'I just find it hard to believe that she is unable to remember anything useful. If it were me, I would want to know. I'd be doing everything I could to get to the bottom of it all.' She added, finishing the sentence with a sigh of frustration.

Tamura smiled.

'Well, she's certainly no Maisie Lockhart,' he said, disarmingly. Tamura raised his cup as a gesture to break the tension, which led to each of them taking a sip of sake. Tamura could see from Maisie's preoccupied expression that she remained dissatisfied with his explanation.

'So, what is it that bothered you during the visit?' Tamura asked, with curiosity.

'Something about when I asked her to recall the one bit of information she claimed she could remember. The collision that forced her off the road.'

'What about it?'

'It never happened.'

'Why do you say that?'

'I read your forensic report. There was no damage to the body work of the car on the rear or the sides. Just the front where it went straight into a tree.'

'So?'

'She said she was hit from the side. And yet she can't remember anything else about it?'

Tamura thought for a moment.

'Maybe she was getting confused. Maybe she was hit head on, and that forced her off the road?'

Maisie shrugged, unconvinced.

'She certainly put on a good show,' Maisie said sarcastically, half under her breath. 'But there were some moments when I found her quite callous. Such as when I suggested she might want to meet Walker's parents and say goodbye to Walker himself. The notion was completely foreign to her. Clearly it hadn't entered her mind until I mentioned it. And when I offered my condolences for her father's death, there was nothing. Not even the hint of an emotion. Like it meant nothing to her.'

'She has had a lot to process. Her father has been accused of her kidnap after all.'

'Which she repeatedly rejected.' Maisie interjected.

'And he was accused of being part of a criminal conspiracy,' Tamura continued, 'and grief can affect people in different ways.'

Maisie was silent for a moment as she searched her mind. 'And what about the photographs?'

'Photographs?'

'Yes. All those photographs, all of her mother.'

'So?'

'Didn't you think it was strange?'

'What, that she treasured the memory of her mother?'

'No. That there wasn't a single photograph of her father. Not one. And that she has chosen to live four hundred miles away from his main residence.'

Tamura shrugged indifferently.

'Not that strange for a daughter to want some independence,' he said.

Maisie's look became more pensive.

'What do you know about the circumstances surrounding the death of Akina's mother?' Maisie asked.

'Only rumours,' Tamura replied, 'I was a child myself when it happened. Apparently, she suffered from deep episodes of depression and had not left the family home in months. Her suicide was attributed to her mental health. Yoshi Oshiro started a charity in her name after her death and very publicly called for more investment and education in mental health.'

Maisie pursed her lips together, forcing her bottom lip to protrude slightly.

'Given what we now know about Oshiro, maybe it would be worth a closer look. Who knows, his links to organised crime could span several decades?'

The pair finished eating their seafood ramen at around half past five, within an hour of being seated. Tamura was keen for Maisie to see Kiyomizu-dera temple before the sun set, and so he caught the attention of a passing rickshaw driver, and the two of them exchanged the seats at the table for another set on wheels.

It wasn't the first time Maisie had ridden in a rickshaw. However, unlike most other parts of the world, where the cart is pulled by a cycle or a noisy two-stroke engine, in this case, a young man pulled them along himself at a gentle trotting pace. Maisie felt quite ridiculous. But as the painkillers were wearing off and her ribs had begun to ache more intensely, she was glad to avoid the walk along the busy promenade.

They navigated the labyrinth of small streets – some no more than several meters wide – with a seemingly infinite number of shops and restaurants on either side. The two storey buildings typified traditional Japan, many of them modest wooden structures with their signature, gently slanting gables and extended overhangs.

The soft murmur from the tranquil crowds that wandered the streets was strangely hypnotic. And they seemed happy to make way for the cheery and respectful driver who would let out the occasional nod, accompanied by either 'doumo,' or 'arigatou.' Meanwhile, Tamura also seemed content to enjoy the journey without the distraction of conversation.

The gradient of the promenade began to rise steadily, slowing their progress, as the driver pushed on through his exhaustion. But gradually the first of the temple's many structures came into view, and the shops on either side relented to reveal the full extent of the complex in all its splendour. Its various elevated levels carved into the hillside, exuded a certain imperiousness over the city.

The road eventually ran out and they came to stop in a large open area below the entrance to the temple. Tamura handed over several crisp bills to the driver, who accepted the overpayment appreciatively, before seeking his next customer for the return journey. Tamura then led them past two lion statues seated at either side of the path and up the twenty or so steps towards the first of the temple's many structures. The large, solitary gateway marked the entrance to the temple. Its vermilion red, curved canopy, spread over them like the wingspan of a giant mythical creature.

After passing through the first gate, Tamura escorted them diagonally across the first level, to another set of steps that led to a slightly larger gate that mirrored the design of the first.

'Impressive, isn't it?' Tamura said proudly as he reached the top of the steps slightly ahead of Maisie.

'Quite imposing.' Maisie replied in agreement, with a faint breathlessness. Even though it had only been a very small climb, the discomfort of her injuries was beginning to drain her strength, but she was determined not to let it ruin their enjoyment.

'Many consider this to be the gateway to paradise.' Tamura explained.

As she reached the top herself, she turned around to enjoy the views. The sun had dropped low enough in the sky, creating a vast silhouette of the mountain range in the distance. Its rays shone diagonally down on the city through breaks in the cloud, completing a scenery reminiscent of biblical depictions.

'I can certainly see why,' she said, somewhat in awe. 'I take it you have visited before?' she asked him.

'My parents used to bring us here when I was young.' he explained. 'Come. It gets even better,' he added, with a hint of childish excitement.

Now at the top level of the complex, they continued on past the multitude of other temples structures, all of a similar design, including a towering three-storey pagoda which claimed to be the tallest in Japan. 'Does the colour red hold a particular significance in Japan?' Maisie asked inquisitively.

'Yes,' Tamura replied, 'it is believed to ward off evil. The same goes for the demonic faces,' he explained pointing at some of the decorative tiles at the edges of the canopies.

'And what about the dragon?' Maisie asked, pointing to a large serpentine copper sculpture, leaning over a stone trough and filling it with water from its mouth.

'That represents the god of water,' he replied, 'here to protect the temple from fire. The structures you see here have been rebuilt many times. Over the centuries fire has claimed almost all of them. Other than the site itself, there is little that remains of the original eighth century buildings. These were all constructed around the fifteenth to seventeenth centuries,' Tamura stated, reciting another tour guide script from memory. Then, with the subtle tilt of his head, he encouraged Maisie to continue following him.

Maisie consumed the atmosphere of the ancient site but, haunted by her recent encounters, she remained wary of her surroundings. The light was dimming and there were now little more than a handful of other visitors visible on the upper level of the complex. There was a middle-aged man who appeared to be capturing the whole experience through his smartphone, in a single, uninterrupted take. Meanwhile, an elderly couple patrolled with tranquil indifference, as though this was part of their daily ritual. Two teenaged girls played between two large boulders. One of them was blindfolded, attempting to walk the not inconsiderable distance between them.

'They are practicing an old tradition,' Tamura explained, noticing Maisie's bewilderment. 'It is said that if you can find the way from one rock to another whilst blindfolded, you are destined to find love.'

'And if you don't?' Maisie asked.

'Then you may need some help.' Tamura said with a smile. 'Would you like to have a go?'

'No. I wouldn't want to embarrass myself,' she replied politely, 'besides I would be just as likely to fall and break another rib.' she added.

'Very well,' Tamura said understandably, 'but this is what I wanted you to see,' he said holding his arm out in the direction of the largest of the temple's structures. 'This is Hon Do, the main hall.'

Stood at the edge of a steep cliff face, the big two storey structure included a large balcony, supported by wooden scaffolding, which extended out over the mountain slopes. The platform provided panoramic views over the distant mountain range, the city of Kyoto and the picturesque woodlands that surrounded the temple, with vast swathes of the red maple interspersed with large thickets of pink and white blossom.

'This is one of the most popular places for sakura viewing in the city. But in the evening, it becomes quite peaceful,' Tamura explained, as the two of them took in the scenery whilst lent over the thick wooden balustrades.

Maisie was suddenly unsettled by Tamura's comment. It took a moment to process where she had heard the word Sakura before.

'So, does that mean Akina's mother's name means cherry blossom in Japanese?' Maisie asked, as she recalled Akina's earlier translation of the plaque beneath the photograph of her mother.

'That's correct. Sakura is a very common name in Japan.' Tamura confirmed.

Maisie shrugged and respectfully returned her attention to the present; to the views and to Tamura himself.

'So, what's next for Sergeant Tamura? I expect you will have lots to do over the coming months. A criminal network to unravel, not to mention potential corruption to weed out from the police force.'

Maisie immediately noticed her words had hit a raw nerve.

'They *are* keeping you on the case, aren't they?' She added fervently.

Tamura shook his head with regret.

'Now that Oshiro is dead, it seems Kishimoto will be continuing the wider investigation without me, from the Tokushima office. I have been asked to return to my duties at the village.' he said, with weighty disappointment.

'But that's madness. You were the one who broke the case. Without you, he would have nothing.' Masie said, unable to stop herself from raising her voice.

Tamura shrugged his shoulders with calm resignation.

'*We* broke the case,' he corrected her, 'I have no doubt that I would not have got to where I did without you. It has been an honour.' he added, turning to look into her eyes.

From nowhere, a series of short, loud cracks ruptured the silence and echoed around the compound. Maisie's heart leaped as she immediately recognised the sound of gunfire and instinctively dropped to a crouch behind one of the thick, wooded balustrades. Tamura did the same whilst forming a protective shield around her. Then another burst of fire … crack, crack, crack, crack, crack!

But instead of screams and yelling, all the two of them could hear was laughter. Tamara and Maisie looked at one another, before cautiously peering across to where the noise had originated, at one of the lower levels. There, two boys had spotted their reaction to the firecrackers, and were pointing directly at Tamura and Maisie as they laughed.

Tamura and Maisie got to their feet once more and smiled to each other with embarrassment before resuming their positions, leaning on the edge of the viewing platform.

'And what about you? What have you got out of this experience?' Tamura asked, still with a faint smile on his face.

Maisie considered the question briefly before answering.

'I certainly hadn't expected to encounter so much death and violence, that's for sure. When I set out from England, this was intended to be a simple missing persons' investigation, to escape the dangers back home. And yet, amidst all the horror and grief, there have also been plenty of moments to celebrate. This truly enchanting country, for one. But, most of all, my friendship with you,' she said, in a moment of unexpected tenderness. 'And there were your lessons in self-defence, which without a doubt saved my life.'

'So, what will you do next?' Tamura asked.

'I will need to convince my editor, but I have a feeling this will provide enough content for a book,' she added. 'All we need to do now is find a way to help you get the promotion you deserve.'

Tamura raised his eyebrows.

'I have learned a great deal from this experience. The importance of building relationships and cooperation; of following your instincts; and, of course, the importance of always having an umbrella,' he said with a wry smile. She laughed.

'There is actually something I have been meaning to ask you about that night in Tokyo,' he added, preparing Maisie for a more serious question. 'When the gang members on the motorcycle were heading straight towards us and you told me to run to the end of the road, how did you know they would miss us?'

Maisie smiled mischievously.

'Lucky guess, I suppose! I had fired one of those weapons whilst in America several years ago. Quite a machine. Something in the region of 600 rounds per minute. The thing is, the recoil of each shot forces the barrel upwards. And our friend, on the back of the bike, was firing one-handed, whilst moving. The chances of him accurately hitting his intended target were almost zero.'

'Almost zero!' Tamura exclaimed, shaking his head as he turned away in the direction of the sunset, now able to see the funny side.

Both remained silent as they took one last look at the views that would soon fade into darkness. Lanterns hanging from the branches of the sakura trees had begun to glow, allowing celebrations to continue well into the night.

Then suddenly Maisie was struck by an epiphany, like a thunderbolt sparking the synapses.

'Jesus!' she exclaimed.

'What is it?' Tamura asked.

'We've missed something that has been staring us in the face since the very beginning. Something that was out of place at the crime scene in the cabin.'

'What are you talking about?' Tamura asked, unable to keep up with Maisie's incoherent ravings.

'The cherry blossom branches that were found at the scene in the cabin. What if it was her that put them there?'

49

The office was sparse and utilitarian. Not what Maisie had imagined at all. She had expected walls covered with oak panelling and oil paintings, shelves filled with leather-bound books. But the reality was very different. It was just another room, not dissimilar to any other you might find in a hospital.

The middle-aged American woman, the director of the institute, sat behind an aged, and very basic-looking desk, made from a simple steel frame and with a cheap, worn veneer wood top. The woman was subconsciously tapping her fingers on the desk as she waited impatiently for Tamura to finish reading Akina's file.

Until now, there had been no reason to consider Akina's medical history, but Maisie had convinced Tamura they should at least delve a little deeper into her theory that she might have, in some way, played a role in Walker's abduction. As soon as they had returned to the station at Takakumi, calls were made to the forensic teams, to get a clearer idea of Akina's movements in and around the cabin. Inquiries had also been made at the Japanese Ministry of Health and Welfare, which had led them here.

'Did you know Akina when she was here?' Tamura asked the director.

She nodded.

'Yes. I wasn't in my current role, but I remember her coming here. It was quite a big deal at the time. We're accustomed to visits from celebrities, but a lot of fuss was made over her arrival. Lawyers accompanied her and all the staff were asked to sign non-disclosure agreements to prevent any leaks to the press.'

'And she was admitted at the age of fourteen, just a few months after her mother's death?' Tamura asked, for clarification.

'That's right. Not surprisingly, she had taken her mother's death very badly. But she had resorted to self-harm. It was never established whether these were suicide attempts, but as you can see from the pictures, they were extensive. I can still remember them. She had cuts to her hands and legs, as well as bruising all over her body.'

'What made you think it was self-harm? Could someone else have been inflicting these injuries?' Maisie asked.

The director shrugged.

'I guess. But staff caught her trying to repeat the injuries. There was never any suggestion from her that she had been beaten in any way. And we do look into that sort of thing.'

'And who was it that admitted her?' Tamura asked.

'Her father. She had become quite a handful. Expelled from her school for attacking another pupil. And she had become prone to outbursts of sudden violence. She even attacked one of her therapists, here at the hospital, after they asked her about her mother. But over time she became more stable and she learned to deal with her grief. She was extremely intelligent. Tested off the charts.'

'What sort of treatment did she receive while she was here?' Maisie asked.

'It's all in the file,' the director said, with a slight huff as she glanced at her watch. 'She would have received a mix of pharmacological treatment and cognitive behavioural therapy.'

'Can you recall what her relationship was like with her father?' Tamura asked.

'Complicated, as I recall. When she arrived here, she spoke a lot about how she blamed her father for her mother's death. But these were incoherent outbursts, nothing more. We knew about Akina's mother, of course, and how she had battled with poor mental health.'

'It says here she was with you for almost twelve months. Is that a long time for this type of condition?' Tamura asked.

'It always depends on the individual. It takes as long as it takes. But it's fair to say that Akina was one of the more extreme cases that I've seen.'

'And how did she respond to your treatment?' Maisie asked.

'Initially, it was difficult. Her outbursts and the need for her to be sedated made things harder. Gradually she responded to treatment, but she was always very quiet. She never said much.'

'Would you say she was cured by the time she left?' Tamura asked, as he continued to read the report.

'Our job here is to help provide patients with coping mechanisms that help them deal with the world around them, so they can return to society. But there is rarely a cure for anyone. It's not that simple. There can often be relapses. But when she was discharged, she satisfied the release board that she was ready.'

'Was there ever any indication of such a relapse for Akina?' Maisie asked.

'We never saw anything of her after she was discharged, if that's what you mean. But in the case of Akina, who suffered the significant loss of a loved one during childhood, who can know what sort of damage that does? A deep childhood trauma of that nature can leave scars. And sometimes they lie dormant beneath the surface for years, invisible to the rest of us.'

Suddenly Tamura lifted his head from the report and stared momentarily at Maisie. His eyes told her he'd found something important. Then he looked across to the director.

'It says here there was an incident during one of her therapy sessions.' Tamura stated.

The director shrugged again, 'As I recall there were many.' she replied, as though no one incident stood out in particular.

'During this session she attacked the therapist and then attempted to use a sharp implement to remove a finger on her left hand!' Tamura said.

The director paused as she searched the ceiling for answers, and then slowly began to nod as the fog lifted on her memory.

'That's right. She grabbed a letter opener, or something similar, and forced it against her hand. Ended up with several stitches and a fracture to the bone. Needless to say, we don't leave those sorts of implements lying around these days.' A hint of levity appeared in the corner of the director's mouth, which she quickly retracted.

'Did you find out why she chose to inflict that type of injury?' Tamura asked.

'It was a long time ago,' the director replied, giving herself more time to think, 'but yes, I think I do,' she said, still searching the depths of her personal archives.

The tension in the room was palpable as both Maisie and Tamura waited for the reveal.

'Yes, that was it … we later discovered that she was trying to recreate an injury that her mother had sustained before her death. The removal of two fingers from her left hand.'

50

'Good morning, Oshiro-san!'

Akina had awoken earlier than usual. She followed the aroma of coffee and burned toast into the kitchen where one of the witness protection officers was making breakfast. He was always chirpy and full of energy, something that Akina found particularly irritating first thing in the morning. But this morning she sensed an awkwardness in his body language, as if he had been caught doing something he shouldn't.

'Would you like some toast or perhaps some coffee?' he offered, pointing to one of the burned slices of bread.

'Thanks, but I can get it,' she replied with a half-smile, as she manoeuvred around the breakfast bar to the cupboard where the cups were kept. 'How about I make the coffee?' she offered.

The officer made a single nod of his head and smiled appreciatively, before continuing to apply accompaniments to his toast.

'Is it just us, or will the other officer be joining us?' She asked.

'Just the two of us. Tanaka is out at the moment. But he'll be back in a couple of hours or so.'

Akina forced another smile as she retrieved two cups from the cupboard, taking more care with the one in her left hand. She had yet to master her imbalance.

Suddenly the officer's phone began to vibrate, causing it to shift slightly over the granite worktop.

'Excuse me Oshiro-san, I must take this.' he said with a sense of urgency as he glanced at the caller ID. Then he walked out of the kitchen and along the corridor to one of the spare bedrooms, for privacy.

Akina waited until he had closed the door behind him, before quietly tracing his steps along the corridor, until she was within earshot of the conversation.

'Yes, I'm with her now … Yes, I can talk freely …You want her to come in? Is there a problem?' there was a brief pause, 'I see. I'll need to wait for Tanaka to come back first … Oh, I see …

how long before you arrive? … No, of course, I won't say anything yet.'

Akina's heart began to thump harder and faster in her chest. Shit, what had they discovered? And why would they be coming here if not to arrest her? Sensing the conversation was reaching its conclusion, Akina hastily tiptoed her way back to the kitchen. There was no time to lose. She needed to get out of there.

She went to the drawer where she kept her medication and removed a box of prescription sleeping tablets. Hearing the sound of the door opening, at the end of the hallway, she quickly liberated a handful from their sachets – hoping the quantity would be a sufficient overdose to induce a swift unconsciousness. The officer's footsteps over the wooden floorboards were deliberate, as if he were still preoccupied with the phone call. Akina hurriedly ground the pills into a fine white powder, using the bottom of one of the cups. Then, using her hand, she quickly swept the powder from the worktop and into the cup, before wiping the surface down and disposing of the evidence.

'Sugar?' She called out, just as the officer was reaching the open entrance to the kitchen.

'Two, please. No cream.' he responded, just as Akina began pouring the coffee.

Akina passed the cup to the officer. He searched her face and thanked her appreciatively. Then he pulled up a stool at the breakfast bar and sat down to a plate of toast.

'Everything okay?' she asked him, as she evaluated his body language for clues.

'Just a routine check-in call. Nothing to worry about.' he replied.

'Have there been any developments in the case of my abduction?' she asked brazenly.

'Not my area, I'm afraid. They don't tell me anything I don't need to know. My job is to take care of you.'

'Surely you would get to hear of something, particularly if there was something significant?'

The officer looked back at her with a faint level of embarrassment.

'I can put you in contact with one of the officers involved with the investigation if that helps?' he said, looking to close the conversation down.

Akina grinned back at him, awkwardly.

'I'm sure they'll let me know,' she replied, 'how's your coffee, by the way?' she asked as she took a sip from her own cup, 'I hope I made it okay? I like it quite strong.'

The officer took his first sip. 'Perfect,' he replied without hesitation, or much thought.

Akina said nothing for several minutes and proceeded to drink from her cup. The awkward silence that ensued, encouraged the officer to finish his toast and drink his coffee, without being interrupted by conversation. It was only when he was reaching the dregs at the bottom of the cup that she spoke again.

'I was thinking I might make a trip into town this morning. I figured it would probably be good for me to get used to being out again. Do you think that will be okay?'

The officer's eyelids were beginning to show faint signs of fatigue, prompting yet another mouthful of his coffee.

'It makes sense that you would want to get out of the house,' he replied, 'but it would be best for us to wait for my colleague Tanaka to return before we make any arrangements.'

Akina was vaguely impressed by the deftness of his lies.

'I understand.' she said as she watched the effects of the sleeping pills begin to take hold. 'Can I get you some more coffee?'

The officer began to lose his balance on the stool, and he placed both palms on the counter in front of him to steady himself. Then he tried to fight the effects by shaking his head and stretching his facial muscles in an attempt to force his eyelids to open wider.

'Are you okay?' Akina asked innocently, after he failed to reply. 'You look like you're struggling.'

He looked back at her suspiciously. Then his hands reached for his phone, which he juggled clumsily before managing to make a call. As he placed the phone to his ear, he got up from his stool and stumbled across the room towards the doorway. Meanwhile, Akina darted around the breakfast bar to intercept him.

'Get here as quickly as you can,' he said, his speech becoming increasingly slurred. 'It's Akina, she's ...' but Akina was too quick for him. She knocked the phone out of his hands before he could complete his sentence.

The phone slid away from them, across the smooth wooden floorboards. The officer desperately leapt after it, but lost his footing and tumbled to the floor. As he attempted to crawl away, Akina straddled his upper back, pinning him to the floor. He struggled against her, but it was no good. With every second that passed, he grew weaker and weaker.

Akina's heart was pounding, fuelled by fear and excitement in equal proportions. She had been unsure whether the dosage of sleeping pills would be enough to cause a loss of consciousness, or whether she would have to speed up the process. But, whilst the officer was continuing to groan in protest, it only took a few more seconds before he was out cold.

Akina jumped to her feet and dialled the number for her driver.

'Hekima, I need you here as quickly as possible. Family emergency!' she said, without putting much thought into the narrative.

'Right away, Oshiro-san.' he replied obediently.

Akina ended the call and then focused her attention back on the officer, sprawled out on the floor in front of her feet. She wondered whether to try and move him or simply leave him. The problem was, he might wake up, or Hekima might come to the door and spot him. So she went to the hallway, picked up a corner of the eight-foot-long rug and dragged it back into the kitchen, next to where the officer was lying. Then she rolled his body onto the rug and used it to slide him out of the kitchen and along the corridor. She stopped in front of the storeroom where the cleaning products and appliances were. This ought to do it, she thought. No windows and a lockable door. She manoeuvred him inside, leaving him on the rug, and locked the door behind her.

Within seconds, she received a text message from Hekima, signalling that he had arrived and was outside. She acknowledged the message so that he would not attempt to come to the door. She went to her safe to retrieve her passport, some cash and details of her overseas bank accounts. Then she put on some comfortable footwear and made her way to leave, taking a quick detour via the kitchen to collect a utility blade, before leaving through the front door.

Outside, Hekima was waiting patiently in Akina's black Mercedes-Benz S-Class. He had parked pointing away from the house, towards the main road, ready to depart – as he always did. Akina got into the passenger-side rear seat and slammed the door behind her.

'Where to. Oshiro-san?' Hekima asked, sensing an exchange of pleasantries would not be required.

'The heliport at Nagano. Quick as you can.' Akina replied.

Hekima responded by pushing down hard on the accelerator and, with an effortless *whoomph* from the engine, they were on their way and proceeding at pace along the rural road leading to the nearest village, Karuizawa.

After fifteen minutes or so, racing along small, meandering lanes, they turned onto Route 18. The single carriage highway was almost entirely straight, all the way to the city of Nagano. Akina looked at her watch. It was a quarter past ten. At busy periods this particular road was an endless string of cars, all the way to the city. If they were lucky, they might get there within the hour.

She phoned the number she had for the heliport and demanded a charter be made available to take her directly to Tokyo. Once they were safely in the air, she would offer the pilot cash to change the flight path. After all, there was no need to make it easy for the authorities to intercept her, she thought, as she felt the corners of her mouth rise up against her cheeks.

After hanging up the phone to the heliport, she turned her attention back to the road. They were travelling at a reasonably high speed, but up ahead they were approaching some slow-moving traffic.

'Don't slow down, go faster! Do whatever it takes!' she demanded.

Hekima used the centre mirror to acknowledge the instruction with an obedient nod, before stamping down on the accelerator. Akina watched as the dashboard readout darted from sixty-five to seventy-five miles an hour. Hekima began weaving through the traffic, prompting the occasional angry toot from disapproving road users. But all that mattered was they were making good progress, and it wouldn't be long before they arrived at the airport.

The weight of the situation began to lift. Akina sat back in her seat and thought of what was to come. What she would do and where she would go, now she had her father's wealth and control of his company? She felt a warm swell of power bubbling up inside her. She realised she could do anything. She would still be able to retain control, even if it meant scaling back operations in her home country or installing an appropriate puppet that could operate the business on her behalf. This would just be a minor setback. She could still take what was rightfully hers. She just needed to get out of the country.

But the elevating and premature sense of victory was dispelled by the discomfiting sight of flashing blue lights erupting from where the arrow straight road intersected the horizon. Their path was made clear by the other road users who subserviently yielded to their authority.

The piercing, high-pitched screams of the sirens grew louder and more unnerving as the convoy drew nearer. She knew they were coming for her. Who else? One by one they screamed passed on the opposite side of the road. Akina followed their progress through the rear window. But they didn't stop. Just kept going.

'I wonder where they're going?' Hekima commented, with a slightly raised eyebrow, as he searched Akina's jittery disposition in the rearview mirror.

Akina ignored the question. She was still checking to make sure all the cars were still on their original trajectory, heading away from them. But before she could celebrate, she noticed that one of the vehicles had broken free from the convoy, aggressively applying its brakes before making a screeching u-turn. It joined the tail of cars behind them, which then promptly slowed to allow it to pass.

As it came within range of the rearview mirror, Hekima caught sight of the vehicle almost immediately and began to apply the brakes.

'What are you doing?!' Akina shrieked, with disbelief.

'Allowing them to pass,' Hekima replied.

'We haven't got time for this; we need to keep going! I need to make my flight!'

'I don't have a choice, they might be pulling us over for speeding.' he said plainly.

Akina reacted by reaching into her handbag. She quickly located the kitchen knife and, clasping it with her left hand, reached forward into the front of the cabin and held the blade to Hekima's neck.

'Faster!' she yelled, 'get us away from that car.'

Feeling the cold steel across his throat, Hekima froze momentarily, the conflict visible in his eyes and emphasised by the three contorted lines on his brow. But he answered without words. Just a gradual push of the accelerator pedal, careful not to create too much G-force that might otherwise cause the knife to be pulled tighter against his skin.

Akina glanced over her right shoulder and could see that there were only two cars between them and the police vehicle.

'Come on, hurry!' she yelled.

But they weren't fast enough. The police car caught up with them and began sounding its horn to get their attention, whilst the officer in the passenger seat aggressively pointed to the side of the road. Hekima ignored them and carried on, still obeying Akina's instructions. Most of the cars in front had decided to pull over, leaving a clear road that he was able to exploit with a burst of yet more power. But they were unable to pull away from the police car, which drew closer still.

Realising Akina and her driver were not going to stop, the officers decided to take more drastic and decisive action. First, they manoeuvred their vehicle to the very edge of the road, giving them just enough room to pull up alongside the Mercedes. Then they positioned the nose of their vehicle parallel with the left rear tyre and turned sharply into their side. The first attempt was unsuccessful, brushing the rear bumper and prompting a minor correction of the wheel from Hekima.

The second attempt was more violent and immediately followed by a burst of acceleration. The Mercedes spun sharply to the left. Then the police vehicle shoved against the passenger side doors until the two vehicles formed a vague 'T' shape, with the

Mercedes now perpendicular to the direction of the road. The tortured tyres screeched painfully until the two on the driver's side burst, leaving the wheel rims exposed to grind excruciatingly against the tarmac. The driver of the police vehicle slammed on the brakes and both cars promptly came to a stop.

The jolts and G-forces had left both Akina and Hekima temporarily disorientated. But Akina was first to partially reclaim her senses. Shit, what now? she thought to herself. Clearly the car was in no state to drive. She retrieved the knife, which had fallen into the footwell, and instantly let out a ghastly scream.

'Help!' she yelled. 'Please help me!'

As one of the officers approached the car door, she readied the knife. But, as they pulled open the door, the officer had a taser gun already trained on her body.

'Please put the knife down, Oshiro-san,' the officer said to her calmly.

Akina realised the hopelessness of her situation. She had exhausted all options for escape. She dropped the knife and offered out her arms, in a gesture of surrender.

51

Akina was still in handcuffs. Being in restraints was nothing new to her, but she realised this was the first time she had ever been handcuffed. They were heavier than she expected and more uncomfortable, particularly where the teeth of the closing mechanism occasionally pinched at her skin. As she sat with her arms resting on the table, she observed the objects that had been placed in front of her by Sergeant Tamura and Inspector Kishimoto. Both were sitting across from her, with their arms folded, watching her. Waiting for some sort of reaction.

There was a sealed evidence bag containing her father's blood soiled tiger pin. Another contained a sample of the cut branches from the sakura tree. There were images taken of the damage to her car, the one she had crashed near Takakumi. And there was a stack of documents and other images beneath them, deliberately arranged in a disorderly pile. It was an almost literal manifestation of a mountain of evidence. But Akina said nothing, just waited for one of the others to break the silence.

'So, how did you do it?' Kishimoto asked, with a heavy frown and elevated pitch of superiority in his voice.

Akina wasn't sure what he meant and frowned awkwardly.

'The pin.' Kishimoto continued, glancing at one of the evidence bags. 'Very clever. Somehow you managed to get his prints in your blood. On a piece of his jewellery, no less. Very clever.' he said again. 'And whilst it's true that we took the bait originally, there's just one problem. We have found no other forensic evidence – no fingerprints, hair follicles, footprints – that proves your father was at the cabin. Only this pin places him at the scene. Strange wouldn't you say?'

Akina remained silent. Then she glanced at her lawyer, who frowned and shook her head.

'But there is plenty to link *you* to the scene.' Kishimoto said.

'My client isn't disputing being at the cabin, Inspector. She was being held captive there alongside Edward Walker.' Akina's lawyer interjected.

'Yes, but who was holding her captive? This pin was left there to suggest that it was Akina's father. We don't believe Akina's father even knew the cabin existed, let alone set foot in it. And we now know it can't have been Edward Walker, given the state we found him in … He was barely alive, having been subjected to a particularly brutal torture.'

'We've been through this in my client's statement, Inspector. She has no memory of being held in the cabin, thanks to the severe injuries she sustained after her escape. An escape that wouldn't have been necessary, had the police managed to successfully locate her in the first place.' Akina's lawyer sounded fed up, as though she was already tiring of the inspector's line of questioning.

Kishimoto nodded, his eyebrows still bearing the weight of his discontent.

'Perhaps then we can start to fill in some of the gaps.' He looked to Tamura and pointed at the evidence as a cue for him to take over.

Tamura sorted through the images on the table and then presented a series of pictures.

'This is your car, Oshiro-san.' he said, pointing at the crumpled remains of Akina's coupé. 'In your statement you said you were rammed off the road by a large, dark coloured four by four vehicle, causing you to crash. A vehicle that could quite easily match the description of this vehicle here,' he said pointing to another photograph. 'This particular vehicle belonged to your late father's estate. You can see that the side of the vehicle has sustained some superficial damage to the left front wing and passenger door. Tyre marks matching this vehicle were also found at the scene of the cabin. When we inspected this vehicle the traces of mud found in the grooves of the tyres also matched the soil found at the scene.'

'Sounds like a good match for the car you believe forced you off the road,' Kishimoto interjected, 'and it belonged to your father.' he added.

Akina made no attempt to confirm nor deny. For now, she remained content to listen, to understand not only what they thought they knew, but what they could prove.

'The problem is, there's no physical evidence that places your father in that car. And his staff say that the car was never used by him, only the groundskeepers. Added to that, there was no corresponding damage found on your car to show the two had collided at all. In fact, our forensic team couldn't find any evidence of your vehicle being forced off the road.'

'Inspector, please,' interjected the lawyer, 'can we dispense with the theatrics and get to the point?'

Akina noticed the subtle glint in Kishimoto's eyes, before he delivered his response. It was clear to her he was enjoying the moment, even if he didn't want to admit it.

'I'm saying there was no car that forced your client's car off the road. It simply didn't happen. Not only that, there was no sign of a struggle and no sign that anyone other than Akina was at the scene. There's no physical evidence that corroborates her story at all.'

Akina felt a sudden tightening in her stomach as her mistakes were laid out before them and her carefully constructed narrative unravelled.

'Let's talk more about the cabin.' Kishimoto continued, nodding again to Tamura to take the lead.

Tamura took a sip of water and cleared his throat, then he picked up the bag of dead sakura branches.

'For a while we ignored these. We didn't really know what to make of them,' he said candidly, 'even though they are not much to look at now, you can see someone went to a great deal of trouble to cut them to an exact length and arrange them in a neat display within this vase at the centre of the room,' he said pointing to another photograph. 'By the time we found them, the flowers had already fallen from the branches onto the floor. But when they were picked, they would have been in full bloom.'

'Any ideas why someone might have done that?' Kishimoto asked, with his uninterrupted stare pointed at Akina once again.

Akina matched the stare and maintained her right to silence.

'Why don't you explain for Oshiro-san, Tamura?' Kishimoto said.

Tamura paused as he took a deep breath.

'There were a lot of tools in the cabin. Most of them were wiped clean of prints, as you might expect. A large hammer, used by you to break open the door from the inside bares your prints, and perhaps may have been used to make your alleged escape. But we also found another implement that bore your prints.'

Tamura picked up another evidence bag, which contained a rusty set of secateurs with wooden handles, and placed them on the table next to the cherry blossom branches. The blades were worn and showed evidence of a resin-like residue.

'We found these at the scene as well. The forensic team found traces of sap on the blades matching the branches.'

'So, we have your fingerprints on an implement that was used to cut the branches from a tree more than fifty yards from the cabin.' Kishimoto's black eyes seemed to cut through Akina's sole. 'Would you like to tell me how you managed that, whilst you were being held against your will?'

Akina said nothing and looked to her lawyer.

'Why did you put them there, Oshiro-san?'

'My client has already stated she has no recollection of the events at the cabin, Inspector.'

Kishimoto and Tamura both looked at each other knowingly. Then Tamura pulled out a wad of photographs from a grey, unlabelled folder in front of him. He placed the pictures out on the table in front of Akina, like he was dealing a deck of cards.

'Your mother Sakura,' he said, 'what can you tell us about her?'

Akina shrugged, churlishly.

'To have lost her at such a young age must have been too painful for someone like me to comprehend.' Tamura continued, genuine empathy in his voice.

Akina lifted her head and glared back at Tamura.

'I didn't lose her. She was taken from me! By him.' She spat the words across the table with disdain.

Kishimoto and Tamura looked at each other, as though they might finally be making some progress.

'You mean your father? You hold him responsible for her suicide?' Tamura said.

Akina's fists slammed violently against the table, as if a wild animal had suddenly awakened.

'Don't you get it yet? He was responsible for her death! If it wasn't for him, she would still be alive!'

Tamura paused and fidgeted in his seat a little.

'Let's talk about that some more,' he said. 'There's growing evidence your father had links to organised crime. And, whilst the majority of his business dealings appear to have been legitimate, these links may have originated from as far back as when he joined the company you now own.' Tamura paused and removed another photograph. 'Before her death, your mother reportedly suffered an injury to her left hand. The removal of two fingers. An injury that is synonymous with punishments administered by the Osore Shirazu crime syndicate. An injury identical to the one you have sustained to your own hand.'

Akina looked up at her lawyer from beneath her bedraggled mop of hair and sighed with resignation.

'He caused it with his stupidity,' she said, hissing the words angrily through her teeth. 'He thought he could cheat them out of their money and get away with it. But instead of punishing him, they punished my mother. They used it as a warning that if he crossed them again, they would kill her or me. They used fear to control him. But he never really cared about us. He only cared about what they might do to him. But he believed, as long as he made money for them, he would be safe.'

'And what did he get out of this arrangement?' Kishimoto asked.

'Initially they gave him funding and helped to remove obstacles.'

'Obstacles?' Kishimoto asked.

'Yes obstacles. When there was a dispute with a supplier, they would solve it. When there was a contract to be won, they would make sure of it. When there was an individual standing in the way of his career progression, they removed them. And in return, my father gave them limitless access to the company's resources, shares in the business and a means to launder vast sums of their money. Over the years, the ventures became more ambitious, making my father even more influential. His network of police and government contacts and the fear of his organised crime connections meant he became almost invulnerable.'

'Is that why your mother took her own life? To escape all that?' Tamura asked.

'I told you, *he* killed her! With his stupidity and carelessness! He didn't care what happened to us. My mother tried to get us out. She went to the police, but they betrayed her. After that, he made sure that she never had the freedom to step out of line. She became his prisoner. She knew there would be only one way to free herself. She knew what had to be done, and she knew it would one day fall upon me to do it. It was both her dying wish and her dying regret.'

Tamura and Kishimoto looked at each other, as if they had both reached the same realisation simultaneously. Suddenly amidst the twisted chaos, it all made sense. The abduction of Walker, the trail relating to the rare earth metal and land being bought up in the village, all pointing towards her father.

'So, you tried to frame your father for Walker's abduction, and your own, so we would find his connections to organised crime and bring him to justice? You drugged Walker and yourself. You wanted it to make it look like your father was trying to silence him. And by being seen as the target of the abduction yourself, you could maintain your innocence?' Tamura said.

Akina sat there vacantly.

'And the removal of your own fingers. You did that too.' Kishimoto interjected. 'You used recognised punishment of the Osore Shirazu to indicate the involvement of organised crime. But why didn't you come to us?'

Akina recoiled and then launched at Kishimoto.

'My mother did that, and look what happened to her. I needed a better way. A way to ensure that it couldn't simply be covered up again.'

'That's why you chose Walker. A foreigner. Someone the British would come looking for. You were the one who found him and recommended him to your father.' Tamura said.

Akina's silence was tantamount to an admission.

'You used your position within your father's property empire to find the evidence linking your father to the land being bought up in the village. The links to the shell companies. Everything.

Then you gave it all to Walker. You made sure he left a trail of the file and the motive for abducting the villagers: the rare earth metal he was employed by your father to verify was there and how to extract it.'

No response.

'So, you befriended Walker, led him to the cabin where you incapacitated and tortured him and harmed yourself. It was so we would think your father was trying to find out what the both of you knew.' Tamura paused momentarily, as the pieces fell neatly into place. 'But presumably your plan was for you to escape, and Walker to be found dead. Otherwise, he could have revealed you were behind everything?' Tamura asked.

No reply.

'The coroner's report shows Walker was asphyxiated. Evidence of bruising around the mouth, where pressure had been applied. Did *you* kill him?' Kishimoto asked.

Akina looked back at Kishimoto; a subtle tear appearing in the corner of her left eye. It was the only remaining trace of her humanity.

'Walker was already dead!' Akina said with another sudden eruptive display of aggression. 'He was dead the moment he signed the contract. Father's associates would have made sure of that. They don't leave loose ends, not if someone's no longer of any use. And certainly not if they're a threat!'

'That may be so, but you were the one who killed him. Not because of some misguided act of mercy or to save him pain, but to make sure your crimes weren't discovered.' Kishimoto said, elevating his voice to a pitch that demanded obedience.

Akina went silent once again. She consulted her lawyer with a look of hopelessness, which was immediately answered with a sharp frown and an emphatic shake of her head. But it was clear Akina was beaten. She had had enough.

'You killed him!' Kishimoto said again.

Akina shrank in her seat, her head tipped downwards to the floor. She nodded faintly prompting the previously formed tear to trickle down her cheek.

'For the tape please Oshiro-san.' Kishimoto demanded, sensing the cusp of his victory.

'Yes, I did it.' she whimpered.

Kishimoto paused, satisfaction radiating from his eyes. He allowed himself to savour the moment as he watched Akina's head fall into her crossed arms on the table. But there was still more he needed to know. Much more.

'I'd like to return to the subject of your father. My colleague here has a theory that his death was not suicide at all; that he was murdered by his inmates. Perhaps acting on behalf of the crime syndicate he had links to.'

'I don't care. He deserved to suffer.' she sobbed.

'But your father was not the only one who caused your mother's death. And there are others out there that are still suffering at their hands.' Kishimoto paused for effect and leaned forward. His eyebrows still underlining his frown. 'So ... how about you help us catch them too?'

52

'You okay?' Tamura asked.

In her daydream Maisie had been oblivious to Tamura's eyes, watching over her with concern. He had probably noticed that she had been tapping her fingers haphazardly against her knee. The involuntary movement that alerted others that something was troubling her.

'Fine.' she said unconvincingly.

Tamura didn't ask again. Just waited for her to change her answer.

Through the rear passenger window of the police saloon, the giant that was Tokyo was beginning to stir from its slumber. The darkness had rescinded, leaving a perfect, unblemished sky. The low hanging sun fired shards of blinding light through the gaps in the skyscrapers. An anxious anticipation hung in the air as though the streets could erupt at any minute, with the demands of millions of daily commuters. But right now, there was only a scattering of early risers preparing the streets for what was to come.

'I was just thinking about Akina and Walker. Wondering whether it was always Akina's plan to murder him.' Maisie added eventually.

Tamura shrugged.

'It certainly seems he was always part of her plan. She needed him to go missing to get the attention of someone like you. Someone outside the system who wouldn't be afraid to ask questions. That was the whole point. She needed someone to come looking for him.'

'And for the trail to lead to her father.' Maisie added.

They approached a crossroads with a red light. The officer at the wheel applied the brakes firmly, causing Maisie's seatbelt to bite into her ribcage. Maisie winced with pain. Every bump in the road or turn from the wheel had been an unpleasant reminder of her injuries, and she couldn't wait for the journey to end.

'There did seem to be some conflict within her,' Tamura said, 'as if she held some regret for what had happened to Walker.'

A crease appeared across Maisie's brow.

'Maybe she had hoped that Walker would be complicit with her plan. Maybe she hoped that he would help her. Akina didn't share any details?' Maisie asked.

'No details,' Tamura said affirmatively, 'she admitted responsibility for his death, but refused to say anything else.'

'So why has she agreed to help with your investigation? Please tell me you haven't granted her immunity.' Maisie said, a slight growl accompanying the words.

'No. No immunity. Her case will go to trial. The help she is giving may help towards a reduced sentence, but that wasn't her main motivation.'

'No. Then what was?' Maisie asked.

'Revenge. It wasn't just her father she wanted to see suffer for what was done to her mother. But, realising her father's death probably wasn't suicide means she will need additional protection herself, now more than ever.'

Maisie noticed for the first time that Tamura was sounding pleased with himself. His confidence was brimming and Maisie could tell that he was riding high on the wave of his first major success.

'So, what has she given you so far?' Maisie asked.

Tamura smiled, his gaze still fixed ahead.

'She's provided details of bank transfers between her father's business and prominent officials.'

'Donations?' Maisie asked.

'No. These are private bank accounts. She's also supplied recordings of conversations between her father and the two individuals. It seems they were made by her father as some sort of insurance policy. Somehow Akina managed to get hold of them. She was keeping them so they could be used for … you would say bargaining, if she was caught.'

'And who are these so called "officials"?' Maisie asked, 'anyone we have come in to contact with?'

'No. One is a politician, and the other is a senior police chief. Both have been close to this investigation, so we cannot release their names yet. Not until after their arrests have been made.' He paused briefly. 'Don't worry, you will know before the press release is issued.' Tamura said with a smile, already anticipating Maisie's next question.

Maisie made no reply but chuckled inwardly at how easy she was to read.

Maisie turned back to the window. She began to recognise some of the buildings and landmarks from their previous visit. 'So, where are we going?' she asked, already knowing the answer.

'The Void,' Tamura replied. 'Kishimoto wanted you to see something.'

'After all we've been through, is that all you're going to give me?' Maisie asked, still with levity in her voice.

'You'll soon find out,' Tamura replied, 'we're almost there.'

Maisie felt a sudden pinch in her stomach. A nervousness. The driver took several turnings, left and right, as they navigated the labyrinth of streets and side-streets. The polished skyscrapers and pristine facades were steadily replaced by more modest dwellings and establishments, each building looking more worn and weathered than the last. Maisie prided herself on her good sense of direction and her ability to retrace her steps, but she recognised none of this. Perhaps it was that, or that they were returning to a place where they had only recently escaped being killed, that was making her feel ill at ease. She wasn't sure which, but Tamura's body language remained calm and composed. His upright posture projected a reassuring confidence, which she had come to trust.

'So, what's next for you?' she asked Tamura. 'I hope now you have been recognised for your achievements?'

Tamura's mouth widened slightly, and his eyes seemed to smile.

'You could say that.' he replied. 'I have been promoted to inspector. I will be Akina's primary contact, partly as she will only speak to a small group of officers who she believes she can trust. My mandate will include investigating Yoshi Oshiro's links to organised crime and to disrupt their network. I will continue to report to Kishimoto, now chief inspector. His responsibilities will include overseeing a separate investigation specifically focused on the events surrounding Yoshi Oshiro's death and the possibility of police corruption.'

'That is fantastic news!' Maisie shrieked with genuine delight, 'I'm thrilled for you. You deserve it! How soon before you begin?' Masie asked.

'We already have,' Tamura said, nodding his head in the direction of the windscreen.

At that moment the Void came into view. It was different during the day. The multi-coloured displays of neon lights, which previously had a hypnotic quality, now looked untidy and cheap. And most of the establishments that had been open, now had their shutters closed. Guarding the entrance was an array of vehicles that collectively emitted pulses of red light from their roofs. There were half a dozen armoured vehicles haphazardly parked around the entrance to the street, and about the same number of police saloons. Officers dressed in black and decorated with tactical weapons stood in lines facing outwards as others patrolled the streets themselves. Men adorned with tattoos on exposed arms and torsos were being led handcuffed into the back of a police van as they protested angrily.

Their vehicle pulled up and Tamura was first to open his door.

'Let's see how Inspector Kishimoto's getting on,' he said with an uncommon enthusiasm.

Maisie opened her door and got out. She stood by the vehicle and retrieved her sunglasses from her purse. She paused for a moment and observed the police presence. She had witnessed raids before, but nothing like this. She counted at least fifty uniformed officers and about the same again in full tactical gear. It was a clear show of force. A message that Kishimoto meant business.

Having identified himself to one of the officers on sentry duty at the entrance to the street, Tamura turned back and called for Maisie to join him. Maisie hesitated. Maybe it was the memory of what happened here only a few days earlier, the images still ingrained within her psyche like an unshakable nightmare. Or maybe it was the sheer abundance of automatic weaponry that reminded her of a war zone. Whatever it was, even with this much police presence, she didn't feel safe, and so she proceeded with caution.

'You okay?' Tamura asked, as she caught up with him.

Maisie produced a convincing smile from behind her sunglasses but said nothing.

A vibrant buzz of victory hung in the air as they passed through the herd of police officers, many of whom had already holstered their weapons. But still there was a sense of formality and discipline. In the centre of it all, they found Chief Inspector Kishimoto stood next to an officer who was relaying his instructions through a loudspeaker. Maisie couldn't work out what was being announced, but it was clear that properties in the area were now being systematically swept, and the occupants questioned.

'What's going on here?' Maisie said, turning to Tamura.

'It was the old lady from the shop in the village – she's given us everything. Details of the gang members who abducted the villagers. She made detailed notes of every meeting she had, including when and where. A lot of them match the timings of the disappearances. But crucially, she made recordings and managed to obtain photographs. Most of these men were known to Tokyo police, so it wasn't too difficult to locate them.'

Maisie smiled to herself. Devious old cow, she thought. 'And who are they, the brains or the muscle?'

'A lot of them are mid-level guys, but crucially we have the leader who ran this whole operation, a man known locally as the Ghost. That's him being led into custody now.' Tamura said, pointing to a man being led away in handcuffs. He was not what she was expecting. Perhaps in his mid-forties, he was lean and below average height. His greying hair was neatly swept over the back of his head. He wore an expensive-looking pinstriped navy suit with a white open collar. Otherwise, he looked pretty unremarkable. No visible tattoos nor memorable features. As he was led away in front of them, he seemed passive, bordering on timid. Maisie took his photograph using her phone as they passed one another. Maisie expected a threatening look, but there was nothing, just indifference.

'Do you think this is Oshiro's contact within organised crime?' Maisie asked.

Tamura nodded.

'We believe he has links to the corrupt officials. The same list of names Akina has provided evidence of being on her father's payroll. But it's now only a matter of time before we uncover the wider truth.'

As they drew closer, Kishimoto noticed them and turned to greet them, with a faint bow of the shoulders, first to Tamura and then for Maisie.

'Konnichiwa, Lockhart-san,' Kishimoto said, with a voice that shouted authority but with eyes that appeared to be smiling.

Maisie struggled with a half bow. 'Konnichiwa,' she replied, as buoyantly as she could muster.

Kishimoto gabbled in Japanese at Tamura, who Maisie noticed had suddenly become more rigid.

'He says that he wanted you to see this first hand,' Tamura translated, 'so that you can see he's serious about cleaning up this mess.' Maisie followed the direction of Kishimoto's extended arm, which pointed to another squad of armed officers entering a property. 'Kishimoto says this has been a dirty secret of Japan's for too long, and it is time for us to reclaim our streets, from the criminals and corrupt.'

Maisie pursed her lips together and nodded unconvincingly, 'It's certainly a strong show of force.' she said, still uncertain of exactly what she was seeing and how effective the raid was likely to prove in the bigger picture.

Tamura relayed the message, prompting a bark of forced laughter from Kishimoto.

'He says it's more than just show. From today, the region known locally as the Void will cease to be a criminal stronghold. The gang leaders will be arrested. And their captives, forced to work in effective slavery, will be freed and allowed to return to their homes or offered a fresh start.' Kishimoto handed Tamura a sheet of paper, which he passed to Maisie. Printed on it were nineteen pictures of men, women and children, accompanied by Kanji symbols that Maisie was unable to decipher.

'These are the missing villagers,' Maisie said, a hint of excitement in her voice as she returned the sheet of paper.

Tamura nodded.

'You've found them?' she continued.

Tamura said nothing, just smiled. And in the same moment something caught his eye from further down the street.

'Here's some of them now.' he said.

Maisie followed the direction of his eyes. A group of civilians were approaching, accompanied by several uniformed officers. They wore dishevelled clothes, and their hair was overgrown and neglected. The men among them were mostly disguised by bushy facial hair. Many of them were crying audibly. The sort of wailing that Maisie had heard before, when witnessing a mother cradling her dead child. At first it seemed they were being led against their will. Perhaps they had become used to their new life, she wondered. Maybe they were afraid to leave, fearing they would be punished by the gang leaders. But as they drew closer Maisie realised these were not tears of fear or loss, but a visceral display of elation. This was the rescue they had thought would never come.

As the crowd of exhausted faces approached, Maisie inspected them one by one. She believed Tamura, but there was no room for error here. She wanted to be sure that these were, without doubt, the missing villagers. Immediately, she recognised the young couple and their daughter, who had grown since her photograph was taken. There were the farmer and his wife, a seamstress. There was the schoolteacher. The list went on. But as the convoy passed, there was one face that was missing. The one that had given her the key to the breakthrough in this case. Tanii. Suddenly Maisie was jolted by an unsettling thought. Had his cooperation with her and Tamura been discovered by the gang leaders? Had they made an example of him as they had so many others? Maisie feared the worst.

Tamura noticed the anxious look on Maisie's face, as she searched the surrounding crowds.

'What's wrong?' Tamura asked.

'Chisato Tanii?' she said without explanation.

Tamura smiled and pointed in the direction the convoy had originated from. Approaching, was a gaunt figure, with straw-like hair. Maisie knew his age, but his shoulders bore the weight of a much older man. The low light of their prior meeting had been kinder to the deep grooves carved across his forehead and beneath his eyes. Unlike the others, there was a solemn resignation to his steps, as if he had endured a heavier burden than his fellow captives.

As he came within ten meters, he spotted Maisie. Through his squinted eyes, straightaway it was clear he recognised her. Slowly his laboured steps became more energised as he walked directly towards Maisie. He stopped and bowed reverently. As he raised his head, Maisie noticed his eyes were filled to the brim, about to spill over. She smiled and bowed her head towards him. Then he held her by both hands and began to speak.

'He says, he knew the moment he saw you that you would be the one to rescue him and the other captives. He will be forever indebted to you and wishes you a lifetime of peace and happiness,' Tamura said, on behalf of Tanii. 'He will make sure the others also know what you risked to free them.' Tanii squeezed her hands tighter and looked into her soul, as the tears streamed down both cheeks. Then he released her from his grip, wiped away the tears and smiled at her.

Maisie found herself without words but could feel a trickle running down her own cheek. She smiled back and his mahogany eyes remained connected to hers until he turned in the direction of the others, leaving the horrors of the Void behind him.

Kishimoto had been watching the whole thing. Looking at Tamura, he barked out a short stream of Japanese.

Tamura smiled with a hint of embarrassment as Maisie looked to him for a translation.

'He says he hopes you'll grant the Japanese police some credit in this outcome, and not claim it all for yourself when you report these events.' Tamura said, relaying the message.

Maisie looked across to Kishimoto. His expression remained stern, but his eyes were still smiling.

'So long as there's the right outcome, I don't care who gets the credit. After all, my job is to report the news, not to *be* the news,' she replied.

Kishimoto nodded and spoke again.

'He wants to know what your plans are. Will you be staying?' Tamura asked. From his tone of voice, it sounded to Maisie almost like he was wishing her to.

'I suspect you've seen enough of me here for the time being. But you can tell Kishimoto I'll be keeping tabs on you both. And that I expect the exclusive when you conclude your investigation.'

Tamura relayed the message to Kishimoto, who smirked and then returned to his other group of colleagues without further comment.

'Are you sure you don't want to hang around to see this to its end?' Tamura asked, turning to Maisie.

Maisie shook her head and smiled.

'No, you've got this. Besides, I need to return to England. I have an editor who will pop a blood vessel if I spend any more time here. And I have important, unfinished business of my own to take care of.'

53

The rain clapped heavily against the windscreen, like a barrage of gunfire. For a second, Maisie was transported back to the streets of Tokyo, crouched behind the wheel of a stationary car, bullets whizzing through the air in all directions. But today, the continuous deluge and gloomy conditions provided a welcome camouflage. Maisie resisted the compulsion to turn on the wipers so her presence would remain less obvious to the casual eye.

The location of the rendezvous point was a small independent café at the end of London's Chapel Market. Maisie had parked just a few doors away, on the opposite side of the road, with a good view of the entrance and both sides of the street. From here she could use her line of sight, and her mirrors, giving her an almost uninterrupted 360-degree view of her surroundings.

The meeting had been arranged under the pretence that the informer would be meeting Hunter, using his phone to exchange text messages. Meanwhile, to aid Maisie's deception, Tamura had reluctantly agreed to delay the release of Hunter's identity and details of his death to the press. Whilst enough of the local police knew the details, the sphere was small enough to limit the likelihood of word spreading this far – at least for a day or two.

Maisie had arrived at 1p.m., one hour before the scheduled meeting time. There was almost no one around. Those who had decided to brave the downpours were either sheltering under hoods or an umbrella, which made identification more challenging. Maisie found herself studying the movements of everyone who came into her view. Their posture, the movement of their legs and length of their steps. Sometimes these could be as unique as a signature, even in these conditions with much of the body concealed under an overcoat.

With only a few minutes left to go, the butterflies began to flutter and suddenly Maisie's nerves were roused by self-doubt. Would she be able to go through with this? Worse still, what if *her* plan had been discovered? What if *she* was the one walking into the trap? Maybe Conway would send another of *his* people. Someone who might finish the job this time. The angst grew inside of her, as if it might even bubble over. Then with a few deep breaths, she rested back in her seat and pacified her subconscious with pragmatism. She had this under control and would see it through to the end. She owed herself that much.

Maisie glanced away from the entrance to check her watch again. Almost two o'clock. When her attention returned to the café, she noticed a figure approach from around the corner of the street. The slightly rounded body, covered by a full-length raincoat, was hunched under an umbrella, trudging through the puddles in a pair of slightly heeled ankle boots. This was it, Maisie thought. Her heart leapt with eagerness and more nerves, mixed together in a cocktail shaker.

She paused and waited. The figure stopped and peered inside through one of the large plane glass windows, then turned and scanned the surrounding area. When her eyes reached Maisie's car, they stopped as if a possible threat had been identified. Maisie froze, even though it must be impossible for her to been seen under cover of these conditions. But the sound of a passing siren, diverted their attention like they suddenly felt the need to escape the open streets. They used their back to push open the door, hurriedly folding the umbrella and shaking it firmly to remove the excess water, before disappearing inside.

Maisie looked across at the grey Audi parked facing her, less than fifty yards away on the opposite side of the road. She flashed her headlights three times. The Audi immediately reciprocated with three short bursts of its own. Then Maisie collected her handbag from the passenger seat, exited the car and cantered the short distance along the pavement to the café.

She glanced through the window and saw Fran sat on a double table near the back of the café, facing the front. Maisie pushed her way through the door, which triggered a bell loud enough to cause everyone to look up from their cups. She swept her damp hair back over her head and stood motionless by the doorway as she glared across the room. Suddenly she felt the rage rising in front of her. Everything seemed to have led to this moment, and there she was staring back at her: Fran Bletchley.

When Fran realised who had walked in, she jumped in her seat, enough for the chair legs to make an unpleasant grinding noise against the floor tiles. It was if she had seen a ghost or something not of this world. Maisie began to relax as she took another deep breath. She smirked inwardly as she likened the scene to a classic Western, with the anti-hero entering the saloon, watched pace by pace by the regulars who were wary of outsiders. Her heels created a loud tap against the black and white floor tiles as she strode past the counter towards Fran's table.

'Not who you were expecting to see?' Maisie asked with an impenetrable confidence. She had practiced the moment in her mind, over and over, since she first learned of Fran's betrayal, and saying the words for real provided a satisfying release.

Fran sat looking up at her with her mouth wide open, struggling to get the words out. 'Maisie? What … how?' she said incoherently, like someone trying to make sense of an apparition.

Maisie pulled out the chair opposite her and sat down. She placed her handbag on the chair beside her, reached inside and stealthily set her phone to record the conversation,

'I'm afraid Hunter won't be joining us.' she said, without answering the question. 'He died last week after abducting me. But not before he told me all about your involvement.'

'What are you talking about? Involvement in what? Who is this … Hunter?' Fran blurted dismissively.

'You can drop the act.' Maisie said. Her words were sharp and cold. There was no anger. No passion. She had become hardened like a blade forged from fire.

'I know it was your idea to coax me to Japan, so I would be more vulnerable. You were keeping tabs on me and feeding him information so he could find me and kill me. And it almost worked. But unfortunately for him, he was arrogant and complacent. In the end, it cost him his life.'

'Maisie, my darling. What are you talking about?'

Maisie produced Hunter's phone from her handbag, selected the only contact in the phone book and pressed dial.

Fran's phone was on the table, but a buzzing noise sounded from her handbag. She looked back at Maisie with shock. Then she retrieved a second phone and inspected the caller ID.

'You know who this phone belonged to, don't you?' Maisie said.

Fran said nothing.

'I recovered this from him before he died. He told me everything, how you helped him by providing my exact whereabouts and specific details about my daily activities. Details that I had shared with only one person … you. All these messages link directly back to you, and your possession of that phone proves the connection.' Maisie said as she returned Hunter's phone to her handbag. 'I'm not here to listen to more of your lies. I now know what they sound like. I just want to know why.'

Fran retrieved a hip flask from her own handbag, removed the top and sloshed a generous dose into her coffee.

'What do you expect me to say? They forced me to do it? That I had no choice?'

'I expect the truth. You owe me that much.'

Fran let out a small sigh of resignation and took a slurp of the whiskey-laced coffee.

'Let's start with who approached you? Was it Hunter?' Maisie asked.

'No. I didn't come into contact with him until later on. I was first approached by one of Conway's people. He didn't tell me his name, but I found it out through one of my contacts. It was Conrad Smith. One of Conway's lieutenants.'

'How did he make contact?'

'He came to my house. He told me who he worked for and that if I didn't help them, they would hurt me like they had so many others. He gave me a phone and told me to keep it on and wait for a call. A few days later, someone made contact and arranged a meeting.'

'How long ago was this?'

'About six months ago. Almost immediately after Conway was arrested. After you exposed his criminal network. At first, they just wanted details about your habits: where you live, work, spend your free time. But then, as time went on, they wanted me to help them keep tabs on what you were up to. They told me they were going to scare you, try and force you to change your mind. I never knew they were going to hurt you; I would never have agreed to that.'

'And yet you continued helping them even after Hunter killed Nathan. And you sat with me over lunch and sold the idea of going to Japan to find Walker. "Doing you a favour", I recall were your exact words. You knew me well enough to know I would never say no to something like that.'

Fran said nothing.

'And what about the money?'

Fran looked surprised.

'I know you've recently paid off a large chunk of your debt.'

Fran looked downwards, ashamed. She nodded timidly, then took another large swig from her coffee mug.

'I suppose there is just one question left to answer.' Maisie said, breaking the uncomfortable silence. 'Why? What was it that drove you to do it?'

'Does it really matter? What difference does it make now anyway?'

Maisie's eyes hardened. 'It matters to me.' she said, now with a hint of cruelty.

'What do you expect me to say, that they made me do it? That I was coerced against my will?'

'I know that can't have been the case. By my reckoning, you far exceeded your remit. If you wanted to make it difficult you could have. Omitted details, perhaps even tipped me off. But you didn't. You went further than you needed to. So why? After all these years of friendship, how could you do this?'

Fran shrugged her shoulders with acquiescence. Emotion bubbled over and tears started to fall.

'I was scared. I knew that if I didn't help them, they would kill me. I knew what they were capable of. And I knew that they would hurt you. But they offered me a simple choice, take the money, enough to start again and clear my debts.'

'And the second option?'

'Or they would torture and kill me. They even showed me pictures of what they had done to others that had disobeyed them. I believed them.' Fran said, her voice reaching a higher pitch as the tears streamed down her cheeks.

'Why didn't you go to someone? To Nathan, or me? Why did you give in so easily? We were supposed to be friends. I trusted you. Idolised you. And people have died as a result of your actions. Nathan died because you did nothing.'

'You have always held me in much higher esteem than I deserve. But the truth is, I'm not the person you think I am. I'm not courageous, nor incorruptible. I knew if I didn't do exactly what they said, I would be dead. I've never known fear like it.'

Maisie observed a frailty she had never seen in Fran before, as her hands shuddered under the weight of the coffee mug. Inside, Maisie remained fired with fury, still begging for blood. And yet she could not help but pity the sorrowful sight sitting opposite her.

She reached into her handbag for a third time, took out her own phone and used it to send a text message. Fran followed her movements curiously without speaking, waiting for Maisie to say something. But Maisie didn't oblige. She stood up from her chair, slipped back into her raincoat and flicked her hair out of the collar with both hands.

'So, is that it?' Fran asked, with confusion.

'Not for you, I'm afraid,' Maisie replied.

Right on cue, the door to the coffee shop burst open behind her, and half a dozen police officers approached their table in a pincer movement.

'Frances Bletchley?' One of the officers in plain clothes asked. Fran looked up at them obediently. 'I'm arresting you for conspiracy to commit murder.'

Fran looked anxiously to Maisie for reassurance, who glared back at her with a stern and unforgiving gaze.

'You'll never be able to undo what you've done. But perhaps there might still be an opportunity for redemption.' Maisie said. Then she turned coolly towards the doorway and left the police to do their job.

54

Ivan Leegood was back in front of his computer after a long business lunch. He rubbed his hand across his forehead where a mild headache was forming. He reached into the top drawer of his desk, took out a couple of painkillers and washed them down with the cold dregs from his coffee mug. Then he scrolled through a long list of articles that had arrived in his inbox since the morning and prepared himself for an afternoon of critiquing the work of his deputy editors and senior journalists. Whilst he hated the idea of showing favouritism, he would have been lying if he said he did not prioritise articles, or even the authors, which were more likely to stimulate his interest. He spotted an email from Maisie Lockhart and chose to ignore the chronology of the others. The subject of the email read: 'Scarecrow Valley (part 1)'.

As he opened the email, the headline continued with: "… where mystic beauty and the bizarre converge. A story of greed, abduction, vengeance and murder." In the article, Maisie described the tech mogul with ties to organised crime; the displacement and enslavement of almost the entire population of a rural village, to acquire mining rights to a precious rare-earth metal; the troubled daughter who would go to any lengths for revenge against her father; and the murder of a young British national, with a promising career ahead of him.

As he reached the end of the article, Leegood looked up from his laptop and out through the glass partition walls of his office. At the edge of the bullpen, the entire office had congregated around the large television screens. The office echoed with an unnatural quiet. There was only the ring from the unanswered telephones and the TVs bellowing out commentary of a breaking news story. Leegood rose from his desk and adopted his default authoritarian stance. As he moved towards the glass partition wall, he saw his secretary, standing in the crowd of his employees. He knocked angrily against the glass. Immediately all eyes turned to him. Leegood used an exaggerated stare to single out Holly from the crowd, his eyes bulging from their sockets and his neck extending forwards. Then he pointed towards the floor of his office. Holly responded instantly to the instruction and ran towards the office as Leegood returned to his chair. Holly burst open the heavy glass door.

'What the bloody hell's going on out there?' he asked.

'It's Fran. She's been arrested!'

'Not Fran Bletchley?' He replied with incredulity, 'what on earth for?'

'It's all over the major news outlets. They're saying she may have been working with Conway's people. And that she may have had something to do with the abduction of an unnamed British journalist.'

Leegood paused.

'They mean Lockhart.' Leegood said, whilst burying his head in his hands, 'Did you know about this?' he added sharply.

'No, no one did. This is the first anybody has heard about it. Some of the guys out there have managed to find out, through police contacts, that Maisie was somehow involved in Fran's arrest. But the details are sketchy at best.'

Leegood developed a wide grin and shook his head in a display of proud reflection.

'Good for you, Lockhart,' he uttered quietly under his breath. 'Where is she now?' he demanded, looking sharply at Holly.

'So far I haven't been able to reach her, but I'll keep trying,' Holly replied.

'Arrange a meet as soon as you can. I want to know what she's planning.'

Holly nodded obediently.

'And arrange a meeting with the sub editors for this afternoon. Lockhart is planning a series of special features on this saga in Japan. I want to make sure that she is supported and that we are ready to go to print straight away. I'll send you the first part of the article for you to circulate.'

'I'll get on it now,' Holly said, urgency in her voice. She turned towards the door and went to leave, but then stopped short, turning back in the direction of Leegood whose attention had already returned to his computer screen, his spectacles balanced on his forehead.

'Is there something else, Holly?' Leegood asked without looking up.

'Yes, there is,' she said hesitantly, 'I was just on my way to tell you … Edward Walker's father is here. He's asking to see you.'

'Has he said why?'

'He just wants a moment of your time. He seems very calm.'

Leegood weighed the decision before giving his answer.

'Where is he now?'

'In the reception area.'

'Well, let's not keep him waiting,' he said, thrusting his arm in the direction of the door.

Holly left Leegood's office and hurried around the corner, only to return half a minute later with Dr Walker. He was carrying two envelopes, both gripped in his left hand and pressed tightly against the left side of his chest. Holly opened the office door for him and remained at the threshold as she provided the introductions.

'Jonathan Walker, this is Ivan Leegood, Editor-in-Chief.'

Walker gently strode past Holly, with a quiet nod of appreciation, and proceeded towards Leegood's desk. Leegood immediately jumped to his feet and held out his hand.

'Jonathan, please come in and take a seat. Can we get you anything? A drink perhaps.'

'Not for me thank you, I won't keep you.' he said as he manoeuvred the chair closer to the desk, before taking a seat.

'Thank you, Holly,' Leegood said, as affirmation she could take her leave. 'First of all, please allow me to offer my sincerest condolences. I didn't know your son, but from what Lockhart has told me, he was an accomplished young man with a bright future ahead of him. For him to have been caught up in this mess is a great tragedy.'

'Thank you. I appreciate the sentiment,' Walker replied solemnly. 'Actually, that's the reason for my visit. My wife and I will shortly be going to Japan to arrange for the repatriation of our son's body. Maisie has already informed us that she has submitted an article that may be published over the coming days. My wife and I have prepared an obituary, which details some of his friendships and achievements. We were hoping that you would publish this in a manner you see fit. We would like him to be seen as more than just an anonymous British national. Instead, perhaps your readers will see him as the man he was. A good man. Through the eyes of a proud mother and father.'

Leegood rocked his head repeatedly forwards.

'Of course,' he said, reaching across the table for the large envelope, 'I will take care of this personally.'

'Thank you,' Walker said appreciatively, whilst mustering a faint smile, 'that will be of great comfort to Edward's mother in particular.'

After an awkward pause between the two men, Leegood was first to break silence.

'Is there anything else that I can do for you?'

'There was just one other thing, if you don't mind,' Walker said, glancing at the smaller envelope still in his hand. 'My wife wrote this letter for Maisie. I'm afraid she's too upset to speak with her just yet. But she wants to thank Maisie for everything she has done for us, and our son. I'm quite sure that the truth about my son's death would not have come to light without her. And it's that small mercy that has at least provided us with some measure of solace.'

'Absolutely, I will make sure that she gets this. Perhaps it would be best that I hold onto it for now, as I am not sure she will be returning to her home straight away.'

'Is everything okay?'

'I believe so.' Leegood replied, not entirely convinced by his own words, 'given everything that has happened lately, and the continued threat on her life, the police are urging her to keep a low profile. But given her nature, I don't expect her to stay hidden for long.'

'She's quite remarkable, that's for sure.' Walker said, with admiration.

'She's my very best journalist. Perhaps even the best there is.' Leegood replied with an emphatic whisper, as if trying to avoid being overheard.

'Well, I really mustn't keep you,' Walker said getting to his feet. He shook Leegood firmly by the hand, and as quietly as he had arrived, he was gone.

As Leegood settled back into his seat, a ping from his laptop prompted him to return to his emails. Two more messages from Maisie. The first had the subject heading: 'Exclusive: renowned journalist Fran Bletchley linked with organised crime'. The second had the subject heading of 'expenses' and was accompanied by three exclamation marks. The message read:

'Boss, hope you enjoy the two exclusives ... more to follow shortly. Details of my expenses attached. Hope you don't begrudge me my plane ticket home!'

Leegood opened the attachment and reviewed the long list of travel expenses and meal receipts. As he got to the bottom, he saw what she was referring to: a first-class flight from Osaka to London.

Leegood removed his glasses and pinched the bridge of his nose. Then he smiled to himself whilst shaking his head, with a casual vexation. Bloody Lockhart, he thought!

Acknowledgements

My thanks go, of course, to my family who have always been so supportive of my endeavours: my father Paul, my mother Angela and my sister Lucy. A special thank you must go to my inspirational wife Michelle: thank you Shelly for your unwavering encouragement, optimism and patience in indulging my newfound passion for writing. For the many hours of lost sleep suffered as a result of the tap, tap, tapping from my keyboard into the wee hours of the morning. And for the many hours debating character traits and plot lines, thank you. You have helped make the journey of completing this novel, as it ought to be, a joy that we could share together, rather than a chore.

A huge thank you to my copy editor Jo Lane, for helping me to develop and polish the story – I learned a great deal from our conversations – and to my proofreading editor Becky Wyde whose knowledge and attention to detail has been outstanding.

As many thrillers have some precedents in truth, so too do numerous themes within this novel. The phenomenon of the 'Johatsu' or "Evaporated People" is well documented, with a whole raft of articles, documentaries and books – too many to mention here, but many of which capture the dilemmas facing thousands in Japan (and indeed in other parts of the world) every year.

Finally, on a lighter note to end, thanks must also go to James May and Amazon's: 'Our Man In Japan' series, which first alerted me to the lure of Japan's fascinating culture and scenic beauty, something that ultimately acted as the inspiration for the setting of this novel.

Printed in Dunstable, United Kingdom